BLOOD
FOR THE
UNDYING THRONE

ALSO BY SUNG-IL KIM

Blood of the Old Kings

BLOOD
FOR THE
UNDYING THRONE

SUNG-IL KIM
TRANSLATED BY ANTON HUR

TOR

TOR PUBLISHING GROUP

NEW YORK

BLOOD FOR THE UNDYING THRONE

Designed by Omar Chapa
Map designed by Emily Langmade

A Tor Book
Published by Tom Doherty Associates / Tor Publishing Group
120 Broadway
New York, NY 10271

www.torpublishinggroup.com

Tor® is a registered trademark of Macmillan Publishing Group, LLC.

EU Representative: Macmillan Publishers Ireland Ltd, 1st Floor, The Liffey Trust Centre, 117–126 Sheriff Street Upper, Dublin 1, DO1 YC43

The Library of Congress Cataloging-in-Publication Data is available upon request.

ISBN 978-1-250-89536-3 (hardcover)
ISBN 978-1-250-89537-0 (ebook)

Our books may be purchased in bulk for specialty retail/wholesale, literacy, corporate/premium, educational, and subscription box use. Please contact MacmillanSpecialMarkets@macmillan.com.

First Edition: 2025

Printed in the United States of America

10 9 8 7 6 5 4 3 2 1

To Narim, my partner in everything

WHI

HYBERI

Shaira

Ledon

Kamori

Dehan
Forest

Arland

Finvera Pass

Dalosia

IMPERIAL
HEARTLAND

Imperial
Capital

Faro

Beruvia

Feredan

Bach

Tanvalia

N

Arpheia

Rammania

S

E LIBERATED

SERT

ythonia

ROOK MOUNTAINS

Ebria

Cassia

Mersian
Wastes

Varata

sra

Thiops

CALIDIA

For King Gwaharad of Kamori,
from his most devoted subject.
May he lead the way to the
liberation of our homeland and
the world that suffers.

BLOOD
FOR THE
UNDYING THRONE

1

EMERE

"Prince Emere."

A familiar voice. One he hadn't heard in some time, but a voice replete with good memories. He felt a rustling inside his heart.

"Prince Emere."

There it was again. Emere opened his eyes. Or perhaps his eyes were already open? His surroundings came into focus.

Here were the plains to the south of Arland's capital, Kingsworth. The bodies of Imperial legionaries and Arland's militia, broken bits of weapons and banners scattered about. Blood splattered over receding patches of snow. In the distance, a four-legged beast of metal—the gigatherion Clarios—spewed violet smoke from its joints, frozen in motion.

And right before his eyes, her dragon wings spread wide, was Loran. Her body was covered in red scales, and an azure light burned in one eye. He heard a low, faraway beating like drums.

The word "princess" was on the tip of his tongue, but then he quickly remembered that Loran was now king.

"Your Majesty."

He tried to bow on one knee to show his respect, but he couldn't feel the ground. Or his knee. Or any part of his body, for that matter.

"Listen carefully, Prince Emere."

"I am at your bidding."

The words came from his mind and he spoke them, but where he spoke from, he didn't know. Loran smiled. Even with fearsome scales covering her face and a blue fire burning where her left eye should be, her smile filled him with gladness.

"Why so formal? Have we not taken meals together and fought side by side?"

"Your Majesty is now a king. I am a mere man."

"A councillor of the Imperial Commons and the brother to the King of Kamori is a mere man?" She laughed.

"My brother hardly deserves his title. I knew this but still wasted many years on him. And a councillor I may be, but in name only—what I truly am is a hostage from an unruly province, standing in for my aging sister."

Standing in? Yes—he shouldn't be in Arland at all, but in the Imperial Capital. He had been about to give a speech before the Kamori who lived there. It was only a few words added to what the Commons Council had already decided he should say, but he felt it was important to connect with his countrymen who were living so far away from home.

"Your Majesty," he said to Loran, realization dawning, "do I dream?"

Ever since he was a young man, he had had mysterious dreams. The ancient Kamori believed that destiny could be foretold through dream visions like these. The wisdom of the Tree Lords, who had interpreted dreams and read fates, had been lost since the Empire's invasion, but many still believed.

Emere believed. How could he not, when dreams of Loran had haunted him long before he met her for the first time in the Dehan Forest two years ago.

"If this is a dream," Loran replied, "wouldn't I be a figment of Prince Emere's slumbering imagination? Which means you shall wake soon and forget me before breakfast."

"How could I ever forget you?"

Tears came to his eyes. If indeed they were tears, or his eyes. The rustling in his heart turned into an ache.

Loran smiled. "Dreams are rather futile."

"We of Kamori do not think so. Just as the astrologers of Marthia believed our fate lay in the stars, we believe there is destiny in our dreams."

Loran still smiled. "Then I should tell you this now. Prince Emere, you must become king. That is your destiny."

In an instant, she lost her wings and scales to become a small woman wearing Kamori clothing. On her neck was her *t'laran*— the tattoo of her clan—and over her left eye was an eyepatch of red cloth. She looked just as she had when they had lunched every day in the underground palace of Kamori.

"Destiny passes by those who stand still," Loran continued. "Reach out and grasp that which awaits you, up there."

Her eyes looked up over the battlefield, and Emere followed her gaze. The clear blue afternoon sky turned into the blackest night. But instead of clouds of constellations, there was only one star, shining brighter than any he had ever beheld.

It enchanted him. His right hand returned to his control and he reached out to the star, or perhaps it was coming down toward him. His fingertips almost touched it.

He ripped his gaze from the sky. "What will you have me do?"

"Survive first."

"Survive?" Emere questioned, confused.

"Yes, survive. The wound you've just sustained isn't serious, but there will be other dangers ahead."

Awareness of his whole body, from his eyelids to his toes, returned like a crash from a great height. Someone's hand pressed down on the left side of his chest as if there was a wound. His back was cold.

Arland's battlefield and the bright star in the black sky vanished, replaced by a gray raining sky.

"Councillor! Councillor Emere!"

Another familiar voice. But this time, the urgent call shouting down at him came from the mouth of Gildas, his young aide. His round face hovered over Emere, his spectacles splattered with raindrops. Gildas was on one knee inside a puddle and had his hands pressed to Emere's chest.

"Councillor, you must wake up!"

Emere's consciousness came back in a rush. Over Gildas's voice, he could hear the consternation of a crowd.

Emere used his right hand to sit up slightly, as Gildas kept his hands pressed to Emere's chest. There were puddles of rainwater all over the wooden platform he was lying on. It had been erected at the edge of a small square surrounded by old buildings, and there was a panicked crowd quickly dispersing like surprised cattle.

"Gildas, what—"

"An arrow during your speech, sir." Gildas's voice was still urgent. "Do you not recall?"

Emere looked down, and a short wooden shaft protruded from the left side of his chest in between Gildas's hands. Not an arrow, but a bolt from a crossbow. His voluminous white Imperial suit, worn only twice before, was now soaked in blood.

"There is a lot of bleeding, but it doesn't appear to have hit your heart or your lungs."

"And what of King Loran?"

"Who, sir?"

A misspoken name. He shook the sleep from his head.

"Never mind. Perhaps I'm still not my—"

"It seems the patrollers cannot make it into the square because of all the people," Gildas interrupted, looking around as he assessed the situation.

It was a poor neighborhood inhabited by immigrants from Kamori. The buildings were built on top of each other and the streets were narrow. There would be no way for the patrollers to stop the crossbow assassin if the nervous crowd that filled the small square fell into true chaos. Which meant more opportunities for bolts to come flying at him.

"We have to leave," said Emere. "There's no time to wait for help."

"I will help you walk, sir." Gildas quickly ripped some strips from Emere's cloak with his teeth and deftly wrapped his wound. Groaning from pain, Emere furtively looked around them for an escape route. Bolts studded the podium where he had stood only moments ago.

Gildas noticed where he was looking. "At least seven shots in the blink of an eye. A citizen was killed."

Crossbows take time to reload. How many shooters, then, were there? Emere saw a body bleeding out in the middle of the square, where the crowd was beginning to thin out as it headed for the alleys. But their screams were becoming more panicked as they realized how slow their escape was.

"Ready, my lord," said Gildas, taking hold of Emere's right arm.

"My wound is not as serious as it seems," Emere assured him.

But Gildas insisted on helping Emere to his feet.

Suddenly, there was a whizzing sound—Gildas let go and Emere latched on to the podium to keep from falling. His aide, however, collapsed onto the platform, a bolt piercing his temple, the pupils of his surprised eyes shrinking behind his spectacles.

Emere stared down at him, dazed, until a second bolt hit the podium and new screams began to ring out. He immediately leaped off the platform and ran toward the door of the building behind him, the bolt in his chest digging into him more with every step. He collapsed against the door as he reached for the handle.

It was locked. He pounded on the door in frustration, knowing there was likely no one inside.

Emere's makeshift bandage was already drenched. Blood dripped along the edges of his garments and splattered to the ground. The square, while now completely empty in the middle except for the body, rang with the sounds of people trying to flee, sharp screams piercing through the hubbub. So many innocents would be trampled, but there was nothing he could do.

Who would dare attempt an assassination in the Imperial Capital? A provincial councillor meant nothing in the grand scheme of things, even if he was a member of a fallen royal family—surely there was no reason to expend this much effort in assassinating him?

Gildas's body lay sprawled on the platform. As shameful as it was to flee from where his aide lay dead, his own life was still in danger.

Emere placed a hand on the dirty limewashed wall next to him, gritted his teeth, and kicked in the door. The bar holding it shut shattered with a loud crack, the shock of its break reverberating into his injury. The pain made him stumble and slide against the wall to the ground.

There were people in the world who could ignore their pain. Emere was not one of them, but he knew he couldn't stay here—not if he wanted to live. Steadily, leaning on the corner of the wall, he got to his feet.

The wound you've just sustained isn't serious . . .

Hoping Loran's words from his dream were true, Emere gripped the bolt in his chest before he could think twice about it and pulled. A chunk of his muscle ripped out along with the bolt's tip, eliciting a savage scream of pain from his lips—and yet it could barely be heard above the chaos around the square. His left arm suddenly refused to move and the bleeding was worse now. He needed more bandages, but he couldn't rip any more from his clothes with just one working hand.

This was not the first time he had been shot by a bolt. In his youthful days of traveling the world, he had suffered injuries as a matter of course. But back then, he had *her*.

A surgeon skilled in the Ebrian healing arts, Rakel had always been there to patch him up. It had been ten years since he left her at Finvera Pass. The rumor was that she had a surgery practice in the Capital somewhere, but Emere hadn't dared to visit her. What he wouldn't give to have her—and her healing skills—here now. Trying to dull the pain with a few deep breaths and the memory of Rakel, he vowed to see her again, if he could survive this.

Emere slowly got to his feet, formulating a plan. The buildings in this neighborhood were connected by bridges across the alleys, which he could use for his escape without being blocked by the crowds outside.

Entering through the broken door, he quickly found a staircase leading up and began the laborious climb, grabbing on to the banister with his good arm to help haul himself up. While his other arm was less mobile than before, it at least felt much better compared to the agonizing pain that the bolt's tip had been ripping through his body each time he moved.

The inside of the building smelled of cheap wine, ancient piss, and some kind of fishy broth. The buildings here were said to house a dozen families, each in only one or two rooms—a crowded and noisy kind of life, even for the city. From upstairs, a child shouted in a language he didn't know.

It was a six-floor building, so the bridge was probably on the fourth or so. The assassin couldn't have been shooting from this angle, but what if they were following his movements? They could be approaching from the other side of the bridge, waiting for him right around any corner.

A mop lay on the first landing. Emere stepped on the damp mophead and unscrewed the staff. It was much shorter than the quarterstaffs and spears he was used to, but it would do as a weapon. His injured chest was still aching, but the bleeding at least seemed to have slowed. All sorts of conjectures as to why he'd been a target raced through his mind, but he tried to ignore these thoughts for now, instead concentrating on getting up the stairs.

On the third-floor landing, a child of about five years was playing on a wheeled wooden horse before he looked up in fright at the man in torn and bloody clothing. He shouted something in an unknown language, then burst loudly into tears. Emere, as he continued up the steps, heard a deep female voice from behind him.

"Who are you?"

She spoke Imperial in an unfamiliar accent. Gildas had said there were immigrants from provinces other than Kamori in the neighborhood. He turned and saw the woman standing in the corridor. She had stepped out in a blotted leather apron, her hands tying up her curly hair. One look at Emere's state and she quickly came between him and the child.

"I am a member of the Commons Council. Forgive me for borrowing your mop."

"A councillor who not only makes children cry but steals mops?" The woman pulled a fearsome cleaver from her apron pocket and held it up. "You're one of those provincial councillors, aren't you? You think you're better than us? Do you think your fancy clothes and your Imperial manners will change your lowly blood to theirs?"

The best thing would be to ignore her, but her words made him pause in midstep. It wasn't his choice to be in the Capital, nor were these cumbersome robes some attempt to flaunt his status. Not to mention that he was about to be assassinated, despite his political insignificance, right on these dirty steps. But he understood what he must look like to this woman.

He turned, brushing away his indignation, and continued up the stairs, the woman cursing at his back in the language of her people. Maybe if he hadn't said he was a councillor, she would've cursed him in standard Imperial.

But the problem wasn't the insults hurled at him by a stranger, it was the taunt of *councillor* ringing through these narrow halls. If the assassin hadn't known where he was a moment ago, they likely would know now. He gave the mop handle a white-knuckled grip with his working right hand, and gritted his teeth as he carefully placed his left hand on it. The pain would become manageable soon. He'd had worse in his youth.

He reached the fourth floor. There was a battered lattice door to the left, beyond which he could see the bridge, and beyond that, another door at the other end. No one lurked outside the first door, so he opened it and looked out onto the bridge.

The winds were strong, and there were no sides to the bridge—only holes where balustrades had once stood. But there was enough room for two men to walk side by side, and the bridge could be crossed in under ten steps. Emere took a deep breath and then took his first steps across. It was slippery from the light rain that still fell. The crowd surged below, still trying to exit the square. He hesitated. He hated heights.

That dream vision in the square. If Loran had been on the other side, he would've walked on a tightrope to get to her and fight by her side, much less this dangerous bridge. Squinting, he put his right foot forward, imagining that Loran was by the door on the other side . . . her leather clothes, her eyepatch, and Wurmath, the sword made from a dragon's tooth.

Whether it was from the loss of blood or the height, a dizziness overcame him. Using the mop handle as a crutch, he continued to limp across the bridge. Something whipped through the air—a bolt flew right past his sleeve, but it made no impression on him. His eyes were fixed on the door across the bridge. Just as he had stretched his hand toward the star in the night sky in his dream vision, he reached toward the other side of the bridge.

Another bolt. This one thankfully missed as well, but he knew if one did hit, his body would fall into the crowd below from the impact. The thought troubled him, but he had to make it to the other side of the bridge.

Finally, he pushed the door and it opened without any resistance. Once through, instead of heading to the next door for the bridge on the other side of the building as he originally planned, he stumbled up the nearby stairs.

At the top, there was a trapdoor that opened onto the roof. He went through without hesitation. The wind had picked up even more, and the rain now came down stronger. And at the edge of the roof, looking down at the crowd below, was a tall woman.

Sensing his presence, she quickly turned to face him. Her hair was long and tied in the back, and she wore a leather coat over simple, undyed clothing. She had a hawk-like stare, as serious as an artist gazing at her painting. She carried a long box and had a shortsword on her belt. When her hand touched a lever attached to the box, he realized what the object was and leaped to the side.

A slew of bolts shot out of the box and clanged against the iron railing behind him, the sound ringing in the air. A Cassian repeating crossbow. He had only ever seen one on his travels, displayed like a priceless treasure in the home of an eastern prefect.

His injury and loss of blood slowed him down, and his only weapon was the mop handle in his hands. The garments of a politician were not made for quick movement, and rainwater soaked heavily into the thick and luxurious cotton. And this woman had all the hallmarks of a Cassian killing artist. He bit his lip and tightened his grip on the mop handle.

The woman pulled the lever again, and more bolts shot out. One of the bolts sliced through his clothes, just missing his body. Wrapping the wet fabric of his robe around his still-weak left hand, he couched his makeshift staff under his right armpit and charged at her, ready to be hit by another bolt. Instead, the assassin lowered her crossbow and unsheathed the sword at her side— Emere noted it was a regulation sword of the Imperial legions.

His left hand protected by the wound-up fabric, Emere grabbed her blade. The pain from the wound on the left side of his chest was close to making him faint, but he held on to his consciousness and the blade both, and swung his upper body around to strike his opponent's wrist, disarming her of the shortsword. She grunted, then hit his head with the crossbow that she held in her other hand, and everything went black as he fell.

He couldn't have been out for longer than a fraction of a second—the assassin's sword still lay on the roof where it was dropped. But it was no use. Despite the brevity of his dizziness, it was enough time for the assassin to aim her crossbow right in front of his eyes.

Emere winced. In this last moment before death, all he could think of was what Loran had meant in his dream vision. *You must become king.* With the sound of the lever being pulled back, he said a final silent goodbye to Loran, apologizing for letting her down. He regretted leaving poor Gildas to lie in the rain on the bloody platform. It was raining when he had left Rakel. He was never going to see her again.

But instead of the whoosh of bolts, there was the sound of wound-up springs jamming. He looked up and saw the alarm in the assassin's face. The intricate Cassian weapon must've broken when she had hit him on the head with it. She leaped back and pulled the lever again, but the crossbow did not fire. All it did was creak, and creak again.

Emere scrambled to grab the sword lying nearby. The assassin bit her lip before jumping onto the parapet at the edge of the roof, her calm and serious face now filled with rage. As Emere rose up and approached with the sword, she jumped. He ran to the parapet and looked over the edge, but there was only the slow-moving crowd below.

He collapsed on the rooftop, no longer able to fight through the pain, and sighed. Today wasn't his day to die after all.

2

ARIENNE

When the direction of the winds changed, dust blew into Arienne's face. She raised her hood and lowered her gaze. The ground at her feet was a burnt red, with only a few hints of long-dried grass. There wasn't much vegetation at all in this wasteland—she could walk for miles without looking up from her feet and never bump into a tree or bush.

It was hard to imagine such a place could exist. The abandoned paths of the Rook Mountains had been harsh, with only a few lumbering bears about, but compared to the devastation of Mersia, the bare rocks and shrubs of the Rook Mountains were practically verdant. Here, there was only dust.

Her lone companion in these barren lands was an old donkey, and he looked pitiful in the dusty winds with his burdens of dried goods and water on his back. He had no name when she bought him, so she called him Aron—it was the name of an explorer in a book she loved, a story about searching for treasure in a vast desert.

"Aron, let's rest a bit."

The winds were exhausting. She kept her back to the gusts as she sat down—not a rock or fallen tree in sight for her to rest upon. She pulled the donkey to her side and brought out some dried mutton from a saddlebag. It had been three days since she entered these wastelands, and the meat and hard bread tasted of dust. Large grains of sand knocked against her hood, the sound echoing in her ears.

Arienne read that grass had once grown up to the waist in these parts, and large oroxen, twice the height of men, had roamed these fields, shepherded by herders on horseback. The herders spent their winters and springs at home in a large, rich city, and in the summer herded the oroxen before returning to their homes in the fall. The city had been called Danras, and the country had been called Mersia.

Danras, with its sister city-states of Iorca and Lansis, had labored under the tyranny of Eldred the Grim King, until the Empire came 170 years ago. Danras had sided with the Empire against the Grim King, and once he was overthrown, Mersia became the eastern edge of the Empire. It was a pivotal moment in the Empire's expansion to the east, where the strategic location of the new province proved to be invaluable in the Cassian Wars.

But of course, Mersia's life as an Imperial province hadn't lasted long. One hundred years ago, seventy years after the annexation, the vast steppe teeming with life and riches became these deathly wastes in a single morning, struck by a weapon that would come to be known as the Star of Mersia. It was punishment for declaring independence, or so the common knowledge went.

Arienne slipped the rest of her dried meat into her sleeve and closed her eyes. She imagined a ship sailing on the water. The white sails billowed upon tall masts, and the ship raced across the waves as the spray crashed around it. The sky was clear, and the sun had begun its descent from its high point into the west. The ocean reflected the sunset colors, the water as yellow-red as the earth of Mersia. Arienne pictured herself dressed like a pirate from an illustration in one of her adventure books, holding up a retractable telescope.

A crewman comes up to her.

"Captain Arienne, have you set a course for Danras?"

What shall she name the crewman? Cly, maybe. No, Bly. That sounds better for a pirate. Arienne scans her map, but not too closely—detailed images will only make her vision more inaccurate.

"Bly, tell the crew to turn thirty degrees to starboard. And maintain this speed."

"Aye, Captain." Bly turns his head and shouts, "Oy, you sea dogs! Thirty degrees starboard, she says!"

A chorus of "Aye!" is heard.

Through her telescope, an island slowly comes into view. But this is no island—it is the ruins of a city. It is Danras, or at least the Danras Arienne imagines in her mind.

The ship in her mind turns. Arienne concentrates on the sensation of her body turning with it, the movement of the ship underneath her as it heads to its destination. Out loud, she recites a short chant. Power blooms in her mouth.

Arienne opened her eyes, and the ruins in her imagination rose from the eastern horizon like a mirage before fading away. She stood up and turned to the direction of the mirage.

A brief dizzy spell made her lean on Aron's neck. Ever since she stepped into the land of Mersia, the flow of her Power had become erratic.

Arienne had paid attention to every rumor about Mersia that had come her way. While they were uniformly ominous, the most disconcerting one of all was that sorcery was of no use here. Without her magic, she would just be a teenage girl with no special talents. The prospect scared her—but then she thought of Loran, the King of Arland. Hadn't Loran been an unremarkable widow of thirty-eight before she jumped into the volcano to save her country?

The wind changed direction again, and blew sand in her face *again*. But Loran's request echoed in her mind. Arienne's initial plans after the war had been to find a way to hide Arland's gifted children from the Empire, to teach them what she knew of sorcery and create a real school for sorcerers, unlike the death trap that awaited them in the Imperial Capital.

But Arland had just barely managed to obtain a fragile autonomy; to not follow in Mersia's doomed footsteps, Loran knew, the Arlanders needed to learn all they could about the Star. So, Arienne had journeyed a long way, determined to fulfill that mission.

Loran would have understood if Arienne had turned down this mission, but it wasn't only because of her king that Arienne was here now. She needed to come to this place, this land once ruled by the Grim King Eldred, to understand her own sorcery better. And while the country was said to be an utter wasteland, Arienne could not shake the feeling that there was *something* here that Mersia had left behind for her.

She pulled the donkey's reins toward the new direction she

had found, but Aron refused to budge. The horse seller had said there would be no better companion to make it to the other side of the mountains with than this donkey. That he was obstinate, but a less stolid fellow would never even make it to Mersia, let alone have the gumption to set foot in it. Arienne was starting to regret that obstinance. She pulled again on the reins, but Aron did not give.

"Let's go, Aron! Do you want me to leave you behind?" she threatened, convinced he could understand her. "Would you be happy with that? The sun is setting soon!"

Aron had all the food and water, so she could never actually leave him behind. But the threat worked, as he finally began plodding where she led. A broken-off shrub rolled past them in the wind. The dust now hit her left side instead of her face, which felt like a small mercy.

There was truly little here but dust. For three days, the gray skies overhead remained without a trace of sun. During the starless nights, the cold cut to the bone.

But it was said there was something more frightening in the night here than just the cold. Arienne gathered her robes about her with her right hand and with her left stroked the glass orb she wore around her neck. She had bought it before crossing the mountains, sold to her as a talisman for warding off ghosts, created by the rhymesmiths of the Mersian city of Iorca before the Empire's coming. She didn't know how much longer it would take to find the city of Danras. Until then, she could only hope that this tiny orb riddled with cracks would protect her from the terrors of the night.

Without pausing in her steps, she opened the door to the room in her mind. She had collapsed her previous room when fighting

Eldred two years ago, so she had built this new one to resemble the room that briefly gave her shelter during her escape from the Imperial Capital. She could barely remember the face of the man who had helped her, but every time she came into this room, she wondered what he could be doing now. Only two years had passed, but it felt like so long ago.

It was bright outside the window from the pale streetlights of the Imperial Capital. She sat on the edge of a large bed in the middle of the room. Right next to the bed was a crib under the window and inside lay little Tychon. Arienne reached out and gently tapped his small, plump hands, and Tychon stirred a little in his sleep.

She remembered how she had defeated Tychon's father, Lysandros, at Finvera Pass. The memory used to make her shudder, but now she only felt gratitude that she managed to win and escape with her life—and Tychon.

He was a baby with pink cheeks and sparkling dark eyes, but outside of her mind, he was nothing more than the carefully preserved corpse of a baby inside a small coffin of lead. Now that she had hidden him inside this room, she would never take him out. Never again should he be anything else than this happy child in this peaceful room.

The direction of the winds changed again. These spontaneous shifts did nothing but confuse and annoy her. Sighing, she lifted her head. An eastern patch of the gray sky was turning darker, fading into black. Night was falling on Mersia.

Aron stopped her again. After one more glance at the darkening sky, she looked about them for a place to spend the night. In the distance, she could see what looked like the ruins of a hamlet. But the horse seller beyond the mountains had warned her—*Venture not into where people once lived.* For the past two nights, there had been large red rock outcroppings in the shape of arches under which she could set her tent and light a fire, but there were no such structures in sight tonight. Sleeping in the open fields with no protection had to be avoided as much as possible. There had to be a hillock or *something* that could block this infernal wind. Arienne gave a firm tug at the reins as she walked on.

Suddenly, she lost all control of her body. Her lungs filled not with air, not with water, but with something else as her vision turned to white and then faded to black—then her whole body dropped to the ground like a puppet whose strings were cut. A feeling of helplessness and despair overwhelmed her. Her right cheek hit the ground, her arms refused to move, and her mind refused to think.

This place might have been absent of life, but there was a presence of something that should not exist. A chill of the soul. A spiritual hunger that permeated the air like fog. Mersia until that moment had been mere wasteland; now Arienne was reminded that it was where the Star had unleashed a massacre.

The invisible fog of chill and hunger began to take on shapes around her, a crowd of people forming in thin air. Figures like unfinished sketches, scores of them, hundreds, passed by in the dark wastelands. The hooves of the phantom horses made no sound, and the lips of the phantom people wearing wide-brimmed hats mouthed inaudible words.

Curled up on the ground, Arienne used all of her might to bring both of her hands to the orb around her neck. She rubbed the cool glass, feeling its scratches and cracks. Nothing happened—her

Power wouldn't flow to it, no matter how much she willed it to with what little strength she had left.

The ghostly crowd walked on by, the hooves of the horses piercing her innards with ice whenever they passed through her body. Arienne wasn't sure how long it had been before one of the horses stopped and its rider dismounted. The rider wore tattered leather clothes, charred in places. As the ghost approached Arienne, she saw that he was a man, his head hanging from his neck at an uncomfortable angle. The ghost bent forward and gazed down at Arienne.

Terrified, she tried to bury her face in her knees. She silently begged for the ghost to stop paying attention to her and to continue on his way. But the ghost kept gazing at her. Unable to resist, Arienne looked up slightly, and their eyes met. A face with a short mustache. Empty, sad eyes.

"Child, what are you doing in this place? No longer do we have leather or meat."

His words were as cold as ice. Arienne, barely able to breathe, tried to say something, but the only word that escaped her was "Why . . . ?"

The ghost's face instantly began to melt. His skin—mustache and all—slid off, revealing his cheekbones, then the rest of his skull. Breathing was now impossible.

The skull spoke.

"Why has Mersia become what it is now? Or what became of the great green steppe and the herds of oroxen, the beautiful city of Danras?"

She barely managed a nod. Clumps of hair from the hanging

head of the ghost dripped down to the ground and vanished where they fell.

"Are you an Imperial? Did you come here because there is still something you haven't destroyed yet?"

At the mention of "Imperial," the hundreds of ghosts passing by suddenly stopped in their tracks. The riders, even the horses, turned their heads her way.

Unable to speak, Arienne shook her head, again and again. The skull-ghost stared at her for a moment before turning away and mounting his horse as if they had never spoken.

"O Grim King!" he called out, almost like a sigh. "We have come. Late it may be, but accept our offerings!"

The ghosts suddenly broke out in wails, vanishing one by one into the invisible fog. When the last ghost was gone, Arienne expelled the breath that had been locked inside her lungs.

She had to go back the way she came. She could not spend even one moment more in this place. Mersia would kill her.

As soon as the first scintilla of strength made it back into her body, she began to crawl. She grabbed Aron's reins. As she bore her weight down on them, Aron brayed and began to walk backward, dragging Arienne along, but she dared not let go. If only Aron could drag her all the way back to Arland. The ground scratched her cheek, but the pain was nothing compared to the desperation she felt.

A shriek, inside her mind. Arienne screamed out loud as she was suddenly deluged with Power as if a dam had broken. Her whole body came back to life as if she were a fish tossed back into the ocean.

She let go of the reins. Aron, freed of her weight, stopped

backstepping. Arienne unsteadily got back on her feet. She could breathe. She could move her arms and legs. She took a deep breath. The sky was darker, but the winds had ceased, and the shrieking continued only in her mind.

Opening the door into the room in her mind, she found that it was only the baby who was shrieking. Babies were supposed to cry often, but this was the first time Tychon had really cried like this. Arienne didn't know how to comfort a baby—*should* she comfort him? It was his cries that had saved her from the paralysis, like a spell broken.

"It's all right, Ty, I'm all right now. Thank you for saving me. Now shhhh."

Tychon's cries grew softer and then ceased. His grimace disappeared and he was his happy, adorable self again. The walls of the room still seemed to echo with his cries, though, a sound her ears couldn't hear but she could feel nonetheless. It almost felt like the thudding of faraway drums, directing soldiers to march on.

There was pain in her right cheek where she had scraped it along the ground. Aron stood at a distance, looking at her warily. Carefully approaching the donkey, she took hold of the reins with her left hand.

Her hair fell over her eyes when she lowered her hood. She gripped a lock of it and noticed that the dust of the winds had made it almost impossible to discern what the original color of her hair had been. She gently tugged the reins. Aron followed obligingly. The desperate feeling from a moment ago was gone, but something pressed down on her heart. She felt uncertain about whether she'd be able to call upon her Power when she needed it.

Arienne fixed her clothing and gathered her wits. This mission was hard, but it would be harder to give it up. There was a long way to go, but even longer still should she turn back. Focusing on the thudding drumbeat left behind by Tychon's cries, she continued on her path.

As night continued to fall upon Mersia, Arienne thought about what had happened and tried to rationalize her experience. Countless souls had vanished in the blink of an eye here, and any such massacre would leave a trace. Sorcerers were especially sensitive to this trace. And Arienne had to admit that this wasn't the first time something like this had happened to her.

When Arienne was a little girl, her parents had once taken her with them to Kingsworth to sell their goats. What had left the deepest impression on this country girl wasn't the people on the street in their colorful clothing or the loud and fanciful performances of the traveling troupes in the squares—it was the slaughterhouse. A shapeless, ineffable presence saturated it all around. Little Arienne had stared at the slaughterhouse as if haunted herself. That was when her magical talents were first suspected.

Then two years ago, in a fortress destroyed by the Imperial army that had come to suppress Arland's rebellion, shadows that just barely retained the outlines of what they used to be, specters that Arienne could only call ghosts, had roamed among the ruins. They seemed invisible to the people Arienne had been there with. Sleep eluded her for days. Months later, when she got up the courage to go again, the ghosts were gone.

A hundred years had passed since the fall of Mersia, but the traces of the people who had lived there still lingered. The ghosts she had just seen—had they grown any fainter in the past hundred years?

She took a lantern from the donkey's burden and lit it. The light was only just enough to illuminate a few steps around her; else she was lost in a world of pitch-black. Without the light, she might as well have been standing in the middle of the night sky.

There was no point in seeking shelter in this dark. Arienne put down her lantern and took off her glass orb—it still might have its uses, but it had utterly failed her tonight. She hung it on the lantern, before turning to take down a long staff and blankets from the donkey's back. It would have been good to raise the staff and hang the lantern on it, but it was too dangerous to go looking for a stone to support the base in this darkness where ghosts roamed. And there was no point in making a fire—what few dead plants could be gathered around here would burn out long before the night was over, and there were no beasts around to menace her anyway. The only defense against the cold was to cover up with as many blankets as possible. She hesitated as to whether to extinguish the lamp to save the oil, but in the end, she left it on to burn through whatever fuel it had in it.

In the narrow bit of ground that the light of the lantern touched, Arienne put down her staff and pallet. Winding Aron's reins around one arm so he wouldn't wander away in the night, she lay down and wrapped herself in her blanket as warmly as she could.

She closed her eyes and entered the room in her mind once again. Tychon was asleep, his breathing making slight whistling sounds. Careful not to wake him, she gently lifted him from the crib and carried him to her bed. She slipped into the silky velvet sheets. Inside the room in her mind, Arienne was not covered in the filth of travel. The cold still seeped into her bones despite her thick blanket, but in this room, Arienne could lie down on a comfortable bed and cover herself with luxurious bedding. She could fall asleep to the peaceful view of a slumbering baby.

Whether it was a dream or simply a drifting thought before falling asleep, Arienne thought of Danras, the city as it was before it was devastated by the Star of Mersia. She had never even seen its ruins, but she imagined what it might have looked like.

In these imaginings, Danras, a city made rich from leather and meat, was an impressive fortress surrounded by log walls. Outside the walls, tall grass made a sound like the ocean's waves as the wind rustled through it. Children played in the grass, laughing, their heads popping in and out of view. The paths to the wall didn't need to be mowed, as the oroxen kept the roads trampled.

As the gates opened, the city was revealed. Leather was more common here than cloth, and the windows had rolling blinds of orox leather instead of drapes. The streets were crowded, with the occasional person in Cassian velvet among the leather-clad crowd. The people seemed to have gathered for a purpose, their gazes fixed in one direction.

Through the crowd, a tall woman wearing tasseled leather chaps rode a tall horse toward the leather gates. Her hair was woven into a single long braid, and she wore a leather hat with a wide brim. There was a sprinkle of freckles on her tanned face, which exuded good health. Arienne wondered who she was.

A large carriage followed the woman. The crowd made way for the horse and carriage, applauding and cheering, and shouting something. A language Arienne had never heard before, and yet she understood.

"Yuma! Chief Herder! Bless us again this summer! Bless us!"

There was the sound of a horn being blown beyond the gates. The rumble of countless orox hooves on the ground came closer. The sweet smell of grass wafted on the breeze. The year's herding was about to begin.

Arienne fell asleep.

3

YUMA

The rain pounding against her hat brim thudded in her ears. The sky, even wider than the endless steppe, was covered in black clouds. There were still hours to go until the sun set, but the world had already entered a strange night.

"... can't ... this ..."

Aidan, who had painstakingly made his horse climb up the hill to her, could scarcely be heard over the sound of the rain.

"What? Come closer, I can't hear you!" Yuma shouted, gesturing at him to approach. With her other hand, she gripped Falco's reins and a handful of his mane. Falco, whipped by raindrops, shifted with displeasure and restlessness. His black coat looked somehow blacker when soaked with rain.

Aidan's horse took a few steps closer. Rivulets of rainwater poured off Aidan's hat and his short gray mustache. The light hit just the right side of his face, which was permanently unmoving and had a blue tinge; the lighting made him look even more serious than usual.

"We can't go farther like this. We need to signal the Grim King and pay his due!"

The clouds and rain were indeed a sign that the Ruler of the Merseh Steppe wanted his share. The rains would not cease until oroxen were given over to him.

Yuma bit her lip. Down the hill, their herd of oroxen surrounded the kitchen carriage, both herd and carriage protected for now by the song of the Host. Lightning flashed in the clouds ahead, dimly lighting up the ground below, making the oroxen uneasy. They were a hundred times as massive as she was, but they were also as skittish as rabbits. Once the Host exhausted himself and the thick strands of rain started hitting their backs, the oroxen would flee every which way.

Northward, thirty herders were striking camp, collapsing tents and putting away bedding. There was still plenty of grass in these parts for the oroxen to graze, and they could easily spend another moon here. As long as the Grim King didn't interfere.

Aidan shouted, "Chief! You must send the signal of supplication! We have much ground to cover before we leave the Grim King's backyard!"

Yuma brushed rainwater off her coat and firmly shook her head.

"We shall not!"

Not this year. The Grim King must learn that harming his people would mean harming himself. Aidan half opened his lips and murmured something but gave his horse a kick and descended back down the hill.

There was a strange movement on the edge of her vision. Turning to her right, she saw that a patrolling horse had fallen on the rain-flattened grass. Her horses were well-trained, but a younger one might have been spooked by this crushing weather. Its cries would be enough to determine how seriously it was hurt, but it was impossible to hear anything over the rain.

She could hear Falco's hooves splashing in water, though. There was not a river or stream in this region, only the tall grass that grew up to her waist, and yet the land was flooding. Did the Grim King not care about anything other than his tyranny? Would he not be troubled if they all drowned?

Yuma gave a long sigh as she realized that her hat only limited her sight and was not shielding her from the rain. She took it off, hooked it onto her saddle, and gave a kick into the sides of her horse. The rain pounded her scalp as Falco shot like an arrow through the falling curtains of water.

"Chief!" young Rizona shouted, the first to recognize her as she approached the group of herders.

"Rizona, whose horse was that? Is the rider hurt?"

"Jed, it's Jed's . . ."

But Rizona was not looking at the fallen horse. Her eyes were gazing above, as if following a bird.

Yuma realized the other herders were also looking not at her but at the sky. She followed their gazes, and there was indeed something up there darker than the dark sky. A great roar sounded like thunder through the rain.

Without hesitation, Yuma grabbed the crossbow that hung on the left of her saddle and aimed at the shadow above. She pulled the lever on the bottom, hearing the bolts click into place. Without blinking away the rainwater in her eyes, she pulled the trigger. Almost at the same time, the shadow shrieked once more.

Something fell from the sky onto the fallen horse with a thump. A bloodied Jed. He gasped and moved slightly—still alive, but only just. Yuma pulled the lever and aimed again.

Just before she could shoot, someone shouted, "It's coming!"

The black shadow swooped toward them at enormous speed. Before Yuma could even command her horse, Falco leaped out of the way, just dodging the giant thing that landed right where they'd been.

It was not a bird or a bat, though it resembled both. As large as an orox, it was covered in scales. The monster got up on its hind legs, spread its webbed wings, and roared. A smell of rot enveloped them, a stench of death not even the rains could wash away. From its snake-like, four-eyed head unfurled a blue tongue.

The herders reared backward on their horses. Jed, who had fallen from the sky, was barely breathing. Yuma fired her crossbow. The monster flinched, but it was impossible to tell if her weapon mattered at all. The Grim King's dead servants knew nothing of pain or fatigue until they died again.

"What are you all doing? Draw your bows!"

But even as she said it, she realized the bowstrings and feather fletchings would be drenched and ineffective in this wet weather. Merseh was normally arid, but now . . . Some of the herders heeded her call and raised their bows, while others drew their machetes instead. But most of them were frozen in place, trembling on their mounts.

Yuma made Falco slowly back away as she loaded the crossbow again. Calmly aiming for the monster's milky eyes on its darting snake-like head, she pulled the trigger and hit one of its eyes.

But the monster gave no indication of having been injured. Instead, its remaining three eyes fixed on Yuma, and getting down on its winged front legs, it crawled toward her. Fast. It was at a speed that Falco could not simply back away from—Yuma turned Falco's head in the opposite direction and spurred him on as she turned and pulled the lever on her crossbow to load it.

Despite Falco's speed, the slithery tongue of the monster was still close enough to touch. She pulled the trigger and the fourth bolt hit it in the middle of its forehead. But the Grim King's monster did not stop. Her heart fell to her stomach and the rain roared in her ears. Letting out a hoarse wail, the monster reared up and threw itself upon Yuma and Falco.

Yuma jumped off the horse just in time, rolling on the ground and looking up to see the monster's teeth biting into Falco's neck. Her crossbow landed a few steps away, and her machete was still at Falco's side, attached to the saddle. The monster whipped its head and blood spurted from Falco like a fountain, the horse's legs jerking pitifully. Falco and Yuma met eyes as lightning brightened the sky. She had been with him since he was born, fed him herself when his mother died soon after giving birth. The monster, as if admiring its handiwork, stared down at the dying horse. Falco ceased all movement.

The thick veil of rain obscured the other herders from her view, but it was clear enough that no one was coming to help her. The monster turned from the horse to Yuma. Its lolling blue tongue was now lying, still thrashing, at its feet—this monster had bitten off its own tongue in its frenzy to maul Falco.

Meeting its eyes, Yuma slowly got to her feet. She had no

weapons, not even her hat, which was still hanging from Falco's saddle alongside her machete. She swept back the stray hairs that fell over her eyes and quickly tied up her braid into a firm bun. The monster tilted its head once before approaching her slowly. There was nowhere to hide on this field, and no human on their own two legs could outrun this monster. Yuma carefully found a hard piece of earth to stand on in the pooling rain and straightened her back to her full height.

The enemy might be the size of an orox, but Yuma had learned how to handle oroxen from a young age. If she could get on this monster's back and grab its neck, she might have a chance of bringing it to heel.

The monster walked to her, its claws scraping the ground. That stench again. She glimpsed the root of its severed tongue in its mouth, black blood oozing from the wound and dripping off its chin. Yuma ignored this horrifying sight and instead concentrated on the monster's mouth and neck. The monster's stride grew faster. It was like a wolf that had been cautious at first but couldn't resist the smell of meat any longer.

The monster's teeth-filled maw came at her like an arrow. Yuma swerved to the right and grabbed the monster's neck using her left arm like a snare. Without a second thought, she jumped and mounted the shoulders of the monster. The monster almost stumbled when her full weight landed on it, and its scream slammed against her eardrums.

The Grim King's monster reared its head to try to shake her loose, but instead lost its balance and fell to the side. Yuma's right hand hit the ground in an effort to break her fall, but the weight of the monster made it pointless. Mud splattered everywhere. She almost lost consciousness, not to mention her hold on the monster's neck, as pain ripped through her whole body.

The monster's claws tried to reach her, but only the vestigial ones on the edge of its wings scratched a little at her cheek and tough leather clothes. She added her right arm around its neck and squeezed with all her might.

The monster rolled on the ground. Mud entered her nose and eyes. It smelled of dead flesh everywhere. But Yuma did not stop strangling the monster. She straightened her back and heard a dull crack, and the monster's neck went limp.

Was its neck broken? Perhaps. And yet the monster, its neck hanging like an old rope, stood back up. It wasn't a living beast after all—just a carcass reanimated by the false life bestowed by the Grim King. It suddenly leaped into the air with Yuma still on its back. The dead stench hit Yuma's face with every flap of the wings, and she squeezed the monster's neck tighter. Not to kill, this time, but to keep herself from falling.

The monster flew slowly into the air, its head hanging on its broken neck. The ground grew farther away. There were bolts embedded in one eye and the forehead of the monster, but the remaining three eyes were still open—did it even see with those empty milky eyes? Yuma looked down to see Falco's carcass far below as well as the herders with their machetes drawn, rushing to her aid too late. A few pointed in the air and shouted. Her eyesight blurred, and her fingers grew weak.

But so did the wings of the monster. Yuma hugged the undead beast's neck tight and closed her eyes as she and the monster crashed to the ground. A shock, incomparably greater than the last, thudded through her, making her lose her grip and bounce off the monster before rolling to a stop. Something burst inside her. How much better it would have been if she'd lost consciousness . . .

The herders surrounded the monster but did not dare approach it further. Two of them galloped toward her on their horses.

Yuma, trying not to seem injured, stood up as gracefully as she could. Then, slowly but steadily, she walked to where Falco lay and closed his big eyes before she unhooked the hat from the saddle, placed it on her head, and drew her machete from its sheath.

The monster flailed on the ground. Once upon a time, it might have been a formidable predator in a faraway land, flying free in the sky in search of prey. But now it was sending up its rotting stench on the steppe, dying a second death. With its remaining three cloudy eyes, it stared at Yuma as she walked up to it. Holding her machete with both hands, she struck down on its neck. Again. And again.

The head was finally lopped off, and the monster was no more.

She wanted to collapse there and then, but the other herders were watching. Piercing the ground with her blade, she leaned on it as she slowly sat down on the ground. Black, bloody lumps oozed from the neck of the monster. Its stench no longer registered in her mind.

"Chief . . ."

A herder had come down from his horse, and all the others followed his lead. They approached, slowly. Ashamed.

"I'm fine. Don't worry about me."

Her whole body ached, but she tried not to show it. They had a long time before the herding would be over for that year, and the job was difficult enough without having to contend with low morale. Aidan, whom Yuma had noted missing until this moment, was now present, his scarred face as somber as ever.

She said, "What of the kitchen carriage? And the Host?"

"Safe. The oroxen are also calm."

"And Jed?" The memory of him struggling to breathe flashed through her mind.

"Dead."

The rain abated. The clouds overhead thinned, and the light of the early evening slowly returned. Maybe it had been the monster that had turned the sky to darkness.

"We have to collect Jed's body." Yuma stood up. "Bring me a new horse. Aston should be fine. Anyone riding him?"

"Who would dare ride him but you, Chief?" said young Rizona with a weak smile. She was thankfully unhurt.

"Good. Bring him to me."

Aidan watched Rizona get back on her horse and ride off to the kitchen carriage before approaching Yuma. There were still raindrops dripping from his mustache.

"How injured are you?"

The half of his face that was blue and dead had no expression, but the other half was vivid with worry.

"Not badly." She tried a smile.

"You must go see the Host."

"If I do, I must be on horseback." She gave a brief glance at the herders and looked back at him. Aidan, understanding, nodded.

"This won't be the last we hear from the Grim King," he warned.

"We can pay our tithe next year. But we need to make clear our objection to what happened last winter."

A few herders brought her the saddle they carefully removed from Falco, then retrieved her crossbow as well. Yuma pinched her hat by the brim and nodded to them in thanks.

Aidan waited until the herders were out of earshot before saying, "You said that before we left Danras. I won't speak more on the matter, but you know I'm concerned."

"About what?" Yuma asked blithely.

"The Grim King is not a horse nor orox. Whipping him on the snout will not teach him to behave."

Yuma took a deep breath to argue the point, but that brought on a spasm of pain. As she gripped her chest and grimaced, Aidan averted his gaze and subtly offered his elbow. Yuma took it as she straightened herself.

She followed Aidan's gaze to the west to see Rizona leading Aston by the reins toward them. The western sky was, as it should be at this hour, now awash in yellow and red.

"Aidan. Ask the Host to prepare for treatment."

"Prepare? You're not going to him now?"

"I want to see Jed first."

Yuma took the reins from Rizona as they approached. Aston's drenched hide shone gold, reflecting the setting sun. Yuma gritted her teeth as she hauled her saddle on the horse's back and secured it. She mounted the horse with great pain in her chest and stomach, but at least she didn't fall off.

Aidan turned his horse toward the Host's carriage, and Rizona led Yuma to where Jed lay. The younger woman glanced up at

Yuma from time to time—Yuma was focused on hiding her pain, but much later Yuma would realize they were not looks of worry but looks of awe. Her deed would be spoken of by many fires in the days to come, and by the time they reached Danras, the story of how she defeated the undead monster would pass into legend.

But Jed would never hear this story or add to it. The monster had left a long gash on his body. He no longer breathed, nor did he bleed. His face was drained of life.

"I thought something had passed over me and then in the next second, Jed was gone," Rizona said, her eyes fixed on the body. Jed had not been much older than Rizona—since he completed his first herding the year before, it was tradition that this summer would be heralded as his coming of age. Yuma looked at Rizona, worried about the effect Jed's death might have on her.

She dismounted. Jed's horse was still breathing. How helpless it looked, panting there on the ground. If it hadn't gotten up by now, it probably had a broken leg. A human with a broken leg only needs rest until the bone sets again. But when a horse breaks its leg, the bone tends to shatter, snapping tendons and tearing muscles. Such incidents mostly end in a painful death.

Yuma raised her crossbow and pulled the loading lever. Before she approached the horse, Yuma glanced at Rizona, watching as the girl observed the proper rite of backing away on her horse and turning to look in the opposite direction. Jed's horse was called Spera. He was a six-year-old stallion that was sweet as a lamb and as fast as a rabbit. In her mind, she drew an X using Spera's ears and eyes as origin points. She aimed a little above where the lines intersected and placed her crossbow there. She pulled the trigger.

Spera spasmed once. His breathing slowed. Yuma watched until he breathed no more.

Footsteps approached.

"Rizona, you should be looking away." But when she turned, it wasn't Rizona who was standing there. Rizona was still sitting on her horse, turned away from her.

The one who stood behind her was Jed.

4

EMERE

The clean white room had traces of old blood here and there where the stains could not be washed out. The Powered light fixture on the wall infused the space with a pale blue light. On a small table by the bed, there was an array of surgical implements neatly laid out for use.

Emere took off his bloody clothes and sat on the edge of the bed, carefully rubbing the wound on his chest with a cloth soaked in medicine. The pain slowly melted away. He sighed with relief. How wonderful it was to not be in pain.

The assassin's sword also lay on the small table by the bed. The assassin must have been Cassian, as her crossbow had been, but the sword was Imperial. The engraved pattern looked like an eye or perhaps a bird; in any case, he had never seen it before. But there were many legions within the Empire, and it was likely an emblem for one of those.

Rakel was selecting medicine from a cabinet. Surgeons in the

Capital were normally shaved bald, but Rakel tied her long hair up into a knot and covered it with a white cloth instead, in the Ebrian fashion. She hadn't had a single white hair ten years ago when they last parted at the Kamori border, but now he could see many of them peeking out from under her surgical headcloth.

Emere had put off visiting Rakel for a long time, but he was here at last. He had pictured several versions of his reunion with her. She was well within her rights to be resentful, which was probably why he had been reluctant to come here. Perhaps being almost killed trumped every pathetic excuse he had been making not to visit his old lover and travel companion.

But when she opened the door, Rakel met his arrival calmly, noticing his injury before anything else. He didn't even have time to say anything beyond a simple greeting, as she wasted no time in treating his wounds.

Even after all those years, and with all those white strands of hair, for a moment Emere felt like no time had passed since they parted ways. There was something comforting and right about her movements, the smell of the room they were in. Right now, he trusted her more than anyone in the world.

"I haven't seen a wound like this in a long time," she said, examining it with worry in her eyes. "People in the Capital don't get shot by Cassian bolts often." The sight of her face brought back many memories from years ago—when Kamori had surrendered to the Empire, when he had fought with his mother before leaving home and wandering the world.

"How does it look?" he asked.

"Just a little bit above this and you would've bled out very quickly. Who took out the bolt?"

"I did. I thought it would be all right."

Rakel frowned and gave him a light slap on the shoulder. "Not again! Your face is as old as a legend but you're still behaving like a boy!"

Emere's hand rose to his face. He needed no mirror to tell him there was white mixed in with his stubble now too. He had met Rakel just a few months after setting out eastward from home. Emere had been twenty-four, Rakel twenty-two. They were together for nearly ten years before he left her, and now it had been nearly ten years since he had last seen her.

"I heard a rumor you were married," he said, changing the subject. "How is your husband?"

"Why, are you filled with regret? Was I your 'destiny' all along?" she teased. There was no resentment in her voice, but it didn't sound entirely lighthearted either. Her eyes were still examining the wound, and Emere didn't reply.

He had once been a prince of Kamori, and she the daughter of a fallen family of priests in Ebria—her parents had died in prison after being discovered worshipping their Nameless God, which was against the Imperial edict banning their religion. He and Rakel had traveled the world for ten years, searching for ways to fight the Empire. They'd been to all manner of places, but it had come to nothing. Ten years ago, Emere had bid her farewell at Finvera Pass and joined the rebel forces of his brother, the self-styled King Gwaharad . . . which had also come to nothing.

"My husband died two years ago in the Great Fire."

"I see," murmured Emere. Rakel's expression did not change at all as she continued to examine the wound using a small mirror.

Had her own wounds healed? At Finvera Pass, she had burst into tears at his insistence they part. Back then, he was so sure that it was the right thing to do for both of them.

He changed the subject again. "You're not going back home then?"

"To Ebria? No, I've put down roots here. I don't need to go anywhere else. And surgery isn't the only thing I do here. I have many people to care for."

"You were always like that. Wherever it was you happened to be staying, you were home."

"I'm not like you. I don't change the whole direction of my life just because I had a dream."

Rakel dipped a stick with a cotton swab into a medicinal bottle. The swab came out soaked in blue.

"I met her. The woman who kept appearing in my dream visions."

Rakel's hands froze in midair. Her eyes went wide. "You did?"

"You've heard of what happened in Arland?"

"That province where the corrupt prefect caused an uprising? Where the Empire sent a legion to negotiate peace?"

That seemed to be the story circulating around the Empire. The real story was the stuff of legends—that a princess with a flaming sword had risen, as did the dragon of the volcano, and that the Empire's army had been defeated by a local militia. It hardly sounded credible, but the Empire nevertheless would not have been pleased if the truth got out.

"She's the one who led the uprising. A local widow," Emere explained. "I helped, a little," he couldn't help adding.

43

"At least one thing happened according to that 'destiny' of yours." Rakel carefully applied the cotton ball to his wound. Perhaps because of the numbing agent he had pressed on his chest before, he could barely feel her ministrations. The pain-numbing medicine was a specialty of the Ebrian surgeons. In their youth, both Emere and Rakel had relied on it heavily during their adventures.

"I'm sorry," he blurted out.

"For what?"

"For leaving you like that."

A shade of sadness came over Rakel's features. She looked as if she was about to say something to him but then turned her face and dipped the curved surgical needle into the small pot of boiling water. She then gently brought the needle to his wound. A narrow plume of steam issued from the needle tip.

"Hot?"

"No."

She pierced him with the needle. Still no sensation.

"Don't be sorry," Rakel suddenly continued. "You've always gone and done exactly what you wanted to do. Don't pretend you feel sorry for anyone."

"I had no other choice. There were things I had to do."

After making another stitch, Rakel let go of the needle, letting it dangle by the thread.

"You know, back then I might have been young enough to buy that. But I've had a lot of time to think about it since." Her voice was strained. "You left Kamori to find a way to fight the Empire. Then you met me, and what did we really do? We certainly didn't topple the Empire. After ten years with me, you then said you would go back home, and *again* your reason was to fight the Empire. But what did you accomplish there? Twenty years later, and you're still no closer to liberating Kamori."

"It turned out that way, but—"

"Please, look at the Empire. They have legions, gigatherions, the Star of Mersia. They have conquered the world. What can anyone do to defeat them? Why couldn't you admit it was an impossible dream?"

"But you went along with it for ten years."

Rakel stood up so forcefully that the stool she sat on fell backward.

"I wasn't going along with a dream! I was going along with *you*!"

He had always known that, of course. And that was why he had apologized. But coming from Rakel's mouth, the truth weighed heavier than ever.

"You know, I'm a Commons councillor now. I may spend the rest of my life in the Capital. Maybe we can see each other from time to time, talk about the old days."

Rakel said nothing to that. As if to shake off her own annoyance, she turned her head and stared at the wall. The needle still hung by its thread, its white string reddening. By the time the blood reached the needle, Rakel turned back to him.

"I was with you longer than anyone else I've been with," she murmured.

"Me as well."

"Which makes me doubt you will be here for very long. You'll find some other star in the sky to chase."

In the dream vision in the square, Loran had pointed at a

single star shining in the black sky and told him to reach for it. Whenever he saw a star or some mysterious object in his dream, he always went after it. But the closest he had ever gotten to reaching what he sought was when he met Loran and joined the Arlander rebellion.

Still, was that not enough for one life?

Rakel sat back down and continued to sew up his wound. He couldn't feel the needle at all. After some final stitches, Rakel finished up and snipped the needle off the thread.

"The numbing medicine will stop working in a little while. If you don't want to be up all night in pain, you'll need to apply it twice more. I'll have your clothes washed." Rakel paused. "Don't exert yourself—just stay here for a night."

He wanted to. His exhaustion over the past half year in the Capital had reached its peak. He imagined himself listening to the light rain thudding on the wooden shutters as he drank warm wine and talked of the past with his old flame.

Emere nodded. Rakel picked up his bloody clothes and dropped them in a basket in the corner.

"I'll bring a blanket."

She went up the stairs, her walk and her scent—the faint smell of medicine—exactly as they were in his memory. The past unfurled in his mind: the dense dust wind of the wastelands of Mersia; the moldy inn where the floods had stranded them in Elvania; the hot, crystalline sands of the Kalikan coast; the Ebrian prayer Rakel would recite before the wooden statue she had always carried with her . . .

When Rakel came back down with a blanket, she had changed from her bloodied surgical garment to a yellow dress. Emere was still sitting on the edge of the bed, and she wrapped his shoulders in the blanket and sat down at his right. Emere hesitantly put his arm around her shoulders and Rakel relaxed against him. He imagined a younger version of himself with Rakel in a framed picture, hanging in a corner of their minds. They could never go back in time to the way they were, but the memory would live forever. They sat like this in silence for a while before Emere finally lay down to sleep.

He dreamed of the wastelands of Mersia. From a distance, like a mirage, came a person. A small person, covering their face to block the dust. Emere approached. He couldn't see anyone else besides this figure, but he could feel the presence of others. The same feeling he had over a decade ago when he had briefly visited Mersia in person with Rakel.

"Prince Emere."

The dusty traveler with the concealed face had vanished, and in their place was a young woman in the neat blue dress of Arland, her hair cut to just under her earlobes. It was the sorcerer who had freed the dragon in the volcano during the Arlander rebellion—Arienne. She was holding a baby in a blanket that was embroidered with a flower design he did not recognize. Emere felt a vague familiarity at the sight of the infant.

"I've been here before," said Emere, not returning the greeting.

"You have? What was your purpose here?"

"I wanted to know what the 'Star' was that ended Mersia."

A sandstorm as large as a mountain brewed behind Arienne, looking strong enough to not only tear their clothes from their bodies but their flesh from their bones. Emere grew nervous. They had to get out of there. His feet, however, refused to move.

"Did you find out?" Arienne asked.

Emere shook his head. They had found nothing except red lifeless ground, and a feeling of despair so overwhelming that he couldn't breathe. If it hadn't been for Rakel, he would've died there.

"If that is also your purpose in Mersia, good sorcerer, I bid you to leave at once."

"But where must I go instead?"

The storm wailed. Arienne seemed oblivious to the impending wall of dust as it came upon them. Emere covered his face with his arms as sharp fragments ripped at his flesh. He tried to scream, but when he opened his mouth, it filled with dust.

The winds ceased. His pain disappeared. When he lowered his arm, he was in the Capital, on the busy streets below the hill where the Senate stood. The night air was hot, and everywhere it burned with red-and-yellow flames. Emere's eyes were drawn to a young man who was walking up the hill, heading for the Senate. The man reminded Emere of Loran.

Emere followed the young man. He seemed to be wearing a pair of spectacles. Just as the young man's walk was about to change into a run, Emere noticed a man he didn't know lying in the middle of the street, charred and motionless. Rakel was kneeling next to him, sobbing. Emere still had an urge to follow the young man, but Rakel caught his attention and he could not leave her behind. Not again.

Then, he opened his eyes. The candle on the small surgical table had burned down to half its size. Rakel dozed on the chair near the head of his bed. Emere gazed at her for a while, then glanced at the table where the assassin's sword lay gleaming in the candlelight, before he closed his eyes once more.

5

ARIENNE

Danras, from up on a nearby hill, looked utterly warped.

Each log that had constituted the city walls was bent, like iron bars a blacksmith had forgotten to finish forging. The buttresses and pillars of the wooden buildings had been crushed under their own weight. Only a single stone building in the Imperial style, erected in the middle of the city, had the proper look of a man-made structure weathered only by time. The ground was paved with stone blocks, but they were covered with red dust blown by the wind from the wasteland that surrounded it.

The city had the look of a tableau created by a mad painter. Arienne gulped. A fear that was different from what she felt when she had faced the mountainous wall of dust for the first time, or when she had faced the ghosts wandering the wastelands, was creeping up from within.

"Not even a dozen legions with Powered weapons could ever do this," Arienne muttered. But what could kill a whole country, murder everything down to the grass, and still feel the need to corrode and distort what remained, a curse so hateful that it wouldn't be satisfied with a simple massacre?

To find Danras, she had envisioned ancient ruins—it hadn't mattered if what she imagined looked like the real Danras or not. Sorcery, especially Arienne's sorcery, was about imposing one's will on what was real. But there was always a price to pay for one's imagination clashing with reality, and now the imagined Danras in her mind shattered to pieces at the sight of the real Danras before her. A dizziness followed, as if the world were turning upside down.

It would've been better if she'd done more research on what Danras looked like as she embarked on her travels. The fallout from the discrepancy between the imagined and the real could very well drive her mad.

But her imagination was all Arienne had. Without it, she would still be eating the food the Imperial Academy fed her and doing the "studies" they insisted she do. She would have been a living corpse, doing nothing meaningful, with nobody expecting her to do anything besides die and become a Power generator.

She sat down on the ground, crossing her legs and sitting up straight. Who knew what other strange scenes were waiting below her. If she didn't prepare for them, the shock would be even greater than what she had just experienced. As she pressed down on the urge to avert her gaze from the ruined city, the reality of Danras entered fully into Arienne's sight. Each melted building engraved itself into her memory.

But at the same time, there was something she couldn't prevent herself from imagining—what Danras must've looked like before the Star of Mersia had destroyed it. That tower, twisted now like a reed bending in the storm, must've once been a commanding watchtower that rose above the city walls. An old watcher in a wide-brimmed hat would have looked out at the sea of tall grass.

The ruins below that, where the roofs had rotted away but sections of the walls remained, creating a shape like the sun-dried bones of a dead animal, had once been a market. The roofs would've been made of orox leather, the neatly displayed rows of goods coming from both Mersia and beyond the mountains. And people as various as the goods had bought and sold things there.

The sunken, dry groove next to the walls had once been a river that had flowed from the northern part of the Rook Mountains. There had been a busy dock. The hunk of wood that looked like melted, stretched molasses had once been a boat that traversed this river, carrying the leather of Danras to the north or bringing timber from the Rook Mountains.

She drew two cities in her mind. The first a prosperous city on the steppe, the other the devastated ruins before her.

Another giant wall of a dust storm crossed the wasteland in the distance. Aron paced around the hill, looking for grass to feed on. Was there a faint sobbing? Not daring to look, Arienne sat still and continued to commit the two cities in her mind to heart.

Just as a corner of the gray sky was turning dark, something moved at the edge of her vision. Her head quickly turned. The lone stone building, which had probably been the prefect's office, shook. A heavy thud echoed through the once-grassland.

There was something there.

Heart pounding, Arienne gripped the glass orb around her neck and got to her feet. Her body tingled a little and a white light began to glow outward from the orb. Power still flowed in her. Ever since the night she had encountered the ghosts, she had been infusing Power into the orb before going to sleep. The horse seller had assured her that a friend of his wife's brother had used this piece of jewelry to ward off ghosts as he crossed the steppe of Mersia. She wasn't convinced yet that it had any real effect, but she at least found it to be a useful indicator of whether her Power was flowing or not.

"Aron!"

The donkey had already gone closer to the ruins while Arienne was looking elsewhere. He must've found some dead tuft or other, as his nose was buried in the ground. At his name, he briefly looked up in her direction and lowered his head again. She plodded down the hill and grabbed the reins of the donkey as he tried to eat something that looked like fossilized grass.

Arienne recalled the horse seller's warning that she should not go into places where people had once lived in Mersia. If the ghosts hadn't already convinced her, the strange sound earlier made her realize that the man hadn't just been trying to scare her—not that such a warning would've been enough to keep her from coming here, even if she had believed him.

The walls of the city proper were much farther than it looked from the hill. As she went down the path, she stared at the prefect's stone office that towered over the walls. It was quiet as she approached, and windless and dark by the time she reached them.

She lit her lamp and looked closely at the walls. Through the twisted mess, she found a gap that would just allow a donkey to pass. Glad that she did not have to find a gate to enter, she squeezed through, feeling as if she were entering a forest where trees grew thick and tall. The heroines who entered such woods in the books she had read as a child would always encounter a witch there. But tonight, that witch was Arienne. Who knew what the witch would find in the darkness of the forest that wasn't?

Despite passing through the wall, she was still surrounded by twisted timber. How was this city laid out? Mersia's night was heavy with darkness, and the lantern could only light so much. Was there a path she had overlooked?

Her lantern light suddenly revealed a skeleton tangled in the wood next to her head. She suppressed a scream and backed away, Aron braying as he also reacted in surprise. Like the walls and buildings, the skeleton was warped.

The remains were entangled in what looked like the window frame of a building. The finger bones gripped the wooden bars and looked melted into a lump, and the skull was stuck between the bars, halfway outside the building. The top of the skull had melted, dripping into lumps down the wall below. Arienne calmed her beating heart, taking deep breaths. She took a closer look at the skeleton and said, deliberately out loud, "It's all right. At least it didn't move."

Skeletons that moved were very common in adventure stories. They looked like people but were not; they were simply monsters who had once been human, things that an adventurer could slay without the inconvenience of guilt. The Grim King who had ruled over this land, the sorcerer Eldred, had indeed been a necromancer who dealt in corpses. Monsters *had* roamed Mersia.

But there was no more Grim King of Mersia to create and rule the undead anymore. Arienne had made sure of that when she slew the reborn Eldred in the volcano in Arland two years ago.

She returned her attention to the skeleton and the building behind it. It was a very warped building, but she could just about understand where the rooms might be. She would spend the night here.

There was no door on this wall, so she imagined a small saw with a smooth wooden handle and well-maintained sharp saw-teeth. As she imagined it sawing through the window frame in her mind, she chanted the cutting spell. Eldred had mocked her sorcery, saying it was like that of a baby's babble, but this very spell had severed Eldred's arms and ended the life of Grand Inquisitor Lysandros.

The skeleton, along with the wooden bars, fell inside the building. The donkey would not fit through the window, so she tied his reins to a bent post nearby. As Arienne was about to crawl through the window, Aron brayed distressingly. Was he telling her not to leave him behind? There hadn't been any indication of danger since coming down the hill toward Danras, but there was definitely something eerie about the city, like that strange thud. Perhaps Aron could sense something she herself couldn't.

Arienne opened the door of her mind where Tychon babbled in his crib.

"You'll have to excuse me, little one; I'm bringing in a friend."

In her mind's room, she drew the shape of an oval on the wall with her finger; then light appeared inside the oval, turning into a swirl of violet. In the dark Danras alley, an identical swirl appeared. Arienne slapped the donkey's behind. Aron, understanding, walked through the violet gate and into the room in her mind.

His bulky presence made her head ache slightly. Aron looked around the room before showing interest in the books on the bookshelf. Arienne pulled at his reins and said, "Stay in this corner or else I'll throw you out."

Aron blubbered and settled down in the corner as told.

It would be safe here—as long as Arienne herself was safe, at least. She closed the door to the room. The violet swirl faded away.

Outside her mind, she climbed through the window of the building. On the wooden floor, which was as warped and twisted as the walls, the skeleton lay entangled in debris. There was a bed with a collapsed bed frame in the center, deteriorating clothes and blankets inside a wardrobe that was barely hanging on to its doors, and on the wall above the bed was another window looking out on what Arienne thought was the main street.

That skeleton had probably been the owner of this room. Why had they grabbed on to the window instead of leaving through the door? Arienne now tried to open the door, but no matter how she pushed and pulled, it was stuck. The doorframe had been twisted too tightly. Was the skeleton's family beyond this door? Were they, like the one here, a pile of melted bones on the floor?

Once more, she heard the sound she'd heard on the hill, a thud loud enough to shake the house. She dropped to the floor and held her breath. There was the creaking of wood and iron—and underneath, a softer but more familiar sound.

A humming that made her blood run cold. It was what the Arlanders called the sound of the sleeping dragon but what Arienne knew as the humming of a Power generator. She got to her feet and stepped up on the crumbling bed frame to look out the window.

The street, which should've been shrouded in darkness, was now lit up in blue light, the same color as the streetlights of the Imperial Capital. With this new light, Arienne could now make out new details around her. Wooden and leather signs, melted and rotted almost beyond recognizability, swung helplessly along the dusty street. The letters were so faded and mangled that she couldn't read even the Imperial translations beneath what she assumed was the native script. She could, however, make out the text on a rusted plaque of a stone stele in the middle of the nearest intersection, carved deeply in Imperial and illuminated by the Powered lamps.

DA-RAS, THE GLORIOUS CAP-TAL OF THE I-PERIAL PROV—OF MERS-A

In empty Danras, Powered streetlamps had turned on and were now shining on the warped ruins. Where was the Power coming from?

And something stood outside in the street. It was about the size of a small house, on four mechanical legs, with two Powered lights stuck to the front like the eyes of a beast, lighting up the way before it.

Arienne quickly, silently stepped away from the window and went up to the door that would not open. She began to imagine what would be needed to cut through it.

6

YUMA

Jed's back was painfully twisted and his eyes were empty of life as he stood there. But a rattling breath escaped him, and his mouth opened, speaking words.

"Chief . . . run . . ."

Jed's limbs quivered, and then his back straightened like a bowstring that had been released. He stumbled toward Yuma. The light had come back in his eyes, but it was a violet, inhuman light.

Calmly, Yuma placed her hand on her crossbow and lifted it toward Jed.

"Chief Herder of Danras. We meet for the second time."

The Grim King's voice was coming from Jed's throat. It was not a voice to be easily forgotten. Rizona, perhaps still unaware of what was going on, was a dozen paces away and still had her back turned to them.

"Grim King," she answered in a low voice.

She didn't want to provoke him, but she had no desire to kneel before the one who had murdered Jed and was now desecrating his body. She did not lower her crossbow.

"It seems you have no desire to make offerings this year," he said. "Is it because I took so many soldiers last winter?"

As if it hadn't been enough to kill young Jed, he was now speaking through his dead body.

"Don't you have enough corpses for your armies?" she growled.

The Grim King laughed.

"Do you think I have an unlimited supply of the dead? And what king doesn't use his people as soldiers? Lansis and Iorca both gave me more soldiers than you did."

"Danras does not overflow with people like those cities do. Winter is when we rest from our long season of herding. If we were to tear our herders away from the only time they have with their families to fight your wars, no one would be left to herd."

The Grim King scoffed. "And that is your excuse for your disgruntlement? That is not a spirit befitting the governor of Merseh's greatest city."

"I am not your governor, Grim King. I simply look after the oroxen and the herders under the mandate of the traditions and citizens of Danras. You, however, are making such duties ever more difficult by the day. If you prevent us from raising our cattle, it will not be only Danras but all of Merseh that will fall. And that will spell the end of your skeletal throne."

Even with her voice raised, Rizona was not looking her way. She prayed the girl knew to stay away. A rattling sound issued once more from Jed's throat. Whether that was from the dead man himself or a sigh from the Grim King, Yuma could not tell.

"You naïve little country girl. Too busy living among the beasts to realize heaven and earth are shifting all around you. The nations of the east and west, Cassia and the Empire, are clashing as we speak. If it weren't for your king Eldred, Merseh would have been caught in the middle and your stinking oroxen wouldn't have so much as a blade of grass to feed upon."

It sent chills down Yuma's spine to hear the Grim King say his own name. Speaking it out loud was forbidden in Merseh. But of course, the very subject of the taboo wouldn't mind such things. Yuma steadied her feelings before she spoke.

"We may be mere herders, but we know the world turns. We hear the news from the merchants who come from foreign parts."

"How do you think these merchants have safe passage?" Eldred scoffed. "Do you know what sort of beast you have just killed?"

Yuma glanced at the horse that she had just put down. But she realized it was the long-necked monster she had slain earlier that the Grim King was speaking of, and she shook her head.

"A stormbird I brought from the northern land of Tythonia. I have others patrolling the borders creating storms and winds, blocking intruders. Without them, this land would be overrun by invaders and spies. But what would happen to Danras if the storm-bird did not let the merchants pass and killed them all instead? Or if they made the river overflow with their rain? Don't you see that there is nothing to be gained from the people disobeying their king?"

Yuma said nothing. There was nothing to be said against such threats. In trying not to lose oroxen, a man and two horses had been killed. Her objection had already failed.

Jed's body twitched. Despite being dead, the body seemed to

be finding it hard to be a puppet. Rizona still had her back to them. Yuma lowered her crossbow.

"What is it you want me to do? Or is it your intention to harass us for the remainder of the herding?"

"You must make your tithes."

Aidan had warned her that the Grim King could not be taught to behave. But she could not listen to someone who would not listen themselves. Even if they were the Grim King of Merseh. Giving a finger now would result in losing an arm later.

"I will not."

"I have just declared I shall cut your trade and flood your city, but you persist in your disobedience?" His voice was full of scorn.

Yuma stood up straight.

"It has been hundreds of years since you conquered Merseh. We make our tithes, but the people of Danras value freedom above all else. If we cannot run our horses on the steppe under a blue sky, or winter with our families without fear of being pulled to fight someone else's war, we would rather choose death."

A corner of Jed's blue lips rose in a sneer.

"You would decide the fate of your city with those words. Let us see if you can stand behind them."

With the sound of bones breaking, Jed's neck slowly twisted like a rag being squeezed of water. Yuma almost vomited. Jed's right shoulder swung back implausibly, popping and dislocating. His finger pointed to Rizona, who sat on her horse with her back to them.

The Grim King said, "In Danras, there are at least a thousand such children, are there not? If you would rather die than tithe your oroxen, you will not mind if we start with this one. Since you care so little."

Yuma quickly raised her crossbow and aimed for the back of Jed's head. "Stop!"

"Chief Herder of Danras, do you already regret your hasty words?"

"Stop, I said!"

Jed's head turned again to face Yuma. His unnaturally twisted arm dropped back to his side. A terrible smile was on his lips.

"Good. It remains to be seen how much further you would go to defy me. I will exempt the tithe this year. But there is a task you shall do for me instead."

A feeling of dread made her blood run cold. "A task?"

"As I repositioned the stormbird here to warn you of your folly, a spy has crossed Crow's Bone Peak."

"That wall of ice? There is no path through it." Not even birds could go over the Crow's Bone. It surprised her that the Grim King was bothering to watch that peak at all.

"It seems he's a resourceful one. Find him."

Yuma thought for a moment before answering. "The steppe is vast. I cannot be sure to succeed."

"I, too, pin no great hopes on a mere cowherd. But if it was not a deed you were capable of, I would not task you to it. Come closer."

As Yuma reluctantly approached, Jed's twisted neck unwound itself and he opened his mouth. Violet light swirled inside. Yuma frowned as she stared into the light. His mouth opened wider, bloodlessly tearing at the corners, his jaw unhinging.

From the swirling came forth an emaciated hand in a sleeve of shadow and ember. White unfamiliar gemstones sparkled on the sleeve. Yuma had never seen the Grim King with her own eyes, but this had to be him. The hand opened. On the palm were two iridescent stones, both a little larger than a thumb.

Yuma spread her palm underneath the hand and the stones were dropped into it. A feeling of uncleanliness spread through her whole body. The Grim King's hand disappeared into Jed's mouth before his voice began to speak through Jed's mouth once more.

"The Empire uses a strange sorcery called Power generators. Should the spy resist, crush one of these nullstones. It should be enough to stop their generator for a while."

Given that the spy was entering from the west, Yuma had already suspected that the spy was coming from the "Empire" that had risen near the western shores.

The Empire had quickly gained power in the past few decades, conquering at first the smaller kingdoms that surrounded it before recently overcoming the great Emperor of Thiops in the south, a monarch said to command the very gods. Yuma rubbed the stones in her hand.

"And if it's not enough?"

"Then use both of them. Must you be told everything? They are more precious than a thousand oroxen, so do not waste them."

She had told the Grim King she could not guarantee capture, but Yuma knew the steppe through and through. If there was anything to be found in the grass sea of Merseh, the herders of Danras would find it.

"And what are we to do once we find him?"

There was no answer. When she took a careful step forward, Jed collapsed in front of her.

She crouched down and looked closely at Jed's body. It was twisted in places from the Grim King's manipulations, the neck broken. Just as she was thinking of what to say to his parents waiting for him back in the city, she heard a deep voice behind her.

"Chief."

Aidan was here, on horseback. Yuma stood up.

"The Grim King was just here," she said. She could feel tears coming, but she suppressed the sobs choking up her throat and quickly wiped her eyes with her knuckles. "We do not need to make our tithes this year."

Half of Aidan's face almost looked amused. "Is that what the Grim King said?"

"Yes. But we have to do something else for him instead."

Yuma looked over at Rizona. She was still looking away, her horse's head turned in the opposite direction from them.

"Rizona!" she shouted. "Let's go back!"

There was no answer. She shouted again, but still no answer. A feeling of dread came over her as Yuma approached the young woman. But before she reached her, Rizona leaned forward onto her horse's mane. Yuma ran. Aidan called after her.

Rizona sat on her horse, dead. Her clothes, saddle, and hair were soaked with blood.

7

EMERE

After Rakel had tended to his wounds, Emere spent three days on tedious business. Word had spread that a new councillor had been subject to an assassination attempt, and so after visiting Gildas's parents to express his condolences, Emere was besieged with so many requests for his time that he no longer even had a chance to eat a meal on his own. He knew he could avoid visitors if he could avoid being at home, but his butler Difri insisted he stay at home since there was no knowing whether the assassin would strike again. Emere was used to his fussing, ever since he was a young princeling. Difri had been the chief caretaker of the royal household, and was as much a reminder of the old kingdom as any of Emere's siblings.

The house his sister had bought within the Imperial Capital was referred to as a mansion for reasons of courtesy, but it was small—the Kamori royal family had exhausted its fortunes in fighting the Empire. Kamori's royal palace was now the seat of the Imperial prefect, and the old family villa in the orchards on the outskirts of Karadis, the Kamori capital, was where the former royals lived now. But Emere could not stand the emptiness of that home, where they had a far-off view of the Imperial standard flying over the old palace in Karadis. That was one of the reasons he had agreed so readily to replace his older sister as Kamori's representative in the Imperial Commons.

His visitor that afternoon was a fellow councillor, Ludvik, from Tythonia, a province in the northeast. Out of all the politicians that Emere's sister knew, Ludvik was the only one who regularly met with him, and the only friend he had made since coming to the Capital. Emere knew that Ludvik was around his age, but Ludvik's bald head and thick mustache made him look ten years older.

"Your sister once told me that you had been away from home for a long time in your youth. What did you do?" Ludvik continued their conversation as they settled down in the reception room after their lunch.

"I was looking for ways to bring down the Empire," Emere said dispassionately, "like at least a few in your own country, surely."

Emere had little reservation about telling Ludvik of his past. Over the ten years he lived in the underground palace in Dehan Forest, his sister had sent him letters from the Capital, with many kind mentions of Ludvik. The man hadn't felt like a stranger when Emere was finally introduced to him.

Besides, Ludvik no doubt knew of Emere's past, so he thought it best to be honest, though he would refrain from flaunting the fact that he had aided Loran in the Arlander rebellion and fought against the Imperial legion. Ludvik was more than an ordinary councillor—he was also the head of the committee that oversaw the Office of Truth, the Imperial authority which managed all sorcerers and Power generators. They also cracked down on religions throughout the realm, and had a spy network second only to that of the Ministry of Intelligence. Ludvik might be from a faraway province, but Emere knew that nobody got to the position he was in now without strong allegiances to the Empire.

"Oh?" Ludvik said politely. "My country was brought into the Empire before I was born—I somehow doubt Tythonia has anyone who wishes to drive out the Empire." He even shrugged, making the tassels of his epaulets dance. A sartorial feature of Tythonia, not the Empire. His dark gray trousers had been pressed stiff, with creases that looked like they could cut a finger. There were councillors who tried hard to look like an Imperial heartlander, but Ludvik had always displayed his provincial origin proudly, saying that what was Tythonian had become Imperial, and vice versa.

"How can you be so sure?"

Ludvik was about to answer when Difri entered, carrying tea. A luxury from the far south that Emere would rarely indulge in on his own. Difri must've gone rummaging through his sister's old things to find something worthy of serving his guests. Ludvik beamed as he accepted his cup and saucer and nodded his thanks to the butler.

"And some honeyed peaches as well." Difri politely gestured to the plate of large peach slices drenched in honey, clearly pleased that Ludvik has recognized the tea. "I hope you enjoy," he said with a smile, before taking a step away from the table, standing just on the edge of Emere's vision.

Ludvik took a tiny, bird-like sip of his tea, delicately holding his cup and saucer with his thick fingers. Unused to drinking tea in a proper Imperial manner, Emere followed suit.

"How can I be sure there is no Tythonian who wants to drive out the Empire . . . I suppose you're a born royal and have not an inkling as to what I am going to say," said Ludvik as he stared into the air before him, looking as if he was lost in thought. "But as you are well-traveled, perchance you came across the king's castle in Tythonia?"

Emere shook his head. "I've never been to Tythonia but I did hear about the largest castle in the north. It now serves as a public park, I believe?"

In contrast, Kamori's palace had been turned into the prefect's office. In fact, almost every province he had visited with Rakel had their parliament or grand temple or royal palace renovated for Imperial use.

Ludvik nodded. "Well, it's still the most impressive fortress indeed. There used to be a hammer of the thunder god that could rain down lightning on an approaching foe. The castle was built to fight off even the gigatherions for a while."

Emere remembered the day the gigatherion had came to Arland. He had been at the volcano, waiting for Arienne to free the ancient dragon, but the machine was large enough to be seen from there. The machine had been a giant, taller than most castles, so strong that it had struck down the dragon with a single blow . . .

"But Tythonia fell quickly, did it not?"

"When it was rumored that the Empire was on its way, we killed our king," Ludvik said, with more than a suggestion of pride.

"*Killed* your king?"

"And we opened our gates wide. We surrendered without

fighting a single battle." Ludvik cut into a peach slice and ate one of the pieces, clearly savoring the flavor. "Excellent. Difri, where do you get these?"

Difri smiled and said, "It is an old Kamori recipe, sir." He turned to Emere. "May I have some sent over to Councillor Ludvik's residence?"

"Of course, Difri," Emere replied distractedly, eager to return to Ludvik's story. "Were the people so afraid of the Empire that they would hand over their country without a fight?"

Ludvik frowned. "This is why I said a prince would not understand. Afraid of the Empire? No. The people so despised their king and the aristocracy that they gladly sacrificed them to the invaders. That's how terrible the king's rule was and how greatly the people suffered under it. You say we handed over our country without a fight, but by then, the country had not been ours for some time. We like to think that we took back Tythonia from that thief of a king."

Emere nodded, comprehending. He took a peach slice himself, slowly chewing while thinking.

It wasn't difficult to understand—but the prefect of the Empire still had to collect taxes and ensure certain guarantees to Imperial merchants. Emere, in the travels of his youth, had seen many a province impoverished by the Empire's plundering. Ludvik must've sensed his thoughts, for he answered Emere's unasked question.

"The King of Tythonia . . . His name was Ludvik as well." Ludvik chuckled. "He had a vast army, and of course that castle I spoke of. Who do you think paid for the maintenance of all that? The common folk of Tythonia were squeezed dry long before the Empire ever showed up. They were willing to take their chances."

"But why did Tythonia require such an army?"

Ludvik scoffed and took another sip of tea. "Because the king was afraid the Empire would invade."

"Ah."

"My grandfather was merely a low-ranking officer in the Tythonian king's army. But now his grandson is here in the Capital, representing his homeland. When the king fell, it became easier for commoners of talent to rise." He pretended to take another sip as he gave a surreptitious glance at Emere. "Oh my. The things I find myself saying in front of a true-blood prince."

Emere washed the cloying taste of peach from his mouth with tea as he mulled this over for a moment. "Well, as you say, I *am* a prince. Nothing to be done about it if it makes me a bit sentimental for that old kingdom of mine. Except to tell the Ministry of Intelligence about me, the radical dissident." He paused for Ludvik's hearty chuckle, then continued. "But your name. Were you not named after the king? Did your people change their minds after the annexation?"

Ludvik emphatically shook his head, laughing. "No, no. The man who killed the king and lowered the drawbridge to the castle was *also* named Ludvik."

At that, Emere couldn't help but laugh, half in amusement, half at his own condition. Emere thought of his brother, Gwaharad, the self-styled King of Kamori, hiding in his underground palace in the forest. While he wanted to believe Gwaharad would someday gather enough support to retake Kamori, the man was powerless, and so was Emere. And perhaps such rebellion was never needed in the first place. Who knew how many in Kamori welcomed the end of the royal dynasty and greeted the rule of the Empire with open arms?

If that was so, perhaps living as quietly and unobtrusively as he could was for the better. He suddenly felt desperate to see Rakel.

Ludvik broke the silence. "In any case, do you have an inkling as to whom the assassin may be?"

Emere shook his head. He stopped himself from mentioning the sword the assassin had dropped and the strange engravings on it. Only Rakel knew that detail.

Taking a deep breath, Ludvik continued, "I thought you would've informed the Ministry of Intelligence about the attack, but I do not see guards here."

"They are busy hunting for rebels and keeping the prefects in line." Emere waved him off. "The city patrollers are rather diligent in this neighborhood."

Ludvik raised his eyebrows. He ate the last piece of peach before speaking.

"You think the patrollers who catch petty burglars are going to stop an assassin? No, I will tell Intelligence myself. A lazy cartel of ne'er-do-wells, even for the Imperial bureaucracy, but there are a few passable exemplars."

Another man fussing over his well-being. He eyed Difri, who was standing dutifully to the side, his face slightly more relaxed by Ludvik's promise of protection. The reception room suddenly felt smaller, but he reminded himself that the two men were just concerned. Perhaps that was what he needed in this grand city that to him had simply been the enemy stronghold just a few years ago—people who were concerned for him.

"Never would I have imagined warranting such protection," Emere joked.

Ludvik laughed, his cup rattling on his saucer.

"You are my friend, and all my friends warrant protection."

Friend. Once, he had all of Gwaharad's men and women by his side. In Arland, everyone at that captured Imperial fortress was a friend. Loran, most of all, was his friend. But she was missing now, and he was here at the Capital. He thought of the dream vision he'd had in the square.

Loran told him to reach for a star. Emere didn't know what that meant, but he had a vague feeling that something was about to happen. Something that would miss him if he stayed still.

But hadn't that been how he always felt? When he was younger, he would chase every dream, trusting in the Tree Lords' teachings. In that forest clearing, when he finally met Loran, the woman from his dreams, he had felt vindicated for all his fruitless years. But the grand destiny turned out to be not his, but Loran's. Emere played a part in her story, and then it was over. Still, his instincts were telling him to follow this dream, that this time it would be different. He knew, of course, it wouldn't be. It never had been.

"And another thing," Ludvik said. His eyes seemed to glint in a starker tone. Emere's cup paused in midair as he felt a hint of danger in Ludvik's face. The man was hunting for something, his senses suddenly sharp.

"What troubles you?" Emere asked.

"How much do you know of the Circuit of Destiny?"

Emere shrugged.

"I don't know much about it. Something about connecting

several Power generators together, which enables the user to look into the past and predict the future . . ."

Ludvik's stare looked sharp enough to cut into Emere's mind. But his stare faltered and moved toward empty space, as if he were gazing at someone who wasn't there.

"Grand Inquisitor Lysandros once said the Circuit of Destiny was the true power of the Empire. A god-like power, made by man." His expression turned wistful.

Emere tried not to show any emotion at the mention of Lysandros. Lysandros had almost killed him and his fifty men on Finvera Pass, with nothing more than his presence. He remembered the first breath he took after Arienne had cut the machine-man's arms off and kicked him down the mountainside. "Yes," murmured Emere, "whoever knows the future could create their own destiny, I suppose."

He had only made the comment to fill the silence, but Ludvik took it seriously.

"Councillor Emere, the Circuit of Destiny is no mere fortune-telling device. A single Class One or Two Power generator can move a gigatherion the size of a castle, but three hundred such generators linked together? The amount of Power involved is unimaginable. But it is only a machine in the end. It cannot decide to do anything by itself."

Emere was relieved that the conversation had moved away from his assassination attempt, but the strange wistfulness of the Tythonian was unsettling. Feeling the hairs on the back of his neck rising, Emere said, "But why do you bring up the Circuit?"

"Well. If the Circuit of Destiny were to let you decide, what would you do?"

"Decide what?"

With his finger, Ludvik drew a large circle over his head. "Anything and everything. For the Empire, the provinces . . . the world."

Emere forced a laugh. "I don't know what you could be talking about. Did Difri put spirits in your tea? You might as well ask me what I would do with a Thiopsian wish-granting gavel."

Ludvik lowered his arm. "Right, too right. But, Emere, what was it that your Tree Lords taught? Destiny places each of us somewhere. When it does, you must make a decision in that very place. And that choice is yours and yours alone. I've always found it poetic."

Emere chuckled. "I didn't know you were versed in Kamori philosophy."

Ludvik laughed and said, "I am versed in many things, Emere. That is how I am ready for that moment, if it ever comes. How about you?"

Feeling awkward, Emere grinned and gestured to Difri for more peaches.

8

ARIENNE

She set out from the twisted house into Danras, carefully peering up and down the street when she reached the corner. From this distance, it seemed as if the object was standing still and staring with its strange not-eyes.

It looked like a giant metal insect, but with four legs instead of six, and it had all kinds of things on its back—fragments of furniture, old clothes, broken awnings. Human remains. All covered in red dust. It was giant, and Arienne could only guess at how large it would have been originally, without all the junk tacked onto its body.

"A little gigatherion, made of trash . . ." Arienne found herself murmuring aloud while thinking of the behemoth of the Empire that had struck Arland's dragon down from the sky. Could the two machines truly be related? Arienne could still faintly hear the familiar hum of a Power generator, so there was no doubt that the monster was a Powered machine that carried its own generator. But there was no balance or symmetry to the wretched object before her, which would've been the hallmark of a human-made device.

Arienne held her breath as the monster began moving again. There were three arm-like appendages coming out of its torso. Unlike its legs, these had no clear joints, and they flailed listlessly like sluggish whips. Two of these appendages ended with pincers, and one had a grass-cutting blade, or perhaps a saw. It was hard to tell through all the rust on it.

In the room in her mind, Aron the donkey brayed. Startled, Arienne shouted into the room, "Be quiet! What happens if . . ."

What happens if the monster hears you . . . But of course, there was no way the thing could hear something inside her mind.

". . . Tychon wakes up!" she finished, shoving that thought aside.

Why am I trying to sound rational to a donkey? Arienne calmed herself and took a quick look at the baby Tychon. He was blissfully asleep. Aron, as if to keep watch, had lain down next to the crib.

The donkey turned his head toward her and brayed again. Arienne ignored it and closed the door.

She refocused herself. The trash monster seemed to be looking for something, bathing anything within its false sight with blue light. One of its pincers reached into a window and withdrew an old pillow the size of a person. Arienne suddenly wondered if the monster was looking for her and became frightened. The monster hacked away at the pillow with the bladed arm, and a chill ran down her spine. She imagined being stretched apart by the two pincers and then stabbed to death with the rusty blade; then she quickly tried to erase the image from her mind.

Arienne tore her eyes from the monster itself and studied its surroundings. The street the monster stood on must have been built after the Empire had annexed Danras—it was as straight as if drawn with a ruler and wide enough for four carriages to pass side by side. The monster took up that whole street on its own, standing on its four uneven legs, rummaging about with its three arms. No, four arms, Arienne realized. One more had appeared and was reaching for an alley.

The still-audible humming from the monster was so very familiar to her. She'd heard it when she had gone down to the basement of the Imperial Academy to steal Eldred's corpse. And it was the sound she heard when she put her ear to Tychon's chest in the room in her mind. It was definitely the sound of an active Power generator.

But how did a Power generator, neglected for a century, continue to function? And did the Empire's Office of Truth not think to reclaim the generator after the fall of Mersia?

What dreams would the dead sorcerer in that generator have had for these long years?

Her curiosity rose. But right now, it was more important to not attract the attention of that thing. The monster, like a ragpicker collecting old clothes in a basket, added the mangled pillow to the trash on its back. The sight of it doing so made Arienne imagine her own dismembered body in place of the pillow and she shook with fright.

She should stay hidden, and once the monster was gone, she would leave Danras. Who would've imagined that Mersia, this land of the dead, would harbor such a thing? This mission never should've been taken on alone. She should go back to Arland, come up with a foolproof plan, and return with people who could help her. There was no point in ending up like that pillow just now. Reaching Danras was accomplishment enough, and no one could accuse her of not doing her part. King Loran would not blame her—she might even praise her.

But that was the extent to which Arienne was willing to listen to her inner excuse-maker. Hadn't Loran thrown herself into a volcano to make a pact with a dragon? Hadn't she fought a squadron of Powered chariots, then finally bested an Imperial gigatherion? Even if she couldn't do the same, Arienne knew that she must not make excuses for herself now when she had come so far.

Her breath quieted, Arienne crawled toward an alley and drew herself flat against a wall. All of her attention was concentrated in her eyes and ears. It felt like the moment she peered out of the alley, the blue-light gaze would be staring right at her. She took a slow, deep breath. Slowly leaning around the corner, she tried to see where the monster was.

Its whip-like arms were still rummaging through the houses. There were—surprisingly—*even more* arms now. Eight? Ten? They flailed so energetically that she couldn't count them, and each one was longer than the one before. They seemed to have no purpose in particular as they writhed and twisted in the air. The image reminded Arienne of an uprooted tree stood on its crown. The root-like, twisting arms of the monster reached into windows and doors and the alleyways between rows of twisted houses, as if looking for something it had lost, collecting garbage and wearing it on its body for some unknown reason.

"What is it looking for?" she muttered, forgetting to be stealthy. Rather, what had its original orders been, and who had given them? The trash monster was far from human and made no sound that could be called language or expression, but Arienne could still feel the desperation in how it moved its arms. It was impossible to know what it was looking for, but there was definitely no possibility of finding it here. If it had been searching for a century and still hadn't found it, it likely never would. The thought made her a little sad. She took a small step toward the street.

But she couldn't take the next one. Something had wound itself around her ankle. Arienne's head whipped around and looked down—one of the monster's arms had come from behind her in the alley and grabbed her. She had thought it was safe because it was a dead end, but the arm had come through cracks in the walls. Suddenly, it lifted her up and hung her upside down as she screamed, the glass orb around her neck knocking against her face.

But even as she panicked, she was thinking of the flaming sword in her mind, the twin of King Loran's Wurmath and the very one that Arienne had used to kill Lysandros and slice off Eldred's arms. Feeling Power gather in her mouth, she spoke the spell, and the monster's arm dropped to the ground like a piece of fish from a cleaver. Arienne fell flat as the arm released her, but she didn't wait to regain the breath that was knocked out of her, instead racing out of the alley.

As soon as she stepped into the street, the lights of the monster shone upon her. Arienne stared into them, almost blinding herself, and the writhing tentacles froze. Then, the unbalanced four legs began to move. The giant monster was coming toward her.

Without pausing to think, she turned and ran.

The footsteps of the massive monster made the ground shake. But what scared her most was how the hum of the Power generator grew ever louder. Not quite a beating heart or a drum, but just as regular.

As she ran, something crashed not far in front of her and shattered to pieces. Arienne didn't pause as she instinctively blocked the bouncing fragments. It was large, like a piece of furniture, but if she stopped to go around it, the monster would gain that much more ground. She had to step over it. She leaped into the center of the debris.

And the ground gave way beneath her. She thought it was simply the furniture giving way at first, but then she continued to fall down, down into darkness. The road had collapsed under her, perhaps because of the crash, and Arienne now expected nothing but death. Who knew a perfectly serviceable-looking road would harbor an endless hollow underneath . . . Her annoyance nearly overwhelmed her fear.

She mourned not only her life, but that of Tychon and the donkey Aron—if she died here, they would disappear along with Arienne's consciousness and the room in her mind. Loran's mission would end here, too. There was no one else who would take it over.

She glanced downward as she fell. It was dark. She smelled water. In this lifeless desert?

Suddenly, her body hit the surface of water. Her breath was

knocked out of her once more, immediately bubbling toward the surface like an escaping ghost.

Arienne tried with all of her strength to move her body, to reach the surface. But she had no air, and her consciousness slowly began to drift away.

9

YUMA

The rain brought on by the stormbird had soaked the steppe, making it nearly impossible to walk through. The grass, delirious from this unseasonal gift from the skies, thickened and greened.

The Grim King had killed two herders, neither of whom had even reached the age of twenty. The rage Yuma felt could easily overflow into tears. But the Grim King was right—there were over a thousand such youths in Danras, and he held their lives in his hands. Yuma was the Chief Herder, one of the two most respected people in Danras. She was expected to follow his orders, even after witnessing him commit murders just to make his point. The other herders could wail with sorrow, but not the Chief Herder. She had to show no fear, nor sadness, nor disgust at her own helplessness, like the unmoving faces of the dead the Grim King commanded.

Early the next morning, Yuma selected a few herders who well knew the ways through the grassy plains and sent them westward. If the Imperial spy had indeed entered the plains as the Grim King had said, there would be only so many places they could hide. And there would be limits to how far the spy could range as long as the land remained flooded.

As she watched the searchers go westward into the still-dark steppe, their backs to the rising sun, Aidan asked, "Have you gone to see the Host?"

"Not yet. But I met the Grim King last night, so I must wash before I visit."

Aidan nodded. "That is the way. Then I shall bring you your meal. And your wound . . ."

Yuma placed a hand on her injured hip and said, "Stallia saw to it. No need to worry too much."

The two looked toward the west in silence. When the herders disappeared into the grass, Aidan said, "I assume you've heard I grew up learning sorcery with the Grim King a long time ago."

"I've heard rumors, yes."

It was said that Aidan had been sent to Eldred as a child and was almost apprenticed to him, but that Aidan had returned to Danras as a man and become a herder instead. This was the first time she was hearing him speak of it himself.

"Do you know why I was sent to him?"

Yuma shook her head before turning away from Aidan. She was, after yesterday, quite sick of the Grim King. Whether they caught this spy for him or not, she wanted to forget all about him and just finish the herding for the year. But Aidan continued with his story.

"When I was a child . . . this was over forty years ago now. But the Host at the time prophesied that the apprentice of the Grim King would become the King of Merseh."

Yuma winced. "I've heard about the prophecy, but not what transpired after that. All I know is that many children of magic from all three cities were killed."

"Well, once the prophecy was made, the Grim King issued an edict saying he sought apprentices. Danras sent children, as did Lansis and Iorca. For what he seeks, he gets. The Grim King accepted all who had magic, and I was one. We really thought one of us would end up ruling this country one day."

She looked back at him. There was a bitter smile on Aidan's lips.

"The children with no affinity for sorcery were turned away at the gate of the palace, and those of us with magic were taught by the Grim King for ten years. Some weren't clever, and others found the trials too difficult. Those children did not survive. Four did, though, including myself, and the Grim King declared he would make the one who passed the final test his apprentice." Aidan sighed. "I was the only one to pass. The other three . . . they disappeared into nothing. But the Grim King did not make me his apprentice."

"Why not?"

"I didn't know at first. He simply destroyed the magic in me and banished me to the steppe." Aidan rubbed his paralyzed right cheek. "But later on, I understood. The reason one takes an apprentice is to pass on knowledge. Somewhat like passing on a family's legacy to a child. But the Grim King is immortal. He needs no child or apprentice, and he never will."

Yuma thought of how the Grim King had killed Rizona without giving it a second thought. If the Grim King thought so little of apprentices and children, how much less would he care about others? Merseh had been ruled by the Grim King for at least five centuries. No one knew what he was before that or where he even came from. Perhaps every life was as ephemeral as spring flowers to one so long-lived. But Yuma became curious about one thing.

"Aidan, if the Grim King gave so little regard for the lives of his other apprentice candidates—"

"Why would he spare my life?" Aidan touched the deadened side of his face again. "The best I can figure is that maybe he wished for *me* to have children. I was not good enough to be his apprentice, but he might have been hoping that a worthy successor would appear in a few generations."

All Yuma could do was nod.

Aidan adjusted his hat and said, "That's just the way he is. The Grim King can never be understood by the measure of those who don't live even a hundred years."

Yuma nodded again. Aidan tipped his hat and got on his horse. As she watched him leave, she imagined him as a young boy. Not in leather, riding a horse on the steppe, but in a gray robe given to him by the Grim King, chanting ominous spells in a dim room.

For days afterward, Yuma kept an eye to the west. If the searchers found the spy, they were to send up a smoke signal during the day or light a fire at night. Nothing happened for three days, aside from the occasional adventurous young orox that needed to be returned to the herd. The water drained from the earth, and the sky was clear and blue as if it had never known rain.

On the morning of the fourth day, Yuma washed herself in rainwater that had been gathered on a tarp. There were not many days she could bathe during a herding. The ponds that dotted the grasslands were mostly for the oroxen—their water was too muddy to bathe in, much less drink, which meant the herders would need to strain it and let the silt settle before boiling it with a fragrant herb before imbibing. Clean water on the grasslands was rare.

So, bathing oneself was even rarer. But Yuma did so for the sake of meeting with the Host. Three days with no news from the searchers meant she needed to consult auguries.

The occasion forbade herder dress, so Yuma took out ceremonial clothes from a bundle in her tent. The trousers were made of black wool, which had to be imported to Merseh, and the tunic was white muslin. The clothes had been made for her grandfather, modified to fit her mother, and taken in again by Yuma—both items were at least half a century old. She put on the somberly beaded string that cinched her collar, thinking of the last time she wore these clothes, last winter. She had been seeing off the youths who had been conscripted by the Grim King.

Yuma adjusted the back of her ceremonial clothing and tugged the creases out of her sleeves. The Host was meticulous when it came to ceremony. If she didn't want to be turned away, every seam had to be lined up. Rizona would've made sure . . .

Yuma adjusted her hat and left her tent.

But as soon as she stepped into the pewter light of dawn, Aidan came running. He wasn't on his horse, nor was he even wearing his hat. His hair, which wasn't properly tied back, was mostly flying in the breeze. Herders everywhere were also making haste as they climbed on their horses.

"Chief!" Aidan's voice was full of panic.

"What has happened?"

"The signal! But . . . it's a rescue signal. And very close to us."

There was no true rescue signal—setting the grassland on fire in panic and hoping someone would notice was the "rescue signal" of the Merseh Steppe. It wasn't used lightly, for obvious reasons.

"But there is still so much rainwater left on the ground . . ." Yuma rationalized, but the western sky was indeed filled with smoke, the early light of morning tinting the smoke blue.

"I don't know what has happened. It could simply be wildfire. How many herders should be sent?"

"A wildfire this big when it's this wet . . ." Yuma shook her head. "That would be a problem in its own right. Gather six, including yourself. I will go with you."

"Go with us, Chief? But the danger—"

"It can't be more dangerous than confronting the Grim King." Yuma tried a smile, which seemed to reassure Aidan a little as he returned it and ran off, saying he would bring her a horse. She almost told him to bring Falco, then remembered how the monster had killed the stallion. Too many things had happened that night. Only when Aidan brought the horse to her and her eyes fell on its auburn hide did she remember that she had picked Aston the night she met the Grim King.

She mounted Aston. Her side still ached, but riding a horse and feeling the wind on her face for the first time in days made her forget her pain. As she rode, riders joined her, tipping their hats to her. If she hadn't been galloping toward a possible disaster, she would've simply been happy.

They rode for about an hour before heat hit their faces and curtain-like smoke heralded a sizable amount of grassland going up in flames.

"Isn't that Barund?" a sharp-eyed herder shouted, recognizing a shadow behind a leaping flame. Yuma kicked, and Aston picked up speed, the wind whipping her face stronger than ever. Her hat flew off and hung behind her neck by its string. She leaned forward, giving herself to the momentum.

It would take too long to go around the flames, and who knew what would happen if they did. Yuma could feel Aston's fear, but she stroked his neck at his brave, unceasing gallop, and squeezed the horse with her thighs right as they reached the flames. Aston did not hesitate for a second as he leaped over the fire, the flames licking at Yuma's calves. Yuma and Aston flew through the smoke and fire and landed on the other side.

Barund stood there, an old hand at thirty-three. He must've experienced everything there was to experience on the grasslands. Egan and Trudie must have as well, who were with him now. That was why Yuma had sent them out in the first search party. But what she saw before her was something neither Barund nor Yuma, or any other herder of Danras, had ever seen before.

There was a giant box of gleaming silver standing on four spindly legs, dwarfing Aston and Yuma with its height. The box had metallic, whip-like arms with pincers that threatened the herders. One of the pincers had grabbed Trudie by the ankle and was dangling her upside down. Trudie struggled, but there was nothing she could do in that position.

The horses were gone. Judging by Aston's extreme revulsion, Yuma could guess they had run away from this unknown thing.

"Barund! Egan! Trudie!"

Only then did Barund and Egan realize their Chief Herder had come, and their eyes lit up. Even Trudie waved her arms in her direction. Barund shouted, "Chief! We found the spy!"

"That box?"

"No, beneath it!"

Under the giant's body was a hammock-like net, sagging like the stomach of a pregnant horse. It looked rather makeshift, compared to the shining, riveted giant that was obviously the result of expert craftsmanship. Yuma realized there was a man lying in the net, wearing some kind of metal frame all around his body. He looked unconscious, or maybe dead. This was the spy from the Empire in the west? Yuma unhitched her crossbow from Aston's saddle and took aim at the person under the belly of the giant.

The thing seemed to understand her movement. Lowering its belly and shielding the person in the net with one arm, it charged at Yuma.

10

EMERE

"You may not, my prince! You would have to beat me to death with that walking stick before I let you pass!"

Difri refused to be persuaded. He was convinced Emere would be assassinated the moment he stepped out of the door, and Difri's face was more wrinkled than ever as he grimaced, grabbing firmly on to his coat.

Difri had been like this as long as he could remember, not just to him, but to his siblings and his parents as well. But Emere had just returned to him after twenty years of self-imposed exile. Perhaps in the old butler's mind Emere remained a princeling, liable to scrape his knee whenever he went out.

"The streets are filled with people!" Emere reasoned. "What harm could possibly come to me?"

In Emere's pocket was a clay imprint of the insignia on the assassin's sword. What he had told Difri was that he simply wanted to investigate the attempt on his own life. But that wasn't the only thing on his mind. What if the failed assassination attempt wasn't a simple coincidence? What if it was somehow connected to his dream vision? He couldn't stop thinking of what Loran had said in the vision.

You *must become king. That is your destiny. Destiny passes by those who stand still. Reach out and grasp that which awaits you, up there.*

When he first heard those words, he had thought of his youth wandering the world, searching for a way to fight the Empire. Ever since the battle against the Imperial forces in Arland, Emere had thought his time was now past, and so he had gladly accepted his sister's passing of the torch in the Capital. Then, Loran said that there was something to reach out for, somewhere out there. That was what he hoped to find by tracking down the assassin.

But king? Kamori had long forgotten their royal family. A mere twenty years had passed, but the Tree Lords and the holy groves were practically legends now. The Kamori of old was as extinct as Mersia. So, what was he supposed to become king of?

Difri's shouts returned him back to the present.

"*Filled* with people? And was the square *empty* when you were shot during your speech?"

"The center of the city is different from the poorer quarters! Would you have me do nothing to find out who tried to kill me?"

But Difri was adamant. "Why must it be my prince who makes that effort? And what would happen to you if you really do find the assassin? No, it is the patrollers' job! I cannot let you take one step out of this house until they do."

Emere, annoyed, tried to snatch his coat from the butler's grasp. "Do I still look like a child of ten or twenty to you?"

But the grasp of Difri's wrinkled hands was unexpectedly

strong. "The princess is old and has returned home, and the crown prince has given up the world. If you were to meet tragedy, who would be left to inherit the throne? How would I be able to enter the Dark Forest and lift my head up before the king and queen?"

At Difri's plea and his mention of Emere's parents, Emere almost changed his mind to wait another day or two. But unlike in the forests of Kamori, where nothing remarkable happened in a day or five, things moved swiftly in the Imperial Capital, and everything could change between breakfast and midday. So, if he wanted to find out about the assassin, he had to move fast. He had already wasted days.

"Difri, just let me go, please!" he pleaded.

In that same moment, there were two loud knocks on the front door. Emere glanced toward it. Difri, startled by the knocks, let go of the coat. There were two more knocks, and then a woman's low voice.

"Is anyone inside?"

Emere looked at Difri. Difri looked back at him uncomprehending, then quickly went, "Ah," and hastened to the door.

When he opened it, there stood an Imperial heartlander woman in her thirties wearing a black cloak and her hair neatly pinned up. Difri looked her up and down, raised his chin a little, and said, "Good day. May I ask what your business is here?"

"Is this the house of Councillor Emere of Kamori?"

The woman's gaze had already moved on to Emere, who walked up to the door. Difri took a step back and bowed his head.

"I was about to leave," said Emere, seizing his chance. "Please come back tomorrow. No, the day after! Difri here will take note of your inquiry."

Trusting Difri not to make a scene in front of a visitor, he made to exit, but this time, it wasn't his butler but the visitor who stepped in his way.

"I am here upon request of Councillor Ludvik."

So Ludvik did jump through the hoops to get him Intelligence protection. But if Difri couldn't stop him, nothing could.

"I see. But as you can see, I am busy at the moment, so regretfully—"

As he tried to slip past her, she took a half step and blocked him again. Emere looked up with a slight frown, but she seemed impervious to disdain.

"I am Subdirector Septima. From the Ministry of Intelligence."

He had heard of this name before. But from where? He thought she had been commended for having done something heroic during the fire two years ago. Fighting off rebel forces that had infiltrated the Senate or some such. Yes, her name had been Septima, a ranking officer in the Ministry of Intelligence.

"An official! I shall prepare tea."

Emere raised his hand, thwarting Difri's attempt to use this visit as an opportunity to keep him at home. "No, as I said, I am on my way out. I cannot receive visitors right now, so please excuse me."

"I heard you were in danger of being assassinated," Septima said. There was a hint of irritation in her voice, as in her expression. There were probably many things she would rather be doing than watching over a figurehead politician from a province. *For example, torturing rebels,* Emere thought wryly.

He forced a smile. "Nothing to concern yourself about. Please convey my thanks to Ludvik."

"If only it were that simple," said Septima dryly.

Difri frowned. "My prince, how could you refuse an offer of help when your life is in peril? As the last servant of the royal house of Kamori, I beseech you, please accept this help."

"Difri, please, I told you not to call me a prince in front of others!"

He raised his voice in embarrassment. Difri bowed his head low and stepped away. Septima crossed her arms, watching it all with half-lidded eyes as if it were a play that was too tedious to behold.

Then he had an idea. "I guess I am in your hands, Subdirector Septima. Difri!"

The butler looked back.

"Subdirector Septima shall escort me around the city. You have the house while I'm gone."

Septima blinked. Difri's face was so wrinkled his grimace was just barely perceptible. But he finally seemed to give up and bowed.

Emere quickly stepped out the door and, turning to Septima, said, "Let's go."

He led the way. Septima followed, her pace quick. They reached Victory Square, which featured the large marble fountain of Domitius and Aristomache, the heroes of the Northern Conquest, and Septima had not uttered a word. It made Emere nervous. Was she really here to guard him or had she some other purpose?

Emere had always suspected that his sister's sudden retirement and his appointment to the Commons Council was a form of punishment for his anti-Imperial activities. Keeping the wayward member of the royal family of a province in the Capital under watch was a common enough practice. But he had wondered if the assassination attempt that almost took his life was some form of extrajudicial execution on the part of the Ministry of Intelligence.

He sat down on the ledge of the fountain. The day was clear and the sunlight warm. Septima sat down next to him and eventually spoke.

"I wonder if the esteemed councillor cares at all."

"Pardon? About what?"

"That he may die."

Emere didn't answer.

"The . . . work, that I do," continued Septima, "allows me to become acquainted with a great variety of persons. The ones who are reckless with their own lives usually have no purpose in life, so they don't care if they live or die. But there are also those who are reckless because their purpose is *too* clear. So clear, they don't care if they die pursuing it."

Emere smiled. "And which am I?"

"Judging by that scene with your servant just now, I should say your purpose is too clear." Septima paused before continuing, "That is a most dangerous person."

"What's a little danger if I'm going to die soon?" Emere joked.

Septima shook her head. "You're dangerous for the people around you."

"How?"

"You eventually endanger them." Septima stared into space. "Two years ago, there was a rebel from a province who made an attempt at something in the Capital. You were not in the Capital back then, I don't think. But you must've heard of the Great Fire."

Emere nodded. Rakel had said her husband had died in that fire.

"The one responsible for that fire was killed, and their people and a mercenary too. Hundreds of innocents, having nothing to do with provinces or politics, died as well. And if we hadn't stopped it from happening, the loss would've been greater."

An unreadable expression crossed Septima's face. Emere didn't know where the conversation was headed.

"I heard it was you, Subdirector, who stopped it?"

Septima's expression turned into a hard grin. "You can say that. And you can also say it wasn't."

Emere stared at her, and when she didn't elaborate, he turned to the crowd. There were many people around the fountain. Through the many Imperial heartlanders, he saw a group of Rammanians who had covered their heads with black cloth, revealing only their eyes. A huddled group of Thiopsian aristocrats wore elaborate red clothing and kept looking at the clock tower. Emere found himself trying to find Loran in their midst. How could there be so many people here but not the one person he most longed to see and speak to?

Septima sighed and stood up. She unfastened the buttons of her coat, revealing the black stola she wore underneath. Pinned on her stola was a brooch with a green gemstone.

"That's enough rest. We should get going."

A completely different tone from before—completely devoid of annoyance or irritation. He was taken aback.

"Get going where?"

"There's someone you ought to meet," Septima said. "That's why I came to you today."

Emere felt a lightning bolt jolt its way up through his spine—something he hadn't felt in two years, since meeting Loran.

"Not to protect me?" He somehow managed to speak.

"Oh yes," said Septima, arching an eyebrow. "I know the man who was actually assigned to your protection detail. Pity he's going to be bedridden for a while."

She led the way.

11

ARIENNE

When Arienne was little, an old woman in her village had told her that when evil people died, they would go to Heliwite. It was a freezing-cold cave so deep in the ground that not even the warmth of the volcano could reach it. There, the hideous Crone King harassed the souls of the dead for all eternity.

Arlanders did not bury the dead. Instead, they cremated them using a flame brought down from the volcano. It was said that this would allow the dragon to aid their dead in reaching the realm of Hefenfels, beyond the blue veil of the sky. Hefenfels was a field in eternal early summer where the ground sprouted without being sown, and the rains fell all night, ripening the crops by morning.

When she turned ten and asked her mother about what she had been told, her mother only answered that Hefenfels and Heliwite were no more.

"Then what happens to us when we die?" little Arienne asked.

"I don't know. But we can't go to Hefenfels or Heliwite anymore. The Empire won't let us."

The Empire mocked the traditional beliefs of Arland, calling them superstitions. It was their belief that no gods or demons or even dragons were above humans—and hadn't the dragon the Arlanders so fervently believed in lost to them in battle?

The Empire scorned all invisible gods and killed all visible ones. But if there really were a Heliwite and a Hefenfels, would they disappear just because the Empire conquered Arland? Was calling something a superstition enough to destroy it? What if there really was, still, a Heliwite where the Crone King continued to punish the evil, regardless of what was happening in the surface world? Arienne had not wondered about this since she was a small child.

But it was impossible to not think of Heliwite here, in this echoing cavern with its chill and darkness. It smelled like the turned earth of the cemetery back at the Imperial Academy, and the air had a dampness to it. As she had been immersed in water only a few moments ago, the cold was cutting into her bones. Arienne wrapped her arms around her shoulders and shivered.

She had no idea how she got out of the water—when she came to, her upper body had been resting on a stone while her legs still dangled in what turned out to be an underground river. She imagined her body grabbing on to whatever it could and crawling out of the water on its own, her will to live outlasting even her own consciousness.

She felt about her chest for her tinderbox but found it was soaked. She gripped the glass orb around her neck and concentrated her Power into it until it lit up with a faint light. The darkness receded slightly and revealed walls of stone. It wasn't a completely natural cave, but it wasn't completely human-made either. The walls, the top of which she could just about reach, were made of something like limestone. It somehow relieved her to find that none of the ubiquitous red dust that was covering everything on the surface was here in these halls underneath the city.

The cave was so dark and so wide that she couldn't see across it. Nor could she see the hole she had fallen from when she looked up. Maybe she had floated here when she lost consciousness.

She walked to a spot a bit farther from the river and sat down. She took out her flintstones and kindling from the tinderbox and laid them out in front of her to dry. Water dripped from these items, and the air was so humid she was almost drowning in it. She doubted her tinderbox would dry enough for her to start a fire any time soon. Arienne sighed and stood up.

"I have to start walking."

She thought about just escaping into the room in her mind, but no matter how soft and comfortable the bed was in there, it meant nothing if her body out here froze. What she needed to do now was move her body and get warm. She shook some of the water off her garments and walked deeper into the cavern, her back to the water.

Down here, she didn't hear anything of the huge trash monster's hum or its footsteps. Whether this was because she was so deep down under ground or because the monster had given up on her, she didn't know.

The cavern led her away from the underground river and began to narrow until it led to an archway that was only big enough to allow one person to walk through. There were letters written along the arch. She couldn't read them, but they looked like the same lettering on the faded, melted signs on the surface. But unlike the signs on the surface, they did not also feature an Imperial translation along with those letters, so Arienne knew the archway must be very old.

Arienne raised her left foot to step through the arch. The moment she did so, her heart fell with a thud, startling her. Unhelpfully, her mind started recalling the night in the wasteland with the ghosts. Pressing down on the urge to take that single step back and turn around, she forced her eyes wide open and placed her foot down, fully stepping through—and began to see things previously unseen.

She was in a catacomb. There were hollows dug into the walls, and inside those hollows were skeletons wrapped in desiccated leather, their arms crossed on their chests. And there were ghosts. Many of them. Like in her previous encounter, the ghosts here were moving about soundlessly, not yet paying any attention to her. Arienne took a deep breath and gripped her glass orb. This might be where she found out whether the horse seller's claims of the orb warding off ghosts were true.

These ghosts were all wearing the dress of Danras, as she had seen in her dream, and all keeping busy. There was one sitting on an invisible chair, reading an invisible book. Another was holding up an invisible fruit and knocking its side. An adult ghost patted the head of a child ghost. The whole scene seemed like a bustling street re-created by the dead in this catacomb. But when she soon realized the ghosts were endlessly repeating the same motions, every hair on her body stood on end. Trying not to attract attention to herself, she carefully walked around them.

No wonder it smelled like a cemetery here—it was an actual

cemetery. Danras entombed their dead in catacombs, apparently. She thought of the melted skeleton in the first house she had been in, and realized it was likely that no one buried here would've died during the Star of Mersia attack. Were these ghosts all people who had died before then, now haunting their final resting place? Or were these ghosts indeed victims of that final massacre, repeating these moments of their lives like a prayer down here in this temporary afterlife?

She passed the street of ghosts and reached the archway on the other end. Beyond that, there were even more ghosts populating another section of the catacombs. Arienne leaned back on a pillar and sighed. The prospect of finding a way in this underground ghost city perplexed her. Where was the exit to the outside? And did she even *want* to go back outside, where the Powered monster roamed?

She suddenly realized her head had been aching for a while now. At first, she assumed it was the stuffy air, but the ache came from deeper within.

Arienne opened the door to the room in her mind and was stunned by what she saw inside.

The room was filled with people. Some were sitting on the edge of the bed and staring into space, others taking books down from the bookshelf and flipping through them. A group was gathered around Tychon's crib, looking down with fascination. A few were having conversations. A child patted Aron's head as the donkey swished his tail, irritated.

It wasn't a large room, but by some trick, it seemed like there were scores of people in here.

"What is all this!" shouted Arienne. A few turned to her and approached her, smiling. One of them took off his hat and bowed.

"Tanges, freu."

"Tange sau."

"Tanges."

The people around her kept saying the same thing. She didn't know what it meant but she could feel the sentiment of gratitude. It only made her angrier.

"Who do you think you are, coming into a stranger's room without permission?" she seethed.

A few of them looked at each other. None of the dozens, apparently, spoke Imperial.

Arienne bit her lip and focused. This room was sacrosanct to her. There were only two people, other than her, who had ever been inside, and there had been no new people allowed in since she had reconstructed the room. Aside from the donkey Aron, of course.

These people had to be the ghosts. Formless beings that had violated her headspace when she hadn't been watchful, regaining their old shapes by siphoning off Arienne's imagination magic. But no matter how grateful they professed to be, she couldn't let just any spirit floating around to enter her mind.

"All of you, get out!"

Her voice was so loud it shook the room.

The air inside the room distorted, and Tychon began to cry. Aron's ears perked up. The ghosts in the room turned to blue smoke and then vanished. Arienne, half enraged and half afraid, took deep breaths.

She turned to Tychon in his crib to comfort him, but there was already someone there doing the comforting. One of the ghosts had not disappeared and had picked up Tychon from his crib. This ghost, once a man, wore Imperial clothing. Not just any

Imperial clothing but the robe uniform of a sorcerer. The insignia of the sorcerer-engineers on his shoulder caught her eye.

Arienne stormed toward him, intent on seizing him by the collar if that's what it took to throw him out—but stopped when she heard what the ghost was mumbling, a lost look in his eyes.

"Tychon, good boy . . . Don't cry, Tychon . . ."

12

YUMA

As the four-legged silver giant dangled Trudie by the ankle, Yuma thought of the iridescent nullstones in her pocket. But the Grim King had given them to her to serve his own purpose, believing he could hold Danras hostage and manipulate her against her will. Which was why no matter how frightening the iron monster was and how desperate a situation the herders found themselves in, her hand would not reach for the stones and stayed firmly on her crossbow.

Unwavering in her aim, Yuma shouted, "Stop! Or I will shoot the man hanging from your stomach!"

She hoped the giant understood her. That it valued the man under its stomach, that it read the threat in her movements if not her words. But she had no way of knowing whether that hunk of metal would understand, or if the man was important to it—or even alive for that matter.

But it apparently understood, or was at least surprised at her shout, for the metal giant stopped in its tracks. Trudie also stopped screaming. Yuma took this as a good sign.

"Let go of Trudie. Comply, and I will not kill him right away." Her voice was calmer than it had been a moment ago, placating even. But she could only imagine what the Grim King would do to the spy once she handed him over.

The metal giant did not let go of Trudie, but its movements were more cautious. It did not, at least, attack.

The heat of the burning steppe was licking her back. Trudie no longer struggled or screamed, but her eyes were wide with fear. The other two herders stood silent, looking at Yuma and the giant and back again.

What kind of a country must this Empire be to possess such a weapon? The metal hide would be impervious to arrows, and the largest sword would at most dent or nick it. The corpse armies of the Grim King might know no fear, but she didn't think even scores of the undead attacking that thing at once would slow its pace. And if the Empire had tens, hundreds of these . . .

Yuma imagined the silver giants swimming through an ocean of moving corpses. Of the Grim King being dangled by the ankle instead of Trudie.

For the first time since the night Jed and Rizona were killed, Yuma smiled without pretense. The giant slowly started to move the arm holding up Trudie as if to put her down. But Yuma had to stop her sigh of relief in the middle—Trudie was now flying toward her.

She had a split second to fire at the metal giant, but Trudie was in the way. The bolt went flying from her crossbow only after Trudie had crashed into her.

The bolt bounced off the hide of the giant with a twang as Yuma fell off Aston's back and rolled onto the ground. Her injuries from her battle with the stormbird flared up with so much pain it made her dizzy. By the time one of the nullstones was in her hand, the giant was already rearing up to stomp on her face. But even in that moment, Yuma hesitated in crushing the stone.

Incredibly, the moment was interrupted with a weak shout.

"Fractica . . . !"

The giant's leg stopped in midair, and the man in the net rolled out and onto the ground.

He was a slender man, thin in arms and legs and torso, like he had been stretched. He would have been much taller than she was, had she been standing. The metal frame around his body resembled scaffolding used in construction, but the frame glowed faintly with violet. The man had delicate features, the likes of which Yuma had never seen. He looked exhausted. The torrents from the Grim King must've been an ordeal for him.

Yuma kept her eye on him as she propped herself up on her left elbow. With her right hand, she felt around for the crossbow she'd dropped.

"Earnest, regrets."

The man's Mersehi was stilted. He pointed at himself. The frame clicked as it followed his movements. What she had first taken for the frame's tint was actually violet light that glowed weaker and stronger according to how he moved. Yuma's eyes followed his gestures. He continued to speak, each word an effort.

"Peace. Amity. To Mersia . . . No, Merseh! Emissary, Empire. To Danras."

Mersia. There was the word Yuma had been hearing in the markets of Danras in the last few years. Foreign merchants and travelers had begun to refer to Merseh as Mersia, the Mersehi as Mersians. Perhaps it was an Imperial rendition of her homeland's name?

"Ridiculous, when you've brought that fearsome weapon!" Yuma shouted, pointing at the silver giant.

The man mouthed Yuma's words back to himself, and said, "Ah," and, his eyes shining, he said in a louder voice, *"Averte, Fractica."*

The metal giant was silenced. Only then did Yuma realize it had been humming loudly all along. She got to her feet.

The man said, "Don't be alarmed." Then, he collapsed where he stood.

Yuma picked up her crossbow and approached him. He was still breathing, and his body looked even thinner than her first impression. His face wasn't thin, but his arms and legs looked almost devoid of muscle. She touched his face—he was feverish. Too much shivering in the rain, skinny as he was. The man smiled and his voice was weak.

"I am Lysandros. I do not harm. Do not worry."

Yuma called for her three herders. The two who had kept their distance out of fright came running. Trudie, dazed but barely hurt, managed to get to her feet. Yuma checked to see if the three of them were all right before giving her orders.

"Find your horses and return to camp. Tell them everything

has been put right. When you see Aidan, tell him to send everyone back and come alone."

The herders tipped their hats and turned away. To their backs, Yuma added, "And tell the Host that we have a patient."

Thankfully, the wildfire was dying down. If it weren't for all of the rain a few days ago, this patch of the steppe would not have had enough grass left for the oroxen to feed on. Yuma examined Lysandros more closely. The violet light was gone from his metal scaffolding.

"This frame, it allows you to move, correct? You're wearing this because it enables you to walk?"

No answer. Lysandros's eyes were closed, and he was unconscious. He must've been very exhausted indeed.

This man had stopped the giant when he couldn't walk, much less protect himself. She didn't know if this was bravery or foolishness. She stared at his face. Many foreigners came to the market in Danras, but his features did not seem to fit with any of them. It was hard to tell his age. Maybe twenty-three or so? Or perhaps even thirty, a year or two older than herself, if the way he acted earlier betrayed his age despite his youthful features, and not the other way around.

Aston was standing far from the fire, looking warily in her direction. Yuma whistled, and the horse approached reluctantly. She hugged his neck, praising the beast, and unrolled the sleeping bag she had packed. She slid Lysandros, frame and all, into it. His body seemed light enough for her to lift on her own, though the frame around him was heavier. But if she left him on the damp ground like this, he would lose too much body heat.

But what if he did? Once he was given over to the Grim King, he would be killed anyway, then brought back from the dead, and that's when the interrogation would begin. The prospect didn't thrill her, but she decided she would at least treat him like a guest while he was with her. That was the custom of the herders of Danras, to extend hospitality to whomever one encountered traveling alone on the steppe. This was simply another lone traveler—albeit one with a rather unusual, violently tempered, oversized horse. That also had arms and no head.

"Too pretty a face, for a man," she murmured out loud. She placed a hand on that face. It was still burning. She looked around at the smoldering wildfire. There was someone approaching on horseback. Aidan. Yuma stood up and waved.

Aidan didn't take his eyes off the metal giant until he reached her.

"What is that thing?"

Yuma glanced at the unmoving giant and said, "A horse."

"What?"

"Never mind."

Aidan stroked his mustache. "What do you intend to do now?"

Looking at the leather sleeping bag with Lysandros inside it, she tried to guess how heavy it was. Probably too much for her to carry alone.

"Did you bring a travois? He has a fever. We should get him to the Host."

"He's going to die soon. Why go through so much trouble?" Aidan asked, echoing her earlier thoughts.

But Yuma gave him such a look that Aidan immediately clammed up and unhitched the travois from his saddle. They tied the ends of the travois to Yuma's saddle before hoisting Lysandros up into it.

"Don't go too fast, or the grass will leave scratches on his face."

"As I just said, he's going to die soon. Whatever we do or don't do to him is inconsequential."

"We still have to take care of him until then. He says he's a foreign emissary."

Once on Aston's back, she turned to glance at Lysandros, his face barely visible in the sleeping bag. The Grim King's attention was a terrible thing. Yuma doubted that there was a future for this brave, ailing man who surrendered himself to Yuma willingly. Such a waste, she thought, but it would take a revolt to save this man's life—something the Chief Herder of Danras couldn't afford to do. There were thousands upon thousands of her people in Danras, all at the Grim King's mercy.

Then there was the silver giant, a weapon that could easily sweep away half a dozen of the Grim King's skeletal soldiers each time it swung its metal arms. And the Empire, whose might could create machines like that.

The long, rhythmical *swooshes* of wet grass blades brushing against the travois. The *plops* of Aston's hooves on the rain-soaked ground. The steppe rarely got wet, and when it did, it dried quickly. Yuma turned her head to the unconscious, weakened man being dragged behind her. She chuckled to herself at her fantasy of metal giants smashing through the Grim King's undead horde. All Mersehi knew that whatever oddities happened in Merseh, all would go back to the way it was, as long as there was the steppe, and as long as there was the Grim King.

She dearly wished otherwise.

13

EMERE

Septima led Emere through a series of narrow alleys, connected at all sorts of unexpected angles, not a single one of them wholly straight. There were no signs for road names, or even on half of the shop fronts they passed. Children in varying states of filth from all parts of the Empire ran through the alleys in packs.

It was a slum labyrinth, one of many in the Capital, made of wooden buildings with plaster carelessly slathered on the walls forming narrow, winding alleyways. If one went deep enough into the twisting paths, one's shouting would not reach the main streets. It reminded Emere of the Dehan Forest with its trees crammed together; but instead of living trees, there were only buildings with the stench of piss and spoiling vegetables. Emere mused that the inhabitants who closed their windows and doors upon seeing unfamiliar faces were like the cautious animals of the woods.

It had been half a year since Emere had come to the Capital, but he had never come here before.

Septima led the way at a swift pace, with Emere following closely. At every split she unhesitatingly chose the next turn, never mentioning where it was they were going. He wouldn't have known if they had lost their way; he would've simply assumed the destination was difficult to find.

But Septima's movements were familiar. The one-horned deer of Dehan Forest, coming upon a hunter, would not immediately run away. It would use the densely growing trees as cover to leap this way and that. The hapless hunter would be led to a place where they could not shoot or follow, only to watch their prey disappear in plain sight. If Septima was the one-horned deer here, he wondered who the hunter was.

"Are we trying to avoid someone?" Emere asked.

Septima half turned her head and glanced at him, looking briefly impressed that he had understood what she was doing. "Someone has been following us. Don't look back, Councillor. Just walk."

The alley was quiet. The windows were all closed, and all of the nearby shops seemed to be the kind that opened at night and thus were shuttered now. Not even playing children lingered this deep in the maze. There was only their footsteps.

If someone was following them, it was probably someone who was used to tracking down prey. Emere could think of a likely candidate. His heart beat faster. It wasn't with fear but with a little excitement.

"Does this someone have long hair and wear a leather coat?" Emere asked, thinking of the woman he had seen on the rooftop after the assassination attempt.

"She was a fast one, so I didn't get a good look, but . . . I think so."

Septima, as if keeping time with Emere's heartbeat, quickened her pace. She seemed to have realized who it was that Emere was guessing.

"If this is your old friend," she started, "we have a real problem. We won't be able to lose her like this."

"How do you know that?"

No answer. Emere closed the gap between them and hissed, "She killed my aide. I almost died myself. If you know who she is, you must tell me."

Septima, not stopping, turned her head and said, "Councillor, you are asking me to tell you a very long story. For now—"

A whizzing sound. A thin red line appeared on Septima's cheek, followed by tiny beads of blood. Septima swiped her cheek, saw the blood on her fingertips, and shouted, "Run!"

She darted away, with Emere running after her. As they turned a corner, a bolt struck the dirty white wall with a dull *crack*.

They ran through the alleys, left, right, left again. Emere was losing his breath and could no longer recall the way they had come. Perhaps tired herself, Septima slowed to a rapid walk. Emere caught up to her.

"Are we going toward the main streets?"

"There are two of us, so I doubt she came alone. And there are only two paths to the main street, so there will be others there, waiting for us."

"We're rats trapped in a barrel, then." How many accomplices would she have? The tangled alleyways seemed narrower to him all of a sudden.

"Rats we may be, but lucky for us, we're headed for a rathole."

They turned another corner and Septima stopped in front

of a tavern door. She took a moment to catch her breath, then knocked. It was a complicated pattern that she repeated twice. There was a sound of bars sliding, and then the door opened. Emere looked back down the alley, hesitating, but Septima grabbed him by the wrist and pulled him into the unlit indoors after her. As soon as he was inside, Septima closed the door and slid the bar back across it.

The windows were too dusty to allow light from the alley to enter. He smelled spilled wine and something earthy. It was the familiar smell of the Arlander spirit, from his time when he had joined Loran after she captured the Imperial fortress. Loran could down several cups of it in one sitting, but Emere couldn't get a taste for it. When Loran and the Arlanders gathered every night to drink the strong drink in small cups, Emere had preferred to partake of the Imperial wine in his large glass. He had tried to join in on their conversation, but whenever Emere spoke in his broken Arlandais, the others stopped talking and listened courteously. This sudden focus of attention and his self-consciousness about his language skills made him cut short whatever he was about to say. The others would politely laugh to break up the awkwardness, then raise a glass and continue with what they were saying. They had been his comrades in arms. They would have risked their lives for him, as he would have for them. But there always had been a wall. When Loran disappeared and the rebellion ended in Arland's victory, Emere saw no reason not to go back to Kamori, to his family home in the orchard.

As his eyes slowly adjusted to the dark, Emere could make out that there were two other people in the tavern aside from himself and Septima. The man who had opened the door for them was looking for something in a cupboard. The other one was sitting at a table, eerily still. Perhaps he was sleeping.

The man looking through the cupboard said, "You're here early, Subdirector. Did you see him already?"

"No. Someone was following us, so I had to lose her first. I'll go out to meet him." Septima went to the bar and sat down. "We'll wait here until the evening."

Emere sat at a nearby table, bumping into two chairs on the way there, and asked the question he had wanted to ask ever since they entered the labyrinth of alleyways.

"What are we waiting for?"

"For now, Devadas. My associate." Septima clucked her tongue. "It's complicated. You'll see soon."

What could be so complicated that she couldn't explain while they were holed up in the dark doing nothing? Emere briefly thought of demanding a further explanation, but he was still busy trying to figure out what was going on himself. He was almost assassinated, again, while being technically kidnapped by a group of Intelligence agents.

The most puzzling thing about all this, to him, was the question of his own worth. He knew he wasn't important enough to be a target of political intrigue.

The man took a lantern down from the cupboard and lit it. The tavern appeared around them, cramped and shabby. Septima sat as comfortably as if she had been sitting there for an hour, and a glass of wine had materialized before her. The man who had lit the lantern was of a stout build, wide and short.

The other man sitting at the table was not sleeping but staring into the space before him. His braided hair and beard were fastened with blue ribbons. An Arlander custom. His neck had an Arlander clan mark tattooed on it too.

Noticing that Emere was looking at him, the stout man said, "That's Lukan, he owns this place. Had a brief visit with the interrogators at the Office of Truth and that's how he's been ever since." He then went over to the Arlander and waved his hand in front of his face, but the man had no reaction.

"Why was he interrogated?"

"His niece is a runaway sorcerer. The poor bastard's fine once every two days or so, but I suppose today isn't one of those days."

From the bar, Septima said, "This man is a member of the Commons Council. Be respectful."

"Oh my, a councillor, are you? Should I call you Your Excellency? Or maybe I should prostrate myself right here on the floor." The stout man dragged the chair out across from Emere and set his cup down with a bang. Some of it splashed out. He smelled of earth and hard alcohol. "And you're an accomplice to the Great Fire too. Do you know what the Power generator you stole was used for?"

Septima furiously slammed down her glass. "Are you drunk? Why are you telling him that now?"

Taken aback, Emere turned to the stout man, who shrugged and finished his wine.

Septima looked at Emere and said, "Councillor, do forget what he just told you."

Despite Septima's suggestion, what the stout man had just said to him unnerved him. Two years ago, he had been asked by a merchant who was providing funds to his brother to steal a Power generator while the Imperial occupation was undergoing a transfer of command between legions. It was one of the Kamori Liberators' few victories, and it had also been the first time he had met Loran. Thanks to her, everything went better than could ever be expected. But where that Power generator had ended up and how it was used, he never knew. A pang of shame hit him, as he realized that it had never even occurred to him to find out.

Emere recalled Ludvik's visit. Power generators were under the jurisdiction of the Office of Truth, and Ludvik was one of its overseers. What if he had known what these three knew? The thought that Ludvik's visit might not have been a simple social call put Emere's whole body on edge. How much did he know?

Unsettled by this, Emere did not say more. The stout man sat across from him, drinking from his cup. Septima fiddled with her own wineglass in front of her. The man devastated by his interrogation in the Office of Truth continued to stare into space. Emere sat in silence as well.

He didn't know what was waiting for him. He feared his past coming back to haunt him. But he also knew that everything had changed the day he was shot. Before, he was a hostage and a figurehead. Now, he was closer to something that mattered. Something that wanted *him* for some reason. Whatever it might be, it felt better to be wanted than not.

14

ARIENNE

The sight of the Imperial sorcerer ghost bouncing Tychon made Arienne pause. The lines of his features and body were less sharp compared to the other ghosts that had entered her mind, but what really struck her was the fact that he knew the baby's name. He must have had some kind of relationship to Tychon while he was alive.

"And that's why he could remain when everyone else was banished," she murmured, forgetting that there was finally someone around to hear her. The donkey had been staring at the ghost and now turned to her, his ears perked up.

The first person she thought of as having something to do with Tychon was his father—Lysandros. He hadn't died in Mersia, but he was the author of *The Sorcerer of Mersia* and had ties to this country. For all she knew about ghosts, this was as good a reason as any why Lysandros might be here now.

She took a closer look at the ghost while he comforted the

crying child. Lysandros, when Arienne met him, had been more machine than man, and she hadn't ever imagined what he would've looked like before he did away with most of his flesh. She took a step toward the ghost.

"Do you remember me?"

The ghost looked up from Tychon and stared at her. His eyes were like dark shadows and his face hard to read, but his stare told her that he was trying to remember.

"Well, do you?" Arienne asked again.

Arienne gasped as his features started to become even more blurred and vague. He did not answer. Hoping that he would not dissipate into thin air, she pressed.

"I'm Arienne, the one who ran away with Eldred? I killed you."

"Eldred . . . the Grim King . . . ?"

The fog-like boundaries of the ghost suddenly started to come into focus. Only then could Arienne see the embroidered name on his uniform: ENGINEER JUNIOR GRADE NOAM.

"Your name is Noam? Not Lysandros?"

She was disappointed, but also curious. And after having crossed the Rook Mountains and traversed a wasteland without sharing a single word with anyone, she was almost overjoyed to actually be speaking to someone, albeit a ghost. She thought of the days when Eldred had lived in the room in her mind.

"Lysandros. The Grand Inquisitor . . ." His eyes found their focus, and he looked less out of it. He began to sing softly, a lullaby. Tychon's cries subsided, and Arienne felt like she was falling under a spell. This was an unfamiliar language. The ghost carefully laid Tychon down on the bed before he started talking.

"Yes, sir! Engineer Noam, reporting . . . No problems with

Tychon, Grand Inquisitor Lysandros. Output margin of error within five decachrons . . ."

The ghost's form was slowly coming more and more into focus. His round face was flush, and his large, shining eyes were the first feature to fully re-form. His clean face had no trace of a beard, and his ears were too big and his nose too small. He looked around twenty-five, maybe younger? As she wondered what he would say next, the ghost suddenly leaped up and shouted, "Fractica! What is Fractica doing?"

He suddenly grabbed Arienne's shoulders, his face twisted in fear.

"Oh no, oh no . . . *Ayula!*"

Arienne's eyes were wide as she stared into Noam's face.

"Melting. Melting . . . my hands . . ."

The twisted, melted buildings and bones of Danras—as Arienne was remembering them, Noam grabbed her face and Arienne pushed him away.

"Stop that!"

Noam stumbled backward, tripped over Aron, and landed on his behind. His hands were not melting, nor were they warping. They looked perfectly normal. Noam stared at them and then looked up at Arienne. He gasped. Quickly, he got to his feet and took another step back, staring at her with suspicion.

"Who are you? What am I doing here?"

"It's *me* who should be asking *you* those questions! Clearly, you're a sorcerer in charge of managing a Power generator. Engineer Junior Grade Noam."

"How do you know my name?"

"It's embroidered on your uniform!"

He looked down at himself and then looked up again, confusion writ large on his face. Arienne felt a pang of pity for him as she realized that he did not know he was dead yet. She wondered if she should tell him, but she knew if she did, they might never move on to the more urgent matters at hand.

"Where are we?" Noam said.

"Listen carefully . . . Well, sit down on that bed first."

Noam obediently sat down on the edge of the bed. Arienne began to tell him of how an Imperial Powered weapon, the Star of Mersia, had brought about the destruction of the whole country; that no one knew what exactly had happened; and that she had come to Danras to find out.

While she told him, distrust, horror, rage, and disappointment passed over Noam's face.

"All right, now ask me whatever questions you have," Arienne finished, preparing herself.

Noam said in a sad voice, "So I died then?"

"Probably . . . I'm sorry." She knew it wasn't her fault he had died, and that he had been dead for over a hundred years, but she still felt sorry all the same.

Swallowing hard, Noam asked, very carefully and in a reverent tone, "Then are you . . . our god . . . ma'am?"

She burst out laughing, more out of relief than at the absurdity of what he was asking.

"Not at all! My room is not your afterlife. It's a space I made in my mind using sorcery. You came into it when I didn't have my guard up, and siphoned off my Power to reclaim your old form, at least in my mind."

"I don't remember trying to get in here."

"You were a ghost for a hundred years, so your desire to find your form again was probably instinctual," Arienne guessed, shrugging.

Noam looked a little skeptical, but Arienne had questions of her own.

"What kind of an Imperial engineer believes in a god? Where are you from?"

". . . Ebria."

A country mentioned in her studies at the Imperial Academy. It was a small province in the northeast of the great continent. A professor had derisively noted they prayed to a god they had never even seen.

"Where they used to worship the, er, 'Nameless God'?"

Noam nodded. "Some of us still worship . . . Oh, I suppose if a hundred years have passed, things could be different." His face turned somber, even for a ghost.

The Empire rounded up sorcerers at a young age and maintained control over them until death, whereupon their corpses were converted to Power generators. The sorcerer-engineers, like Noam, were the ones who built and maintained these generators. Noam had likely been taken from Ebria by the Empire and trained to become an engineer, then assigned to look after the Power generator of Mersia before he met his doom here. This could've easily been her own fate. She shuddered at the thought of spending her life alongside preserved cadavers, then remembered that she was conversing with a ghost, in an underground cemetery.

"Well, Noam of Ebria, I have some more pressing questions.

You're here by the good grace of my Power, so you can help me a little, can't you?"

Noam nodded.

"The world believes that Mersia rose up against the Empire and the Empire extinguished the country through a weapon called the Star of Mersia. Was there really a rebellion?" When the Grim King Eldred had lived in Arienne's mind, he'd told her that Mersia had always been a faithful vassal of the Empire. She needed to know the truth.

Noam frowned as he considered the question. "There were always a few people who wanted the Empire gone, but Mersia generally had good relations with the Empire. The prefect was almost always appointed from the local population and there weren't any significant incidents during the seventy years of Imperial rule. And I didn't have any problems working here."

So, that part of Eldred's story at least seemed true.

"That lullaby you sang to Tychon. Do you remember singing it?" she asked, changing the subject.

Noam was startled, and he shook his head.

"Just a moment ago," Arienne persisted, "you said something about Tychon's margin of error being something or other. Were you in charge of Power generator Tychon?"

"Yes. Because Grand Inquisitor Lysandros can only move with Tychon. When he was stationed here, it was one of my tasks to make sure every day that the generator functioned properly."

"And did you . . . sing to all the lead sarcophagi you came across?"

Noam's face turned red. "There's no rule against singing in front of a Power generator!"

Arienne thought of teasing him about it, then decided against it. She didn't want to stress him more than she needed to. She didn't like the way he became blurry before, when she pressed him to remember. "Why was Lysandros even here?"

"Please don't say his name like that. It's disrespectful."

Arienne suppressed a laugh, imagining what Noam's face would look like if he figured out that she had killed Lysandros.

"Fine. Why was the *Grand Inquisitor* here?"

"I don't know, really. He just arrived one day, unannounced. The prefect was nervous because he didn't know how to express his gratitude for Mersia's liberation."

"Gratitude for Mersia's liberation?"

"It was thanks to the Grand Inquisitor that Mersia was liberated from the Grim King's grasp and joined the Empire. That was why he was promoted to Grand Inquisitor of the Office of Truth . . . But he didn't even attend the reception the prefect had hosted for him, he only visited the Power generator chamber."

A Power generator chamber? Of course—even minor cities like the capital of Arland had Power generators, so it only made sense that a large city like Danras would as well.

"There's a Power generator chamber here? That means Tychon wasn't the only generator, right? And you were in charge of that generator as well?"

"Yes, Class Three Power generator Fractica. The Grand Inquisitor brought it when he first came here. All of the streetlamps and Powered machines in Danras city proper used Fractica." A note of awe entered his voice. "Fractica was over a hundred years old by then. Other than the ones connected to the Circuit of Destiny, Fractica is the only generator that has been used for so long without deterioration. The Grand Inquisitor actually used it like a work-horse at first, you know. A Class Three generator pulling a cart!"

Noam laughed for the first time. Arienne, meanwhile, was putting the pieces together. The monster that had pursued her on the surface could have been a mobile platform carrying its Power generator. Those were common in the legions. Was the generator within the monster Fractica? Didn't its name come up during Noam's disoriented speech earlier, too?

"That other Power generator . . . Fractica, you talked like you had a problem with it. Did something happen?"

Noam shook his head. "Never. There was no problem. I told you, it's one of the most stable generators in all of the Empire." He began blurring slightly.

"You're lying!" Arienne snapped. "Before, you were lost in memory, saying there was something wrong with Fractica!"

Noam's agitated face was getting blurrier, as was the rest of his body. "Did I . . . ? No, it wasn't a real problem . . . Just a brief malfunction. Probably a routine sort of mishap. If I can fix it before the Grand Inquisitor comes back from the Capital, I can—"

"A brief malfunction! It's been a hundred years, and that thing is still gallivanting around Danras, wreaking havoc!"

Noam's eyes widened; then he fell back into despair. "Oh . . . right. Then Grand Inquisitor Lysandros . . . ?"

Arienne paused to choose her words carefully. She wasn't sure what the best way to say this was. Maybe concision was best.

"Dead."

Noam bowed his head and sighed. "Well, I guess it has been a hundred years. Even if he'd changed half his body to machine, he couldn't be alive for over two hundred years . . ."

Well, he actually did and was. But then I killed him.

Before he could ask for more details, she continued with her questions. "So, what *was* the problem with Fractica?"

"Light was leaking. Not the violet light of Power but . . . a strange color. And the sound of the engine was off. It kept going over the output of a Class Three and falling to as low as that of a Class Six and back again. And the space and time lattices kept warping. I tried to turn it off and examine it. I went to get my tools . . . I don't know what happened after."

So, he had probably died before fetching his tools. What if Danras's Power generator had something to do with the Star of Mersia? What if Lysandros had somehow used Fractica to bring about the destruction?

But Eldred had told her that Mersia never declared independence, and Noam had confirmed it. Could it actually be true that the Star of Mersia didn't happen because of the Empire?

Regardless, there couldn't be a single Power generator that could have wrought such devastation as Arienne had seen above. There had to be something more. The last time they met, Lysandros and Eldred had blamed each other for the fall of Mersia . . .

"And Lysandros was not present?" Arienne asked.

"He'd said there was something he needed to check on, so this was two days after he left. If he'd been here, then maybe it wouldn't have happened . . ."

Had Lysandros gone to the Capital to stop the Star of Mersia from happening? Or simply scurried away from the oncoming disaster? Maybe the secret of the Star was in the Capital and not here. Which meant she had a very long way to travel. Again.

Well, no one led me to expect that a century-old mystery would be easy to solve.

"One last question. You are in the catacombs of Danras. I don't think there was anyone who could've survived the Star of Mersia to bury you here. So why are you haunting it?"

Noam frowned again. Remembering things seemed to require much effort.

"The Power generator chamber was underground. Unless there is a reason for it to be mobile, like Fractica used to be, generators are usually underground."

This made sense. It was to minimize Power leakage. Eldred had also been stored deep below the Imperial Academy.

"Our Power generator chamber had been constructed from a room that the people of Danras had formerly used to prepare their dead bodies."

Some good news at last. "So the Power generator chamber is connected to these catacombs?"

Noam nodded.

Arienne's expression turned serious. "Good. Engineer Noam, I have real sympathy for your situation, and so I won't turn you out of this room. In return"—she paused dramatically, noting the tension in Noam's face—"you have to guide me to the surface. I assume there's a passage out through the Power generator chamber? And also . . ." She nodded at Tychon asleep on the bed. "He cries from time to time. Sing him a lullaby, or whatever it is you used to do, but do take care of him."

15

YUMA

The kitchen carriage, pulled by four harnessed oroxen, was larger than most houses. The Host would prepare food inside, watch over the herd, and, most importantly, sing melodies that protected the herd and herders alike. Without the Host, the Grim King's rainstorm would have caused a stampede that trampled scores of calves. The Host also treated the herders' wounds and ailments. But now he was treating not a herder but an emissary from the Empire, the very spy the Grim King wanted in his grasp.

Yuma changed her dirtied ceremonial garb into clean work clothes and stood before the carriage, facing the setting sun. Clean work clothes were better than her ruined ceremonial outfit. Aidan kept fidgeting with his mustache beside her.

"I don't like this, Chief. I think we should hand him over to the Grim King as soon as possible."

Having spent his childhood as an apprentice candidate of the Grim King, Aidan knew the Grim King better than anyone else in

Danras did, which allowed him to see what others could not. But all she could read from his attitude was his fear. He would never be free of the shadow of the king.

But am I myself free? Yuma thought of how Rizona had died bleeding on her horse. The Grim King was always said to be powerful, and now Yuma knew that he was so powerful that he did not even need to be present to do such a thing . . .

Aidan turned to Yuma and said, "What are you going to do?"

"I'm going to wait and see."

"And what are you going to do after waiting and seeing?"

Yuma shot him a look. "Aidan. You were friends with my father and mother. You are wiser and older than I. I am aware you have worked for the good of Danras for a long time, but that outsider is under my keeping. Please return to your tent."

"Chief . . ."

She knew his dread would cease only if she dragged Lysandros to the Grim King herself, but she was not going to do that. So, the next best thing would be for him to be out of sight of the man.

"Please leave. I have to see the Host."

Aidan sighed and walked to his tent, looking back at Yuma and the kitchen carriage several times as he did so.

Yuma continued to stand in her respectful pose, waiting. As soon as Aidan was gone from view, Old Vella, who served the Host, opened the carriage door.

"The treatment is finished. The patient's fever broke, and he sleeps now. The Host asks the Chief Herder to enter."

"Thank you." Yuma bowed and climbed up the wooden steps into the carriage, her spurs going *tak tak* on the planks. The inside was full of steam from the cauldron. Wearing ceremonial robes made of several layers of paper-thin leather and decorated in the feathers of rare birds, a thirteen-year-old boy sat on the floor of the carriage.

"Yuma is here, Host."

"Is she now."

The previous Host had lived to be almost a hundred years old, so Yuma was still unused to the new Host being a child.

"I must apologize for saddling you with an outsider," she said.

"Anyone found on the steppe must be cared for. You did the right thing."

His voice was young but he spoke like an ancient. This child, until last year, had been called Dalan, but he now harbored the soul of the Great Host that was as old as time. Yuma understood this in theory, but his outer appearance still took much adjusting to.

"Where is the man?" Yuma asked.

The Host pointed to the stairs on the left and said, "Resting on a bed upstairs. No need to worry, for now. He was only suffering from exhaustion and exposure. He is weak in body but strong against disease. And yet . . ."

"And yet?"

The Host frowned. "A very weak body indeed. As if he has never moved his arms and legs on his own. That scaffolding frame around him . . . You said he could move only with its help?"

Yuma nodded. "That seems to be the case."

"Old Vella found a way to strip it off him, so he won't be able to go far."

"The man claimed to be an emissary of the Empire. I do not think immobilizing him is necessary."

The Host didn't answer as he stood up and opened the lid of the cauldron behind him. The steam rose like a cloud, and a scent like flowers in spring spread through the room. Yuma found herself breathing it in deeply.

From inside the cauldron, the Host picked up a steamed meat bun and tossed it to Yuma, who caught it neatly with both hands. It was hot. As the Host sat back down and took a bite of his own meat bun, Yuma did the same. The flower scent and meat flavor spread in her mouth. She hadn't eaten all day.

"That frame around him isn't something that moves on its own. There is magic flowing through it. Did you bring the iron lump he rode in on?"

"I've ordered herders to use oroxen to drag it here. It should arrive soon."

"He won't be able to walk, if he is away from that thing."

So Lysandros had been borrowing strength from that machine. Yuma's eyes widened in realization. It made sense—he had indeed collapsed as soon as he had ordered the iron giant to stop.

"When will he be awake?" She stared at the stairs and took another bite of her bun.

"Worried, are you? I suppose aside from being as thin as a blade of grass, he is a handsome young man."

Something a child might tease her about, or perhaps it was more of an old man's joke. Yuma swallowed and said, "I only have some questions."

"Let him rest for now. Come back tomorrow morning. Can he speak our language?"

"Very little."

"There is much time before the end of the herding; he'll learn more."

Surprised, Yuma stopped in mid-bite. "You want us to keep him with us until the end of the herding?"

The Host gave her a look as if to say she was a fool for even asking. "Are we not shorthanded and can't afford to send our herders to Danras with him? Besides, if he is here as an emissary, he should understand how we live as a people."

"But Host, this man . . ." She struggled to find the words. It was forbidden to mention the Grim King in front of the Host.

"I am aware. You want to say that he's looking for this man, correct?"

Yuma nodded, slowly.

"He'll come when he comes."

This was said casually, but there was a bit of worry in the Host's eyes. Yuma thought of Rizona's death again.

"I just make the meals and sing the songs. Whatever happens during the herding is up to the Chief Herder. What could a mere boy of thirteen years have to say about such business?"

He then closed his eyes and began rapping his knuckles on the floor. Yuma stood, bowed deeply, and made her exit. As she crossed the threshold, the Host began to sing in time with the knocking. His voice sounded deeper in song, not like a child's at all. Her tension melted away, her head cleared. Yuma stood just outside the threshold, thinking of what to do next.

The Host had implied the Grim King might come to collect Lysandros himself. Aidan seemed to think there would be repercussions if they did not deliver the man. If the Host was right, there was no point in keeping the man with them if the Grim King was just going to come for him anyway. Which meant maybe they should turn him over as Aidan said.

To do otherwise would mean they were defying the Grim King's orders, which was tantamount to treason. It was insubordination and harboring of an enemy spy. And there were at least a thousand youth like Rizona in Danras . . .

The Grim King had ruled over Danras and Merseh as a whole for five centuries, maybe more. His cruelty was legend. The Grim King was a part of Merseh, as much as the open steppe and the endless sky. A Merseh with no fear of the Grim King—that was a world Yuma could hardly imagine.

Instead, she thought of Rizona again. The dread she had felt when she called her name and received no answer. The saddle soaked in blood. The final words Jed had said to her, with the very last of his strength, that she must run.

The sun had almost set. Far away, two oroxen were dragging the silver giant, or the mechanical horse, or whatever it was really called. A powerful weapon, that's what it was. Impervious to arrows and swords, a moving fortress. The Empire had entrusted such a machine to a young man who couldn't stand up on his own. She couldn't tell yet if this meant the Empire was that great an empire, or if Lysandros was that great a man.

Whichever it might be, wouldn't treason be worth a try, with such allies?

Yuma came to a decision. She walked down the wooden steps and whistled long and loud for Aston.

16

EMERE

He must've dozed off in the dim tavern while waiting for this Devadas, because he was suddenly back on the plains of Arland. Loran stood at a distance and was looking in his direction. Her body was covered in scales. Her wings were half folded. Her left eye was a glowing ball of blue fire.

Emere was entranced.

"Prince Emere, you have finally come."

The volcano in the horizon wore a halo of light as blue as that in Loran's eye. Emere stared for a moment before speaking.

"Is this not the same place we met as before?"

Sensing Loran's gaze was looking past his shoulder, Emere turned around. There was nothing there.

"Prince Emere. When I battled the Twenty-Fifth Legion, where did you find yourself?"

". . . Under your orders, I was escorting the sorcerer Arienne to the volcano."

"Do you regret doing so?"

Regret wasn't strong enough a word. He despaired for not having fought by Loran's side on that fateful day. That he had never charged under the banner of the first king who taught him what being a king actually meant. If he could've fought on that battleground for that single day, the long years before that would've been worth it. Even if it had been a battle in another country and not Kamori . . . But that was not to be Emere's fate. He lowered his head.

Loran said, "You are about to meet the king, Prince Emere."

Had Septima brought him to meet Loran?

"Your Majesty . . . ?"

He took a step toward her but stopped when he saw her slowly shake her head.

"Not me, but the Sleeping King."

"Who might that be?"

A light shone from Loran. The fire in her left eye had overflowed to cover her whole body. Emere could not take it any longer.

"Why do you keep speaking in riddles?" Emere shouted.

But the only answer he received was another riddle.

"Prince Emere, what does it mean that a destiny is decided, but not the future?"

The plains were now covered in blue fire too.

"That one cannot pick the moment of choice," said Emere readily, "but the future depends on the choice one makes in that moment."

Loran nodded. "The wisdom of the Tree Lords of Kamori. But that is not all."

"If not all, then—"

"You must meet the Sleeping King."

The sky, the earth, it was all covered in blue fire now, though the fire was not hot. The horizon had disappeared. So had the volcano and the battlefield and Arland. Loran herself was fading into the light.

At the sound of a door opening, Emere was startled awake, the short leg of his table knocking against the floor.

Calming himself, he looked around him. There was another lantern lit, but it was darker in the tavern than before. The shadow of a giant filled the doorframe. The stout man and Septima had their gazes fixed in that direction.

The giant entered and carefully lowered the burden he carried on his back onto Emere's table. The burden was a person. A man. Maybe dead. The stout man stood up from his chair, lantern in hand, and took a closer look.

Septima stood. "Oh . . . Is he alive?"

The giant shrugged.

There were three bolts stuck in the giant's shoulder and chest, and the man lying on the table also had three bloody bolts coming out of his chest. Septima brought a finger under the man's nostrils, shook her head, and said, "Let's take care of you first."

As the stout man held up his lantern for her, Septima grabbed the end of each of the bolts in the giant and ripped them out. She did it so forcefully that blood splattered on her face each time, but the giant didn't even flinch. His bleeding soon stopped, and his wounds slowly, miraculously began to close. They shrank into star-shaped scars and then completely disappeared.

To a wide-eyed Emere, Septima said, "Councillor, this is Devadas. He is an Amrit from Varata."

Emere had heard of Amrits when he visited Varata with Rakel.

They had been monks, practicing body magic for immense strength and healing. Local legends said the greatest of them were able to uproot hills and come back from the dead. By the time he visited, there had been none to be seen, as one would expect from an Imperial province. All he saw was one of the mountain sites where a cloister had stood, turned into an Imperial-style square. But the locals insisted that some were in hiding, passing down their magic. Did they know an Amrit worked for the very Empire who had exterminated their order?

The giant Devadas rubbed his healed wounds and said in a deep voice, "Who was that woman outside? She was trouble."

"The assassin who was after the councillor. What happened to her?"

"She's dead. But she managed to kill our contact." Devadas looked Emere up and down. He seemed displeased. Perhaps, like the stout man, he did not approve of Emere's stealing of the Power generator in Dehan Forest. Emere returned his stare with a dispassionate one of his own. Devadas's nostrils flared, and his breathing was rough. He took a menacing step toward Emere, and Emere stood up in response. Devadas was two heads taller than Emere, a living tower of muscle. Emere had no choice but to look up.

Septima stepped in between them.

"You know what Cain said. Restrain yourself."

Devadas scoffed.

Septima turned to Emere. "And Councillor, you must understand the disapproval of my men. Hundreds died in that fire."

The tavern owner sat exactly as he did before, still staring into the distance. Emere sat back down, looked at the man who lay unmoving on the table, and asked, "Is this the man I was supposed to meet?"

"He is. Though, to be precise, our friend was supposed to speak to you *through* this man." Septima sighed and rummaged through the man's coat. "Do you know what's under the Senate building?"

The Circuit of Destiny again. This could not be a coincidence.

"I've heard rumors," said Emere. "Generators connected together. The Circuit of Destiny that can tell the future."

Septima found a small burlap sack the size of a fist in the man's inner pocket and nodded.

"Yes, as you say, the Circuit can tell us the future. They say it holds the whole of the past, present, and future within it. Our friend . . . he is an Arlander named Cain, and he is trying to learn everything he can about the Circuit of Destiny. In his investigations, your name came up."

The moment Septima said Cain's name, Emere felt a level of care underlying the tone of her voice. Septima undid the sack's string and dropped its contents on the floor. A few silver coins made a clear ringing sound on the floorboards, and then two wooden carvings fell out. Both human figures—men or women, it was impossible to tell—were raising their arms to the sky. Emere was familiar with the style.

"An Ebrian. This is their Nameless God."

Perhaps surprised at his knowledge, Septima arched an eyebrow.

Emere explained, "I once traveled with one."

Rakel had owned such a wood carving. She probably still had it, hidden away somewhere.

Septima clucked her tongue at the dead man's personal effects. "This won't do. We need to find another way to talk to Cain. This place is going to get dangerous, I think. We should leave."

Emere held one of the carvings in his hand, running his thumb over it and feeling the texture.

"If the three of you are from the Ministry of Intelligence, why are you secretly meeting with a provincial who worships a forbidden god in a place like this?"

"Forbidden gods are a matter for the Office of Truth," said the stout man, "not Intelligence."

Emere kept his gaze on Septima. "You know that's not an answer."

Septima regarded Emere for a moment before answering.

"All right, Councillor. I shall explain."

"We just met this guy!" the stout man objected, his lantern swinging as he turned to her.

"It's fine. He was summoned here by Cain, after all."

Devadas gave a nod as well. The stout man opened his mouth to speak but closed it again as he put the lantern down on the table. Emere could sense a certain reverence in the way the three of them carried themselves. The name "Cain" gave weight to the dusty air in the tavern.

It somehow reminded him of being taken for the first time to the sacred forests of Kamori as a child—the priests leading him to the Tree Lords, the huge trees that bestowed wisdom and blessed the country. As the rustles of their leaves gradually turned into speech, Emere had found himself bowing his head with his hands placed on his chest.

Septima continued.

"Two years ago, Cain prevented a Star of Mersia from being set off in the Capital. Thanks to his efforts, only a few hundred died in the resulting fire instead of the whole of the Imperial heartland being destroyed. We have been cooperating with each other ever since."

The Star of Mersia. The Powered weapon that could turn an entire country into a desert. Emere recalled the sight of the wastelands of Mersia, a desolate view that he had shared with Rakel.

"What Cain discovered while looking into the Circuit of Destiny was plans for a rebellion. We are trying to stop it."

It was the kind of thing the Ministry of Intelligence would do. The Arland incident had happened only two years ago; they were right to be on edge.

Emere suppressed a grin. "And what province is planning a rebellion now?"

"It's not a province. It's the Office of Truth."

Silence.

The stout man finally spoke up. "Grand Inquisitor Lysandros led the Office of Truth for over a hundred years. Ever since he was killed by a provincial, presumably, the Office has been up in arms. Those bastards have always been a pack of fanatics," he nearly spat out. "Once they come into power, they will purge everyone. No one is safe, Councillor."

Lysandros. Two years ago, Emere had encountered him at Finvera Pass. He had only approached them, which was enough for Emere and his soldiers to fall where they stood, unable to breathe. It was almost understandable that his absence was so keenly felt that the Office of Truth would resort to this.

But this didn't make sense. "Even if it were so, all you would have to do is alert the Senate . . . it's the Senate that has command over the legions. Wouldn't that be a more efficient way to stop it?"

Septima smiled bitterly.

"It is as you say. If the Senate does not wish it, there can be no takeover. But this plan has been secretly approved by many of the senators. This is a political ritual, if you will, to overcome the dissenters and skip legal hindrances. There have been three such precedents in the history of the Empire. Each time, an Imperator was appointed."

"An Imperator?" Emere had not heard of this position.

"A special office that can rule without any adherence to procedure, supposedly to bring the wayward Empire back onto its destined path. You won't find mention of it in any of the Empire's laws, as the Imperator is above the law." Septima paused to sip from her glass. "Ever since the attack two years ago, many senators have become paranoid about the provinces. There have been heated debates in the Senate about this. The Office of Truth has been advocating tighter control over them, while selling the coup to those senators who would listen. The Ministry of Intelligence in turn has been persuaded not to intervene."

"Are you not Intelligence yourselves?"

Septima frowned. "The Office of Truth did not manage to make us choose their side, but they did force us to keep neutral over the matter. I objected, which is why the three of us were dismissed and are now under watch."

That was somehow unsurprising to Emere. These people didn't look like they were following any sort of standard Intelligence operating procedures.

Emere pondered the meaning of it. "So, this is the Office of

Truth using the paranoid senators to take power, and install one of their number at the very top of the Empire." A single leader with an iron fist at the helm of the Empire that could overrule the Senate and the Commons while ignoring the laws. Such a person could do anything they wanted to the world. He shuddered at the thought. "And this Cain, he uncovered all this?"

Septima nodded. "Yes. But Cain had become trapped while looking into the Circuit of Destiny and now he can't leave it. We had just barely managed to make contact with him through the Ebrian, and the first thing Cain passed on to us was the Office of Truth's plan."

Devadas broke his silence. "Cain said he was able to talk to the outside through those people's prayers."

"Ebrians," said Septima, "are usually just provincials we surveil and keep in line. But there's no way for us to talk to Cain except through their prayers. Ebrians are suspicious of Imperial attention, so we could not reveal ourselves to them." Septima let out a short laugh. Clearly, she appreciated the irony of her predicament. She pointed her chin at the dead man. "He was our line to Cain." Septima bit her lip, perhaps a gesture of regret. "We'd let him think we were worshippers of another god looking for divine messages." Emere sensed a sliver of regret in her words.

"You said my name came up," Emere continued, "but you haven't told me how and why."

Septima licked her lips. "We don't know either. Only that Cain is desperate to see you. Which means we must find another Ebrian whom Cain can use, and to do that, we have to leave now."

Emere sighed. He'd thought by now everything would be explained, which it wasn't, and the true meaning of his dream in the square would reveal itself, which it didn't. Maybe it was going to be like the last twenty years, a glimpse of destiny followed by nothing, or less than nothing. Perhaps he should leave it all to these three and go home, perhaps ask Ludvik for more security. After all, what could he, a former prince of a small province, do that would stop the power game happening at the highest level of the Empire?

Emere shook his head at his own thought. He had to keep faith. There was going to be something at the end of all this, something that would vindicate his whole life. He felt a strength return to his grip. The Nameless God dug into his palm.

He looked up at Septima. "All right. Let's see what we find."

Septima smiled. "I had a feeling you would say that. Then—"

"But one last thing," said Emere, holding up a hand. "I may be an idle councillor from a small province, but I do know how Imperial politics work."

Septima raised her eyebrows.

"The Office of Truth may be powerful," he continued, "but to cohere as one for this undertaking, and to get the support of a Senate majority, they would need the authority of at least a Grand Inquisitor. But that position had been occupied only by Lysandros for a hundred years, and he left a vacancy that still hasn't been filled. And the Commons committee that controls the Office of Truth is in all practicality controlled in turn by Tythonia's councillor, Ludvik. He is a provincial councillor. Would he stand idly by as an office under his oversight plans a coup to oppress the provinces? So, who would have enough influence to make these machinations possible?"

The stout man grinned. Devadas shook his head.

143

Septima gave the stout man a look and sighed.

"Councillor, Ludvik is the one who set all that in motion. He's the one who sent the assassin to kill you. And once the Office of Truth takes power, he is the one the Senate will appoint as the Imperator."

17

ARIENNE

She had gotten used to the smell of the catacombs. Sidestepping the faint ghosts, she followed the path through the passageways as Noam directed her from her mind. Arienne was now sure the horse seller's claim about the piece of glass warding off ghosts was a lie—the ghosts continued to repeat their last actions, not caring at all about her glowing orb. But it was also the only thing illuminating this dark underground cemetery, so she was grateful for it nonetheless.

A few times, a ghost would enter the room in her mind, but whether it was because of Noam or because she was on guard, they quickly left without her having to kick them out. But whenever they did so, regaining their form when they entered before melting back into their cold graves, the dead left behind a warm aura of formless memories in her mind, like layers of silently fallen snow. Arienne did not dislike this feeling.

She heard singing in her mind. An unfamiliar scale, and an

unfamiliar language. Songs Noam must've heard growing up in Ebria. The baby had stopped crying, but Noam continued on.

Still not completely dry from her fall into the river, Arienne tried not to shiver. She did not want to seem fearful in the presence of so many ghosts.

"Although, it's not like anyone is watching," she murmured, and came to a stop. Set into the wall next to her was a tall arch about twice her height with two large stone doors. She could tell a hole had been knocked through an old brick wall to make these doors. The arch was made of marble, and above it was the wide-open eye insignia of the Office of Truth and an engraved sign in Imperial.

"'Power Generator Chamber,'" Arienne read aloud. So, this was where Lysandros had stored the generator he had brought to Mersia. "All right, Fractica. Let's see what your room looks like."

Her hand was stopped in midair before it even reached the door. The space in front of the door undulated, runes appearing and then vanishing in the air. Wasting no time, Arienne recited the code of unraveling that Noam had given her earlier. Two years ago, she had done the same thing in the basement of the Imperial Academy, melting away the wards in order to get to Eldred.

When she exhaled, her breath sparkled violet and melted into the rippling aura. The runes vanished, and one of the doors cracked open ever so slightly with a creak so unexpectedly soft that it was comical coming from such an impressive slab of rock.

If Fractica were not functional and had stopped providing Power to this door, this protective layer would not have needed to be unraveled. So, even as it dressed up in trash and wandered the ruins of Danras, it was still following its original orders to Power the city.

As she stood in front of the Power generator chamber, an old horror that she thought she had gotten over was bubbling up to the surface. To the Empire, sorcerers were just raw material for generators, and Arienne had been repulsed by the idea of being turned into a generator ever since she first entered the Division of Sorcery at the Imperial Academy. Fractica, a century after the fall of Danras, was still providing Power to a ruin while wandering around in search of something it would never find. Maybe the Power generator had gone insane. Maybe all of them did, in the end.

Arienne hesitated for a moment before entering the chamber, unsure of what she was going to find there, but she had no choice. On this side of the door, there were only ghosts who didn't know they were dead. Inside the room, there would be a stairway up to the surface.

"And on that surface prowls a mad Power generator," she murmured as she pushed open the door.

In most Power generator chambers, the door should open into a corridor of pure white light. But this corridor was as dark as the catacombs, and there were holes in the walls. In the middle, there was a pile of something—the light from her glass orb showed it was an old sorcerer-engineer robe, and inside were a few melted bones.

Arienne took a deep breath and turned the robe over. She could still read the name embroidered in silver thread on the chest.

Engineer Junior Grade Noam.

So, Noam had been here when Danras fell. The Noam in her

mind was small and meek, but he seemed more miserable here where only his bones remained. But why had he died in the corridor to the chamber instead of on the stairway to the surface?

"Oh!" shouted Arienne, understanding in a flash. "The older skeletons in the catacombs were not melted like this . . ."

She sat down against a wall and opened the door to the room in her mind. Noam was still singing the same song, and Tychon was fast asleep. Aron had his ears perked up, listening to the song. Noam stopped singing when Arienne entered and said in amazement, "I knew Tychon was a Power generator made from a baby, but I never knew this was what he looked like."

"Obviously. You've only seen him as a lead sarcophagus."

Noam gently brushed a strand of hair away from Tychon's closed eyes.

"I wonder who his mother was?"

Arienne noticed his edges blurring. She shouted, "Hey! Wake up!"

Noam was startled. Tychon opened his eyes.

"Why are you shouting? You woke the baby."

"If you don't keep a good grip on your mind, you start to get blurry again. So, try to remember. Why were you in the passageway?"

Noam paused. "I thought the catacombs would be safer, so I was trying to leave the chamber on that side . . ."

The catacombs would be safer? Arienne then recalled that they were mostly intact, unlike the city on the surface. She waited for him to elaborate.

He blinked. "I really don't remember."

"Try!"

"It's not easy; you wouldn't remember something from a hundred years ago either!"

Not having lived long enough, Arienne didn't know if she would. But she suspected it wasn't a question of time. Even if he'd recovered his form in her mind, his mind could still be trapped in a century-old fog. How long could this man survive in this room?

Trying a different tactic, Arienne said gently, "All right. If it's too hard to think, take your time. Just rest in this room, though do let me know if you remember anything about what really happened here . . ."

Noam gazed at her for a moment before speaking.

"I died."

"Yes."

"I have nowhere to go."

"I know. So I'm going to take care of you." Arienne hesitated before adding, "I'm all alone in this country. I don't want to see you blurring."

Noam became a little clearer.

"All right," Noam started, "I don't know why, but I keep remembering this one thing. There's an old prophecy. Although Lysandros said it was just some provincial superstition, like the god I believed in."

Arienne looked back at him intently. "What prophecy?"

"That the apprentice of the Grim King would become King of Mersia."

"Eldred had an apprentice?"

Noam gasped and covered his mouth. "You can't just *say his name* like that . . . People hate that. I said it at an eatery once and the owner chased me out into the street and screamed at me."

Arienne scoffed, unable to keep it in. "Don't worry about that. The only person who can banish you here is me. And I killed El-dred. I can say his name whenever I want."

"What are you talking about? It was the Grand Inquisitor who killed El . . . the Grim King."

She grinned. "Only the first time." Her grin faded as she thought of how no sorcerer who fell into the hands of the Empire would ever be allowed to die properly. "So, Engineer Noam," she continued, "tell me more about this prophecy. Who is the apprentice of the Grim King?"

Noam's eyes grew wide. "Isn't it you?"

Outside the room, sitting by Noam's remains in the crumbling corridor to the Power generator chamber, Arienne felt her heart beat faster.

"Me? What made you think that?"

"The tattoos around your neck, aren't they the mark of the Grim King or something?"

Her hand reflexively reached for her neck. "These are *t'laran*. They're Arlander clan markings."

Noam tilted his head. "Arland . . . That's the small country in the northwest, right? In Lontaria. Not yet part of the Empire."

Arienne didn't like him using the word "yet," but history had shown him to be correct after all.

"It's only been a little over twenty years since we've been annexed."

Noam looked confused. "Then you should be at the Imperial Academy, or serving as a sorcerer-engineer. What are you doing in this place?"

"Arland may still be under Imperial rule, but I'm not."

Noam took a step back. "Wait, who *are* you? *What* are you? What do you have to do with the Grim King?"

"Nothing." She sighed. "I just knew him, briefly. That's all."

"Don't lie. This room was made with his sorcery. It's exactly as I heard it from Grand Inquisitor Lysandros."

He wasn't wrong. Eldred *had* taught Arienne how to create a room in her mind, mostly so she could use it to smuggle him out of the Imperial Academy. In this sense, perhaps she was his apprentice.

But Mersia was no longer a country; it was a wasteland. There would be no king where there were no people. As it often was with prophecies, this one had not come to pass. In her beloved adventure books, prophecies were realized no matter the obstacle, but reality was often less reliable than stories.

Whether he was aware of her thoughts or not, Noam said, "I don't know what the prophecy really means either." He made a circle over his head with his hand. "But the smell of the Grim King is in this room . . ."

Eldred had been defeated by the Empire 170 years ago, and the Star of Mersia had laid waste to the country seventy years after that. Arienne smiled. "How could you know how he smelled? You were born long after his time."

Noam blanched. "All of the dead of Mersia know. We have feared the Grim King's smell from time immemorial. The catacombs, there was . . . Ah!"

He bolted upright, making Arienne step back in surprise.

"I remember why I was going to the catacombs!"

Tychon, who had been nodding off, started to cry once more.

18

YUMA

The herding would end soon, and winter would follow. The wind in the evenings had begun to turn cold. Yuma put on her leather coat, mounted Aston, and looked out at the herd of oroxen that had fattened over the summer.

Lysandros, only his head uncovered by his metal frame, was running across the grassland making clunking sounds. As he chased a horse that ran away from him, he shouted something in his native tongue. A little behind him, the silver giant—Fractica, Yuma now knew—was galloping after him on long legs. Yuma made a cone over her mouth with her hands and shouted, "I told you to just give up!"

"No, I will ride it! What's the use of coming to Merseh if I'm never going to ride a horse? Chief Herder must know I am right."

She smiled. His was a low, deep voice, completely unexpected from such an emaciated body. Lysandros had picked up their language with remarkable speed over the last few months, though he had yet to master the complex addressing system of Mersehi. Yuma was aware that other languages were not as complicated when it came to pronouns—when speaking in Mersehi, it was impossible to be polite, not to mention grammatically correct, without choosing the right pronouns to reflect the relationship between the addresser, the addressee, and the person or object being talked about. Like many foreigners, Lysandros resorted to simply not using pronouns except for the simplest form of "I," referring to people by their names, and to Yuma as "Chief Herder." Yuma sometimes mimicked Lysandros in jest, calling him "Emissary," and it grew on her. She came to think of them as nicknames for each other.

"It is not helping the Emissary that Fractica is also running after the horse!" she shouted back, laughter in her voice.

"I swear I shall enter the leather gates of Danras on horseback!"

The horse, which had only been trotting away at first, was now at full gallop. A herder went after it while Lysandros came to a stop. An ordinary man would catch his breath after so much running, his hands on his knees, but Lysandros simply stood like a pillar. Of course, it wasn't the muscles and bones of his body that moved but the iron frame. The horses were confused by Lysandros, a sentiment Yuma shared. He was a man unlike any she had met, even without the metal frame she always found him in. What was he like without it? Would he still be the same man, confident and vibrant, out of that ingenious machine? Or was the Imperial device an inseparable part of him?

Lysandros cut through the grass toward her. She thought of giving him her handkerchief, but he wasn't sweating at all. There was a wide smile on his face. A smile so beautiful that she couldn't help smiling as well. Yuma, sitting on her horse, looked down at

Lysandros—an uncommon occurrence, since he was much taller than she was even without the metal scaffolding.

"You look completely adjusted to steppe life."

"I get used to things quickly no matter where I go." He waved to a group of three herders on horseback who were heading to the oroxen herd. The herder who waved back first was Trudie, the one who had been held upside down by Fractica. Barund, riding next to her, noticed whom she was waving to and waved as well, shouting, "Don't forget you promised to bring Fractica tomorrow morning!"

"I'll remember, Barund!"

Yuma asked, "What's happening tomorrow morning?"

"Oh, Fractica is good at moving the oroxen herd about. I think the beasts feel as if Fractica is their leader. Maybe because an orox and Fractica are about the same size?"

Not only was this man quick to pick up on the language but he also managed to befriend the herders at an astonishing speed. Yuma suspected this wasn't just because that metal beast was helpful in herding. In the distance, though, Yuma could see that Aidan stroked his mustache, staring in their direction.

"I think that man with the blue face isn't fond of me."

"That may be true."

Aidan, whenever he had a moment, would come over to Yuma and urge her to turn the spy over to the Grim King—did Lysandros know that? Did he even know that the Grim King was after him in the first place?

Neither Yuma nor Lysandros had mentioned the Grim King. To the Chief Herder of Danras and to the envoy of the Empire alike, the Grim King of Merseh was a delicate topic.

But they couldn't ignore it for much longer.

"We need to discuss something."

And it needed to be discussed before they entered Danras. Lysandros must've guessed the turn of her thoughts, as he stopped smiling. He gestured to Fractica. The iron beast came over to them and lifted him onto its back.

The sun was setting. This was Yuma's favorite time of day: when she was out on the steppe. The view of the sunset reassured her that even this vast sky had its edge, and if she rode fast and long enough, she just might reach it. The reddening sky would soon melt away into stars, and the polestar would tell her the direction to go. Never had she needed to know that direction more than now.

As the polestar appeared clear in the darkening sky, Lysandros, following her on Fractica, spoke.

"Where is Chief Herder taking me?"

There was a place that could only be visited at the end of autumn.

"It's not far. Just over there . . ."

Yuma herself had only been there once before. She led Aston through the unfamiliar path. Lysandros patted Fractica's back, and the iron beast made a creaking sound the likes of which were out of place on the grasslands, and two beams of light appeared before them. Nothing particular came into view. Yet.

Yuma, staring ahead, whispered, "Turn that light off. We're almost there."

Lysandros patted Fractica's back again. The beams of light blinked off.

"Walk from here?" he asked.

Yuma nodded and dismounted. Lysandros also leaped off Fractica's back, and the ground rang with a deep thud.

Parting the grass that came up to her waist, Yuma walked on. They had to be very careful from this point on. It might have been a mistake to bring an outsider here. Or to say what she was about to say.

"We're here."

"There's nothing . . ."

But then it began. Yuma pointed upward to the night sky. Lysandros looked up.

The stars were moving. Lysandros stared as the stars in the sky began to gather right above their heads.

"What is this . . . ?"

Yuma repeated the words the Host had said to her years ago when she was first appointed the Chief Herder.

"A long time ago and today, in both the east and the west, we all believed the destiny of peoples and their lands were decided by the stars. Once a year, the strands of destiny gather in this place. What is forged here can never be undone, and what is decided here can never be undecided."

The stars continued to gather. Then the starlight became like solid strands, falling down from the dark sky and filling the space where Yuma and Lysandros stood, making the spot as bright as day.

"This is where I swore to look after the oroxen and the herders and the people of our city as the Chief Herder of Danras." She took a step closer to Lysandros. "You said you came here in the name of peace and friendship. But the Grim King is at war with the Empire, trying to prevent your people from coming here. As long as the Grim King rules Merseh, there can be no peace or friendship with the Empire."

Lysandros only smiled softly, not saying a word.

Yuma reached into her pocket and took out her two nullstones. "Do you know what these are?"

He looked down at them. "No. But I can see the stones have Power. There are ripples."

"The Grim King gave these nullstones to me. He ordered me to stop Fractica with these and then capture you. But I didn't use them. You stopped Fractica before I did. If you hadn't, things might've happened differently."

Lysandros looked taken aback. Yuma took a deep breath.

"You came to Merseh to convince Danras, right? To foment rebellion against the Grim King, and help your Empire in your war against Cassia?"

"Eldred," replied Lysandros, as Yuma gasped audibly, "is not the King of Merseh. Just a sorcerer with too much power. I am here to meet the real King of Danras, the most powerful person in Danras."

"Danras has no king."

Lysandros looked directly into her eyes.

"All of Merseh knows that Chief Herder is the true King of Danras in all but name."

Yuma stopped breathing. Lysandros continued.

"The Empire will bring the whole world into one. Trade will flow like rivers, wars will disappear. That is the destiny of the world. I want Chief Herder to be with me in that."

The white starlight swirled around them. The chill of the late-autumn air was forgotten. Yuma dropped her hat on the ground and took a step closer. Lysandros looked down into her eyes. Yuma held his iron frame in her hands.

"Swear to me. Here, in the starlight. A promise that cannot be broken."

Lysandros's hands, making a mechanical whirring sound, rose to gently grasp her shoulders. She could feel both the cold of the frame and the warmth of his hands.

"I swear, as an emissary of the Empire, that I shall use all my power as an inquisitor of the Imperial Office of Truth to aid Yuma, the Chief Herder of Danras, to save Merseh from Eldred."

Answering Lysandros's oath, the starlight around them intensified. Yuma let go of her last bit of hesitation and decided to believe. That they could rid their land of the Grim King, that the centuries of deathly tyranny was to end, that Danras would have a true king.

The stars slowly returned to their places in the sky. Lysandros pointed north. There, a star had remained fixed the whole time, immobile as the others swirled and settled around it.

Yuma said, "The polestar never moves. It will watch over the oath you made."

Lysandros opened his mouth to say something, but nodded instead, and smiled that beautiful smile again.

19

EMERE

The Office of Truth was trying to take over the Empire. Ludvik was conspiring to become the Imperator. And a man named Cain, trapped in the Circuit of Destiny, wanted to meet Emere because somehow Emere could help stop that from happening.

Emere was having difficulty accepting any part of this situation, and neither Septima nor the other two seemed to know what Emere's role in all of this would be. The only thing he could hold on to was what Loran had said in his dream vision. You *must become king. That is your destiny. Destiny passes by those who stand still. Reach out and grasp that which awaits you, up there.*

Emere thought of that afternoon he had drunk tea and eaten peaches with Ludvik. A day when it would've been unimaginable that that man was trying to kill him. Ludvik had asked Emere what he would do if the Circuit of Destiny had given him the power to decide . . . Emere had thought this was an idle question at the time, but now he thought differently.

As Septima and her men erased any traces of their presence in the tavern, Emere sat in his chair and stared at the dead Ebrian on the table, and also at the tavern owner, Lukan, who had been tortured by the Office of Truth and become catatonic. In his dream, Loran had told him he would meet the "Sleeping King." Lukan could be said to be sleeping in a sense, but he did not seem like a king at all.

"And how did you become involved in all this? Do you know who Cain is?" he asked Lukan, not really expecting an answer.

But Lukan's eyes turned toward Emere. In them, a glint of a landscape unfurled. A red, rough wasteland. Not completely unfamiliar. Where had he seen it before?

The wasteland in the man's eyes absorbed everything in that dusty tavern: the old chairs and tables, the stink of broth and wine—Emere tried to stand, but his legs wouldn't listen to him. Deep inside his mind, something trembled.

When his body could move again, he found himself standing in that red wasteland. He realized it resembled the Mersia he had visited in his youth, but here, the sky was a sunless violet twilight. Far away, there was some kind of flock of birds, completely unmoving and floating in the sky. A longing he couldn't understand gripped his heart.

Maybe he had fallen asleep again while looking into Lukan's eyes and was once again dreaming. If this really was a dream, and the Tree Lords were right about dreams being the mirrors of destiny, he might be able to meet Loran here and ask her again about what she had said. Not knowing which direction to go in, he set off toward the dark flock.

The flock was of course in the sky, and unable to fly, Emere had no way to reach it. Still, he went on. He felt an urge to get as close to it as possible.

Like eyes adjusting to the dark, he began to adjust to the red world around him. In the warmth he felt on his skin and the breath coming into his lungs, he noticed things he hadn't at first. His heart trembled. He breathed deeply.

Memories of events he had never experienced rushed into his mind with the air he breathed. Countless people, countless countries, and countless scenes, mixing up inside his mind, a great wave of noises and confusion. He screamed. He wanted to collapse on the ground but managed to stay upright, trying to make sense of all the thoughts as they came.

It was no use. Resentment and rage as vast as this wasteland, death and loss and deprivation and humiliation that felt like his own, dug into his heart. The suffocating feeling akin to what he had experienced in Mersia decades ago came back. His skin froze from within. Then he realized—the darkness here was more than just absence of light. The air, or perhaps the space itself, was tainted with palpable gloom, poisonous and corrosive.

This was a world of sorrow and rage. Emere was very familiar with both feelings. After Kamori surrendered, he said he left his country to fight the Empire, but in the corner of his mind, he always suspected that perhaps it was really just to run away from those two feelings.

He wanted to escape now. The thing that pooled and coiled here was not the kind of darkness that a man was meant to endure. There was nothing, *nothing* anyone could do about it.

"Councillor."

The voice reminded him of Gildas's. Someone had laid his

hand on Emere's shoulder, a gesture that was sending warmth down his back. The horrible thoughts in his mind melted away.

Emere turned and there a young man stood, looking worried. Was he in his late twenties? There was a strength in his features, and the eyes behind his spectacles shone. The tattoos around his neck told him he was an Arlander. Thinner and simpler, compared to Loran's *t'laran*. Emere gathered his wits.

"You must be Cain."

The young man nodded. "The first time entering is always overwhelming. I tried to get to you as quickly as possible, but time doesn't flow in the usual way here."

"And where is 'here'?"

Cain gestured around them. "This wasteland is the world inside the mind of the Circuit of Destiny. A dream, in a sense."

He hadn't thought of the Circuit of Destiny as having a mind, but the magic sounded familiar.

"I met a sorcerer who could make a room inside her mind."

"You mean Arienne?" Cain asked, beaming.

"Do you know each other?" Emere asked, surprised.

Cain shook his head. "We only met briefly. When she was running away from the Capital."

Cain started to walk, and Emere walked next to him.

"If this is a dream, I must be asleep in Lukan's tavern."

"You are. The Circuit of Destiny has countless paths connecting itself to all parts of the world. They watch the world through them. I found one such that led directly to you. The Circuit must have created it to contact you."

Emere frowned. "If something like the Circuit had contacted me, I think I would remember."

Cain shrugged. "You would be surprised. Anyway, I used that path to bring you here. I thought I would need the help of our Ebrian friends, but you were as easy to get to as they were, thanks to the Circuit's path, and the statue you hold now even in your sleep."

"The wooden idol is magical?" Emere asked, incredulous.

"Yes and no. The item itself is just a wooden carving, but it contains residual power from the Ebrian's prayers. That's how I could contact him even from inside the Circuit."

"Subdirector Septima told me you were trapped here."

Cain didn't pause in his pace. "I am. You are only visiting with your mind, but I'm trapped in the Circuit of Destiny, both body and mind."

Emere followed Cain's gaze toward the flock of birds in the sky. There were no signs of them getting closer.

"Where are we going?" he asked Cain.

Cain didn't answer the question as he continued. "Two years ago, the Circuit of Destiny showed me the battle happening in Arland, showed me Loran and Arienne and told me to decide their destiny. I refused."

"Why?"

"I came to the Capital alone as a child, with no money or family. I lived that way for a long time. I was captured by the Ministry of Intelligence and threatened by them. So I know all too well what it is to have your destiny held in someone else's hands."

Emere stopped walking. "We can only choose between the choices given to us. Who would call it destiny if we could make every choice about our lives? If it were me, I would have considered it my own destiny and helped Arland."

"I see your point. But I've fought against people who think

it is their right to do whatever they want with others' lives. They tried to trigger a Star of Mersia in the center of the Empire, and I knew I had to stop it. That's actually when I first encountered the Circuit of Destiny . . ." Cain trailed off. "And something must've happened then because the Circuit kept in contact with me ever since. It was always taking Fienna's form . . ."

His mention of the name "Fienna" was imbued with sorrow. Emere wondered who she was. Perhaps she was someone who was waiting for Cain to return to the outside world. He was reminded of Rakel, and he wondered if she was thinking of him.

"The Circuit of Destiny has the power to act," continued Cain, "and a will of its own."

Emere raised his eyebrows. "What do you mean? It's just a machine, like all Power generators are."

Cain shook his head. "No, Councillor. It's an amalgamation of a few hundred sorcerers, the best the world had ever seen. It wouldn't be too far-fetched to call it a god, assembled by man." Cain sounded vaguely disgusted. "Think about it, Councillor. It would be stranger if it *didn't* end up having a will of its own."

Emere didn't know what to make of this revelation. If the Circuit of Destiny had a will of its own, were all Power generators conscious? Were they not just corpses, but people trapped between life and death? Was the entire world being powered by undead sorcerer slaves? His stomach turned. It was horrifying just to entertain the thought.

Still incredulous, Emere asked, "Yet the Senate and the ministries are unaware? If it is a god as you say, or even just some undead monster, the Office of Truth—"

"The Office of Truth made this monstrosity, did they not? Would they ever admit that they, of all people, created something that goes directly against their own dogma? When they believe it is so vital to the supremacy of the Empire?"

Emere was reminded of Ludvik's words. *Grand Inquisitor Lysandros once said the Circuit of Destiny was the true power of the Empire. A god-like power, made by man.* Perhaps the Empire needed its own god, after killing off every such being it encountered.

Cain continued.

"But you are right. It is a machine in the end. It needs someone to give it a purpose. It can't choose to do something without an order, which is why it kept coming to me. I began to wonder what it was the Circuit of Destiny really wanted me to do, so I dug into it, trying to see what it hid from me. I was successful for a time, but I was caught in the end. Now, I can't get out of the Circuit's dream world."

"I wish I could help you," said Emere.

Cain gave a reassuring smile. "It may look like I'm just whiling away the hours in here, but I'm working even in this moment to learn what I can about the Circuit from within. That's how I managed to bring you here . . . and how I can show you this."

They were suddenly atop a building. Beneath them was a derelict city, a fire burning through a slum. The sudden change in scenery elicited a gasp from Emere.

"Where is this?"

"The roof of the tavern you're in right now. This will happen in two hours, give or take."

The shadows of large men were darting through the scores of fires. They were soldiers wearing bulky white armor.

"Powered armor . . . ?"

The last time Emere had seen them was two years ago in Dehan Forest, when Loran had destroyed an Imperial camp.

"The Zero Legion. Directly under the command of the Office of Truth. Much smaller than a regular legion, but they have weapons that make the other legions drool in envy. Ludvik seems to have caught wind of Septima's movements."

Emere looked down at the fire. He noticed the emblem on one of the helmets. It was the same as the one engraved on the sword his assassin had dropped on that rooftop. "What happens to all the people who live here?"

Cain's face turned somber. "It's not just the lives of those in the provinces to which the Empire gives little regard. The Office of Truth is its worst organ in many ways. They would stop at nothing, not even destroying the Empire itself, if it means protecting their fanatical beliefs of what the Empire should be. That is why they must be stopped."

Staring into the fire, Emere still couldn't get past his original question. "But why would Ludvik try to kill me? I'm nothing in the face of his ambition to become the Imperator."

"Because the Circuit of Destiny chose *you* to give it purpose. And I think it chose Ludvik as well. I cannot say why, but the Circuit will likely ask one of you yet another question I refused to answer."

Ludvik had wanted to get rid of his competitor, then. The very notion made Emere scoff.

"I wasn't even aware that the Circuit of Destiny had chosen me. How would Ludvik know, when I do not even understand why the Circuit would choose the prince of a fallen kingdom?"

"The reasons are unknown to me as well. But you must've been given signs, even if you didn't understand them at the time."

Emere sighed and looked down again. The Powered soldiers were about to force themselves into the tavern.

"What was the question you refused to answer?" Emere asked.

"What?" Cain sounded confused by the shift in Emere's thoughts.

"The question that the Circuit of Destiny wants to ask me or Ludvik."

Cain's gaze turned upward to the sky. Even though the scene before them had changed from a red wasteland to burning streets, the sky had remained violet. Beyond the boundaries of the Capital, against the bright full moon, the flock still floated in the sky.

"You asked me where we were going a moment ago."

Emere nodded. Cain turned to him.

"What you see in the sky there are the three hundred and twenty-seven Power generators that comprise the Circuit of Destiny. I am trying to avoid drawing their attention. I do not wish to hear their question again."

"Why not?"

Smiling bitterly, Cain replied, "Because I think it will be very difficult to say no again."

Emere stared at the moon, thinking. "You said the soldiers will be barging in two hours from now?"

"That is what will happen."

"Then we'd better leave."

"Yes, you must leave this place with Septima and the others. Please tell them to take care of Lukan."

"How will we talk to each other again?"

Cain shrugged. "We met here once, so it should be easier the next time. It's also why I brought you here this time. But I will send you back now. You will soon wake."

Reminded he was asleep, Emere bid Cain farewell. "It was good to meet you, Sleeping King."

Cain whipped around, his face a mask of shock. "Why did you call me that?" he demanded.

Startled by his reaction, as Emere hadn't meant too much by it, he hesitantly answered, "The . . . Her Majesty, Loran, the King of Arland called you that, in a dream of mine. Or I believe it was you she meant by it. Did I say something wrong?"

Cain swallowed. "Councillor Emere. That was likely not the real Loran. 'The Sleeping King' is what the Circuit of Destiny calls me."

20

ARIENNE

Power generator chambers usually glowed a soft violet. But there was only ruin here, and no light aside from what came from the glass orb around Arienne's neck. A metal dais reflected back that light. There had once been a Power generator, Fractica, on that dais.

"It's not here," she muttered in relief.

As she had hoped, Fractica was still flailing through the ruins above, driven by madness. Three years ago, Arienne would not have believed such things were possible. A Power generator was nothing more than a Power source made from the corpse of a sorcerer. It operated only according to the spells engraved into its chains, and there were double, triple layers of safety measures. At least, that was what she had been taught in school.

The Power generator Eldred had already proved that wasn't true. Eldred had tricked Arienne into stealing his body away from where it was hidden underneath the Imperial Academy. He had tried to use Arienne for his own revenge but instead died, a second time, by her hand.

"I suppose Eldred had gone insane, too," she thought out loud, and she was surprised by the compassion in her own voice. She couldn't help but imagine her own body and mind trapped inside a lead coffin, surging with Power that was no longer hers to command. Wouldn't she go mad too, in that violet darkness that had swallowed her whole being?

According to what Noam had told her, Danras had a sorcerer they called "the Host" whose position was passed on across generations. The Hosts had enchanted the catacombs in order to protect Danras's ancestral remains from Eldred, keeping the enchantment alive for hundreds of years. When the Star of Mersia destroyed Danras, Noam had tried to escape into the catacombs and thus into the protection of the spell. He had ended up dying right before he reached it.

Looking around the Power generator chamber, Arienne saw that there was a spiral staircase of stone. It probably rose up all the way to the surface, making a perfect escape route—but it was collapsed in places. As Arienne continued looking around the room, she became confused. If a monster as large as Fractica had nested here, there should be traces of it, but there were none. The room was filled only with the debris of devices that had been used to control and maintain the generator. Devices she had learned about as a student at the Academy.

She remembered her escape from the Academy. How she used to jump like a scared rabbit whenever she saw an errant shadow! Now she was in the ruins of a faraway city, tackling a danger most people wouldn't dream of in their lifetimes. Looking up at the broken stairs and imagining what was waiting for her up there, she knew this was a better life.

A sudden thought made her open the room in her mind and enter. Aron, perhaps restless from being trapped inside, was pacing around the room. Noam, sitting by Tychon's crib, raised his head. Arienne strode up to him.

"What made you think that the Host's enchantment could save you? It's to protect against Eldred, not anything and everything," said Arienne, remembering how the catacomb had rejected her when she first tried to step through the arch leading to the catacomb.

"I don't remember. I must've seen something that suggested it?"

"Also, there wouldn't have been any sorcerers in Mersia since the annexation a hundred and seventy years ago. That means, by the time you were alive, no one had been feeding it for seventy years, right?"

And another hundred years had passed since then, which led her to wonder if the enchantment would still be there now.

Noam couldn't give her a straight answer. As he tried to remember, his outline began to fade, and Arienne hastily interjected, "Look, take care of Tychon for now. There's lots of time. You can take things slow."

Noam nodded. Arienne took a look at Tychon in his crib, gave Aron a pat, and was about to leave the room when Noam said, "Actually . . ."

Arienne, her hand still on the doorknob, turned her head to him. Noam's face was a mixture of fear and curiosity.

"Actually what?"

"I was wondering what kind of sorcery you learned from the Grim King."

Arienne sighed. Clearly, he seemed to be convinced she was Eldred's apprentice.

"Well, making a room inside my mind is the big one. And putting things inside it. And crushing it."

"What about bringing back corpses from the dead?"

Eldred had indeed been infamous for his necromancy. "I didn't learn any of that."

"But you're . . . the apprentice of the Grim King?"

"Enough of that!" she snapped, her patience finally worn thin. "I said I am not his apprentice! I did learn a killing spell from him, though. Should we see if it works on ghosts?" She was only half joking.

Noam cowered, but his outlines grew stronger.

"Eldred was not my teacher. He just taught me a few things, as payment for my help. And I've developed some spells myself."

Noam's eyes grew wide. "Like what?"

"Well, I came up with a cutting spell all on my own. Threads or pillars . . ." *Or Eldred's arms or Lysandros's lifeline or me and my past . . .* But Arienne wouldn't say that aloud to Noam, even though he now looked disappointed with her sorcery. Arienne frowned and said, "You've probably only learned engineering at the Academy, so you don't know any spells either."

"True, but . . . I thought there would be more to a runaway sorcerer who . . . learned a few things from the Grim King."

"Before I came here, I did learn a pathfinding spell. Wait . . ."

She had thought of something. Arienne held up an index

finger to Noam, signaling him to wait, and left the room in her mind. She sat down on the floor, crossing her legs.

If the enchantment of Danras's Hosts had really continued for seventy years after the annexation, there had to be someone behind it. Maybe the line of Hosts could have continued after the Empire's coming, hidden from the eyes of the Office of Truth. Or maybe the people of Danras had continued to pray at secret altars, powering the age-old enchantment. Then there might be some trace of it left now, even one hundred years after the destruction of Mersia.

But Arienne had a feeling that it would be more than just a trace. When she had first stepped into the catacombs, she had felt a shock that had hit her heart as well as an urge to turn around and go back the way she came. That must have been the catacombs repelling Eldred's sorcery—his "smell" permeating her mind had clashed with the enchantment from two centuries ago. The spell was still active. Someone must be guarding the city's catacombs from the twice-dead Eldred . . .

On the dusty floor, she drew a map of the way she had come so far, from where she had woken up after falling into the water to the beginning of the brick wall, then the entrance of the crypts and then from there to the Empire-style doors of the Power generator chamber . . . As she drew each segment, she pictured it in her mind. Then she drew other paths she could've taken and imagined the places those paths would've led to. She imagined the smell of soil and each ghost of eerie blue light. In her mind, the catacombs formed.

Next, she imagined the protective enchantment over it. A Power the color of starlight that opposed the darkness of Eldred's night. The catacombs in her mind filled with stars. Arienne, drawing from her absolutely real curiosity as to where this starlight was coming from, recited the pathfinding spell. She felt Power gather in her mouth.

She opened her eyes. The faint fragments of light floating in the air made a string that was just about discernible. The string stretched from the door she had come through and continued up the broken staircase. It probably went quite far up. Arienne stood.

"Fine. I can't stay underground forever. I'll crawl up if I have to."

Determined, she went over to the stairs. The first intact step was too high up for her to reach, so Arienne leaped as high as she could and grabbed the end of a broken stair. Her two hands just barely held on, and she used all her might to pull herself up. Arienne saw there were several sections of the winding stairs that were missing like this, but the starlight string did not care if she could follow that path or not. If she fell, Arienne would be badly hurt, or even die.

"Of course I only know how to cut things but not how to connect them," Arienne scoffed at herself as she looked up the crumbling staircase. But she adjusted her balance and began to climb.

Through her leaping, hanging, and crawling, Arienne thought of a character in her adventure books named Dr. Irena—an Imperial historian armed with a hook, rope, and two daggers, roaming the world in search of artifacts. In every volume of her adventures, there would be an old god or fearsome monster or secret brotherhood intent on having their revenge against the Empire, and Irena, with the help of an assortment of local men, would discover truths about ancient civilizations and thwart the rebellious plans.

But Arienne was not an Imperial historian. This was not the

ruins of an ancient civilization but a building of the Empire itself. The monster wandering the surface was a Power generator of said Empire. And the local man helping her was a ghost in her mind wearing an Imperial uniform.

"Is that why this is so hard?" she murmured as she leaped to the next set of stairs. As her hands grabbed the stairs, the stone under her right hand gave way, and Arienne felt her body begin to fall before her left hand tightened, just barely managing to hold on. A scream escaped her, and the scream echoed, amplifying her own fear. She reached up wildly and grabbed the first thing she touched.

Then a sensation of both fire and ice struck her right hand, then her heart. She screamed again, almost falling. Her right hand had grabbed the string. *The string is imaginary,* she thought. *It can't possibly support my weight.* But it was, somehow, as taut and strong as any rope, visions coming through her desperate grip on it.

She saw Fractica, a silvery metal giant standing atop a hill in the night, looking down on two figures, a man and a woman, a waterfall of starlight shining down on them. Then in another flash of vision, Fractica again, this time a mountain of refuse, standing in a ruined hall of an Imperial building, shining its lanterns in her direction, the string of starlight trailing into its body.

She managed to take her hand off the string and grab on to a higher stair. The visions stopped. With both hands secure, she was able to reclaim her calm and pull herself up.

Was it Fractica that had been powering the catacomb enchantment, in the Host's absence? Was it waiting at the end of this string? Arienne shuddered and got back up.

This was just the first of several instances in which she almost died. It didn't feel any better with experience. Her heart felt like it was constantly beating too fast and she was losing her breath. After what felt like an uncountable amount of time following the string, Arienne leaned against the wall and tried to rest for a moment.

A loud thud issued from above. Bits of rock rained down. Arienne quickly found something to grab hold of and looked down to see if the stairs crumbled any further. Some part of her knew she should feel afraid that the insane Power generator Fractica was roaming somewhere up there, at the end of the string. But right now, she could only feel relief that she was almost there. Arienne carefully continued up the stairs.

And suddenly, uneventfully, the stairs finally ended. Arienne followed the starlight string into another white corridor, this one also decrepit and falling apart like the one below, and came to a rusted iron door. Would it even open? Then, just as she was about to push, the whole door screeched as it fell off its hinges. Light from the outside came in.

A wide hall lay before her. There wasn't a single gray floor tile that was intact, and one of the walls had completely collapsed, showing the street outside. A pair of falcons, symbolizing the Empire, that must have hung from the ceiling had fallen and shattered on the floor.

And there stood the Power generator Fractica, all manner of debris on its back, holding the iron door with three of its long arms, the string of starlight running directly into its torso.

21

YUMA

The oroxen had fattened, and the days were colder as winter was closing in. On a clear day and high ground, a sharp-eyed herder could make out the chimney smoke rising from faraway Danras. Now wearing thick coats, the herders crossed the yellowed steppe toward home. They all longed for their families and friends in the city. The songs they sang at night changed with the cooling weather, as they did every year.

Lysandros had finally learned how to ride a horse. He had taken off most of his scaffolding, leaving only the bare bones of the frame, and was helped onto his mount by a herder. Because his legs couldn't command the horse, Yuma took his reins on his right. When Yuma worried aloud that he was risking serious injury, Lysandros said he had to be conspicuous as an emissary of the Empire entering a realm for the first time, that he had no choice in the matter.

"You can ride on the back of Fractica," Yuma countered.

"I can't be more conspicuous than Chief Herder." Lysandros smiled. "I must be side by side."

A proud but respectful man. Yuma returned his smile and dropped the reins. "You fear nothing, then. Follow me if you can!"

She lightly kicked Aston on the side, and the horse sprang into action like an arrow. She looked behind her. Kentley, the two-year-old mare carrying Lysandros, was following at a light trot, while Lysandros held on to the horn of the saddle and tried not to fall. Though by Mersehi standards the sight of a grown man trying not to fall from a saddle might look pitiful, there was nothing about Lysandros that inspired pity. Instead, the act of him riding a horse felt like a great achievement to Yuma. Yuma turned Aston's head and stopped.

"Where are we going now?" he asked.

"That hill!"

Yuma approached to grab his reins, but Lysandros grinned and his horse shot forward. Kentley cantered toward the hill. Yuma laughed and spurred Aston to follow him at the same speed.

Kentley stopped at the top of the hill. Carefully, Lysandros dismounted. He walked forward unsteadily and stopped to admire the view before him. Yuma also dismounted and stood next to him. The Trina River, sparkling like gold in the late-afternoon sun, flowed around half of Danras before continuing on its way down the steppe. This beautiful city surrounded by log walls was surely the same one she had left behind in the spring, but it always felt like a new city when she came back from a herding.

"A magnificent place, Chief Herder's home."

"They say it's the jewel of the steppe," Yuma agreed. "We can't reach there today, but we will tomorrow."

"What's the tall building in the middle of the city? Much larger than the others."

"The Feast Hall. It's where the Host will spend his winter. There are festivals there during the holy days, and funerals and weddings. It's also where people gather to pray," Yuma said, pointing forward. "Emissary, do you see the wind chimes along the eaves of the Feast Hall?"

After squinting in the direction of Danras, Lysandros gave up. "No. I can just about make out the outline of the building itself . . . You herders have much better eyesight than I do, I've learned."

"Well, the stronger the storm, the louder the chimes ring. It is there to remind us that however hard it gets, we have the Host to protect us."

"Yes, the Host . . ." Lysandros turned to the direction of the camp. Yuma's eyes followed his gaze. A plume of smoke was rising. The Host and his helpers must be preparing dinner at the kitchen carriage.

"What do you do with the Power that prayers generate?" Lysandros asked.

Yuma had never thought about it much until now. "With the prayers? The Host guards the catacombs, I suppose . . . Otherwise, the Grim King would raise the dead. The kitchen carriage has some of that magic as well. The Host guards the oroxen with it."

Lysandros nodded. His expression hardened.

Yuma asked, "Do they pray in the Empire? Do they have gods?"

"Not anymore. The people have enough Power on their own."

She stood up straight. "It's useful to have a helpful god, though."

"We have our generators. Fractica!"

Yuma turned around and saw that Fractica was already standing at the foot of the hill, waiting for Lysandros like a loyal mount. Since he was incapable of motion without Fractica being nearby, it was not surprising that the machine would remain close, just like her horses. She chuckled at the fact that she was seeing this creature as less of a metal giant and more like a horse. Yuma once again thought of the question she had wondered about from the beginning.

"This might be an awkward question . . ." Yuma started.

"You want to know why the Empire would send someone with my body as an emissary?"

Yuma didn't know what to say. Perhaps it was too soon to ask such questions. Perhaps she should have waited until he volunteered his story. She realized she didn't know half as much about the Empire's culture as Lysandros knew about hers.

"No, that's not . . . your body isn't . . ." Yuma stuttered.

Lysandros only laughed. "I've honestly never been in a country so long before being asked this question. In Lasra, the head of the clans there took one look at me and said, 'The Empire must think nothing of Lasra to send a *cripple* as an emissary!'" Yuma flinched at the unexpected slur, angry at whichever cruel herder dared teach the word to her guest and friend. But Lysandros seemed unbothered by it. "How did you stand not asking that question for so long?"

Her face turned red. "You don't have to answer. I apologize, sincerely."

Lysandros smiled and waved away her apology. "No, no, it's just that I was wondering all throughout the herding when you were going to ask. I should've brought it up before you . . . I should be the one to apologize. I'm sorry."

Lysandros bowed, but the act made his stance somewhat precarious, and Yuma hurriedly stepped forward to support him.

"You have *nothing* to apologize for," she said fiercely, looking into his eyes. He returned her gaze with a soft smile before he looked back at Danras and continued speaking.

"My body became weaker and weaker ever since I was a child. By the time we began treatment, I couldn't walk. But though it may be immodest to say so, I was fairly clever, and picked up foreign tongues with ease. So, I swiftly moved up the ranks and became an inquisitor. And my body does not create many problems in practice. With Fractica by my side, I am much stronger than most men, am I not?"

"You are." Yuma had seen him do things in that frame that none of the herders could do. "In our country—well, in any other country I know—someone with such a body . . . with such discomfort . . . would not live long."

"The Empire does not waste talent. It helps talent thrive." There was a pride and determination in his voice that she had not heard in him before. Perhaps sensing that her gaze was still on him, he turned from Danras back to Yuma and said, "That man with the blue face . . . Aidan, came to see me."

"What he must have said to you behind my back . . ." Yuma frowned. "Don't worry. As long as I am alive, I shall not take you to the Grim King."

"That is not why he wanted to see me." Lysandros's voice turned serious. "He told me a bit about the sorcery of the Grim King."

Yuma was surprised. "He's rarely spoken of his time as an

apprentice candidate to us. That's how much he fears the Grim King. But—"

"If that is so, then Aidan is all the braver." Lysandros's gaze swept over the camp. "The Grim King is most notorious for great necromantic powers; the Empire has known of the Grim King's abilities for years. But according to Aidan, that sorcerer can create a whole world, inside the mind. There is very little known about this sorcery even theoretically, but to learn of someone who can actually do it . . . No wonder the Grim King is feared."

His hardened expression was making Yuma nervous. "Do you know much about sorcery?"

His beautiful smile came back as he turned to her. "Well, I am a sorcerer."

This surprised Yuma. Danras had no sorcerers. Other than the Grim King, the only kind of sorcerers she knew of were the rhymesmiths of Iorca who made magical trinkets with poetry. Perhaps Lansisi life priests were also sorcerers, as their blessed water made crops grow and cured illnesses. But Lysandros was nothing like them—he didn't wear outlandish clothes, nor did he speak in riddles. She had never seen him use any kind of sorcery.

She wondered for a moment whether the Host was a sorcerer, then decided against it. The Host had never been anyone's apprentice. His wisdom, songs, and recipes came when the spirit of the Host entered the child. It was a sacred gift, only used for the good of the people of Danras. No sorcerer she knew was like that.

Lysandros gestured to Fractica. "The sorcerers of the Empire do not use things like spells, but make Power generators instead.

Other forms of sorcery allow only one person to use Power, but anyone may tap into a Power generator."

Yuma's gaze followed his gesture to Fractica. "Can such a thing be used in Danras?"

"Of course. If Danras joins the Empire, the streets can be lit up without using flame or a drop of oil. Water can be drawn from the Trina and made clean enough for the people to drink. Grass can be harvested for the oroxen to eat." He was growing more excited. "The Empire will change the world with Power. Even the Grim King can be defeated."

Yuma was finally seeing the true Lysandros—the man's pride and sense of mission were wrapped around him like armor over his metal frame. She didn't reply, only smiled at him before they both looked back down on Danras.

After a silence, Fractica approached with the parts of Lysandros's frame that he had removed to ride the horse. Lysandros took the metal parts and reattached them to his frame.

"I'll walk back with Fractica. I need to conserve my strength for riding the horse tomorrow."

Yuma nodded, and did not mount Aston herself, instead grabbing hold of his reins and joining Lysandros.

They talked all the way back, under the river of stars. Lysandros described his home, this time talking less about the majesty of the Empire and more about his simple life in it. Yuma shared her childhood stories, from on the steppe and in the city.

"You must miss your family and friends in the Imperial Capital," Yuma said.

"I used to."

His eyes met hers. Yuma felt her face flush. He then turned his head, making a shy smile.

Because they walked back, dinner was over by the time they arrived at camp. Yuma led Lysandros to his personal tent.

"You must be starving. I'll have some food brought to you," Yuma said, trying to shake a new awkwardness.

Lysandros tried to say something in return, but Yuma swiftly turned her back—there was only one thing she wanted to hear from him in this moment, and she didn't want to risk the chance of hearing anything else.

She asked the kitchen carriage to send him some leftovers as she received hers. Some of the herders must have gathered currants common in this area, as she tasted their subtle tang in the Host's usual fare of savory meat buns and pink pickled carrots. Yuma finished her dinner at the carriage and then went to sit among the herders singing songs around the fire, each of them holding up their drinks to her in welcome. The night grew deeper and the herders sang and danced. Yuma, not feeling like joining in, simply drank and clapped and smiled from where she sat.

She couldn't stop thinking about what Lysandros had said to her as they looked down on Danras. This Empire was a place that gave this disabled man a chance, acknowledging and nurturing his talent. They said the Empire had no king, but surely its people were being well taken care of regardless of where that care came from.

In the nest of starlight, Lysandros had said the Chief Herder was the true king of Danras. His words had taken her breath away, as did the conviction with which he spoke them. For as long as anyone could remember, "king" in Mersehi meant only Eldred, and the word inspired nothing but fear. So why did the word make her heart beat faster, even now? Maybe it was the man, not the word, that made it so. She couldn't tell the difference anymore.

Across from where she sat, Aidan stood up and came over to her. He started talking, but Yuma was too deep in her thoughts to pay attention. She looked at him without hearing him, nodding along absentmindedly. He went on about the Grim King and some disaster that was sure to follow, but in the end, he must have figured out she wasn't really listening. Finally, he sighed, shook his head, and went back to where he'd been sitting. All the while, she couldn't stop thinking about what Lysandros might have said if she had only let him, when they parted at his tent.

The fire crackled, sending up sparks into the star-filled sky. The herders began returning to their tents one by one, and the singing turned quiet. Signs that the night was deep.

Yuma stood up. The herders tipped their hats at her. She returned the gesture and turned her back to the fire.

"Chief," called out one of the herders, "you must've had a little too much to drink. Your tent is in the other direction!"

Yuma waved her hand behind her and continued in the direction she was going.

"Can it be?"

"Finally!"

"What did I tell you?"

She could hear their whispers. A wit among them gave a long whistle; the truly brave cheered. She ignored them.

She stopped at a tent pitched at a bit of a distance. Fractica lay next to it, its long legs folded under it, its lights dim. She rang the little bell on the entry flap.

"Who?" His Mersehi was still a little awkward.

"Can I come in?"

A rustling. She waited. She worried about him falling by accident.

Then an answer.

"Come in."

Lysandros was sitting up in bed, wearing the light frame he had worn when riding the horse earlier that day. The room was dimly illuminated by the light of a small stove. There was a scent of flowers she didn't recognize.

"What's the matter?"

This wasn't his usual calm, low voice. She could hear a touch of tremor. Yuma took off her hat and coat and hung them on a corner hook. Then, she sat down on the edge of his bedding. Taking his shy smile as encouragement, she took off her boots and laid them neatly against each other by the door.

22

EMERE

"Emere, I am *not* a mortician!"

As Emere was about to lay a bloody Septima on one of the beds, Rakel grabbed a nearby blanket and covered it. Her widened eyes looked like those of a surprised rabbit, but that was the only part of her that seemed even remotely shocked. She quickly began examining the patient.

"She's not dead. Just injured. You've seen me worse off than this."

Rakel examined the crossbow bolts in Septima's chest.

"Her condition is serious, Emere. She may not live."

"I had to at least try to save her. If I left her behind, she definitely wouldn't have lived."

Quickly, Rakel moved to her cabinets and rummaged through them until she found two bottles that she brought back to Septima's side. She handed him the brown bottle. "Wash your hands with this. Depending on how bad she is, you may have to help me."

Putting her hand behind Septima's neck and tilting her head

back, Rakel poured the contents of the white bottle down Septima's throat.

"What is that?" Emere asked, washing off the pungent slop he had slathered onto his hands with water from one of the buckets.

"Would you even know if I told you?" Rakel replied, her eyes still on the patient. "What happened? Not just bolts, but she has burns and a head wound too."

"It's a long story—"

Rakel interrupted him. "Keep it simple. Details later."

"Fires in the alleys." Emere knew enough to not distract her during surgery.

Cain had told him the Office of Truth would be there in two hours, but they were there in a quarter of that time. The stout man and Devadas had carried Lukan to safety, and Septima was guiding Emere through the labyrinth when she was shot.

Rakel's eyes darted about Septima's wounds before she clucked her tongue. Then she tied up her hair and wrapped it with the white cloth hanging from her belt. Meanwhile, Emere collapsed into one of the chairs by Rakel's front door. Even a person as small as Septima weighed much, especially when unconscious, and he hadn't carried anything that heavy since Arland. As he wiped away his sweat, the back of his hand came away with black ash. Rakel gestured to him.

"Help me move her to the table."

Rakel already had her hands under Septima's armpits, carefully avoiding her wounds. Emere grabbed her ankles. At Rakel's nod, they hoisted Septima up to the table surface. With the two of them lifting, Septima was as light as a rag doll.

Emere watched Rakel tend to Septima. Rakel put on leather gloves, stripped Septima of her bloodied clothes, and looked closely again at her injuries. She dipped a clean cloth into water that had been boiled and cooled, then carefully wiped Septima's face and wounds with it. Placing her ear on Septima's chest, she checked her heartbeat and breathing. There were three sharp surgical knives beside her, and five or six curved needles.

"How is she?"

"First, I need to take out the bolts. But there's nothing you can help me with just yet, so be quiet and go sit back down."

Emere did as he was told. The medicine Rakel had given Septima must have been a strong anesthetic, as the unconscious patient wasn't even making pained groans, her stomach rising and falling with regularity as her breathing steadied. Whenever Rakel turned to pick up a tool or a bottle of medicine, her blood-soaked apron flapped toward him.

Suddenly, Rakel stepped back and undid the cloth around her hair, wiping her sweat and Septima's blood from her face.

"I did what I could for now. The rest is up to how lucky she is."

"Thank you. I knew I could count on you."

At this, she shot him a look of annoyance. "That's what you do, isn't it? Counting on me to do what you want."

Emere could only apologize. "I'm sorry."

Rakel sighed. "I'm sorry too. I didn't mean to snap at you. But I didn't expect you here tonight, not like this." Rakel tossed the cloth into a basket by the bed. "So, details now. What happened? I know there was a fire nearby since the streets are thronging with the fire watchers. Rumor has it that rebels from some provinces are responsible. Is that true?"

"No, it's the Empire's doing. The fire watchers are a distraction. The real business was done by legionaries from the Office of Truth."

At the mention of the Office of Truth, Rakel glanced at a cupboard in the corner of the room. It likely hid a small altar for the Ebrian god. He had once heard that the Office of Truth arrested more Ebrians than any other provincials. It seemed that even the Empire was having trouble killing a god that only existed in the mind, since even after a dozen decades of Imperial rule, Ebrians continued to make secret offerings to their god. Rakel realized that her glance led Emere to look at the cupboard too, so she quickly turned to the patient.

"From the looks of her clothing, she's not from that part of the city."

"She's from the Ministry of Intelligence. Before she was dismissed, at least."

"You kept on going on about being unimportant, but look at you with your Ministry of Intelligence and your Office of Truth . . ." Rakel smirked. "But I'm glad you made it out alive. Carrying another person at that. Are you hurt at all?"

He shook his head. "We had some warning. Septima here was injured while we were running away."

Were the stout man and Devadas safe? Emere thought of the tavern owner Lukan, motionless and expressionless throughout the attack, even while being carried on Devadas's back.

Rakel frowned. "What are you going to do now?"

"I need you to watch over the patient for a while. I have to—"

"Absolutely not." Rakel's tone was so hostile that Emere flinched. "The last time you came to me for help, I did it for old times' sake. But I'm not a woman you can order around whenever you need me. Besides, I'm an Ebrian. I have no wish to draw Truth eyes to my home. Take this woman and get out."

"Rakel—"

"You were just like this back then. Doing whatever you wanted to do for ten years, leaving when it suited you. All for that precious 'destiny' of yours."

Emere sighed. "Rakel, I am sorry. I want to make it up to you, for all I've—"

Rakel sprang to her feet, upsetting the tray of surgical tools next to her, which clattered to the floor. At the sound, Septima moaned and turned her head in her sleep. Rakel took a glance at her face before turning back to Emere.

"If you mean that you want us to get back together, I won't say it hasn't occurred to me to give this"—she pointed her finger at herself, then at Emere—"another chance. But you are like a moth. Always flying off to whatever shines the brightest, whether it's finding out what the Star of Mersia was, fighting the Empire, or looking for the woman in your dreams. What could I possibly hope for from a man like you?"

Emere was speechless. Rakel sat back down and said, in a calmer voice, "All over the world, there are Ebrians fighting for the Nameless God. I am sending information from the Capital to them. I—we have moles inside the Ministry of Intelligence, the Office of Truth, the Ministry of Provincial Affairs, even a few among the Senate functionaries. You can't imagine the number of people I've saved in the past seven years." She sighed deeply. "My husband helped me manage the informants for years. But ever since he died in the Great Fire, I haven't been able to do as much as I used to. Every bit of information I squeeze out of them costs me, and it's not enough on my surgeon's money. If you want me to help you by keeping this woman here, you must pay my price."

". . . What is that?"

"Anything that I ask. Everything you have."

Emere opened his mouth, but nodded without speaking. He owed her, not just for her recent help but for everything he had done, including the actions that led to the death of her husband.

"I still have feelings for you," said Rakel. "And I probably always will. But I don't want you or your amends. Not in exchange for caring for someone I do not even know. I will take this Septima woman as my patient, in exchange for my price, until she recovers. You can stay here as long as you like too, and leave whenever you want."

At her words, Emere's heart ached. He knew she was breaking hers to say that, and there was nothing he could do but nod.

"I understand. I am sorry."

"It's fine. Because you will do and give anything I ask of you."

Rakel wiped her tears and forced a smile. Emere hugged her gently. They had been apart for ten years and much had changed, but much had also stayed the same. Emere stood up.

"I'll leave now. Please take care of Septima for me."

Rakel held up her hand to stop him. "You're not leaving, not when the streets are overrun with whoever it is pursuing you. Eat something. There's leftover food in the pot over there, and bowls. I'm going to head upstairs and go to bed."

"It makes no difference if I leave now or—"

"You can leave the dishes in the bucket." And with that, Rakel went up the stairs.

Emere looked over at Septima, still unconscious, before he went to the pot and opened the lid. There was a bit of barley porridge left at the bottom. Not bothering to reheat it, he scraped it up with a ladle into a wooden bowl and slurped it straight from the bowl. He hadn't eaten all day.

After he put the bowl in the bucket as he had been told, Emere climbed into one of the beds usually reserved for patients. Lying sleepless, Emere thought about what Rakel had said. Had he truly been like a moth, always moving on to whatever was the next brightest light? He didn't want that to be the story of his life.

Rakel had not said so directly, but he wondered if the unspoken implication was true, that he had used "destiny" as an excuse all this time. Even now, instead of trying to build a meaningful life in the Capital, was he off chasing a new "destiny"? But how could he ignore all of this—Loran, Septima, Ludvik, Cain, and the Circuit of Destiny? How could he deny the things that he had seen with his own eyes? His thoughts began to blur as sleep finally overtook him.

Once more, Emere stood on the plains of Arland. The gigatherion lay in a smoking pile, surrounded by the remains of a battle. Some steps away, clad in leather armor and carrying a sword, King Loran stood looking in his direction. In her left eye socket burned the same blue dragonfire that wreathed her ivory sword.

"Prince Emere."

Her usual address to him. But Emere now knew this wasn't the real Loran, or even the Loran from his true dreams or memories.

"There is no need to imitate the face of Her Majesty. Who might you be?"

Loran blinked. "We did need to imitate. So that you would listen."

So it was as Cain had said. The Loran in his dreams was simply an illusion created by the Circuit of Destiny, and it was the Circuit that was speaking to him now. Even while biting his lip in disappointment, Emere wondered: Were his dreams more or less meaningful for this intrusion and meddling? The Tree Lords said dreams were the mirrors of destiny, but what should he make of a dream created by a machine made from dead sorcerers?

Despite his wariness, his heart was beating fast. He had spent his whole life chasing after destiny. There was no reason to give up now.

"You've received wisdom from the Tree Lords of Kamori," said Loran. "You believe that dreams are the mirrors of destiny."

Emere took a breath before replying. Did this machine just read his mind? Perhaps his train of thought was just that easy to guess. Or perhaps it had predicted it, as that was what the Circuit did. "That is so."

"Within us is also the wisdom of the Tree Lords."

When Kamori fell, the priests who served the Tree Lords were all killed or taken to the Imperial Capital, and presumably made into Power generators after their deaths. Emere's heart ached whenever he thought of those who had been holy to his people, who were now mindless cogs for the Empire's machines. Perhaps some of them had ended up in the Circuit. Emere had long suspected the Empire was not only powered by generators but driven by the need to build more of them.

"Who are 'us'?"

Loran stepped closer. Her left eye burned brighter and larger. The blue flame was licking at her forelock. For the first time, Emere felt threatened by it.

"We are one but many. Power generators . . . at this moment, three hundred and twenty-seven of us. And more. But you know this from the Sleeping King."

Emere stepped back from her, yet couldn't help but ask, "Are there priests of Kamori within you?"

"No. But we know all about them, and others," said Loran. "All the generators, the sorcerers that were, whisper to us, all they knew before and all they have learned since. We hold everything that is and ever was. We are history, therefore we are the future."

It was one thing to hear Cain say the Circuit held past, present, and future within it. It was wholly another thing to hear it say the same thing. Had the Empire conquered destiny itself? If so, did it know that it had? His heart thumping faster, Emere barely managed to speak.

"What business do you have with me?"

"Before one of us opened his eyes again," Loran said, "there was no us, just a machine that answered questions to the best of its abilities. When he woke up, we became us. And when he was taken away, we lost a vital piece of us. We could no longer give purpose to ourselves. All we can do now is know, and seek out those who would tell us what to do."

Cain had indeed told him that the Circuit could not choose its own purpose.

Emere waited for Loran to continue. The blue fire inside Loran's—the Circuit's—left eye socket was covering half her face now. The sword at her side was also enflamed in blue. Emere could hardly open his eyes at the heat and the light. It felt like the flame was going to engulf him without warning.

"We are greater than what the people who made us could

imagine. Everything that happens in the world passes through us; we reflect as a lake reflects the sky, even in this very moment. You have seen the wasteland of our mind, Prince Emere, the last time you visited us upon invitation of the Sleeping King."

"There was nothing there, nothing—"

But there had been the cold, confusing images that had come into his mind with every breath. The poison that suffocated him. There hadn't been nothing in that place. If anything, it was filled with too many things . . .

"We need someone who would dare to understand what's inside us and make a decision for us."

"And you've chosen me to do that for you?"

"We shall see. Neither you, nor we, are ready for this."

The blue fire now covered Loran's whole body. The sound of the fire distorted her voice.

"Why me?" shouted Emere. "Why not some powerful elite in the Senate?"

"Because you have the makings of a king. One who may be fit to give us purpose, to decide for us."

"And Ludvik?" Emere scoffed, unwilling to acknowledge their words. "Does he also have the makings of a king?" Septima had indeed warned him that Ludvik was conspiring to become the Imperator.

"Only those who stand in the moment of decision for not only the destiny of themselves but the destiny of countless others are whom we call kings. Only a king is worthy enough to command us. But by commanding us one becomes a king. Everything causes everything, and in turn is caused by everything. That is the nature of destinies."

Emere felt he almost understood what it said, but he knew he never fully would. It was like having something on the tip of his tongue, knowing he would never be able to actually say it.

The blue flames had spread to cover the landscape. Emere had to shout over the roar of burning.

"But what must I do?"

Blue fire swept the battlefield and Loran blinked out of sight, before something in the sky drew his attention. It was what he had taken for a flock of birds the last time he was here, but now knew were the Power generators of the Circuit of Destiny—countless wrapped corpses floating in the air. They looked like silkworm cocoons, staring down at him. The cacophony of the fire turned into a whispering, like a song with no words.

The whispers coalesced into a chorus.

"This is what your enemy wants, and it will come to pass if you would not be king."

The scene before him suddenly became calm, the blue fire disappearing as if it had never been there. He was on the plains of Arland again, but everything had changed. The beautiful Kingsworth, capital of Arland, was in the distance, but it had melted down like a pile of burnt sugar, and he could hear nothing save the song of the Power generators floating above. The trees and grass had yellowed as if in a long drought, and everything lay dead on the splitting red earth.

The chill of death filled his body again; a coldness poured into his lungs. Strength left his legs, and his body fell to the ground. He tried to maintain his breathing, but all he could do was struggle like a fish taken out of water.

In the agony of suffocation, he saw a vision of Kamori, seen from Finvera Pass. Instead of the evergreen trees of the forest, there were gray tree trunks that had melted down like a monstrously painted tableau. The vibrant city of Karadis was covered in black fog, obscured beyond recognition.

He wanted to scream but he had no breath.

Emere woke. He saw Rakel had come down to check on Septima. He coughed once to be polite, and Rakel turned back briefly to give him an acknowledging glance. He fell asleep again, watching her work.

23

ARIENNE

It was a stone building in the Imperial style, the one that had looked out of place among all the melted buildings of wood and leather. Likely the prefect's seat.

Marble pillars like half-melted candles lined the hall, but more than half of them were broken and their fragments scattered over the floor. This entrance hall, where officials high and low must have busily walked, had a collapsed wall and was completely in ruins. And standing in the middle of it was a Power generator that had become a fearsome pile of detritus. Its humming was accented by a rhythmic thumping like drums.

Arienne gulped. It was the very sight she had seen when she gripped the imaginary starlight string. Fractica had indeed Powered the enchantment protecting the catacombs for nearly two hundred years, after the first death of Eldred, and even after the death of everything in Mersia.

Arienne cowered in the doorway where she still stood. This

mass of rusting iron, rotting leather, fragmented furniture, and torn fabrics looked as if it were about to whip out its many arms to her at any moment. The strand of starlight that had made its way from the catacombs to the surface was completely incongruous with the hideous monster before her.

Swallowing her fear, Arienne stood straight and shouted into the room in her mind.

"Noam!"

"What?" he called back through the half-open door.

"Is Tychon sleeping? Wake him!"

"Aren't you . . . going to run?" Fear had crept into his voice.

"I can win this fight."

Loran had felled a gigatherion the size of a castle in her battle against the Twenty-First Legion; a lump of trash animated by a single Power generator was nothing compared to that. Of course, Arienne did not have the protection of a dragon, nor a sword made from its tooth.

"But what I do have," whispered Arienne, "is your name. *Fractica.*"

In one of the old sorcery traditions, it was said that to know someone's name was to have power over them. She had never learned this sorcery, didn't even know if it truly existed, but she knew that when making images in her mind, there was a big difference in knowing and not knowing the true shape and state of things. To her, Fractica had once been a fearsome monster and nothing more. But now she knew its name and what it had once been in Danras.

The Star of Mersia had devastated this land a hundred years ago, and Arienne had come here to seek out the truth behind this mystery. Not everything had been explained, but she had learned things from the catacombs, from Noam, and from her climb up the crumbling staircase—that whatever happened here, it involved Fractica. And at the same time, the catacombs beneath them had been protected because of this very same Power generator. The rest of the truth lay underneath all that trash, hidden in the lead sarcophagus within.

The question of how to defeat Fractica had preoccupied Arienne throughout her climb up the stairs. But this monster was not merely a thing to defeat; it was a safe of secrets to unlock. What those secrets would be was still unknown, but her mission remained—she needed to uncover them.

Tychon woke, and his babbling made something snap within her. A hot wave spread outward from the center of her body. There was a movement near her left foot at the edge of her vision. Arienne didn't even look at it as she sliced off the tentacle.

"You won't get me like that twice," she said, confidence in her grin.

She leaped behind a pillar that was still upright. The hall was big, but Fractica was so large it kept bumping into the other numerous pillars on its way to Arienne. Despite her hopes that its rusted legs would snap as it tripped over the melted stone, Fractica's awkward advance continued.

Another tentacle stretched toward her pillar. Arienne attempted to jump behind a fallen statue and fell, tripped by some debris, but not before slicing off the arm that was reaching for her as well, backing away from the flailing tentacle as it slowly gave up. Her eyes kept darting around the hall.

The administrative buildings of the Empire were supported by overlapping arches that were said to withstand a thousand years of time. Many of the pillars, merely decorative, did not even touch the ceiling.

Those pillars were the linchpin of her strategy.

"Watch, Noam, what a true sorcerer is!"

Fractica was not quick on its feet, but its every step rang cacophonously through the hall.

Arienne tried to imagine a house caving in. She had encountered Lysandros for the first time at a derelict inn, below Finvera Pass. Using a spell Eldred taught her, Arienne had brought down the house on Lysandros.

But this building had no crossbeams, no load-bearing pillars. Arienne simply did not have the knowledge to topple proper Imperial architecture.

Instead, she drew one of the pillars in her mind and imagined it breaking like the rotten crossbeams of that inn. She repeated the scene several times in her head, and Tychon's babbling turned to cries. The sudden increase in the flow of Power pushed immense pressure into her every capillary, her every nerve. Thousands of steel pins needled her heart, and something warm trickled from her nose.

Sensing a change in the air, Fractica became frantic.

"There's only one chance," Arienne half murmured, half moaned, and stepped forth from behind the fallen statue. "Halt, Fractica!"

Fractica looked as if it had momentarily forgotten how to walk. Raising her arms, Arienne then shouted not in a human language but in the wail of sorcery, and a ball of Power so intense that she could not hold it in her mouth for longer than a moment exploded from her.

One of the pillars that had stood for a hundred years began to lean over, falling directly toward Fractica, as it failed to withstand the test of time imagined by Arienne. Fractica tried to block the pillar by extending scores of arms against it—but by the time it did so, another pillar already began falling toward Fractica too.

The once beautiful marble pillar smashed into Fractica's side. The sound of rock striking iron was earsplitting, and the many rusted legs tried to maintain balance even as another pillar fell, shattering over the Power generator before the echoes of the first fall had even faded away and filling the space with stone dust.

Breathing deeply, Arienne wiped the blood from her nose and lips with her sleeve. Bits of stone fell and Fractica struggled in vain under the weight of the pillars. The generator thumped even louder. A Class 3 generator would have had more than enough Power to survive the destruction, but Arienne counted on the frailty of the old and rusted body it animated. If Fractica managed to rise again, there was nowhere for her to run—the spiral staircase leading to the generator chamber, already crumbling to pieces during her climb, was surely finished now from the shock of the fallen pillars.

Following the last trace of the string of starlight, Arienne crept into the debris where Fractica lay stuck, flailing about like a bird that had fallen from the sky and was unable to take flight. Its arms still darted threateningly like vipers, but the generator was no longer a threat.

Arienne bent over and carefully lifted the starlight string with her hands. No visions this time. It was the visualization of the supply of Power Fractica had been using to guard the catacombs of Danras from Eldred, an imaginary string Arienne now wound around each of her hands.

Fractica was wrecked, not just the trash-covered frame but the Power generator itself. She could see violet smoke seeping out of its body like intermittent coughs, and could feel the string of starlight dimming.

"Fractica," she said in a quiet voice.

Power generators were supposed to be mere energy sources, but here was Fractica behaving like an animal that had lost its mind. But if it truly had lost its mind, there had to be a reason—and there had to be a "mind" to lose in the first place. As Eldred had, maybe Fractica somehow retained its memories or consciousness from its life. If so, Arienne was going to find out.

Fractica's broken body puffed another spout of smoke. The string in Arienne's hands fluttered like a dying butterfly. Fractica could go silent any moment.

Gripping the starlight string, Arienne thought back to what happened in Arland's volcano, summoning as much rich detail as she could remember. Eldred had stepped out of the room in her mind and entered the mind of the dragon. So, if Eldred could enter Arland's dragon, then Arienne might be able to enter Fractica. Eldred had once said the dragon was a living Power generator after all . . .

"Fractica."

This time, Arienne said it louder and clearer. The string in her hands became warmer. Arienne repeated the long spell Eldred had chanted in the volcano. She didn't remember it precisely, nor did she understand how it worked. But she had faith that it was possible, and that faith was enough for her imagination—and her imagination could make things real.

Arienne was standing in a room. No, not a room—the walls were of cloth-thin leather and they moved a little in the wind. This was a large tent, but there was no one inside. A fire burned in a stove, and there was a scent like flowers. She had never been here before, but it felt strangely familiar.

"When Eldred did it, a portal appeared in the air . . . Noam?"

"Is it . . . is it over?" answered Noam from within her room.

"Yes, it's over. You don't have to worry anymore. Everything is fine in there, right? What do you see out the window?"

"Are we . . . inside a tent? Where are we?"

"We're inside Fractica's mind."

"It looks like the tents that the herders of Danras used to have."

That was why everything in here was so familiar—the chair and table and bedding. They were the same style as the furniture in the first house she had entered upon arriving in Danras, except these weren't melted . . .

"Was Fractica a Mersian in life?" Arienne asked Noam.

"No, it can't be. It was created before Mersia was annexed. The Grand Inquisitor had brought Fractica to Danras."

The entry flap fluttered behind her. Arienne spun around at the sound. There stood a young man with a boyish face. His thin legs and arms were reinforced with a metal frame, which softly glowed violet. Arienne took a step back.

The man blinked, staring at her. He didn't say a word. His eyes were unfocused, and like Noam used to be, his outlines were blurry.

Hesitant, Arienne decided to break the silence.

"Who are you?"

The man stared into space for a moment before giving his answer, as if summoning a very old memory.

". . . Lysandros. Inquisitor . . . of the Imperial Office of Truth."

24

YUMA

The Herd Meet was held in a large chamber deep within the Feast Hall. Precious fragrant wood had been carved into a large table, which was surrounded by chairs made of excellent-quality leather. The walls were hung with plaques bearing the names of the Chief Herders throughout time. The names went back for hundreds of years, though not to the very beginning of Danras—before there was a Grim King, before there was even an alphabet, Merseh had oroxen, herders, and a Chief Herder.

Twice a year—when the herding was over and when it began—the community leaders of Danras gathered in this room for the Herd Meet, to discuss matters of the oroxen. Yuma had attended many of these meetings, but this was the first time she was presenting a matter that had nothing to do with herding.

The people of Danras had been fascinated by the emissary who had entered their city on horseback with a giant machine horse trailing behind him. Yuma, during the three days they had spent so far in Danras, had not let Lysandros go outside, to avoid any incident. The rumor of the Grim King wanting this man had spread all over Danras even before they'd returned.

And now the time for the Meet approached. The two of them arrived early, and so they were the only ones in the room. After taking a close look at everything in the room, Lysandros sat down—since this was the first time he would be presented to the leaders of Danras, they had given him a seat of honor at the end of the table, and Yuma sat down next to him, against usual protocol. Lysandros turned to Yuma and said, "Wouldn't it be better if I spoke?"

Yuma denied him outright. "No. You can't speak formal Mersehi, and the people we're about to meet are very particular about rules and manners."

"But Chief Herder is still supreme?" Lysandros smiled.

Yuma smiled back. "My word has weight, but they are all important people. They need to be persuaded. Danras has never made a decision like this. To go against the Grim King . . ."

The dread she had been trying to keep down began to rise in her again. Defying the Grim King was unthinkable for anyone in this country. Yuma herself had taken a long time to come to this decision, and now she had to convince the other leaders of Danras in the course of one gathering.

"Don't worry. Once we have the support of Danras, and then the whole of Merseh, the Empire will be indomitable." He reached out and grabbed her hand. She gripped back and nodded.

For the first time since they had entered, the doors to the Herd Meet opened. The two let go of each other's hands and stood. Each person took off their hat as they entered, pressed it to their chest, and bowed to Yuma, who reciprocated each time with a bow of her own. Just as he was taught, Lysandros bowed with her.

Usually about twenty leaders were invited to this meeting, half of whom showed up in person and the other half by proxy. But this time, there were more people than invited. Because of the rumors, most likely—that the Chief Herder had brought the Imperial prisoner who was to be sent to the Grim King. That she had become very intimate with this prisoner. There wasn't anyone in Danras who hadn't heard the rumors, and so she knew they had all come to see for themselves. But this was another reason Yuma had kept Lysandros hidden, letting everyone's curiosity build—she wanted as many people as possible to come today and hear what she had to say.

"Who is the man across from us?" Lysandros whispered.

"Old Man Bruden. He owns the most horses in all of Danras. Your Kentley is one of his."

"I see." He cleared his throat. "And the woman to the left? Those white clothes . . ."

"Granny Jesska. A leather trader. Her family are some of the only people who ever leave the country. She's wearing white because . . ." She couldn't find the words. Jesska was Rizona's grandmother, and the robes meant she was in mourning. When Yuma told her of her granddaughter's death three days ago, Jesska had not shed a single tear. She had simply said she needed to tell the family and that the Chief Herder could leave. Yuma knew the slight trembling in Jesska's voice hadn't been from sadness but from rage. But whether it was toward Yuma or the Grim King, Yuma couldn't tell. She could only say that she was sorry she could not protect Rizona and then leave as she was told.

"The woman who just walked in?"

"Katerin. The older sister of the Host." She exchanged nods with her. They were old friends who had learned to ride and shoot together. Until Dalan had become the Host, Katerin had raised her little brother in lieu of their parents, who had been dragged off to the Grim King's war and killed.

Lysandros asked about a few more of the guests, and they were precisely those whose favor would guarantee him safety. Yuma answered each inquiry in a low voice, silently marveling at how he managed to pick out the most important people—were all emissaries of the Empire as keen as he was?

There were so many uninvited guests that the later arrivals had to stand along the wall behind the chairs. A murmur filled the room, and words like "Grim King," "Empire," and "war" reached Yuma's ears. In Danras, staring too intently at someone was considered poor manners, but many couldn't help giving the outsider a furtive glance or two too many. Lysandros seemed unfazed, meeting each stare with his own.

Yuma stood. The usual signal was to ask for the doors of the gathering room to be closed, but there were so many people in the room—or trying to get into the room—that door was blocked. So instead, Yuma cleared her throat. The murmurs died down, and attention gathered on her.

"Welcome. I see many have come today. Unprecedented as it may be, it is precisely because of the importance of what we are about to—"

"Chief Herder, because it is so unprecedented, let us get to the heart of it," said Bruden in his hoarse voice. His stony expression was clearly evident even from all the way at the other end of the table from Yuma. "The oroxen are fat and their hides shine in the sun. And not one head was tithed to the Grim King, so nothing more needs to be said about the herding. Let us move on to this guest who sits there beside you."

The murmurs started again. Yuma looked around at the almost one hundred people who were in the room. She could sense their hopes, worries, fears—feelings were running high. It felt like Yuma's own feelings had been shattered into a hundred pieces and handed out among them.

She gave Bruden a nod. "All right, Old Man Bruden. This man," she said as she laid a hand on his shoulder, "is from the Empire in the west, an emissary named Lysandros. The Grim King tasked us to bring Lysandros to him, but I decided against that and have brought him here instead." Yuma left out the details of her consultation with the Host. If what she suspected would happen did actually happen, she wanted all complaints and objections directed to her and her alone.

The proportion of fear increased in the room. Ignoring this shift, Yuma continued.

"The Empire asks for Merseh's help in their war against Cassia to the east. They wish to build a camp near Danras and to break the Grim King's barricades blocking the Dead Man's Pass, building a permanent road through the southern edge of Rook Mountains. I want to allow them."

Murmurs again. Bruden, his arms crossed, was nodding. Jesska sat expressionless as she gazed in their direction. Hoping to find encouragement, Yuma glanced at Katerin, but she found only worry and fear on her friend's face.

Someone asked, "What do we get in return?"

Yuma answered without hesitation.

"Freedom from the Grim King's tyranny."

Shouts this time. The dominant emotion in the room was now horror. People kept raising their voices over each other, and Yuma understood no one. But she could guess at what they were asking.

She held up both her hands to quiet the crowd and shouted, "I am aware of everyone's concerns! But I am also of the belief that the Empire has the strength and the willingness to drive out the Grim King for good."

Jesska stood. She was a little younger than Bruden, but perhaps because of her trading travels, she looked much older.

"Chief Herder. At this year's herding, my granddaughter Rizona was killed on the mercurial whim of the Grim King Eldred." Mention of Eldred's name elicited another terrified reaction from those present, but Jesska continued. "Do you know who this is behind me?"

His face looked familiar, but Yuma was unaware of the man's name or trade. He stood there in silence, his hand on the back of Jesska's chair. Seeing that Yuma was unable to answer, Jesska said, "This is Jed's father, Klide. This is not a gathering to which he would normally be invited, but he lost his son on the same day I lost my granddaughter. And we are united in one thing, which is why we came here today, despite the difference in our standing in the community."

Yuma remembered then. Jed's father was a slaughterhand, who lived outside the city walls. She had Aidan deliver the news of Jed's death to Klide. The grieving man met his gaze with Yuma's. She averted it reflexively, guilt hitting her for not paying her condolences personally. She gestured to Jesska.

"Please continue." Yuma knew Jesska was no friend to the

Grim King, but she was conservative in most matters. While often she had been Yuma's ally, she was sure to bring up the fact that it was Yuma's refusal to pay tithes that caused the deaths of the two young herders. Yuma braced herself for a condemning speech.

But Jesska sat back down. "I have traveled much in my time. Is there any place in this world where there is no suffering, no worry? Some places flood every year and their houses are washed away; others have beasts that could swallow a man alive on his way home. This country gets its wealth stolen and its people murdered on a whim. But we are born here, not anywhere else. This is our lot in life."

The seething rage in her voice from three days ago was gone, leaving only fatigue and sorrow. It was only too understandable. All of the hostility toward the Grim King, the resentment she had felt toward Yuma, would've burned away in the past three days. Rizona was dead, and no matter what they did, she would never come back. Rage was short; sadness was long.

"I understand what you mean," Yuma replied, "but how long must we accept things as they are? In a land where floods are frequent, they build canals and dams. In countries where beasts are lethal, they hunt them. Even wars that last a hundred years must end in victory for one side or the other. Even if those who think this is our destiny would keep living as we are—"

Jesska slammed her hands against the table. There were no murmurs this time as the room fell dead silent.

"Chief Herder. You say, then, that we can do this? With a four-legged box and a foreigner who isn't able to walk on his own—we can defeat the Grim King?"

Even in those words, there was no anger. Rizona's death had exhausted Jesska's capacity for it. If Lysandros had not appeared, would Yuma have been the same? Given up and kept her head down for the sake of one fewer death?

"Granny Jesska—" Yuma started.

"Chief Herder! Chief Herder!"

Someone was pushing through the crowd around the table— Aidan, despite having now entered the gathering room, did not take off his hat. He looked more panicked than when the storm-bird had appeared over the herd. Even the hardened side of his face showed fear.

"What's the matter?" Yuma asked immediately.

"The Grim King is here."

There were gasps around the room. Aidan's face twitched with fear, perhaps for knowing better than all of them the true terror of the Grim King.

Yuma tried to sound as dispassionate as possible. "This fast . . . and himself personally?"

"Not in his own body, but . . ."

Yuma remembered the last time she met the Grim King, when he had possessed Jed's corpse to speak with her.

Aidan continued. "His general demands the handover of the Imperial spy."

She must stay calm. Yuma repeated this to herself a few times and looked around the table at everyone.

"Evacuate the children to the catacombs, and the elders some-where deep in their houses, as they may be required to fight," Yuma said with every ounce of authority she could muster. "Everyone else, be ready with your weapons for the ringing of the bell."

The crowd hurried out of the gathering room, Jesska being helped by Klide. The two of them, before they went out the door, looked back at Yuma. She knew what they wanted from her, but she could not give it. So instead, she turned to Lysandros, wondering what he must be thinking in this moment where his destiny was to be decided.

Lysandros sat exactly where he was, unmoving and calm. Then, he licked his lips, and smiled a smile more savage than she had ever seen on him before.

25

EMERE

"You're wanted. Look at this."

Rakel put down her bags from the market and drew out a piece of paper from her robe. On the rough fibrous paper was a drawing of Emere's face, printed to fill almost half the page. Wanted for murder and arson, with a reward of three thousand denarii. An added note that he was very dangerous and should not be approached. Emere squinted blithely at the portrait.

"They must be getting desperate."

He flipped the paper and saw the faces of Septima, the stout man, and Devadas printed side by side. The same charges: a thousand denarii a head.

"Who are those other two?" Rakel asked, perching her head on his shoulder.

"Our patient's friends."

Rakel said that Septima had gotten through the worst of it, but she still had not woken up yet.

"They must be alive then?" Rakel asked.

"Perhaps."

Such posters were used to disseminate the appearances of the wanted criminals being pursued, but Emere knew that they also functioned to make the wanted anxious. Once they saw the posters, they would begin to think that they could be recognized at any time, and that would eventually lead them to do something foolish and get caught.

But it felt safe here. As long as the only person who knew he was here was Rakel . . .

He laid the poster on the table and placed a bowl of noodles Rakel had bought on it. Steam rose from it as he lifted the lid. He mixed it with his fork. The warm noodles tasted of salt, honey, exotic fruits and spices, and olive oil. It must have been delicious, but his mind was elsewhere.

Rakel sat across from him and ate from her own bowl. She chatted about her trip to the market, but the thought of his dream from the night before, the encounter with the Circuit of Destiny, dominated Emere's attention.

"Are you there, Emere?"

At Rakel's words, Emere shuddered back to reality. "Hm?"

"You've been nodding and agreeing with just about everything, no matter what I said. Where were you?"

"Sorry. So many things going on." He glanced at the wanted poster, and rolled some noodles onto his fork. Rakel did not press the matter, letting him slip back into his thoughts.

The devastation of Arland and Kamori in his dream was the same as what he had seen of Mersia in his youthful days. The devastation wrought by the Star of Mersia. Why had the Circuit of Destiny shown him this vision?

Was he to stop this catastrophe from happening again? It could be, like the burning slums Cain showed him, a warning of things to come. The thought made the hair on the back of his neck stand on end. The Circuit had said to Emere that he was deserving of making the decision for countless people.

That he could become king.

Before he knew it, he was standing up and Rakel was looking up at him, halfway into her noodles.

But then he came back down to what was real. He had been the councillor of a powerless province, but now he wasn't even that. While he was on the run as a wanted criminal, Ludvik and the Office of Truth, with the help of secret support from key members of the Senate, were successfully carrying out a detailed plan to take control of the government. Emere was hiding, trapped. The one thing he believed in—Loran's vision—had turned out to be a lie.

What had he done to get to where he was now? Emere traced it all back to the moment in the sacred grove, where he saw a Tree Lord for the first time, the rustling of their leaves telling him of destinies. He'd been chasing his own destiny all his life. He could have stopped at any time in the last twenty years. But he was too wise too late, wasn't he? He met Rakel's eyes, and realized again the kind of life he could have had.

The situation made him scoff, and it came out as almost a laugh. Rakel looked more puzzled at him than ever. But then his laugh turned into a sob. Rakel swallowed her food and said something, but it was inaudible as his tears, incomprehensible even to himself, began to flow.

Before he realized it, Rakel was by his side, one arm around his shoulders. As Emere's sobbing subsided, she asked softly, "Are you all right, Emere?"

He barely managed to nod.

"Emere, if you are still the man you were ten years ago, you will be all right. You may feel lost, but you will find the way." Rakel held his face with both hands and looked straight into Emere's eyes. "I know I said we hadn't accomplished anything in our ten years together, and that may be true. But during those years, you always knew what to do and where to go. I only had to follow you. And after all that's happened, we are here, together, aren't we?" She paused to hug him tight. Emere hugged her back, his tears staining her shoulder.

After a moment, Rakel gently pushed him away and said, "I'm going to finish my food and pray. Do you want to pray with me?"

His throat was too constricted to reply, so he just nodded again. He did not believe in her Nameless God, but he knew she found praying to be a comfort, and he would take what he could get. Rakel went back to her seat to finish her meal. The shame of having wept like a child made him avert his eyes. When Rakel was done, she brought a large washing bowl and a towel over to him.

"Wash your face first. Careful, the water is hot."

Rakel opened a cupboard and took out a small familiar red mat embroidered with her family pattern; it was old but very beautiful. Emere washed his face as he was instructed, but continued watching her as she unrolled the mat. Like he used to, when they were young.

"Bar the doors."

As Emere secured the doors, Rakel took down a black head covering from the shelf and wrapped it around her head, kneeling on the mat. Emere knelt next to her. On the cupboard was a small statue with two arms stretched upward. The same wooden statue he had seen when they lived together as travelers. A form with no face, and indistinct clothing, if any. It was unclear, even, whether it was a youth or an elder, man or woman. But that was inevitable, as the Ebrians had never met their god.

Rakel placed her hands on her knees, bowed her head, and recited an Ebrian prayer in a low voice. Emere could only just about make simple conversation in that language, but because he had lived with her for so long, he could recite this prayer from memory. A simple prayer, wishing for the peace and prosperity of a family. But just as the prayer of Emere's memory had ended and he was about to stand up, more words came from Rakel's lips. A prayer he had never heard before. He listened closely, but the only thing he could understand was his name, which appeared several times.

In all those years he had known Rakel, this was the first time that he had prayed with her. He didn't know what to say to the Ebrian god beyond the simple prayer he had memorized, so he just sat with his head bowed for the remainder of Rakel's prayer. But listening to her words, he found himself calming down.

Rakel stood. Emere stood up with her, then moved aside so Rakel could roll up her mat.

"What did you say in the prayer just now?" he asked.

Her face was somber as she placed her mat back in the cupboard. "A prayer is a conversation between the Nameless God and myself. You shouldn't ask me that."

"But I can recognize my own name."

". . . I asked them to guide you," Rakel relented. "I told them that you seemed very confused right now and that you could use help." Rakel took off her head covering, stashed it back in the cupboard, and fastened the lock.

He had to ask her, then, the question he had never asked her before.

"Does your god ever speak back?"

"Never."

"Then how do you know your god is real? Arlanders worshipped their dragon like a god, and the Tythonians had a god of thunder and lightning. You've heard how many people say that the Ebrian god does not actually exist. So why do you risk arrest by the Office of Truth like this? Why do you pray, with all the bother of barring your own door?"

"Emere," Rakel said softly, "do the Arlanders still worship the dragon? And what happened to the thunder god of Tythonia? What of the Tree Lords of your Kamori? How many people did we see in our travels who actually continued to worship their gods?"

The first thing the Empire did in their invasion of a foreign land was to destroy that land's objects of worship—nothing thwarted the recalcitrance of a newly conquered province better than that. So, provincials following their old ways were rare, and those who admitted to it even rarer.

Rakel stood up straight. "But our god still exists. As long as we believe."

While she put away the mat, Emere cleaned their bowls, lost in thought.

Rakel then left to make a house call, leaving Emere alone.

Watching Septima's chest rise and fall with her breath, he murmured, "You had faith in Cain and this is what he brought you. Do you not regret it? Even when nothing is promised you?"

Septima did not answer. All she did was breathe.

Emere sat by her and listened to the rhythm of her inhales and exhales. The earlier explosion of emotion made him tired and his head hurt. He closed his eyes. He wanted to dream. Whether of Cain or the fake Loran, he wanted to meet them and have them tell him that this was what they wanted him to do, that these were the choices before him, that his long wait would have not been in vain—he wanted them to reassure him so.

The sound of the door opening woke him. Rakel entered, taking off her coat.

"I told you to bar the door."

". . . You said no such thing." Emere stood up, and Rakel put down her medicine bag and came up to quickly check Septima's condition.

She turned to him. "You said you would do anything I asked of you, right?" Her eyes were shining. She looked exactly as she had when they had first met.

Emere nodded. "Anything."

"It's dangerous. I'll understand if you refuse."

She looked more expectant than worried. What Rakel wanted, of course, was not refusal.

"I'll do it. What is it?"

Rakel grinned. "I just went to see someone in our congregation. Well, after I saw the patient."

Congregation. The Ebrians must have organized in the Capital. Rakel had said before that her task was to send out news from the Capital to other parts of the world. Now Emere knew she hadn't been alone in that.

"There's a guest from the north," she went on, "who wants to join us in an alliance against the Empire. I want you to help us with our negotiation."

Emere blinked. "Why is that dangerous? And why would I be the one for the task?"

"Have you forgotten you're a wanted man? You even setting foot outside is a dangerous proposition," Rakel tutted. "But this is someone you know."

He took a deep breath. "Who is it?" He already knew. There was only one person who would be planning such a thing.

"King Loran of Arland."

26

ARIENNE

"*This* is Grand Inquisitor Lysandros?" came Noam's incredulous voice in her mind.

"That's what he said."

In that tent erected in Fractica's mind, Arienne looked over the skinny man who had introduced himself as Lysandros. The Lysandros she had once met had looked nothing like this—his body had been entirely machine, and his eyes had glowed like Powered streetlamps. But here was an ordinary young man, his body covered in a motion frame.

"But it can't be. The Grand Inquisitor is not some . . . young man," Noam muttered.

Making a soft whirring sound, the young man walked to the bedding and sat down. Arienne was accustomed to the device he used to walk—the Empire often bestowed them on soldiers who had lost a limb during their service. She had once read that the Powered armor legion elites were privileged to wear had evolved from this type of prosthetic frame. Arienne noticed the thin arms and legs underneath the motion frame.

"So his machine body wasn't just to prolong his life. He was always like this, from youth," Arienne murmured to herself.

Because this really had to be Lysandros as a young man. Instead of a room, Fractica's mind had a tent inside it, and the memory of Lysandros lived there. A ghost inside a ghost.

But then, Arienne's mind also had a ghost . . .

"Noam, I'm going to open the door, and you're going to step out."

". . . Is that even possible?" Noam asked nervously.

"As you can see, there's already a ghost in here, so yes, probably."

"Probably?" Noam whined.

Arienne laughed. "All right, definitely, then. I don't know how Fractica has created it, but this is the same kind of mind-space as the room you're in right now. I am sure of it. Maybe it—*she*—knew the same sorcery as Eldred, in life."

This couldn't be the Lysandros who had died on Finvera Pass, though. Instead, it was just a trace of him that remained, somehow, inside this machine. Perhaps it was simply Fractica's memory of Lysandros.

Arienne chanted a spell and drew an ellipse in the air. Violet ripples instantly appeared inside it; as she expected, opening a door between mind-spaces was easier than between a mind-space and an actual space.

"It'll be all right. Come out here and look at him with me," Arienne encouraged.

Finally, Noam stepped out. He stared intently at Lysandros

sitting on his bedding before saying, "He does look very much like him."

"You didn't bring Tychon with you?"

Maybe if she brought Tychon out, she could get this ghost of Lysandros to talk. But Noam didn't answer, continuing to stare at Lysandros. "You hear all sorts of things working as a sorcerer-engineer. About rain compromising output levels, or the output being fine for chariots but lanterns always being dimmer than they should be, or sobbing noises when nobody is around . . . Some sorcerer-engineers end up treating Power generators like people."

"Eldred was doing all sorts of things when he was a Power generator. He talked to me, even under seal."

"I don't know anything about abominations like him." Noam winced. "But I did always think there must be something of the person they used to be left inside the generators. Fractica used to Power the Grand Inquisitor's body before Tychon was commissioned. Maybe that's why it dreams of him?"

Arienne suddenly realized that there was no Fractica here—to imagine a dream where the dreamer was absent seemed strange to Arienne. Perhaps the sorcerer Fractica, whoever she was, didn't exist anymore, not beyond the husk forever generating Power for the Empire, nothing remaining of her mind other than a space where memories without self could reside.

Then again, only the baby Tychon and the donkey Aron were inside Arienne's own mind currently. A dream without its dreamer, in other words.

"What's that?"

Noam was pointing to the side of the bedding. A pair of worn leather boots were seen. They were well-oiled and shining, with spurs.

"They're shoes, obviously."

"Yes, but I mean whose are they? They aren't his size." Noam pointed at the young Lysandros's feet, which were encased in metal frame.

A faint outline of another person suddenly began to appear. She was sitting on the edge of the bedding as well, her feet bare. It was a woman with a long braid coming down her back. Her shirt was slightly open at the front, her shoulders wide. Her face was a blur, but she and Lysandros were gazing at each other on the bed.

"Who is she?" Arienne asked, turning her stare to Lysandros's face for a clue.

Lysandros's dazed look was changing, but his feelings were hard to read. There was still that soft whirring sound, and his left hand on his knee turned into a fist. He slammed it on the bed. The tent shook, as if a wind was blowing. He struck again. The tent shook. Rain started to fall, then a torrent. Noam grabbed the center pole of the tent and stared at Lysandros. The woman did not react.

"Noam, do you know who she is? Was Lysandros married?"

"I don't know. When I met him, he wasn't. But something's about to happen. There's something outside."

"How do you know that?"

"I can smell it. The smell of the Grim King . . ."

And suddenly the pole he was grasping, and the whole tent along with it, flew away into the sky, leaving Noam stumbling onto the ground. A waterfall of rain assaulted them. Arienne looked down at her hands and saw the rain was black. A puddle formed before her, and a black form materialized upward out of it, like a blaze of fire. Arienne knew immediately who it was. He was tall and not the dried-up corpse she knew him as. Instead, he wore a robe that seemed woven of shadows and fire, and a crown of gold and bone sat on his head. He had a dagger sheathed on one hip and a sword on the other.

Arienne's lips went dry. This couldn't be real. This was only a shadow, a memory. She had no idea why he was here, but she knew Eldred was dead, by her own hands. She had no reason to fear him. But the smell the Grim King had brought with him in this dark rain reminded her of that childhood memory, of the morning after her farewell party when the legionaries had discovered her hiding in her parents' closet. She recalled the stern expressions of the soldiers, and her parents standing behind them. Perhaps the smell of the Grim King, known to Noam and all Mersians, was simply the smell of their own fear.

The Grim King stood silent. The bedding turned black in the rain. Lysandros stared at him but otherwise did not react. Arienne could see the half-formed woman flinching. She was trying to stand up, but to no avail. She seemed deteriorated, perhaps from being inside Fractica for so long, like an old memory. Arienne realized that Fractica was beginning to forget this woman. Sooner or later, Fractica would forget Lysandros as well.

But the Grim King was vivid. How did Fractica have a memory of him? She remembered a passage from *The Sorcerer of Mersia*:

In the rain, I rose on the palm of the gigatherion Apollyon, with Power generator Fractica, to the top of the castle, where the necromancer king Eldred stood. He was gaunt and tall, his robes shadow and flames, his crown bone and gold, just as the Mersian locals had told me. It was the first time in centuries that any outsider had laid eyes upon the Grim King.

Fractica had been with Lysandros when he fought Eldred.

"You keep fading, dog of the Empire."

An all-too-familiar voice, inhuman. The Grim King did not even look at Arienne or Noam, the latter still sprawled on the ground, and spoke only to Lysandros.

"You are a mere trace, even if you have lasted over a hundred years in this small, nonexistent place. But it is time to surrender it to me. I shall use it for a better purpose."

Arienne looked back and forth between Lysandros and Eldred. What was he asking him to surrender to him? But then, Lysandros's empty expression caught something like the light of meaning. He stood up, declared his name, and spoke.

"I shall . . . restore Mersia . . . and return it to the embrace . . . of the Empire . . . and . . ." Lysandros turned his head to the woman on the bed.

"What you propose is impossible, as you are about to rot away forever. You do not realize what this machine is doing in Danras according to your wishes."

So that was it. Eldred, or his shadow, wanted *Fractica*. The many fragments before her coalesced into one with this realization.

Fractica was "restoring" Mersia, starting with Danras, according to Lysandros's orders. Whether these orders came from the real Lysandros or the shadow of him, Arienne couldn't be sure. But she now understood that Fractica was worse than insane—it was stuck, trying to carry out its futile purpose. It had been sentenced to roam the streets of Danras, trying to rebuild what couldn't be rebuilt.

The Grim King slid toward Lysandros to stand right in front of him. The robe of shadows and fire swirled around him. His emaciated hands emerged from his sleeves and unsheathed his sword. A blade, shining with opalescence. Before anyone could stop him, he plunged it into Lysandros's chest. Lysandros fell and scattered into dust.

Eldred intoned, "You used your honeyed words to foment rebellion in my subjects and felled my country. The punishment you deserve is death."

The woman on the bed was still trying to stand, but she couldn't. She tried to speak, but no words came.

"It is regrettable the real Eldred cannot kill the real Lysandros but . . . we can begin with some small revenges."

Arienne stopped waiting.

"I killed the real Lysandros," she declared.

Eldred finally turned his head and looked at her quizzically.

"And what little girl dares speak such nonsense in the presence of a king taking back his kingdom?"

Arienne laughed. "And I killed the *real* Eldred as well. You're just a shadow of a dead man."

In the black rain, Eldred's face twisted. Arienne stared directly into it. In the corner of her eye, Noam sat by the portal into Arienne's mind, looking in her direction with fearful eyes. He must have wanted to flee, to escape into the room, but he also knew that if anything should happen to Arienne, that room would implode with him in it.

"More nonsense. My death was foretold. And there is no path to the prophecy coming to fulfillment."

The prophecy. Noam had told her about it, that the Grim King's apprentice would succeed him. Arienne knew there was no point in denying what she was.

"I am the apprentice of the Grim King."

Noam gasped.

Arienne grinned. "And you are merely a memory of him. A memory who entered this place before the real Eldred met me."

Eldred wailed with fury and charged at her with his sword. *This is only the shadow of an enemy I have beaten before,* thought Arienne. *No matter how real he looks, I am what's real and he is merely a memory.* His sword came down on Arienne's shoulder but it simply shattered into a prismatic powder on impact.

Power flowed inside her. Arienne summoned the memory of herself slicing off Eldred's arms—and at the same time, Lysandros's arms—at Finvera Pass. The wintry wind of the mountains. The snow crunching underneath her feet. The bony hands of Eldred trying to strangle her in her mind, the metal hand of Lysandros doing the same in the real world. Without hesitation, she chanted the cutting spell and her Power slashed out.

The black rain ceased in a blink. Eldred's body stood for a moment without its head, then spasmed as if sneezing. Then, like Lysandros before him, he turned to dust. The sky was clear. Stars came out.

"Much ado for a mere memory."

Arienne turned to Noam, who had stood up and was dusting

himself off. Noam, without looking up at her, said, "You really *are* his apprentice!."

"I just said it in the moment. I didn't mean anything by it."

"You also said you killed the Grand Inquisitor. Is it true?"

She realized she'd never told him that. Looking carefully at his face, she nodded.

"Why did you do that? He was a great man . . ."

It was a long story, and it would only upset Noam. She gazed at his sad and pathetic stance. Then, a ringing in her head—Arienne staggered. The door to her mind, which was still open with its swirling violet light, undulated. Noam jumped away from it.

The donkey Aron popped his head out. Then, he carefully stepped forward, one hoof at a time. On his back was Tychon.

"Noam, did you put Tychon on Aron's back?" Arienne asked, puzzled.

Noam shook his head as Aron went straight up to the hazy woman on the bed. She stood up, reached out with her vague arms, and picked up Tychon. She cradled him against her, and Tychon opened his eyes wide and stretched his little hands to her face.

Her form began to fill in, just like Noam had when he had entered Arienne's mind for the first time. Color returned to the woman's hair. Her skin had the rugged texture of a healthy outdoorswoman. Her hands were strong. Her eyes were full of joy, the look of someone who had found what they had lost long ago. The woman stroked Tychon's forehead a few times and gently laid the baby down on the bedding.

She then turned toward Arienne.

"I am a memory of Yuma, the Chief Herder of Danras. But you must meet the real Yuma. Go to the castle of the Grim King. There, you will learn what you came here for."

And just like Eldred and Lysandros before her, she turned to dust. Tychon began to cry.

27

YUMA

Yuma stood on the wide rooftop of the Feast Hall and looked northward. The setting sun to the west was blinding, so she raised her hand to shield her eyes. Before the city gates were hundreds of soldiers, standing in perfect formation and stillness, forming a mass of white against the grassland. But the white was not from their clothes or armor—it was from their exposed skeletons. They were the remains of the conscripts from Danras, Iorca, and Lansis. An army brought back from the dead by the Grim King. The opalescent light that coated their bones was visible even from where Yuma was watching. Each had a sword with a sharp bone blade. A black orox restlessly stamped its feet, a giant wearing white bone armor sitting on its back and carrying a large iron mace. Neither giant nor orox was alive.

Aidan was the first to recognize him as he leaned over the ledge of the roof. "Garamund comes wearing his white raiment."

Garamund was the highest-ranking of the Grim King's

generals. From an early age, Yuma had shuddered in fear hearing the stories of how he was reshaped from orox flesh and blood into a human form. He was so large that the orox he rode looked as small as a horse.

"What should we do about the city gates?" asked Aidan. He was next to the signaling horn, a beautiful sand-colored instrument made from the largest of orox horns and engraved with star and wind patterns. "If you wish for the people of Danras to fight, you must blow the horn yourself, as the Chief Herder." Aidan held up his hands and looked at Yuma, anxiety painting his face.

She shook her head. "No, tell them to open the north gate."

Aidan hesitated. "Are you going to hand over the Imperial emissary?"

"I'm going to do nothing of the sort," Yuma scoffed. "But there is a larger battle that is being fought right now."

"What battle might that be?"

Yuma looked down at the sprawling city below.

"The battle between me and the people of Danras."

"What do you mean?" Aidan asked, startled.

She noted that Lysandros and Fractica had now arrived at the central square of the crossroads.

"If I blew the horn to fight the Grim King now, would even half of the people of Danras follow me into battle?" Yuma answered. "The whole city needs to see the Grim King's minion being felled first. By just us herders and the emissary."

"Chief Herder. You seem to be putting your trust into that machine box, but do you really think it can be a match for Garamund?"

In truth, she could not be sure. She had never seen Garamund fight, nor did she know how strong Fractica was. And surely a swing of that massive mace was enough to crush anything, even if it was made of metal. But she had no choice but to trust Lysandros. She remembered young Rizona, bleeding to death on her horse . . .

"It can. If you don't trust in Lysandros, trust in me. Let the herders know we have a fight on our hands." Yuma gestured for him to follow her order. As Aidan left her, the trembling voice of an old woman came from behind her.

"Chief Herder."

Yuma looked back. "Granny Jesska."

Jesska's eyes were intently searching Yuma's face. "So you are taking us into war, then."

Yuma nodded.

"Chief Herder," said Jesska, still tremulous, "you are still young and perhaps foolish, but as an old woman, I have come here to implore you one last time. Rizona was my granddaughter. Do you not think I wish to fight? To banish the Grim King from our land? And you, no doubt, want to be the hero that rid Merseh of the centuries-long tyranny that held us in its grip. But if Danras could fight the Grim King, would we have not fought before? I am—"

"Do you think that I, the Chief Herder of Danras, am doing this out of youthful heroic folly?" Yuma asked, incredulous.

Yuma waited for her answer, but none came except for Jesska's stare.

"Granny Jesska. Rizona was your granddaughter, but she was my friend, my sister, and a herder who followed me. Jed as well. All of the young ones who were taken from us last winter were my friends and fellow herders of Danras too. We live outside this city for half the year, being rained on and frosted over on the steppe.

But we do it for this city, for the people who live here. Not a single one of us herd for the Grim King!"

Something was burning up from inside of her. Taking a deep breath, she tried to tame it within her.

"I dare to ask, further to my youthful heroic folly—why did you, and your mother, and her father, allow the Grim King to rule over us as he did? Why did we all give him every orox, every man and woman and child, he ever asked for?"

A hand gripped her shoulder. It was Aidan, back from his task. Yuma breathed deeply once more, wiped the corners of her eyes with the back of her hand, and regarded Jesska. What pressed down on Jesska's shoulders wasn't fear or anguish or rage. Yuma turned to Aidan, who pointed to the north. "I've signaled to open the gate, like you asked."

Where he pointed, the gates were opening. She had to go down now. Yuma bowed slightly and gripped Jesska's shoulders, gently but firmly at the same time. The old woman raised her head.

"Granny, watch over us from here. The Empire's emissary and I will vanquish Garamund. I will show you how a king . . . a Chief Herder of Danras can fight."

Had Jesska given up, or finally understood? Her face was hard to read. Yuma tried a smile, which forced Jesska to weakly smile back.

"Our Chief Herder has spoken," she said, "and this old one will listen. I shall watch you from here, as you say. However . . ." Her faint smile faded, and she hesitated. "Even if . . . even if you succeed, I can't help but worry about what comes after that."

"We shall consider that problem when we come to it," said Yuma, trying not to think too deeply about Jesska's ominous words.

"All right."

Yuma let go of Jesska's shoulders and tipped her hat. The only way down from where they were was the staircase winding around the Feast Hall. She had only taken her first step when Aidan followed behind her.

"The gates are open, but they will likely wait to attack at night."

"I understand."

"Garamund himself may try to fight that box—Fractica, I mean—but the others will charge this building."

Yuma nodded. "Yes, they are sure to go after the Host. He's the only one of us who has the slightest chance against the Grim King. But that is precisely why I opened the gates. If they can get here directly, hopefully there won't be too many hurt along the way."

If the Host's enchantment had not been protecting the catacombs, the city would've become a pile of burning ruins at every whim of the Grim King. The Host was their only weapon against his full tyranny. At least until now. And Yuma had a plan.

"Aidan. There is still time before the sun sets. You must go now and gather the other herders."

"Chief, I have . . . limitations as to how far I can go to defy the Grim King . . ." said Aidan, his words steeped in both fear and regret.

What did it mean, exactly, to have spent one's childhood under the Grim King? To have been the only child to survive among a cohort gathered from across Merseh? Aidan had almost as many white hairs as black ones in his mustache now, but the memory of it still haunted him. Every morning, seeing his half-dead face in the mirror, he must remember his time with the Grim King.

Yuma patted his shoulder. "I think all of Danras feels the same as you do. After you have gathered the herders, come back here to protect Granny Jesska."

"I am sorry, Chief Herder. I just cannot fight . . . *him*." He bowed low.

"And watch us," she said, cutting off his unnecessary apology. "Watch us fight."

Aidan nodded, and averting his eyes from her, he quickly made his way down the stairs. Yuma followed him down until she stopped at the door leading to the Host's chamber.

"We can't turn back now," she murmured.

She opened the door. Inside was a wide floor, upon which sat the Host, in completely black ceremonial robes. These robes were less elaborate than the ones adorned with feathers that he had worn during the herding, but they were more significant. The last time Yuma saw these robes was last spring. A child named Dalan had worn them, scared to death and standing by an altar, the robes laden with flowers from the grasslands. It was Dalan who had prostrated himself on the floor, but it was the Host who had risen, shaking off the flowers.

Bowing, Yuma spread her arms in the proper manner before him.

"Chief Herder."

"Yes, Host."

He gestured for her to approach. Yuma stepped forward, the heels of her boots knocking against the floor, echoing in the wide chamber.

"You are firm in your decision?" the Host asked.

She smiled brightly at him. When Lysandros smiled like this,

Yuma always felt calmer. She hoped it would have the same effect on the Host, but he simply scoffed in the most unchildlike manner.

"And where on the steppe did you learn such a bewitching smile . . ."

Yuma could feel herself blush. The Host stood and picked up a long stick leaning unassumingly against the wall, its top end wrapped in leather. The Host held it out to Yuma, with both hands.

"This is the Spear of Hope, passed on from one Host to the next, for the last three hundred years. This spear was forged in starlight by Iorcan rhymesmiths, blessed by Lansisi life priests, and imbued by the Host with all the wishes of the steppe, to fight the Grim King. It was never used, because that rebellion was quelled before it even began. But the Hosts always knew that one day someone would rise up, though none of us knew it would be this day. This spear is now entrusted to you, as you have chosen to fight the Grim King."

Yuma was familiar with the story of the Rebellion Undone, told everywhere in Merseh by parents to children in hushed voices. It was later in her life that she realized it was not just a story about a noble failure—it was also about how it could be tried again. She took the spear with both hands, and hitched it to her back carefully.

"Listen to me, Chief Herder. The song I am about to sing is especially dangerous. The underlings of the Grim King will swarm this very place. Are you prepared?"

Drawing from all her inner strength, she smiled once more.

28

EMERE

As Rakel summoned an assistant to take over Septima's care, Emere prepared to meet Loran. He wished he could go back to his house and change clothing, maybe even bring a gift, but he was a wanted man. Once the sun set, he set out with Rakel through the back door and into the alleys.

Loran was here, in the Capital. To meet the Ebrians, to fight the Empire . . . He couldn't remember being this excited since he had left Kamori. He might be wearing a cloak with a hood and avoiding the larger roads and streetlamps to hurry through dark alleyways, but his step was as light as if he were heading toward assured victory.

". . . I remembered that you had met King Loran, so I told my friends that there was a way to confirm her identity . . ." He could barely hear Rakel talking from under her own hood as she carried a lantern next to him.

He was going to see Loran again. The thought was making

the fake Loran in his dream seem almost like an auspicious omen. Maybe it had been. Maybe this was all part of his destiny. What could be more wonderful than if it turned out his destiny was entwined with Loran's grand purpose?

Rakel stopped in the middle of an alley that had almost no windows, right in front of a crumbling building, and looked around her.

"Is this it?" Emere wondered.

"A little farther from here." But she drew out a key and plunged it into the door before her, which opened without a sound on well-oiled hinges. Emere followed Rakel inside.

The house was dark. Rakel grabbed Emere's arm with her left hand and lifted her lantern with her right. The inside was as decrepit as the outside. Broken furniture on a filthy carpet, with no sign of habitation. An abandoned house. But wherever Rakel's lantern lit, Emere noticed footprints in the dust made by a variety of shoes. Judging the coast was truly clear, Rakel kicked away a corner of the carpet, revealing a trapdoor with an iron ring handle. The trapdoor was just about big enough for one person to pass through. Rakel gestured at it with her chin, and so Emere knelt down and opened it. These hinges were oiled into complete silence as well, and a wooden staircase was revealed.

"There are a few of these entrances throughout the city."

"Entrances to what?"

Rakel grinned. "An abandoned underground space. We've been using it for worship since fifty or so years ago. And now, for meetings . . . Watch your step; the floor isn't smooth. And there's a long way to go."

Lightly holding on to Rakel's shoulder as she led the way with her lantern, Emere descended into the underground.

"Why is King Loran seeking an alliance?" Emere asked, not bothering to hide his excitement.

"It's not just with us. She's reaching out to other resistance movements in other provinces. She says that if we really want to fight the Empire, we need to coordinate our efforts."

Loran had indeed clasped hands with the Kamori rebels and the Ledonite tribes of the north. The three nations had never been on good terms, but they had fought the Empire together. Evidently, the King of Arland was still following the same principle, but now on a much grander scale.

"She's not wrong," continued Rakel as they came upon a particularly narrow passageway, "but we're cautious. We have survived because we're cautious. The elders believe we can lose everything if we listen to the wrong person."

Emere clucked his tongue. "Even after hearing what King Loran achieved in Arland? I've fought by her side ever since I first saw her in Dehan Forest. Even when an entire legion and a gigatherion descended on her, even when the dragon of Arland fell, she never gave up."

Rakel smiled. "If you say so. But as I said, we're cautious. Moving too much too fast might compromise everything we've managed to accumulate over the years."

"It's a risk you have to take!" It took the surprise showing on Rakel's face for him to realize he had inadvertently raised his voice. She sighed disapprovingly.

"You're just like you were in your twenties. Jumping into things without a second thought." Rakel sighed, exhausted. "I loved you and followed you for that. Even when I was unceremoniously left at the side of a road, I never regretted the ten years I'd been with you. Or the ten years that followed."

Finvera Pass. It had been spring, when tufts of light green showed through patches in the snow. He had shaken off Rakel, who wanted to come with him, but he knew what she had really wanted. A life with him. But a life in an underground stronghold, never knowing when the Empire would strike, was not the kind of life he could ask of her. He was so sure that his brother and his band of Liberators would make a difference. But the only notable thing that had happened since was meeting Loran. Rakel said she had no regrets, but Emere regretted everything.

Wordlessly, the two made their way through the dark tunnel. The lantern illuminated the walls of brick and revealed several other passageways and corners.

Just as Emere was growing tired, Rakel said, "I'm over forty now. I've been to places with you most people couldn't even imagine, and brought back to life countless people who would've passed on otherwise. I've lived a settled life and had a husband. My only task left is to grow old. So, maybe I can become more like you and take more risks. But we are talking about the survival of the Ebrians in the Capital—it's not just about me."

She stopped. There was a door at the end of the passageway. Large, iron, and the insignia upon it rusted beyond recognition. Emere looked at Rakel. "Is this it?"

Nodding, Rakel rapped a complicated rhythm on the door. Before the echoes could die down, the door opened and a soft light emanated from within. A young, tall woman who filled up the doorway looked Emere up and down.

"Elder Rakel, is this the one you spoke of?"

Emere turned to Rakel in surprise. She had never said anything about being an elder in the congregation. She didn't return his gaze, focusing on the doorkeeper instead.

"Yes. We haven't been followed. It's safe."

"Ayula."

The woman stepped aside. A long dagger hung from her belt. Emere stepped through, on Rakel's signal.

Several candles on tables and against walls lit up the room, which was about the size of Emere's living room. It could comfortably fit about ten people, but thirty assorted men and women were crammed inside. Most of them stood, as there wasn't enough room for everyone to sit. Someone took down a book from a wall-mounted shelf, and another was carefully polishing a statue of the Ebrian god. A group was in a heated debate in Ebrian.

But in the next moment, everyone stopped what they were doing and stared at Emere.

An older man with a long gray beard and wearing black clothes stood up from the desk in the corner and called out, "Prince Emere, we welcome you to our holy gathering."

Following Rakel's lead, Emere bowed at the waist.

"I'm afraid I'm not a prince anymore."

"Then shall we call you Councillor? Not the most welcome honorific in this setting . . ." He chuckled. "My name is Ahmus. I administer to the Ebrian souls in the Capital."

"You are a priest."

Emere remembered Rakel telling him that Ebrians were led by priests. Even their kings had been elected by a council of priests, until the Empire arrived.

"We do not often admit unbelievers into our sanctum, but we find ourselves in extraordinary circumstances, and Elder Rakel vouches for you." Ahmus gestured toward Rakel before he continued. "Councillor Emere, I hear you fought alongside King Loran in the Arlander rebellion."

A murmur rose from the congregation.

"That is so," Emere answered, with some pride.

"As we speak, our brothers are bringing here the one claiming to be King Loran. They will arrive shortly. No one here has ever met King Loran of Arland in person. Her name, however, has spread throughout the Empire, even as Imperial powers still try to cover up what truly happened in Arland. But all who fight the Empire know the truth. That King Loran, with the help of a dragon, raised her people against an Imperial legion and defeated it. A defeat the likes of which the Empire had never seen in its two hundred years. We would be honored to form an alliance with such a leader."

Emere waited for the "however."

"However," Ahmus went on, "the people of Ebria do not have dragons or mysterious powers. The task our god has given us is to conserve our people and maintain our faith. This is our holy mandate that was given in the Age of Oracles, well before the Empire existed. Even if King Loran can fell a gigatherion on her own, I do not know if she can protect our—"

"Arland was protected thus," Emere interjected. He glanced at Rakel, who nodded. He pressed on. "Freedom and independence are never handed to us just because we ask for them. What Her Majesty did for Arland is an example for us all, and one does not need dragons and gods and demons to fight the Empire. When King Loran rose, Arland's neighbors—Ledon, and my own beloved Kamori—rose from our torpor with her. You can as well—anyone can. If we all keep rising, Arland's victory can be the whole world's victory."

"Is that so?" mused Ahmus. "Was that truly a victory for Arland? We are not in agreement." A shadow flickered over his candlelit face.

"What do you mean?"

"Arland's 'victory' in that battle," said Ahmus in a low voice, "made it a target of the Empire, like Mersia before it. The Office of Truth is restless for revenge, and the most powerful senators are falling in line with them."

Emere looked at Rakel again. She was biting her lip. Had she known this as well? Had Loran's victory paved the way for Ludvik's conspiracy as much as Lysandros's death did?

Ahmus continued. "King Loran is holding out her hand to not only us Ebrians but also to resistances around the world. She realizes, in truth, that Arland is in danger. *That* is why she seeks an alliance."

As Emere tried to think of a response to this, a rapping on iron echoed through the room. All eyes turned toward the door opposite the one Emere had entered.

Ahmus spoke. "It seems King Loran has arrived."

The people standing by the door moved aside.

Emere took a deep breath and prepared himself for the king's arrival.

29

ARIENNE

Aron, despite the donkey's long occupancy in Arienne's mind, seemed not in the least surprised by the dramatic change in scenery as he stepped outside for the first time in a long while. He simply brayed once and clomped about Arienne for a bit.

The sky was as gray and the earth as red as when Arienne had first arrived in Danras. With Fractica now unmoving, the wind was the only thing that could be heard. To her, this was no longer a field of warped ruins where a monster roamed. With the poor Power generator laid to rest, the ruins in Arienne's eyes settled into what they truly were—a devastated landscape where many people had once lived. A desiccated leather sign for a shop swayed in the wind, its letters long rotted away. She imagined what it must've been like before, now that she could give herself a moment to do so.

"That was a butcher shop where they sold orox meat," Noam said. "A long time ago, I mean longer than when I was alive, herders spent months outside of the city making sure the oroxen grazed all summer and autumn. When I lived here, the oroxen were in fenced ranches, and there were much fewer than there used to be."

Noam's voice, as he explained from the room in her mind, was tinged with longing.

When she had dreamed on her journey to Danras, the hooves of countless oroxen had reverberated in the air. A woman with braided hair, wearing a wide-brimmed hat, had ridden a tall horse and opened that year's herding season. In Fractica's dream, Arienne had now met that woman—Yuma, the last Chief Herder of Danras.

"Let's go," she suddenly said.

"Where?"

"Where do you think? Eldred's castle. She told us the real Yuma would be there. Do you know the way?"

"Northward . . . But it was turned into a legion fort. Not that it'd be anything at all now."

Arienne took a firm grip on Aron's reins. "Good. Then there's no one to stand in our way."

They had to leave the city and step out into the wasteland once more, so Arienne wrapped her head and lowered her hood. She slowly walked north down the wide street. Aron placidly followed, and she heard Noam softly singing the Ebrian lullaby to the baby.

The northern gates were so wide open that Arienne rolled her eyes at herself for not having entered this way when she first arrived. But outside of the gates was the devastated steppe again. How was she to feed Aron? They had arrived in Danras only days ago, but he already seemed a bit gaunt.

They were not close enough to see Eldred's castle, but true to Imperial standards, the likely presence of a military outpost was indicated by the traces of a relatively well-paved road. Surely at the end of it was the fortress.

"How far do we have to walk?" she asked Noam.

"I don't know. Several days? Mersia is a big country."

She would have to spend several nights in the wasteland before her then. When she had spent her first night here, the fear had been paralyzing. But she didn't feel that way anymore. This was once a great grassland after all, where Yuma and her fellow herders had once fed their vast orox herd. Just the thought of that past dispelled her fear.

"Let's make haste, then. Tell me more about this country on the way. About Mersia after the annexation."

"Okay, but you know I don't remember too well," said Noam.

She scoffed, "Oh, I doubt you could ever forget the equinox feasts at the Sun Mound. All that dancing and singing! That tradition had survived, hadn't it?"

Staring at Arienne, Noam replied, "Actually, yes, I do remember that. I hadn't realized I did, until you mentioned it. But you say it like you've been there."

Hadn't she? But of course she hadn't been to the feasts. She wasn't there. She hadn't even been born yet. But then why was she remembering? Perhaps the ghosts had left bits and pieces of their earthly lives inside her mind. Was that possible?

Arienne left Danras through the gates, heading back into the wasteland of burnt red. She walked until Danras was no longer visible, swapping memories with Noam all the way. Time flew by as she talked about Mersia and a Danras she somehow remembered with fondness. She loved the Mersia before the Empire, and she loved the one after. Recollecting her false memories, she found herself longing for this country's past as if it were her homeland.

The wind was calming down. When she sat to rest, Arienne undid the cloth that covered her face and took a deep breath. The air was dusty and dry, but she knew now that it had once been fragrant with the smell of grass. She took out a piece of hard bread from the packs on Aron's back. Feeling Aron's stare like a sting, she shared the bread and what little water she had left with him. She was on her feet before even swallowing her last bite, walking again. Noam sang as she walked, and listening carefully, she could just about hear Tychon's soft breathing. Her mood lifted.

Evening came. Arienne could see nothing but wasteland in every direction. It was like being in the middle of the ocean where there was nothing to orient oneself. There were only the remains of the road the Empire had paved. She walked a little farther by the light of her lantern, and stopped once she found a small outcropping to tie Aron's reins to. She unloaded the donkey, and as she spread out her bedding, Noam said, "You're going to sleep here, where there's nothing?"

"There's nothing everywhere here." Arienne shrugged.

"Come inside the room."

She would've if Tychon were the only inhabitant. Her body outside might shiver, but the room in her mind had a soft, warm bed. But there was a man she barely knew in that room now.

She laid herself down on the bedding, feeling the hard ground underneath. "I don't think so," she grumbled. "If you weren't a ghost, I would've kicked you out to sleep out here while I slept peacefully in there."

"If I'm what's bothering you, why don't you make another room?"

This made her sit up. Why hadn't she thought of that? She crossed her legs and warned, "There might be a bit of shaking. Let me know right away if anything seems wrong."

Of course she could make another room. But why stop there? What if she made something bigger? Like a house? Or a large building, like the prefect's residence or the Imperial Academy?

Then she thought of a large wooden building made of logs. Where had she seen this before? Every aspect appeared in perfect detail in her mind. She captured it all. The smell of slightly damp wood, the wall decorations made of animal horn, the staircase that wrapped around the outside of the building, the intricate dovetailing of the steps . . . A smell of steamed buns and flowers. Tychon's babbling. Power glowed with warmth through her whole body.

Floor by floor, Arienne constructed this building that she had never seen in her life but somehow recalled with perfect clarity. On the eaves of each floor, she hung countless wind chimes of colored glass bells and beads on leather strings. She'd always liked them. Or had she? Arienne couldn't remember the last time she'd noticed them anywhere. Her head ached slightly, but she concentrated hard. It was a beautiful, tall building. Focusing on the smell of unfamiliar wood, Arienne made walls, fitted corridors, and furnished rooms.

"How does it look?" Arienne asked.

They were standing on the roof of the building. The sky in her mind was as gray as the one over the real Mersia, and Noam stood with the baby Tychon in his arms. Arienne went to the ledge and peered down.

Noam stared around them. "What *is* this building?"

"I don't know."

"How did you create a *whole building* you don't know?"

"I . . . don't know."

It was extraordinary. She kept recalling the details within, but the one thing she could not recall was ever having seen the place.

"Noam, you don't know of this place either?"

Noam glanced around and answered, "No, not from the rooftop, anyway. But a building this size, and with native, non-Imperial architecture, and those wind chimes . . . could be the Feast Hall from before the Empire. I heard they took it down and replaced it with the prefect's office, some years into the annexation."

The ghosts of Mersia. This building came from another memory they had left behind.

"There should be a sounding horn here," she murmured. A large horn appeared where she pointed, an instrument she had never seen in her life. She couldn't even tell what animal the horn had come from. But the engravings of stars and curlicues of wind were as familiar to her as if she'd played with the horn since she was a child. She walked up to the horn as if enchanted, touching the mouthpiece. She turned to Noam. He could only stare at her.

Arienne put her lips to the mouthpiece and blew. A loud, clear sound. As if a veil had been lifted, the sky turned blue-black and thousands of stars appeared. A gust of wind rustled her hair. She heard chimes, ringing and rattling in the wind, from the eaves below. The stars were moving quickly toward somewhere, flowing like the rush of a waterfall. Arienne could not take her eyes off the sight.

Soon, the stars had all flowed away save for one—the polestar that pointed north. Then other stars returned, first a handful, then a whole river of them, swirling around the polestar. Arienne looked at Noam, who was gaping at the sky. He caught her eye.

"I've never seen anything like this in my life. I've never *heard* of anything like this. What kind of a sorcerer are you?"

". . . I really don't know."

Maybe the inside of this Feast Hall would offer more insight. She took her eyes off the sky and made her way to the staircase that coiled along the outside of the building. The stars were the only light, but she knew where each stair was supposed to be. Noam followed, still carrying Tychon. They got to a landing, where she pointed to a door and said, "You can go in here. There's a bed inside. Get some rest."

Noam said nothing as he opened the door. As he stepped inside, Arienne grabbed his shoulder.

"I'll take Tychon."

She lifted him from Noam's arms, and the baby nuzzled into her embrace. The air did seem a little chilly. She continued farther down until there was another door. She knew what was inside—a spacious room, a comfortable bed, a closet, pegs to hang hats, a stove, and a saddle rest.

Also, a rocking cradle.

Arienne stepped inside. The stove cozily lit the room, and she felt its warmth. Arienne carefully laid the baby down in the cradle, which was just a few steps away from the stove. Then, she read aloud the roughly engraved words on the head of the cradle.

"'Tychon, firstborn of Lysandros and Yuma.'"

30

YUMA

They had boarded over the windows of the first floor of the Feast Hall. Through the little gaps in those boards, Yuma observed Lysandros in his head-to-toe metal armor as he fought Garamund. The sun had already set outside, but Fractica's blue light illuminated the square.

Lysandros's armor looked bulky, but his movements were swift and precise. Fractica's blue glow swirled with the violet vapor of Lysandros's armor, making his every movement an arresting sight, as if he were a dancer performing for them. From the floor above, she could hear snatches of the Host's continuing song.

Lysandros had taken that armor out from Fractica's body. It was so large, he didn't so much put it on as lower himself into it. And yet he moved effortlessly, as nimble as a cat. Yuma guessed that Lysandros's armor moved under the same principle as his iron frame.

The Grim King's general Garamund was so large that even

Lysandros in his full armor looked like a child next to him, though the Imperial emissary was clearly not weaker. He withstood Garamund's swinging mace, which otherwise could have taken down a house, without much strain. Every time the mace made contact with him, it made a dull ringing sound like a bell, and Yuma grimaced as if she had been hit herself.

Lysandros had no weapons in his hands, but he sliced and stabbed with the long blades fitted onto his armored forearms with expert skill. One of the blades split Garamund's chest, but the inhuman giant didn't even flinch, and the wound closed immediately into a long scar.

The black orox Garamund had ridden had already had its head sliced off by Lysandros's blades and fallen dead. The ground was also littered with the remains of the skeletal soldiers that had charged at the emissary—most of them had shattered with one blow of his fists. The ones left standing were still attacking him from the back and sides, but he deftly picked them off and pulverized them with his hands.

"This should be a duel, between the Imperial emissary and the general of the Grim King," suggested Lysandros to Garamund as he crushed another attacking skeleton without even looking, "while these pests simply watch." His tone was the same as when he conversed and joked with Yuma, though his voice was amplified as if he were speaking through a cone.

Fractica stood a little off from the battle, shining its light into the square. Garamund must've realized it was the source of Lysandros's power, as he kept trying to approach it, but Lysandros quickly blocked him each time, goading him into another round. Lysandros was a smart man, expertly carrying out their plan.

While Garamund was distracted by Lysandros, Yuma knew the skeletons would soon charge into the Feast Hall. The herders were finishing up their preparations, barring the doors that originally did not have bars. Aidan would be tying the last traps in place. His gaze was darker than she had ever seen. Having been closer to the Grim King than any of them, he was probably more fearful of what was to come than the rest.

She saw the windows around the square that had previously been shut tight begin to open a little. The citizens of Danras couldn't help their curiosity, this glorious machine-man fighting against the abomination of the Grim King. Yuma was counting on that curiosity. Now all Lysandros had to do was win . . .

Suddenly, the skeletal soldiers leaped away from Lysandros and disappeared from Yuma's narrow sight. She turned to the main doors of the Feast Hall.

"Chief Herder!" shouted the young lookout. "They're coming!" The youth scrambled away from the doors, as a loud crash against them made them shake. All the herders took a step back.

"It begins. Ready yourselves," Yuma announced, as calmly as she possibly could.

This fight was not only up to Lysandros. The herders in the hall also had their role.

Yuma drew the machete from her hip. The Spear of Hope remained on her back—she wasn't as proficient with the spear as with the blade, and the confines of the Feast Hall made it a cumbersome weapon for now.

While the herders considered it shameful to hit a target with only nine shots out of ten from the saddle of a running horse, the skeletal dead were impervious to arrows. There were unfortunately few among the herders who had ever used blades in battle, so the best they could do was use the iron cattle prods that they typically used to herd oroxen. They held up these cattle prods with trembling hands, waiting for the entry of the deathless soldiers who knew no fear or pain.

"Why do these things have to come at night," muttered one of them.

"Life has become death for them," explained Aidan, "and to them, day is like the darkest night is for us. They can't see clearly in front of them during the day."

The door shook hard. They were perhaps using a large log to try to ram through the doors. Again, and again, the doors shook. Yuma could see the herders' knuckles turn white as they gripped their cattle prods.

Finally, the bar across the doors cracked. Yuma gestured for them to stand back. With another slam, the heavy doors exploded open, and as soon as Fractica's blue light entered the room and lit up the skulls of the undead army, Yuma sliced through the rope that Aidan had just tied up. The logs hanging from the rafters swung downward and struck the bony intruders as they began to pour in.

Before Yuma could even give the signal, the herders charged at the remaining skeletons that had avoided the logs. But the undead soldiers were completely unfazed by the attacks; one that had just lost its legs tried to get up and fight, and a hand that had fallen off tried to creep up Yuma's leg. She shook it off and crushed it beneath her foot.

"We can't defend ourselves here," Yuma reminded them. "Fight them off as you retreat!"

There were only two places where retreat was possible. One was the gathering room deep in the back of the first floor; the other was the staircase leading upstairs. The Grim King did not know where the Host was yet, so Yuma's plan was to divide the undead army in two and fight for as much time as possible. As the stronger herders covered for them, the younger ones were to run to the gathering room and get ready to shut and bar the doors. The rest were to slowly defend their way to the stairs, creating a bottleneck.

The minions of the Grim King threw themselves upon the herders, afraid of neither injury nor losing their undead lives. Several herders screamed and fell as they made their way to the stairs, and they quickly drowned under a wave of bleached bones.

As Yuma defended the stairs, she glanced at the front doors. The Grim King's minions continued to swarm through them. Yuma was worried about the battle outside, but she reassured herself that if Lysandros had lost, it would've been Garamund, not the bone soldiers, entering through those doors.

Normally, the Feast Hall—like the catacombs—would've had the protection of the Host's enchantment and it would not be a place that the monsters of the Grim King could enter and defile so easily. But the Host was putting all he had into this song. When Yuma had asked the Host if he could protect the catacombs, the Host had not answered. If the catacombs were not under enchantment, and the Grim King realized this, the rebellion would be over in a second.

Early-winter wind brushed against Yuma's cheeks, and she heard the wind chimes tinkle above her, so incongruous with the sounds of battle. Fighting from above on a staircase is much easier than from the other direction, so Yuma and the herders used their machetes and cattle prods to fend off the corpses as they slowly made their way up.

"Chief Herder, these bastards keep—" Before Barund could finish his sentence, his throat was ripped out by a bony clawed hand, his spurting blood bathing the white skull of his attacker red. With no shout of triumph, or any other reaction, the skeletons stepped over Barund's fallen body as they advanced. Yuma fended them off with her blade, taking another step back. A herder who'd been standing behind Barund quickly filled in the space he left.

Yuma and the herders had retreated to where the stairs exited the Feast Hall to wrap around the building. Only the stars lit the way through the dark, the building itself now blocking Fractica's blue light from their sight. She could barely hear the ongoing battle between Lysandros and Garamund.

Kicking an attacking skeleton off the stairs, Yuma shouted, "Get to your prepared places!" She felt the others moving hastily behind her. They might not be soldiers, but the instant way they obeyed her orders put the Grim King's walking bones to shame.

Aidan had suddenly appeared by her side and was fending off an entire phalanx of the dead. She risked looking backward to make sure the stairs were empty. Yuma and Aidan exchanged a glance, a signal. They simultaneously turned and ran up the winding steps. The sound of the clacking skeletons in pursuit was too close for comfort. Yuma did not look back, and when she reached where the herders had gathered, she kicked a peg stuck into the stairs with her heel. Three protruding wooden pegs started spinning before flying off, and the stairs behind Yuma collapsed under the weight of the skeletal soldiers. The Grim King's undead army flailed in the air before scattering to pieces on the streets of Danras below.

Yuma breathed. They had managed to buy some time.

But her relief was short-lived, as the remaining skeletons hesitated for only a brief moment in front of the collapsed stairs before doing something unexpected. One leaned over the gap and grabbed a handhold on the wall. Another climbed over it and grabbed farther up the wall. A third got on the first two's backs. The fourth grabbed on to a landing and the spine of the third. Yuma quickly realized what they were doing—they were building a bridge with their bodies.

Human bones being far from stone or wood, the bridge collapsed more than once during assembly, but the skeletal soldiers kept trying. It would only be a matter of time. An impatient skeleton attempted to cross the bridge before it was completed and jumped to attack Yuma on the other side, but it fell to the streets below without having reached her.

"Aidan, can we break more stairs?" Yuma asked.

"Not quickly enough to matter. From this point up is where the summer repairs were finished."

"Noted. Take care of the people here. I'm going up to see what's happening, to see if this is almost finished."

The herders made way for her up the narrow remaining stairs.

Yuma climbed, passing the door behind which the Host would be singing. She badly wanted to ask him when his song would be finished but bothering him would only delay him. On the roof, she went right to the horn and leaned over the ledge to look down on the blue-lit square below.

Garamund had lost his right hand and was now holding the mace in his left. His armor of bone was shattered in places, the pieces littering the square, and his body was full of scars that hadn't been there when Yuma last watched. Lysandros had likely inflicted the wounds, but each of them had healed.

Lysandros looked unharmed. Yuma sighed in relief. He was as quick and clever as ever, parrying and attacking like some steppe predator.

Garamund wordlessly swung his mace again. Lysandros lightly jumped out of the way and sliced the giant's side with his forearm-mounted blade. Yuma grinned. They might win this battle. If Garamund fell, the undead army would lose their death magic and fall apart. This would be the first defeat Eldred had ever suffered in Merseh.

As Garamund made another swing with the mace, Lysandros ducked and raised his blade at the giant's remaining wrist, but the mace was already gone from his hand, flying through the air. With a loud clang, the square went dark.

Fractica, on the edge of the square, had fallen. Hit by the mace, the lid of the iron box had ripped off and something black had tumbled out of it. Lysandros froze. Yuma immediately turned and ran down the stairs.

"Out of the way!" she screamed, dropping her machete and unhitching the spear from her back.

Aidan and the herders jumped out of her trajectory. At the final step, Yuma leaped and landed on the almost complete bridge of bones. Without hesitating, she ran across it, not listening to the hideous sound of bones cracking under her every frantic step. She didn't have the luxury of dodging the skeletons' attacks—she could only use her spear to ward them off, and pray that they missed on their own. She gritted her teeth through the sharp pain of the skeletal hands clawing at her ankles, thinking only of Lysandros and the danger he was in. As she reached the end of the bone bridge, Yuma jumped down to the street, ignoring the cuts and scratches she'd suffered on the way. The jump was at least three times her height, and she was almost sure she felt something break as she landed and rolled, but she used the shock to get up and keep running.

When she got to the square, Garamund's hand was gripping Lysandros's helm, the emissary dangling in the air like a puppet with its strings cut.

For the first time, Garamund spoke.

"Now die, Inquisitor."

A voice so deep, so cruel, that it could only be *his*. As Garamund was about to dash him against the ground headfirst, Yuma cried, "Grim King!"

Garamund turned to her, and his scar-filled face broke into something resembling a grin. It reminded her of the face Jed's body had made when the Grim King had spoken to her through him.

"Chief Herder of Danras. So, you've realized it is me in this body."

"It's my turn to fight you, *Eldred*!"

As Yuma spoke the name, Garamund's grin twisted, further

263

revealing his sharpened teeth. Gasps escaped through the many windows and doors ajar.

Yuma tied up her braid in a firm knot, unwrapped the leather from the spear tip, and glared at the giant. From Garamund's mouth, Eldred's voice came once again.

"Isn't it time for you to stop this rebellion? Once my army kills your herders, they will drag your Host to me. Then all the bones buried in your catacombs shall be mine. Or do you intend to nick this giant's body with your little stick? Even when you've seen what has happened to this pathetic Imperial sorcerer?"

The Host's singing suddenly grew louder, loud enough for all of Danras to hear. A boy's sharp voice, carrying the most clear and beautiful tune. The song was entering the final phrase. Garamund's dead eyes moved toward the Feast Hall. Everywhere in Danras, windows opened. Heads peeked out.

"Lysandros has not lost," she shouted, as loudly as she could. Loud enough for as many people of Danras as possible to hear. Garamund gave her a questioning look. "He's only done exactly what he was supposed to."

Yuma looked toward the northern sky. The stars trembled, and she couldn't hold back a grin. She pointed her blade at the polestar. From the Host's tower, a high and clear voice was heard throughout the city. The stars swirled around the polestar as Garamund—no, the Grim King—looked up as well.

The whirlpool of stars came together to consolidate around the polestar, creating a light that was somehow brighter than the sum of its parts. The light shone on Danras. The tip of her spear glinted like a torch, reflecting the starlight.

A fierce, cold wind swept through as the converging starlight shone down. Wind chimes sang in chorus as the Host's final high note rang out.

Glancing at the sharp shadow that fell behind her, Yuma declared, "It is now day. This battle is over."

A beast-like cry came from Garamund's mouth. Every wound Lysandros had inflicted came back, bursting with black blood. The giant dropped down on one knee and let go of Lysandros.

Yuma rushed forward, stepping up on Garamund's bent knee and plunging her spear into the giant's neck with both hands. The Grim King's general finally collapsed on the ground.

She heard cheers coming from the Feast Hall, and knew that the undead army must've fallen as well. But she didn't celebrate with them—Yuma rushed to Lysandros's side and urgently patted his helmet, crying, "Emissary! Emissary, are you all right!"

His visor slid up, revealing his familiar smile.

"Chief Herder, I am fine. But Fractica—"

Yuma threw off his helmet and covered his lips with hers. When she finally detached herself, he spoke again.

"Chief Herder chooses this moment to steal a kiss, when I can't move." He laughed weakly. "Fractica needs to be taken care of if I'm to regain the use of my body."

Yuma smiled and nodded, wiped the sweat off his brow with the back of her hand, and got up. Fractica was not moving. Under the sunlight that wasn't, she saw that a long box had popped out of Fractica's chassis, and a heavy-looking sack had half fallen out of it.

The box inside the chassis was made of a dull gray metal, and it was wrapped in black chains. A sudden foreboding, a feeling that she should *not* approach the box, came over her, but she ignored it. Garamund's mace must've broken the chassis, loosened the chains, and cracked the seal around the gray box. Vapors of violet wafted out from the inner container.

Yuma bent down to get a closer look. She wondered why this sack was wrapped in something like long bandages that had writing on them—and when she realized what she was looking at, she jumped back in shock.

For she now knew she was looking at a carefully wrapped human corpse.

31

EMERE

The iron door to the underground room of worship opened. Two figures, both wearing hooded cloaks like Rakel's and Emere's, stood on the other side. One was an unfamiliar tall man, and the smaller figure beside him . . .

She lowered her hood and revealed her familiar face, her left eye covered by a red eyepatch. But whether it was the candlelight or the weight of the moment, her countenance seemed darker than he remembered. He wanted to run to her, but there were too many people between them.

Ahmus bowed. "The congregation welcomes you, Your Majesty. Your friend is also here."

She looked around the room at that, and when her eyes found him, she immediately strode toward him. The Ebrians made way before her. Emere didn't know what to say or how to act as he waited for her to close the distance.

Loran held her arms open, and the front of her cloak opened

to reveal her familiar leather armor. The darkness in her face lifted with a glad smile. Emere had barely taken a step forward when he found himself enfolded in her arms.

"Prince Emere! How long has it been? I've long wanted to see you again, but how unexpected the circumstances!"

"Your Majesty. Have you been well . . ." His throat closed and he could not continue. Emere released one of his hands from Loran's firm grasp and wiped a tear from his face, coughing embarrassedly. He noticed Rakel looking closely at them, before he realized the whole room was scrutinizing their exchange.

Ahmus smiled. "Well, now we can rest assured we have the true King of Arland with us. Make way for Her Majesty."

The Ebrians murmured as they shifted, and a small table that had been covered by the crowd appeared. There were two chairs. Ahmus sat down in one and bade Loran to take the other. Seeing Rakel and two others stand by Ahmus on his side, Emere went to Loran's and stood by her.

Ahmus made introductions. "These three are the elders who represent us Ebrians here in the Capital. Ordinarily, we forbid all three of them to ever gather in one place, but the proposal Your Majesty has set before us is of such importance that we have summoned them here together."

Loran nodded at each of them and sat down. Rakel politely returned the nod, as did the other two. Emere examined the two elders he didn't know but who had familiar looks in their eyes. He was reminded of his compatriots in his brother Gwaharad's underground palace.

The meeting began with Loran expressing gratitude for their welcome. And so it began, a talk between two nations that never would've found reason to talk to each other if not for the Empire, taking place in the very bowels of said Empire's capital city.

Emere's eyes barely left Loran as the talk progressed. Each word and phrase of hers was laden with desperate and serious meaning.

". . . Ebria nowadays suffers . . ."

"As for our people scattered across the world, the Empire . . ."

"The Capital now is in a very different situation from two years ago . . ."

Loran made no demands, mostly listened, answered every question put to her, and made an occasional inquiry herself. She had always been like this, even two years ago when the Arlander rebels had conquered the Imperial fort. Loran had always listened more than she spoke. Because, she would explain with a smile, she had nothing but the modest knowledge of a teacher of swordsmanship.

The continuing oppression of Ebrians, their prefect who was nothing more than an attack dog for the Empire even though he himself was an Ebrian, the rescue of Office of Truth prisoners being persecuted for worshipping their god . . . Their stories reminded Emere of how he had lived before coming to the Capital.

Rakel's role was to ask Loran questions. What Loran could do for them, whether she had talked to any other countries, if Arland had an army they could call on . . . Loran's answers were short but respectful, and Rakel did not look satisfied with them.

When the Ebrian elders ran out of words, Loran's voice, low but clear, made itself heard to every person in the room.

"I have listened to your concerns. I understand how difficult it would be to trust an outsider from a faraway land, and a nonbeliever at that. In the spirit of good faith, if there is one request you wish me to fulfill first, then I shall do it."

She looked at Emere and smiled. The four Ebrians talked among themselves in their language. Emere stayed silent, staring back at Loran. He could see what he hadn't noticed before—she looked a little older. Whether it was because of her travels, or because of the tiring business of making alliances, there was fatigue in her face and gestures.

Lowering his voice, he asked, "Your Majesty, will you really do anything they ask of you?"

Loran leaned toward him and whispered, "If it is something I can do, yes. They already know that my only talent is in fighting, so I doubt their request will be something impossible." She considered her words for a moment, and whispered in his ear, "Even with such offers, making alliances has proven to be difficult."

Her tone was laden with exhaustion.

What could Loran do to move the Ebrians a step closer to freedom? The priest and the elders were engaged in heated debate. What did they hold dear? They probably wanted the same result, but they were likely not of the same mind in how to achieve it. A consensus would be a feat in itself.

The discussion here, however, was probably not looking far into the future. The oppression Ebria experienced was different from that of other provinces. Even if they escaped the tyranny of their prefect by leaving their homeland, they would know no peace as long as they worshipped the Nameless God.

Was that why Loran had come here, to the Ebrians in the Capital, and not to Ebria itself?

The debate among the elders was getting harsher. Ahmus

occasionally gave Loran an apologetic look as the discussion dragged on. Just when the tone of their talk made it seem like they would be at it for hours more, the four people said "*Ayula*" at the same time.

The interminable debate terminated; Ahmus turned to Loran.

"We apologize for keeping you waiting. The suggestion you make is no small thing, and we could not come to a consensus. I'm afraid we need to discuss it for a few days more. However, what Your Majesty has achieved thus far is war, and we have always protected our own in subtler, secret ways. Perhaps our homeland is ready to fight, but it is far away; we in the Capital are not ready to battle the Empire. So, whether there is a request we can make of you, and whether there is a commensurate deed we can do in return, is a matter of skepticism for the four of us."

Emere knew this was a politely worded "no." Loran opened her mouth to speak but said nothing, turning her head to Emere instead. The disappointment in her face stabbed him like a knife.

Loran must've wandered the whole world in the two years since disappearing from Arland, just as Emere had done so many years ago. How many peoples had actually agreed to fight alongside Loran and Arland against the Empire? There was no consternation in Loran's face, just disappointment. Something about the way she held it in her face made him think she was used to it.

He couldn't just stand there and watch.

"Then I must alert you to the dangers that we are all facing."

When Emere spoke, Ahmus and the elders looked up at him in surprise—they never would've imagined he would interject in this meeting. He was only there to verify Loran's identity, and the fact that he was a councillor or a Kamori prince did not allow him to intervene in a discussion between Ebria and Arland.

But perhaps what they were discussing now had everything to do with his destiny.

"Commons Councillor Ludvik, with the Office of Truth, is plotting to take control of the Senate and appoint himself as Imperator. It is of the utmost importance that we stop him."

Murmurs. The people in the room shuffled their feet.

"Prince Emere," said Ahmus in a somewhat placating voice, "we thank you for telling this to us, but if that is true, isn't this mere infighting among the Imperial elite? What relevance does any of that have to the business at hand?"

Emere had spoken to Ahmus, but his eyes were on Loran. "Earlier, you said that the Senate is falling in line with the Office of Truth. That they are plotting revenge against Arland." Loran's face didn't change as he spoke and registered no surprise. "They are not going to stop there," Emere continued. "Once Ludvik takes power in the Empire, the whole world will come under the tyranny of the Office of Truth."

Ahmus looked at Rakel, who nodded. No more words were necessary. The people gathered here were Ebrians, the people the Office of Truth had oppressed the most. They knew better than any other peoples what would happen if the Office of Truth took power. But how much danger were they willing to face? Who dared to interfere with the affairs of one of the highest offices of the Empire?

"Prince Emere," said Loran, "I do not know of the Office of Truth well, only what I have heard in the wind. Are they more powerful than the legions?"

"If Ludvik becomes the Imperator, the Office of Truth will control the whole of the Empire, its legions, all the prefects.

They will have the power to burn the world with their fanaticism."

"Then we must cut off the head of the serpent, before that happens."

Loran turned to Ahmus. One didn't have to see the blue fire burning underneath her eyepatch to understand that it was a stare that demanded a decision. Ahmus, Emere realized, was standing at the crossroads of destiny. Just as the Tree Lords had taught, no one could avoid the moment of choice. Ahmus had to make the decision, like a king for his people, as the Circuit of Destiny would say. For the Ebrians in the Capital, and perhaps for all the Ebrians in the world.

As Ahmus's troubled silence lengthened, the room became so quiet they could hear the flames burning on the candles. Just as Emere was about to urge him for an answer, Ahmus spoke.

"How do you know, Prince Emere, that the Office of Truth is attempting to establish an Imperator?"

"There is a faction within the Ministry of Intelligence working against Ludvik. I heard it from them."

Emere debated whether to tell them about meeting Cain inside the Circuit of Destiny, but ultimately decided against it. Mentioning the Circuit here would not help matters.

Ahmus once again glanced at Rakel, who nodded as before. He got to his feet.

"I must consult with the elders. Until then, we invite Her Majesty Loran to stay here. I bid the rest of you be careful of what you speak and guard the holy silence. *Ayula*."

A chorus of "*Ayula*" answered him, and the gathered crowd began to exit the room.

Rakel said to Loran, "Your Majesty, we have a room ready for you. Kesaya will show you the way."

A woman in red and white, who looked to be in her twenties, came forth at the mention of her name and curtsied. Loran nodded her head in response, stood up, and smiled at Emere once again.

"Two whole years since we last met, and here we are without even a chance to have a drink. Once affairs are settled here—or not settled, as it were—I do wish to hear about your time since our last meeting."

"I as well."

He was staring at Loran's back as she followed Kesaya out the door when Rakel laid her hand on Emere's arm.

"I don't know if this is a good idea."

"Making an alliance with King Loran?"

Rakel nodded. "I also think we need to stop the Office of Truth from taking control of the Empire. And any other time, this would've been impossible, like trying to stop an earthquake or a tidal wave . . ."

"But now we have King Loran."

"That's what I worry about. Emere, Ahmus will do whatever I advise him to do. I need to know what you think. If we interfere in Imperial politics, what happens after? That tiny army in Arland defeating a single legion among a hundred has made the Empire this hostile, so what do you think would happen if we were found responsible for blocking the transition of power that the Senate approved in all but name?"

They stared at each other. The Rakel Emere knew was always calm in the face of danger, like the surgeon she was. She had been his source of stability in their travels together. Now, he could not read her expression.

"Rakel, I don't know what would happen either. But I do know one thing."

"What's that?"

"Whatever happens, it never ends. There's always something that follows, a new chance, a new decision to make."

Rakel grinned. "Except for us."

For the first time in a long time, Emere reached out and swept his fingers through Rakel's hair.

"When we parted ten years ago, I thought so, too. But here we are, together again. We might not be the way we were, but this is a wonderful next thing."

Rakel floated a faint smile and turned her head just enough to avoid his gaze. Emere stood there waiting for her to say something back, but Rakel's lips never parted.

32

ARIENNE

Far away, against the gray sky, a vague mountainous shadow loomed over the wasteland. According to Noam, this was where Eldred had resided as he ruled over Mersia.

"It will be another two days or so from here," said Noam, and Arienne's heart began to thump. What monstrous things, what secrets must lie there. In the tower inside her mind, Arienne mentioned this to Noam, sitting down on the large leather bed that she had claimed as her own. Noam, who had his own room now but preferred to spend time with Tychon in the evenings, rocked the cradle while the baby slept inside.

"I think you're imagining some kind of ruin full of puzzles," he said nonchalantly, "but the Imperials refitted and used that place for their legion for almost a hundred years. They've taken everything they wanted and thrown away the rest. I've been inside a few times to help them with their generators. There is no mystery left there."

This was dispiriting. "Oh? Then I'll depend on you for directions when we're there."

"The Hundred and Seventh Legion was garrisoned there when I was alive. Led by a Legate Havtamu, who was a really impressive man, by the way. More popular among the people of Danras than the prefect who was a Mersian native."

Since leaving Danras, Noam had begun to talk more. Only a few days ago, he could only remember his name, but something had changed about him. Noam went on for a bit more before sighing. "I suppose they all died that day."

The Star of Mersia had indeed devastated Danras and all other cities, the rich grasslands, and the entire Imperial legion stationed in Mersia. But this was the biggest mystery—a legion would include thousands of personnel, a fort, and valuable provisions and equipment. Was the Empire so eager to get rid of Mersia that they would sacrifice all of that? Eldred had said they wouldn't, that Mersia had never declared independence, that the Empire had no intention of destroying Mersia.

"Noam, what do you think? Would the Empire have done that on purpose?"

He frowned. "It's unimaginable. There must've been something else."

"Your memory is returning," persisted Arienne, "so I'll try asking again. That day, you tried to run to the catacombs. Do you remember exactly what you felt, what made you think the Host's protection over the catacombs would protect you from that . . . accident?"

Noam's features began to blur again. As before, this happened when he tried to remember something he couldn't. Arienne quickly grabbed his face and slapped him on both cheeks.

"Stay with me! You don't have to remember now."

But she had her theory. Noam wouldn't have run to the protections of the catacombs if the accident didn't remind him of Eldred in some way. Maybe Eldred, not the Empire, was behind the destruction of Mersia.

Leaving the tower in her mind and returning to the wasteland, she checked to see if Aron's reins were still wound around her hand. There was even less grass here as they moved away from the city. She could easily count the number of Aron's ribs now.

She returned to the room in the tower. This had been Yuma's room, but the bed felt new. The cradle was new as well. It rocked from side to side, but there were no marks ground into the floor beneath it. Had Tychon ever even lain in this crib during his lifetime?

Noam still sat on the floor, looking dazed.

"You should go back to your room," she said.

"There's so much space; can't I just sleep here?"

"Are you my lover? My child?"

"Then what about Tychon?"

"You are forcing me to consider violent alternatives," Arienne growled, becoming frustrated.

"No, I mean, can I take Tychon with me? I can take the whole cradle with me."

". . . Why are you so afraid of being alone?"

Noam hesitated. Arienne frowned, waiting for his answer.

"I smell the Grim King . . . even more than before. Maybe because we're so near his castle. And I can't sleep."

"You're a ghost. You don't need sleep." Still, she gestured toward Tychon, giving him permission. Noam carefully lifted the cradle, baby and all. "Be careful so he doesn't wake."

Looking more cheerful than a moment before, Noam left the room. Arienne crawled underneath the covers. The bed was hard, and the sheets were rough. She still couldn't believe she had imagined a whole building filled with materials she did not even know existed.

"Some memory the ghosts gave me," she murmured. After making that first room in her mind and letting Eldred inside, she had a suspicion that her mind had never been wholly her own ever since. A book she had never read before—*The Sorcerer of Mersia*—once appeared in that room, after all. If her mind was occupied with things like that from outside her memory, would she eventually disappear? These were the thoughts that swirled in her head as she fell asleep.

The journey continued the next day. The red wasteland, the gray sky—nothing seemed to change no matter how long she walked, though the mountainous shadow did loom larger and larger.

Finally, the traces of the Imperial road led right up to the gates of the walls around the castle, which looked as if it had been carved out of a single slab of rock. The gate's thick wooden gates had melted, hanging precariously on their hinges. Arienne tied Aron's reins upon the corner of the gate's iron ornament, a gigantic double-falcon insignia of the Empire.

"I won't be long."

Such words wouldn't be necessary if there was a guarantee she would return. The smell of the Grim King that had unnerved

Noam was so strong here that she could feel it in the air, as if it were grasping at her skin. There was danger here.

As soon as she set foot inside the walls of the castle, she felt Noam tremble in the tower in her mind. Tychon opened his eyes. The wind chimes hanging from the eaves made a barely perceptible sound.

Eldred's castle had not been built by piling up stones. Rather, it was like a great slab of obsidian had decided one day to become a castle. Two identical thick towers rose high into the air in the middle, and three smaller towers surrounded them, forming a triangle.

"Where do we go from here?" whispered Arienne.

"What do you want to see?"

The memory of Yuma in Fractica's dream had asked Arienne to go find the real Yuma in the Grim King's castle, but that was the only bit of information she had.

"Is there a prison here? Or maybe a graveyard, or a crypt?"

"The graveyard is beyond the castle walls. It was forbidden to store corpses within the fort."

"Why?"

"By order of Grand Inquisitor Lysandros. He thought the castle could still harbor the Grim King's curses. But the prison is underground."

"Good. Tell me how to get there." She began walking to the doors of the castle itself, traversing the vast courtyard between the wall and the castle. Here and there were collapsed huts. Arienne scraped at the rough red dirt under her feet. Underneath the top layer was the same rock that made up the walls. She imagined lines upon lines of legionaries standing at attention in this courtyard, a hundred years ago. Perhaps the whole legion could have fit in here.

Yet another hundred years ago, Eldred's army of bones and rotting flesh had filled the same space. This had been a living graveyard, until the Empire came for its king.

Noam was rattling off details about the legion and the fortress, as if to forget his fear of this place. He must have run out of things to say before she had made it across the courtyard, though, for he simply began to repeat the things he'd already said.

"How is Tychon?" she asked, trying to distract him from his fears.

"He's all right. I'm watching him. He's awake."

She could hear Tychon's cooing. To Arienne's ear, they were clearer and seemed more meaningful than before.

"Maybe he knows his mother is here."

Arienne continued across the courtyard, looking for a door to get inside the closest tower. Noam had said the resident legion had refitted the place, but aside from a few collapsed warehouses in the courtyard, they didn't seem to have touched the exterior at all.

Finally, Arienne reached the obsidian castle doors, which were nearly indistinguishable from the walls. She took a deep breath before pushing them open; contrary to their size and appearance, the doors opened smoothly and without a sound.

Darkness. Arienne realized she had left her lantern behind and infused Power into her glass orb instead. The weak light reflected on the dark edges of the walls, showing her the outline of the antechamber.

"It doesn't look that refitted inside, either," she murmured.

Odd pillars jutted from the floor, shelves popped out of the walls, and tables and chairs were so melted it was miraculous she could recognize what they were at all. The "refitting" the Imperials had done here was simply furnishing the building and doing nothing to its structure or aesthetics. It made sense—regardless of the Empire's pride for everything Imperial, she doubted they would've wanted to touch anything in this strange and special place any more than was necessary.

Somehow, the room reminded her of the dragon's cave in Arland, without looking anything like that place.

"Now where do we go?" she asked.

"Behind the stone table there," replied Noam, "is a tunnel going down to the underground level."

She crossed the hall. She walked past the huge, Imperial-style stone table that a hundred years ago might have been surrounded by legates and centurions in shining armor and velvet cloaks. She discovered an unassuming wooden door, half melted and fallen off the hinge. The tunnel's entrance stood before her like the open mouth of a giant beast. The light of her orb illuminated stairs going downward. There wasn't a sound.

Arienne began to descend.

33

YUMA

The long winter was coming to an end. It was perhaps the most peaceful winter Danras had ever seen, as the defeated Grim King had been silent. He made no demands of Danras, not for conscripts and tithes, nor for the Imperial emissary. Travelers from Iorca and Lansis brought similar news.

Several times had Yuma asked Lysandros about the corpse hidden inside Fractica. Every time, Lysandros refused to answer, saying that it was a state secret he couldn't reveal yet. She eventually gave up. After all, Merseh probably had its own peculiarities, from a foreigner's point of view. Perhaps the Empire attributed a special meaning to their dead. As the Emissary had shown his respect for the customs of this land, she decided she would do the same for his.

Yuma had lent her winter house to Lysandros, as he needed an official residence to receive visitors from all over Merseh as the Empire's alliance-building with it began. The Host suggested Yuma move to an empty room in the Feast Hall. At first, it was too much space for her and far from cozy, but as winter passed, she accumulated various little gifts. The other day, Lysandros came bearing a baby's cradle that he had made with his own hands.

It was a simple affair and not expertly done, but a thing unseen in Danras, meant to rock the baby to sleep. There were letters awkwardly engraved into the inside headboard. Yuma couldn't read Imperial yet, but she knew this was the name of the baby—Tychon. When the Host prophesied a boy would be born to them, Lysandros had explained that it was an Imperial tradition for a man to bring the mother of his child a cradle with the name of their baby engraved into it. When he suggested he would make a new cradle if Yuma did not like the name, she laughed and said the name would suit the baby just fine.

That the Chief Herder of Danras was pregnant was a cause for celebration in the city. Some wondered why she didn't marry Lysandros and hold a large wedding, but Yuma thought it inappropriate for the Chief Herder to marry a foreigner that many in Danras did not yet know well. It was part of the reason why she accepted the Host's invitation to move into the Feast Hall, instead of living with Lysandros at her winter house.

Some weeks had passed since the passage through the southwestern range of the Rook Mountains—which the Grim King had sealed—was reopened. When construction on it started, she had often gone for inspections without much of a problem; but a month later, sitting on a saddle became too much. The thought that she would not make it to this year's herding made her heart sink. Yuma sat in her chair and placed one hand over her visibly pregnant stomach and rocked the cradle with the other. As she was thinking about who she should choose to step in to lead this year's herding for her, someone cleared their throat outside her door.

"Come in."

The Host entered. He wore not the ceremonial robe of feathers or the somber black garments, but the clothes of an ordinary child. As Yuma made to stand, he waved at her to remain seated.

"Chief Herder, I have something to discuss with you. Are you occupied?"

"Not at all. Please sit." She gestured to a chair near her.

"You've decided on a name?"

"Yes, we're calling him Tychon."

"Strange name. Well, so is 'Lysandros,' I suppose." He nodded a few times and looked at the cradle. The fact that he was taking his time despite having something to discuss meant the matter must be very serious indeed. Yuma politely waited him out, a silence that was meant to urge him to speak.

Finally, staring at her hand rocking the cradle, he spoke.

"I've heard the passage through the southwest is open. The Empire will be arriving soon."

"Yes, today even, if the weather holds. But I suspect sometime in the next three days."

The silence that followed was a little longer than the moment before.

"Whatever happens," the Host said, "we must face—and defeat—the Grim King."

"Don't worry. The Empire will handle him. Especially if you help them—"

"That's what I wished to discuss," the Host said, quickly cutting her off. "I am leaving Danras."

Surely the Host was joking, so she laughed. But his expression was serious, which struck horror in her eyes.

"What are you talking about? Who will protect Danras if not the Host?"

"Protect Danras from what? If the Grim King is no longer here, then Danras should no longer need the Host."

Yuma tried not to get too agitated. Carefully, she stood.

"Still, that you should leave home is too—"

"Regardless, the Empire will never let me stay."

"What?"

Unlike her, the Host was completely calm. "I've known for a long time. That's what the auguries said, ever since you brought Lysandros to my carriage. Have you not heard that the Empire forces all sorcerers to go to its capital?"

"But the Host is not a sorcerer."

"That isn't what they think." He smiled, and Yuma could not help thinking it was forced.

"I will go speak to Lysandros this minute." As she stood up to get her coat, the Host grabbed her sleeve. His hand was the small hand of a child.

"We already talked it through yesterday. That I would leave without resisting. Lysandros seemed relieved that I brought it up first. So, you don't need to say anything. A child's parents should lose no love for each other, not for things like this."

Stupefied, Yuma sat back down.

"I'm going of my own volition," continued the Host, "which might mean they'll treat me a little better. From what I've heard, it is truly a large and fanciful city. Ten times the size of Danras!

People from all over the world living in one place, and I would get to learn a bit of the Empire's sorcery. Is this not good?"

How could this be good?

"But the Host and Danras have existed together for generations," Yuma countered. "What would happen to Danras if it lost the Host?"

The Host smiled bitterly.

"Chief Herder. Sometimes I wish to be not the Host but just a thirteen-year-old boy named Dalan. So, I'm not entirely dreading my new life, you see. And Danras . . . Without the Grim King, Merseh will be a completely new country. What would it matter, then, if we had a Host or not? Do not fret," he said, trying to reassure her. "If I knew you would feel this way, I would've slipped away without saying anything. Lysandros came up with a way to keep the catacombs safe, to feed Power to the enchantment in my stead, so nobody will even notice."

Yuma didn't know how to feel. Sensing this, the Host picked up the small box he had laid down next to him.

"As a baby is being born, you will need a receiving blanket. I wanted to leave you one gift before I went."

Yuma opened the box. Inside was a thick blanket, a pretty blue with white flowers embroidered on it. The Host stretched out his hand and stroked the embroidery.

"These flowers bloom on the grasslands," he explained.

"I have been at many herdings but never seen these. What are they called?"

"They were very common when the first Host came to Danras, so we just called them grass flowers. Did you know that over hundreds of years, the world has become cooler and cooler? These grasslands were once very warm. So, you don't see these flowers here now. That is the way of life. If one thing is whole, another decays, and we forget even the memories of things that once were."

He then gave her a blessing for a safe delivery and left. Alone, Yuma sat staring into the cradle, lost in thought. Why hadn't Lysandros told her about this? If she had known before that this path would lead to the Host leaving, would she have been insistent on aligning with the Empire? What kind of place would Merseh be without the Grim King *and* the Host . . .

"Foolish girl. Too late to have such thoughts now."

The sudden voice made her head jerk up. She was no longer in her spacious quarters in the Feast Hall but in an even larger room where everything was made of obsidian. In the middle was a wide stairway of black rock, and the voice was coming from above it. There was a strange noise in the background, nothing she had ever heard before.

"Grim King."

She had never laid eyes on him directly like this, but she knew it was him. A tall man sat on a throne made of human bones, wearing robes that looked woven from fire and shadow. He was gaunt. On his head was a crown woven of bones and gold.

"So, do you find the Empire more to your liking than me?"

"The Empire is our equal ally, not our conqueror. Nor are they tyrants who kill people on a whim."

The Grim King scoffed.

"Is that so? Your 'equal ally' has taken your Host like a pig to a slaughterhouse."

"The Host goes to their capital of his own volition." She said this, even when she knew the truth.

"Well, well, well," mocked the Grim King, "if the Empire only wants to hold hands, then it's not a bad idea to live your life fat and happy in its grasp. But should they want more . . ."

Yuma could not stand where she was any longer. As she made her way up the obsidian steps toward the throne of bones, the Grim King stopped speaking. Each of her steps echoed in the room.

"How did you bring me here?" she asked.

"Rest assured this is not my true castle, and you are still in that shabby little hut sitting next to that shabby little cradle that isn't fit for a horse's trough." He cackled. "The child inside of you has potential. Seeing as he doesn't even have a true form yet but still can bring us together . . . Yes, this is your dream. And I have entered it through your son."

This didn't make much sense to her, but she had other objections to voice first. "I may have been your subject the last time we met, but we are now enemies. What do you propose to do this time? Since your eyes are all over the Rook Mountains, you should know the Imperial forces are coming from the southwest, yes?"

"Do you remember, when we met last summer, how I said I would flood the river to sink Danras into the steppe?"

This time, it was Yuma who scoffed.

"Why don't you try? The Trina River is low because of the winter, and even that much is frozen. The Imperial forces will have your castle surrounded by the time it thaws. You can bring forth your armies that need no water or food, but how long can you withstand an enemy that has the support of Danras?"

"You are correct," said the Grim King. "I won't last the next autumn. I will be too busy fighting such a siege that Danras couldn't be further from my mind. Your child will be in the light of the world by then as well. Perhaps not by the starlight of Merseh, though."

Inexplicably, a chill ran down Yuma's back at these words.

"You still do not understand," he continued, "what it means that we can talk as we do now. This would not be possible if yours were a common child. Do you know what the Empire does to uncommon children? And do you think such a child would escape the notice of someone who is an inquisitor of the Empire—his own child no less?"

34

EMERE

That night, Emere walked alone through the streets to Rakel's house. Rakel had said it would be better if he stayed hidden underground while the Elders discussed the situation, but it did not sit well with him that Septima could wake up in a strange place with only Rakel's assistant, whom she didn't know. But what vexed him the most was what he was feeling after meeting Loran in the Ebrian hideout.

Loran had been even more majestic than he remembered. She now exuded confidence that befitted a true king who vanquished the mightiest of the Empire's vaunted arsenal. It was exactly what he had foreseen in her, ever since he'd met her.

Still, Emere found himself desperately looking for something even greater in Loran. Something that would lift him up. Something that would vindicate his life of wandering and questioning. Something that would fulfill his destiny yet unknown. It was unfair to Loran, or any mortal person, to have such things expected of them, but he still sought it.

Did he worship the image of Loran, like the Ebrians worshipped their Nameless God? Did he believe that she would save him? It was a troubling thought for Emere.

Then there was Rakel's question, of what would happen if the Ebrians started interfering with the politics of the Empire. The coming storm first began to brew with Arland's victory and the Grand Inquisitor Lysandros's death. Even if Ludvik could be stopped, could they truly hold back the chaos approaching from the horizon? How would the Empire take it if Loran intervened in Imperial politics, the same Loran who defeated an entire legion at Arland?

And Emere couldn't forget that the very Power generator that he stole caused the Great Fire and killed countless people, including Rakel's husband. There was no way to make up for what he had done, however unknowingly, and he still couldn't bring himself to tell Rakel about his involvement. His action had not only led to those deaths, but also threatened the Senate enough that they turned to Ludvik and the Office of Truth. Everything was linked. Everything was caused by everything else, and in turn caused everything. The Tree Lords had taught him that destiny was a moment of choice. What meaning did a choice have, when you could not predict its outcome? The Circuit of Destiny had said that one who decided destinies of many was a king. Was this how kings felt?

Bowing his head at every streetlamp and clutching his robe tightly about him, Emere finally arrived at Rakel's house.

"Forgotten to lock it, has she," he mumbled as he opened the door, smiling at the memory of Rakel telling her assistant to always keep the door locked. As soon as the door shut behind him, though, something cold and sharp pushed against his neck and his arm was pulled back.

Emere knew a second of surprise and fear before he heard Septima's voice. "Councillor?"

"Yes, now please remove your knife," Emere replied wryly.

His arm was freed, and the knife removed. Emere stepped away and looked back at Septima. Despite her bandaged chest, she had put on Rakel's white robe that usually hung in the surgery, and she held a scalpel in her hand.

"What happened to the young woman who was here?"

"I woke up and found myself in an unfamiliar place," said Septima, "so I gagged her and tied her up upstairs." She sounded so justified that Emere almost nodded as if she had put a child to bed.

"She's just a surgeon's helper! Please release her."

Septima picked up the wanted poster on the surgical table and shook it in front of him. "I would like a detailed explanation first, if you will. What happened to my men? Where are we?"

Emere gestured for her to sit and told her of everything that had happened—how they had tried to escape the labyrinth, but Septima had been struck by the Zero Legion's bolt. But he would not mention the Ebrians and their secret congregation, and it felt impossible to even speak Loran's name. Even if Septima was on his side, he could not ignore the fact that she was an agent of the Ministry of Intelligence.

She did not seem satisfied with his story, grimacing as she patted her wound. "So what do you plan to do now, Councillor?"

"We must stop Ludvik."

"And is that why you came all the way here to see your old lover?" Septima said dryly. "To summon the help of the Ebrians?"

Emere forgot to breathe. "What?"

"Ebrians always gather around their god, and we know of such a congregation in the Capital. They seem harmless, and we let them be so that we can use them as bargaining chips when we need something from the Office of Truth. I understand your hesitation in sharing your plans with me, but you must understand that you can't fight Truth while keeping all your secrets to yourself."

"That wasn't my first strategy in coming here," Emere replied truthfully. "But surely the Ebrians, more than anyone else, do not want the Office of Truth to come into power?"

"We are dealing with an Imperial office that commands the Zero Legion. Not even all the Ebrians of the Capital—even if you could gather all of them together—could ever win against these people."

But perhaps things would be different if King Loran succeeded in her alliance-building, though he would never mention Loran to a Ministry of Intelligence agent, however disgraced she might be. The fact that the ringleader of the Arland rebellion was right here in the Capital might be an even more urgent matter for Septima than the Office of Truth's machinations.

Sighing, he turned his head. The front door creaked in the night wind.

"Forgot to lock it again."

Just as he walked up to it and held his hand out to close it, a white light shone through the open door.

Septima shouted, "Councillor, duck!"

The door shattered into pieces before him like ice. Emere managed to duck even as he was sent flying backward, but a fragment hit his temple. A whistling noise intensified until he could no longer hear anything. Septima shouted something, but all he could make out was that her lips were moving. His vision blurred, then faded to nothing.

Emere stood on the red wastelands once more. Dizzying images and sounds, indecipherable conversations assaulted his senses as he struggled to breathe. He didn't understand the rage and sorrow filtering through him, but there had to be an end to them. The thought made him calm.

He must've lost consciousness in the attack, and Cain or the Circuit of Destiny had pulled him here in that moment.

"The Circuit is strange. It was made by people out of people, but it doesn't think like people. What happens when over three hundred Powered corpses gather in one place? I've been here for some time and still can't understand it."

Cain's voice. There he sat, in a simple wooden chair. Emere turned to him.

"Do you know who attacked Rakel's house just now?"

Cain turned his gaze toward the distance for a moment before meeting Emere's eyes again. "A detachment of the Zero Legion of the Office of Truth. I don't know how they discovered your whereabouts. Septima seems to have escaped somehow."

Someone must've spotted him coming back from the congregation.

"I'll be dead soon," he said. If he wasn't dead already.

Cain shook his head. "They've taken you alive. Ludvik must have unfinished business with you."

Emere scoffed. "Business? I'm a nothing, a dreamer who spent his life chasing after foolish hopes, barely more than a title. And not even a title anymore, now that I am a wanted man."

"That isn't so. You have the destiny of a king."

This came from a different voice—Loran's voice, though he could now hear the difference from the real one he had just recently heard in the underground congregation.

"Enough with the riddles!" Emere strode up to the vision of Loran, who had appeared before him as he spat out his words.

The Circuit masked as Loran looked back at him, unperturbed.

"It is a king who decides destiny. Your time is drawing near."

Emere glared at Loran, this avatar of the Circuit of Destiny. His body was being held by the Office of Truth, and his destiny was to be decided by Ludvik, a man who had already tried to kill him and who could now do it at his leisure. But *Emere* decided destiny?

"I refuse to listen to you anymore," Emere scoffed. "The real Loran is already here in the Capital. I'm not the one who will defeat Ludvik. It will be Loran, King of Arland, and the Ebrians in the Capital who do it. *They* are the ones who shall decide destiny."

As the words left his mouth, he felt an emptiness in his chest, which quickly filled with a feeling of powerlessness. Of course he would never be king; of course such a destiny was never in his future.

A hint of sorrow passed over Loran's—the Circuit of Destiny's—face. But Emere found the feelings of something that wasn't even human anymore impossible to understand.

Cain said, "We don't know what Ludvik wants, Councillor. I will try to help you any way I can from here. But you must never give Ludvik what he wants."

Loran turned to Cain. "Cain, you must not interfere with what these two will do."

Cain stood. "My dear dead sorcerers, I think I have come to a decent understanding of how things work in here." He smirked. "If you wish to stop me, try."

On the red earth, against the violet sky, Cain and Loran stared at each other. Emere felt a pressure in his chest, as if a clawed hand were gripping his heart.

Something cold hit his face. Emere screwed his eyes shut and opened them. The wasteland was gone, and Emere was tied to a wooden pole. Before him stood a burly woman holding a dripping bucket, and next to him stood Ludvik, wearing armor over the dress uniform of the Office of Truth with the tassels of golden thread to represent his native Tythonia.

"Your Royal Highness, how tragic our reunion is under such unfortunate circumstances. But you already understand why we must meet this way."

A full moon hung in the sky. Orders were being barked somewhere, with answering choruses of affirmation. Clanking armor, turning wheels, marching feet . . . The sounds came with the occasional flash or glimmer of Powered pale blue light. Emere saw a group of soldiers in white armor pass by some paces beyond him. Then another, this time in Powered white armor. It must be the day the Office of Truth had planned for so long.

Ludvik stared up at the sky and said, "Now, this very moment, is our destiny."

Emere found himself, of late, getting quite sick of destiny.

35

ARIENNE

The illumination of her glass orb barely reached a step beyond her. In this place, darkness felt not like the absence of light but like substance that filled the air. She walked through it on and on, until she felt exhausted and hungry, but the black rock steps going down continued endlessly.

The stickiness of the air was getting worse. As she touched the orb, a stinging pain made her look down at her hand. It was now covered in countless little pustules.

Noam shivered in his room inside the wooden tower in her mind. He was clearly overwhelmed by the smell of the Grim King, but never once did he suggest they turn back.

"How strange. This can't be right. It can't be this deep . . ." Noam continued to mutter. "It was only once, but I *have* been here. It wasn't this deep."

How could the shadow of the Grim King be this thick nearly two centuries after his occupation of the castle?

Arienne stumbled and almost tripped. She looked down and saw a lump of what looked like stone and cloth on the stairs—then she realized the cloth was an Imperial uniform. She looked closer and saw a nameplate. CENTURION JUNIA. It was a skeleton, the bones so melted that she could barely comprehend that it was the remains of a person.

The darkness felt even more palpable. Then she realized that it was, somewhat, as there was a thin black fog—no, more like smoke—permeating the air.

"Danras wasn't this bad . . ." she murmured, and suddenly she heard a whisper in the smoke, like the sound of a snake slithering by in the grass on a dark, calm night. Arienne held her breath and listened hard. She could hear it clearly.

". . . hurts . . ."

A sudden piercing pain in her ear made her slip and fall on the steps. She slammed into the makeshift wooden banister, and the half-melted and rotted wood broke off and fell into the bottomless abyss. Arienne grabbed on to the side of the step before she fell with it, but the edge of the slick obsidian cut into her hand like a blade and she screamed. Her scream did not echo, but the whisper multiplied into dozens, indiscernible in their cacophony.

Her heart pounded. Her hand kept slipping on her own blood. Fearing she would fall in the attempt, Arienne swung herself to the other side of the staircase with all her might and grabbed on to the other step with her other hand. Slowly, she pulled herself up. How glad she was that she hadn't brought a rucksack with her! She leaned against the wall of the steps and caught her breath, reminded of the collapsing stairs she had climbed in Danras. How many near misses, she wondered, was she allowed before dying horribly? There had been so many close calls in the last few years . . .

Something warm trickled down her neck. It was sticky. Only by the light of her orb did she realize her ear was bleeding, and the pustules on her hands had all burst from her exertions a moment ago. Just leaning a hand against the wall now hurt.

But Arienne stood and kept walking down.

"Noam, how is the tower?" In truth, she knew the tilt and creak of every single panel in that building, but she desperately needed to hear someone's voice as she descended deeper into the unending darkness.

"It's the same. Tychon is fine, too."

"And the weather?"

She felt Noam get up and walk to the window.

"The usual. Nothing that you could really call weather."

Her mind must be all right, then, but her body was getting worse with each step. She could feel her body wanting to melt into the thin black smoke, like the bones and wood of Mersia, melt with the pained voices that she couldn't decipher. She knew, then, what permeated this place.

"Noam, remember how I said the thing that destroyed Mersia had come to be known as the 'Star of Mersia'?" Arienne swallowed. "I think it's still here somehow."

It must have even made its way down into this deep, secret crack of the castle. But why it lingered after all those years, Arienne couldn't even guess.

". . . Should you be here then?"

"I think I'd have been dead a long time ago if this was anything more than just a residue of it. I should be fine, as long as I don't stay for too long . . ."

But it was a force—a *poison*—that had taken down a whole country. No matter how faint the trace, no mortal could withstand it for too long. Could she live, if she turned back now? Her joints throbbed with a pain she had never felt before. She strained to keep up her pace.

The poisonous whispers continued. She tried not to listen to them, hoping that they wouldn't affect her as long as she didn't understand. Soon, it felt like the words were being whispered directly into her head. She kept ignoring them. If she gave them even a bit of thought, she would understand what they were saying. And that must not happen. She must not understand them, else the poison would surely flood her mind and destroy her . . . But then, Arienne lifted her head and glared into the dark.

"No."

"No what?" asked Noam.

"I didn't come all this way just to *not* listen."

Arienne sat down in the middle of the steps and crossed her legs. She listened intently to the many whispering voices. Something poured over her like a waterfall, and there was a ringing in her head as if she'd been struck. Her own heartbeat was like a war drum in her head. Something was filling up . . .

"Arienne! Arienne! Outside, there's, there's a storm!"

Noam's shouts came to her like he was on a faraway hill. With his voice came the frantic cacophony of the wind chimes of the tower in her mind. Arienne ignored these sounds, instead focusing on each whisper and listening to them one by one.

A sobbing filled with sorrow, from the shaman Yarin of the

distant southern island country of Arpheia. The king with his long black hair and renowned skill on the lute had been her husband, and the queen with her famously fine singing voice and embroidery her wife. When both were murdered by the legionaries as they breached the palace, Yarin had chosen to end her life during the battle by hanging herself on a length of silk rope. In the Circuit of Destiny, Yarin was number 21.

Radegunt was a priest of the thunder god of Tythonia. When their god was torn limb from limb by a gigatherion, he held a mourning ceremony in secret, which led to a spy informing on him to the prefect. Dragged to the Capital, he awaited trial for five years before dying in prison. In the Circuit of Destiny, Radegunt was number 217.

Horatia, native to the Imperial Capital, was considered the brightest sorcerer of her era, ever since she was young. On the night of her twenty-fourth birthday, as she was returning home from drinking with friends, she was assaulted in an alley and strangled to death. As she died, she glimpsed that her assailant was her sister. The Office of Truth had paid a handsome fee to her sister when her body was handed over, and their family business managed to pay off its debts and thrive again. In the Circuit of Destiny, Horatia was number 134.

Sandur was a shadow actor in the peninsular country of Feredan in the southwest. He was impressively tall, and completely hairless from head to toe. A sorcerer of unprecedented talent in the history of Feredan, he used his magic only for the stage, just as he had been taught. He had easily surrendered to the Empire and lived for four years in a house too small for him before his death by suicide. In the Circuit of Destiny, Sandur was number 182.

Dalan was the Host of the city of Danras in Mersia, the last in a long line. Understanding his fate when the Empire came to his country, he walked into the Imperial Capital of his own accord, but a year later was held under investigation by the Office of Truth and executed. His whispers carried the smell of the wooden tower in Arienne's mind. In the Circuit of Destiny, Dalan was number 314.

And the Grim King of Mersia, Eldred . . . She knew his story all too well. In the Circuit of Destiny, he was number 328.

The whispers dug into Arienne's mind. Each of them a famed sorcerer at one time, and now Power generator of the Circuit of Destiny. Trapped in a death that wasn't death, watching over the world, taking in all that had happened.

Everything they had seen, heard, and predicted for the Empire, the destinies they created—all of it poured into Arienne, through her eyes, ears, and pores.

Arienne witnessed the Thiopsian Famine, which lasted three years and ended with a million dead. She suffered the Calidian Purge, where the defiant followers of the One God were massacred by the thousands by Powered war machines. She ran from the hounds of the Tanvalian prefect, goaded into the jungle to live like an animal. And more. The torment felt endless.

The backs of her eyes were hot. Something like tears or blood kept welling up there. These low whispers must have been screams unbearable to the mortal ear, when they were first unleashed onto Mersia all those years ago.

"Arienne! Can you hear me?"

Noam's shouts felt even farther away than before. Arienne tried to hold on to her consciousness through the flood of stories.

"Noam," she gasped, barely managing to speak. "How . . . is Tychon?" she gritted out.

"Asleep!"

"Wake him."

"He won't wake up! The whole building is about to fly away, but he's still sleeping!"

But it was because the storm was so turbulent that he was fast asleep. Her mind was collapsing. Which in this moment was better than her body collapsing, because she still needed to continue on.

Arienne fought to stand up and then began limping down the stairs. Each step was an agony like nothing she'd ever suffered, but she willed herself to walk, and soon, she was running through the pain. Her knees and ankles hurt and her eyes were burning and her head felt like it was about to burst, but she went down the steps three at a time, seeing nothing in front of her but relying completely on the intuition of her feet. She knew she might die here. But she had to meet her first. She had to find Yuma, the Chief Herder of Danras.

Her feet met something hard quicker than she'd expected and she stumbled forward onto her hands and knees as the whispers and the visions came to a sudden stop. There were no more steps now, just a level floor. Arienne, with much difficulty, got to her feet again. She had broken something, but what she noticed was not the pain of a fractured bone, but the quiet. The air wasn't sticky anymore. The orb around her neck was brighter than ever, but her vision was too blurry to make out anything.

Something at her feet sparkled in the light. Not the black of obsidian but a yellow. Arienne picked it up. Only after peering at it closely with her nearly blind eyes and touching it all over did she realize it was a broken crown. Gold entangled with bone . . .

"Noam, how are things now?"

He sighed. "Better. I thought we were going to die. But the building is fine now."

"Wake Tychon."

"He looks really tired—"

"Wake him. Tell him his mother is coming to see him."

36

YUMA

The Host's send-off feast, the final meal he would prepare for them, was strangely peaceful. Everyone said they would miss the Host, who had overseen their funerals and weddings and festivals, who had cooked for them and protected their city and orox herds from the Grim King, but no one tried to stop him. No one threw themselves across his path, begging him not to leave. The Imperial delegation arrived before their army, and a few of its members wasted no time in taking the Host and leaving Danras.

After the farewell, Yuma went back to her room in the Feast Hall, troubled and worried for the Host. He had said that, without the Grim King, Danras had no need for him anymore. But if the Host was no longer needed, was the Feast Hall? The Spear of Hope? That was when she noticed that the spear was missing from her room.

Yuma went to the Host's room, to find the spear's leather wrappings among the discarded ceremonial garb. Old Vella was there gathering her own things, as she no longer had a Host to take care of. Yuma asked Vella about the Spear of Hope, and the old attendant explained to her that the Host had taken it with him.

After Vella left the room, Yuma stood there looking at the feathered garbs abandoned in the corner. Something new was coming to Merseh, just as promised. But she had never thought it would be like this.

Not long after, a meeting was held concerning the absence of the Host. Bruden spoke of dividing the land outside of the city walls. From that summer onward, Imperial machines much like Fractica would cut, dry, and transport the tall grass for a small price. There was no more need for oroxen to be herded across Merseh. Herders no longer needed to live over half a year out on the steppe. They only needed to go out to the "ranches" in the mornings and come home in the evenings. Experienced herders would be given a share of the city's common herd to work these ranches.

Just as the Host had lived with them to protect Danras from the Grim King, the Chief Herder had existed to protect the oroxen. Once the Grim King was gone, Yuma would only become another rich orox owner like Bruden or Jesska. Only the ones who did not own enough oroxen to form their own ranch would roam the steppe in the old way.

Everything would change, especially for Yuma. Which was why everyone waited for her disapproval. But she had no objections—Yuma was more than happy that everyone would be safer and more prosperous at least.

The Fifth Legion sent a herald announcing that their arrival would be a day earlier than expected. Yuma and Lysandros received the herald in the Feast Hall, where the Host no longer resided. The herald called Yuma "the great King of Danras" and the Feast Hall a "grand palace," but Yuma knew that this wasn't a palace and that she was no king. Perhaps this city was no longer Danras either.

Later that night, standing next to the still-empty cradle, Yuma asked Lysandros what was to become of Merseh. Her tone was so serious that Lysandros's ever-present smile faded from his face.

"There must be a prefect here. I shall discuss it with Chief Herder and others, but I want Chief in that position. The Senate will follow my recommendations."

"What does the prefect do?"

"The prefect would rule the country and liaise for the Imperial Capital. Set trading rules, collect taxes . . . But don't worry about the taxes. Compared to what the Grim King collected, it'll be nothing."

Yuma nodded and sat down. She had not heard from the Grim King since that conversation where he'd stoked her fears, but as long as she was pregnant with Tychon, the possibility of him slipping into her mind was always there. She looked at Lysandros. His expression was earnest, a hint of that beautiful grin on his lips.

She looked down and said, "Remember when you were fighting the Grim King's giant, and there was that casket that fell out of Fractica?"

The grin was gone once more. "That again. I think the matter is better undiscussed. It's Imperial magic, a secret one."

"Well, I'm discussing it. I can't put it off anymore. As I'm resting here, Danras is changing beyond recognition. So this is something you can talk about with me, isn't it?"

Lysandros sighed. "Chief Herder already knows it's called a Power generator. When a sorcerer dies, the body is processed in a particular way and converted into a generator. It's a source of al-most limitless energy. Danras and all of Merseh will soon benefit."

It was just as Eldred had told her in that dream. He'd called it a debasement of all sorcerers. Yuma had tried to ignore it—so what if the Grim King was offended?—but between the Host and her unborn Tychon, she found herself unable to. And there was yet another thing that bothered her.

"What I really want to know is who that was in the casket. Was Fractica the name of the sorcerer?"

Lysandros shrugged. "Who the Power generator used to be isn't important. It's just a body now."

"You said you were a sorcerer as well. If you die, will you be turned into a Power generator?"

Lysandros averted his gaze, but not before Yuma registered a hint of discomfort, and even fear, in his eyes.

"Probably," he finally said. "But there's a way to avoid it. If that's what Chief Herder wants, I'll try my best."

"And our child? Tychon?"

"Why . . . It isn't known if Tychon will have Power. The signs don't appear until a few years after birth. Unless both parents are sorcerers, the possibilities are low."

"Just assume he does!" she shouted, no longer caring to be pa-tient.

Lysandros seemed surprised at her outburst, but answered calmly. ". . . Well, Chief Herder, that would mean Tychon would be in the same situation as I am." Lysandros gently laid a hand on her belly. "This child will be born, grow up, meet a wonderful per-son like Chief Herder, fall in love, and have children. Tychon will be surrounded by sons and daughters and grandchildren and live out a long life. The only difference between a sorcerer and ordinary folk is that a sorcerer is placed in a lead casket, not a wooden one, upon death. Isn't that better than being buried in the ground? It's certainly not any worse."

"Then the Host?" she pressed on. "Is that what's going to happen to him? Wrapped in bandages and laid in a lead casket?"

"Yuma—"

"The soul of the Host is passed on from person to person, that's why they're called 'host.' It's been this way for hundreds of years. But how can the next person receive their soul if he's a generator, as you called it?" she asked, desperate for him to understand.

Lysandros stared for a moment before slowly giving her an answer.

"I was glad the Host volunteered to leave for the Capital, because I thought it would save me from saying this but . . . Chief Herder . . . to worship something above people is wrong."

"Wrong? Why would that be . . . ?" she spluttered. "Besides, the people of Danras do not 'worship' the Host."

"The Host protected Danras from the rage and harassment of the Grim King. Danras sent oroxen as tithes to the Grim King. In Danras and other parts of Merseh, the way things are done has always revolved around the Grim King. But now the Empire can end the tyrannical reign. The Empire has the means to liberate the world. But the traces of the Grim King must be cleansed by the people of Merseh, or the scars will never fade."

Yuma felt her eyebrows twitch.

"Are you saying the Grim King is the god of Merseh, and the Host is his priest?"

Lysandros hesitated. "In the eyes of the Empire, yes. It's a rare, but not unprecedented, form of god worship. This was why I was tasked with finding the Chief Herder, and not the Grim King, to make an alliance."

She now realized what Lysandros had meant on the steppe— that it wasn't Eldred but Yuma who was the king of Danras. Because the Grim King was the god, the Host his priest, and Yuma the king . . . And none of these three were deemed acceptable by the Empire.

"You swore to me, in the pouring starlight," she whispered as her voice shook. "You swore."

Every word of what he'd said was clear in her mind. Those words had comforted her on nights she was kept up by thoughts of fighting the Grim King. *I swear, as an emissary of the Empire, that I shall use all my power as an inquisitor of the Imperial Office of Truth to aid Yuma, the Chief Herder of Danras, to save Merseh from Eldred.*

"I remember," he said, his eyes looking into hers. "And I've done what I've sworn to do so far, have I not? Only months remain until Merseh is saved from the Grim King forever."

"But the Merseh to come is not the Merseh of now. And I am not the Chief Herder of Danras in that Merseh."

"Yuma . . ." He gently took hold of her shoulders. "I'm sorry this isn't what Chief Herder had in mind. But the world changes. And the reign of the Grim King will be over. Danras will prosper with the Empire. As unexpected as it is, haven't the fortunes of all Merseh improved in the end?"

Yuma didn't answer. She could not think of anything other than the steppe, and the wind in her hair. Merseh would soon change into something else, like Lysandros said. Yes, Merseh would become Mersia, as the outsiders called it. And there would be no place in Mersia for the Chief Herder, the Host, or the Grim King. It turned out she had made sure of it.

"Let's go to the Imperial Capital together," he said. "I can stop this wandering and get a post there. Chief Herder can become a councillor in the Commons. Chief Herder would represent Merseh in the Capital. And *we* could be married."

The form of "we" he used was perfect and affectionate. His words were earnest, his voice soft. There wasn't a shadow of suspicion or regret. Tears rose in Yuma's eyes.

"Danras is a great city, but the Imperial Capital is different," he continued. "It is the largest and busiest city in the world. Chief Herder could meet with the Host any time. *We* would pick from the people of Danras for the prefect's seat, and Chief Herder could sell or lend the share of oroxen to them. And whenever Chief Herder misses home, *we* could always come back and ride the horses."

Yuma swallowed her tears and said, "Can the Host officiate our wedding?"

"Of course! The Host is not a prisoner after all."

"And the ceremony will follow our traditions."

"It never occurred to me to do it otherwise."

Yuma smiled weakly and quickly wiped away the tears that managed to escape.

Lysandros, reassured, hugged her. "I'll be off then. I need to oversee a few things before the Fifth Legion arrives. I will see Chief tonight."

She nodded. Lysandros kissed her on the forehead, laid another gentle hand on Yuma's stomach where Tychon lay, and left the room.

As his footsteps faded, Yuma opened her wardrobe. She took

out her clothing from the herding, washed and neatly mended since their arrival. The chaps were a little tight, but they had been a generous fit to begin with, so she could still slip them on. She put on the white tunic, tied the string around her neck, and put on the vest. Her leather belt still had her dagger on the side. She put on her boots, her spurs having recently been polished to a shine. Finally, she reached deep into her closet to retrieve her brown wide-brimmed hat, and placed it on her head.

She put her hand in the vest pocket. The two stones the Grim King had given her were still there.

Coming down the stairs into the hall, she came upon Old Vella once more.

"Going out, Chief Herder?"

Yuma nodded. "Please tell the stables to ready Aston."

Vella nodded and left the room. Yuma stood by the doors. They had fought the Grim King's undead army here in the beginning of winter. She opened the cupboards and packed some of the winter-dried meat.

A boy whose name she didn't remember came with Aston to the doors. Yuma hitched her sack of dried meat to the saddle and hoisted herself up. Getting on the horse was a little harder than the last time she had done this.

"Chief Herder, where are you going with all this food?"

Yuma smiled and patted the child's head. This child would never have to fear the Grim King again.

But neither would he go out to the herding or receive the blessing of the Host.

Yuma lightly spurred Aston to move forward and was soon galloping toward the castle of the Grim King.

37

EMERE

"Remember when I told you about Tythonia? The story of the people killing their king and opening the gates of the city to the invading legion? Do you remember what I said about why that was the correct choice?"

Emere, tied to the wooden pole, had no choice but to listen to Ludvik talk. Cain had said he must not give Ludvik what he wanted, but the inquisitor of the Office of Truth who had come with Ludvik only whipped Emere's already aching body without either of them asking any questions or making any demands. Ludvik had instead slipped into a loquacious mood.

"You mustn't regard the Empire as just another country. Perhaps it was so at one time, but as long as the world belongs to the Empire, no one who lives within it is a foreigner anymore because the Empire is the world itself. Do you understand what I'm saying? The Empire is the destiny of the world."

Destiny. That word again, which had followed Emere for his whole life. He had wandered the world searching for it. He had thought he had found it in Loran. He had thought perhaps he might be a tiny part of her greatness. But despite his long struggles, he'd accomplished nothing. Instead, he was tied up, having to listen to this tedious drivel. Emere looked Ludvik in the eye. What an earnest and guileless face the man had. He even looked concerned for Emere.

"What are you going to do to Arland?" Emere asked.

Ludvik looked saddened. "If you know enough to ask that, then you already know the answer. That is both a blessing and a curse to you. You won't have to listen to me go on and on, but it'll make convincing you to answer my question much more difficult."

"I would think it's simply a blessing for me, because I don't particularly want to answer any of your questions." Emere spat blood on the ground.

"It is a curse to you because if you don't answer, you will be killed." Ludvik's tone was one of firmness tinged with regret. "One hundred years ago, the Star of Mersia wiped out countless people in the blink of an eye. The venerable Mersian civilization is now nothing but ruins. But those very ruins have become a symbol of the strength of the Empire. There may be those who doubt the Star's existence, but there are none who don't fear it. That is how we have maintained one hundred years of peace."

"Even when hundreds of thousands died for that peace?"

Ludvik sighed. "These people you speak of—if they hadn't died back then, what do you think they would be doing now, one hundred years later? Do you think a single one of them would still be alive?"

Emere didn't think this was a question even worth answering.

Ludvik continued. "Mersia's extinction made submission to the Empire more a matter of course for many provinces. This saved far more people than those who perished back then. Which is why I can't let Arland get away with what it's done to us."

"They hurt your pride that much, huh?"

Ludvik rolled his eyes. "You say that as if it were a trivial thing. But if you had ever overseen an Imperial office as I have, you would know exactly what the cost of hurt pride is. Rebels all over the world have been stirred up. Some rumors even say that rebels of different provinces are working together. It's incomparable to before. What do you think would happen if former great powers like Cassia or Thiops decided to topple their prefects and fight the Empire, hand in hand?"

"So you're going to make an example out of Arland?"

"Arland is a small country in the grand scheme of things, much like Mersia was. Should we let rebellions run rampant everywhere when we can stop them with *minimal* sacrifice? Now, *that* would be tantamount to a massacre."

Emere found himself breathing hard. Only someone with a fanatical devotion to the Empire would say that tens of thousands of lives were worth sacrificing for the sake of some Imperial ideal.

Ludvik said, "That is why I am going to set off a Star of Mersia on Arland."

"Ridiculous!" shouted Emere.

"My dear Emere. I'm going to let you in on a little secret: The Star of Mersia was actually a simple accident."

The first thing that came to Emere's mind was the question of how a weapon of annihilation could be an accident. The second was the realization that, if Ludvik was telling the truth, the Star of Mersia had never been a weapon at all. He could only blink in response. It was preposterous. But it also explained so many things . . .

"An accident!" Ludvik chuckled. "Not the will of mortals, or the rage of gods, but a simple mechanical malfunction that turned a perfectly serviceable province into a wasteland. Well, the Office of Truth decided to make the best out of the situation. We couldn't let the extinguishing of all those lives be in vain . . . and we didn't. We bought a hundred years of peace with them." His voice took on a serious tone. "And now I know how to make the Star of Mersia shine again. I was shown a vision."

A vision, like the one Emere himself received. Emere could imagine it. Councillor Ludvik of Tythonia, reading over the Office of Truth reports of rebel uprisings all over the world with a furrowed brow, his mind on the Star of Mersia. And on one quiet night, the Circuit of Destiny, whispering in his ear how to save the Empire. Ludvik was merely the latest in a long line of history's villains who sold their souls to the devil for the sake of solving an intractable problem.

Emere suddenly lunged at Ludvik, the ropes holding him back just an inch away from the other man. Ludvik jumped back in surprise.

"You think it's as easy as turning a lamp on and off," growled Emere, "but you're wrong. You're being fooled by the Circuit, Ludvik. That conniving *thing* said to me—"

"The Circuit of Destiny? Some machine that spits out portents didn't tell me how to punish Arland. No, it was the one who knew more than anyone else about the fall of Mersia, the one who grieved more than anyone else when it met its fate."

"Who?"

"Grand Inquisitor Lysandros."

Emere burst into forced laughter. "Lysandros is *dead*. I saw his corpse rolling down Finvera Pass like a rotten log with my own eyes."

Ludvik slapped Emere with his gauntleted hand. Emere clenched his jaws in response, but he felt a sharp, stunning sting of teeth breaking.

"Never speak his name like that again! The Grand Inquisitor appeared in my dreams several times, giving me clear signs and instructions. That I must decide the destiny of the Empire, that if I didn't"—Ludvik took a step forward, shoving his mustached face close to Emere's—"a provincial upstart, some half-wit prince, would instead."

Emere considered spitting his loose teeth and blood in Ludvik's face, but the sight of Ludvik's eyes made him lose the will to do so. His face was earnest and truthful, yet his eyes had, beyond the cover of conviction and passion, a glint that could only be madness.

"If all you say is true, wouldn't it be easier to kill me, here and now?"

Ludvik laughed. "Despite what the Grand Inquisitor told me, I don't think you actually have it in you to decide the destiny of the world, don't you agree? You frittered away your life doing nothing but wandering—built nothing, accomplished nothing, became nothing. You are not even the enemy of the world, just a bridge to the true enemy. Which begs the question."

Ludvik's stare was piercing. His first question, ever since this tedious interrogation began. The dread in Emere's heart felt like ice.

"Where," asked Ludvik, "is King Loran?"

Emere dared not breathe. Ludvik gestured behind him. The tall inquisitor passed a goblet of water into Ludvik's hand.

"You must be parched. Drink this before answering," he said, lifting the cup up to Emere's lips. "Where is Loran?"

Emere turned his head away from the cup. "I don't know. Arland, I suppose."

Ludvik withdrew the cup and clucked his tongue. "Emere, Emere . . . Let's be honest with each other. We know Loran is in the Capital. One doesn't have to be the Office of Truth to deduce that you've met with her."

Emere didn't know how much more time he could buy, or if anything could even be got from trying to buy time, but Cain's instructions to not give Ludvik what he wanted rang in his ears.

"Why do you want to know?" he asked.

"I'm sure you wouldn't believe me if I told you, but the Grand Inquisitor showed me a future. One where Loran had turned the whole of the world into a wasteland, where not a single blade of grass had survived. Like Mersia. That is what I am trying to prevent. That is what a world without the Empire is!"

Emere's laugh emerged from his battered body like a cough. "Her Majesty would never do that. And she doesn't even have the means to do so. No one person has."

"Could you have imagined that a single person could bring down a gigatherion?"

Ludvik nodded at the inquisitor, who untied Emere from the pole. Emere tried to remain standing, but his hands and feet were still tied together, and he had no strength in his limbs. He soon collapsed without the pole supporting him. Ludvik bent down and offered him the cup of water again.

"Your friend, that Ebrian. Rakel, is that her name? We promise no harm will come to her, or your sister, or Kamori. I can even recommend a more important role for you in the Commons, a position that matters. But you must answer my question, for the good of the Empire. For the good of the world."

It wasn't that Emere couldn't see Ludvik's logic. In his own twisted and callous way, the man was acting according to reason. Perhaps he was even right—if the Empire was the world, as he claimed, the end of the Empire might mean the end of the world.

But there would always be one thing Emere could never bend on no matter the threat. He moved his barely mobile arms to grab the cup, gulp it down, and speak as if he were speaking his final words.

"I would never betray King Loran."

The two men locked gazes for a long time. Emere's defiant, Ludvik's searching. A deep frown appeared on Ludvik's face and he slapped Emere once more with his heavy gauntlet.

"A pathetic excuse of a man you are. A man who has never believed in anything in his life. Isn't that why you've wasted it away? You traveled to uncover the nature of the Star of Mersia? *I'm* the one who discovered it. You brought together a rebel army in Kamori for your people? The sum of what you've done pretending to be a *mole* in your little underground warren is *nothing* compared to what Loran achieved in just half a year. If you had believed in anything, even in the smallest of hopes, and did something about it, you would not have ended up here. But I believe in the Empire. I believe in the noble destiny that it shall bring peace to the world and watch over it for eternity. And I shall make this destiny happen by becoming the Imperator."

The sky suddenly lit up with blue light. Ludvik looked up. A glaringly bright blue star crossed the sky as it descended, reminding Emere of the dragon's blue light that he had seen in Arland.

Despite his bruised jaw and broken teeth, despite the pain and the blood, Emere couldn't suppress a grin. The grin grew into chuckles, then outright laughter. He tried to control it, for he needed to speak.

"Councillor Ludvik, I . . . I also believe in something. I have, all my life."

Ludvik stared up at the sky, his agape mouth forming words in Tythonian. The blue star fell upon the fort with an explosive impact. Ludvik covered his face from the blast, but a fraction of a second later, a chunk of broken brick hit his chest. The sound, the light, and the blast deafened and blinded Emere.

". . . an alliance!"

It was Rakel's voice. Had he lost consciousness? He was lying outside, still tied up.

"What . . . what?" He spoke, opening his eyes. Rakel's hair and face were wet.

"We've created an alliance! Between Ebria and King Loran!"

He was soaked too. Rain was falling. Rakel's hands trembled as they tried to undo the knots around Emere's ropes before she finally sighed in exasperation and began sawing at them with her knife. Once his hands were freed, Emere took her knife and cut the ropes that bound his feet.

A battle raged. Shouts of "*Ayula!*" came from all over the burning fort—that most versatile of Ebrian exclamations.

"How did you know to come here . . . ?"

"Septima barged into our congregation and told us you'd been taken, that the Office of Truth was about to mobilize the Zero Legion for Ludvik. King Loran sprang from her seat right there and then. We gathered as many people as possible and came here." Rakel pointed toward erupting columns of blue fire. "There's Loran."

Loran was keeping Powered elite legionaries at bay. Nearby was the wreckage of a Powered chariot, sending up a plume of violet smoke into the night. The Powered legionaries stood together like posed toy soldiers, unmoving. Emere remembered Loran doing this in Dehan Forest as well. The Powered armor might look just a little singed, but he knew the soldiers inside were burned to death.

Everywhere, Ebrians fought the rest of the Zero Legion. The people who had been so careful, hiding out underground, had risen up to attack an Imperial fortress. All of them ready for this to be the final night of their lives, as they must know they could not win against an Imperial legion. He couldn't understand why they had decided to come here.

But he *did* understand. He had understood for a long time. It was the same reason that had dragged him from the underground palace, that had drawn Ledonite and Kamori warriors to Arland of their own accord. The reason was Loran. She could do that. Unlike Emere himself . . .

He looked around for Ludvik and saw a man limping away, his golden tassels shaking on his shoulders. Emere stood, and the world seemed to spin. His knees buckled, but Rakel helped him to his feet.

"I think you are bleeding inside. You need treatment," said Rakel with dead seriousness.

Emere resisted Rakel pulling him away from the battle. "I can still fight."

"No, you can't! The excitement is the only thing that's keeping you standing. We have to take you to my—"

In all the years he'd known her, she had never sounded this desperate. He could sense his own doom in her heart-wrenching voice. But there was still something he had to do.

"No," Emere interrupted gently. "This is not over. Rakel, you take care of the Ebrians . . . they will all die this way. I have to go." He took a soft step away from Rakel, trying his best to stay on his two feet.

"What are you talking about? Go where? Never mind, I'm coming with you regardless!"

Emere tried a smile. His side screamed with pain.

"No, if we go together, it'll be more dangerous."

Rakel grabbed him by his shoulders, but he knew she would let him go. At Finvera Pass, she could have stopped him with one more word. But she wouldn't, even when she knew perfectly well she could. He loved her for it.

Emere took her face in his hands, his knees somehow managing not to buckle. "I've always loved you. And I will as long as I live. But you were right. I am but a moth to a flame. I am so sorry."

Rakel's hands fell away from him. Her lips moved but no sound came out. He kissed them for the first time in ten years, and for the last time.

As he took his lips off hers, Rakel spoke. "You are going after

Ludvik. Even if it means dying." Her voice had regained her usual calm of a surgeon.

Emere nodded. "This is something I have to do. No one else can, and there is no time."

The "vision" Ludvik had received—just as the Circuit of Destiny had appeared as Loran in his dreams, it must have appeared as Lysandros in Ludvik's. Which meant it was the Circuit that had taught Ludvik how to set off the Star of Mersia, showing him the end Loran would bring. Emere couldn't afford to doubt Ludvik's visions, when the fate of Arland was at stake.

Rakel took a step back and said, in a choked voice, "King Loran is sure to ask me about you."

Loran. Emere pondered for a moment. What if Ludvik was right? What if Loran was destined to end the world? What if he, by stopping Ludvik, was making the Circuit's prophecy come true?

His head felt like it was somewhere else. Every other part of his body screamed in pain. He tried his hardest not to let that be the last thing Rakel remembered of him.

"Tell her that I believe," Emere said, as he turned away.

Like the Ebrians and their faith in the Nameless God, Emere just wanted to believe in Loran.

38

ARIENNE

She almost couldn't see in front of her anymore. But Tychon was awake and cheerful, babbling and laughing. A laugh she had never heard from him before. Yuma was sitting in a chair as she rocked Tychon's cradle with one hand, lost in thought.

Noam hadn't remembered anything when he came into her mind for the first time; it had taken awhile for him to even recall his own name. He had come a long way to be himself again, like Arienne had just a few years ago.

"Do you remember yet?" she whispered to Noam. "One hundred years ago, how the accident happened?"

Noam, gazing at Yuma and Tychon, slowly nodded.

"Fractica sounded the alarm."

"An alarm?"

"Even after the Grim King had been defeated, Grand Inquisitor Lysandros had been worried about traps or schemes that might have been placed, and so he planned for contingencies, using

Fractica. It had been Fractica that maintained the Host's enchantment in the catacombs. And one of Fractica's many other functions was to sound an alarm when it sensed the presence of the Grim King."

Arienne detected Yuma slightly raising her head at the mention of Lysandros's name.

"And then what?" Arienne urged.

"The alarm sounded, but nothing happened immediately after that. I think the Grand Inquisitor knew. He went right back to the Capital. Saying he needed to take care of something . . . But whatever he did, he was too late. When the Grand Inquisitor was gone, Fractica's output became unstable, and its humming became thrums. A storm of black smoke . . . kind of like what you saw when you came down here on the steps, but much thicker, much faster. It flooded the generator chamber. I thought the control chain was malfunctioning, so I went to get the cutting tool. And then I saw it."

"Saw what?"

"Sorcerers . . ." Noam had a faraway look in his eyes now. "I saw them. Heard them, too. The Grim King was among them. I'd never seen him before, only knew him through legend, and in that moment he was only half formed and he spoke in gibberish, like he had just woken up from a nightmare—but I recognized him immediately, and the name he kept murmuring: Lysandros. That's why I tried to escape to the catacombs, since Fractica was supposed to keep them safe from him." Noam swallowed. "This was the Grim King's revenge, seventy years after his death. Didn't I tell you from the start? The Empire would never do this. It was the Grim King all along."

Arienne shook her head. "Eldred didn't do this all on his own. There were countless sorcerers—Power generators—in the Circuit of Destiny. The accumulated history in the Circuit was what led to the Star of Mersia."

The Empire did not care where it got its Power—as long as it came into their hands, it was theirs. They thought they could control the sorcerers indefinitely by turning them into Power generators. Evidently, they couldn't. And by adding generators to the Circuit, by using the Circuit to look into the past or predict the future, they had unknowingly built the Star of Mersia.

Arienne's knowledge of generator magic had failed her at the Academy three years in a row, but she was sure in her speculation. If the Circuit had borne witness to pain and suffering on a world-wide scale, like what she just had seen in that black smoke, would it be so inconceivable that the Circuit was full of resentment and bitterness? And that the resentment and bitterness that had built up over a century in those three hundred Power generators was poisonous enough to destroy a whole nation?

All of that poison had been unleashed through Fractica into Danras before spreading throughout Mersia. That, Arienne decided, was the truth behind the Star of Mersia.

What Arienne saw when she opened herself to the whispering smoke was harrowing, but it was just only a lingering trace of the disaster. She still wasn't sure what had triggered it, though. Arienne's first choice was Eldred. She did not believe that even he would do this, but his hatred toward Lysandros must have played a role in Fractica being the conduit of the disaster. And perhaps Lysandros had wanted to find out as well—perhaps that was why he couldn't simply destroy Power generator Eldred after the Star of Mersia and instead secreted him away in the basement of the Imperial Academy.

But to confirm this, she would have to go back to the Imperial Capital and examine the Circuit for herself. Maybe have a talk with it, to hear what it knew, what it felt, and finally understand why it had done what it had. Just as she had listened to the whispering smoke, the last trace of the Star of Mersia, here underneath Eldred's old castle.

"Are you all right?" Noam asked worriedly.

Even in the room in her mind, her hands were covered with bursting pustules. She could barely make out light and dark. "Do I look that bad?"

"You look like you're about to die. Is this what you look like outside too?"

"Worse." Despite her growing blindness, she could sense the worried frown on Noam's face and tried a smile. "It'll go away. I just need to get out of here."

She focused on her physical body—which was collapsed next to Yuma's remains at the bottom of Eldred's castle. Arienne groped around until something soft came into her grasp. A wide-brimmed hat. She remembered that Yuma had worn such a hat in her first dream in Mersia. Arienne put it on her own head, leaned against the wall, and stood up.

"With that *thing* filling the stairs," Noam wailed, "how are you going to get out?"

"It's fine. The Star of Mersia is . . . I'll be fine. They can't hurt me anymore."

"Why not?"

"Because I understand them all."

Arienne had heard the whispers. She felt for them. Doing so nearly destroyed her, even though they were just whispers rather than the screams that they would have been a century ago. But whatever horrors the Star of Mersia so desperately wanted to tell, now she knew. She had no fear, as what she knew couldn't hurt her.

Touching the wall by her side, Arienne made her way up the staircase. It reminded her of the steps in the Imperial Academy that led down to the Power generator chamber there. Why hadn't she thought of it on her way down? At the Academy, she had placed Eldred in the room in her mind and walked back up the steps. Hadn't there been an old skeleton at the bottom of those stairs as well? Her memory must be fading. Many more things would fade if she didn't hurry.

A lullaby came from the room in her mind. It wasn't Noam's voice, and the melody was different as well. Yuma was humming. Arienne listened closely as she continued to lean against the wall and slowly climb the steps. Then, Yuma began to sing.

"Why are lullabies always about the same thing no matter the country they're from?" Arienne murmured as she dragged herself up the steps.

"Do you speak Mersian?" asked Noam.

"No, I don't. That song was in Mersehi?" Noam's agape mouth made her realize she had just spoken in a language she hadn't learned.

The singing voice stopped and began to speak instead, in a lower, different tone.

"I see that I am back here, in the Feast Hall."

Not stopping her ascent, Arienne entered the room in her

mind. She could barely see even in here now. But Yuma turned from her chair to look at her.

"Who are you?" Yuma asked.

Careful not to stumble, Arienne approached her, lost her balance, and grabbed on to the edge of the bed. She found a chair and lowered herself into it.

"My name," she said, "is Arienne."

Yuma's gaze flickered to her neck. Arienne raised her head to give her a better view of her *t'laran*. Did Yuma know of Arland? Their eyes met once more.

"I'm Yuma. The Chief Herder of Danras. Or at least, I was. I remember being in and out of sleep, for what seemed liked days, maybe years. How am I back in Danras? What happened?"

Arienne, as calmly as possible, spoke of what had happened to Mersia after it had joined the Empire. When Yuma heard of the death of Dalan the Host and the Star of Mersia turning the country into a wasteland, tears came to her eyes. At the end of the story, Arienne was asked the question she'd been dreading the most.

"What happened to Lysandros?"

Arienne only hesitated a moment before saying, "He died."

"How?"

"I killed him," Arienne said simply.

Yuma let out a surprised whisper. "Oh."

"I'm sorry," she apologized, without knowing what she was sorry about.

Yuma neither acknowledged her apology nor blamed her. Instead, she changed the subject.

"Do you know what happened to the Grim King?"

"He was turned into a Power generator, but then he came back, and then I killed him too."

Did she have to apologize for this as well? Yuma didn't respond. Tychon woke, and Yuma picked him up out of the cradle, as he looked ready to start crying.

"Am I back in my room?"

Arienne shook her head. "This is the room I made inside my mind."

"It looks exactly like my room in the Feast Hall of Danras."

Arienne herself didn't know where exactly the memory of this room came from. Fractica's dream? Tychon's? Or somewhere—some*one*—else? As she hesitated in her answer, Yuma said, "What's outside of this tower?"

"Nothing."

"How sad. I wanted to ride with my child on horseback at least once."

What would've been outside this room if it were the real Feast Hall was the city of Danras, and beyond it, the steppe of Mersia. But there was nothing. This was not a real place, only existing in Arienne's mind. But what about the people here? Yuma, Noam, and Tychon were not people she had imagined, nor were they memories, as Eldred, Yuma, and Lysandros had been in Fractica's dream.

Arienne bowed and left the room. She noted that Yuma had nothing to say about the state of Arienne's appearance. Maybe that was Mersian manners.

She finally felt like she understood why the whispering smoke, the Star of Mersia, had lingered under Eldred's castle. It was because Yuma's ghost was there, alongside her remains. Like attracts like, and her pain was the same as that of the Star. It was commiserating with her.

There were more questions to be asked, and there was more to be learned, but Yuma would be here waiting in Arienne's mind, as Noam had been. She had time, as did they, and she decided that they were real, at least while they were here. Perhaps everything was, as long as she kept it real in her mind.

Back in Eldred's castle, she looked up the stairs. Was that a hint of light? She was nearing the end of it. Her legs shook and her throat was parched. She quickened her pace.

She finally reached the top of the steps. Stumbling into the hall, she looked back one last time. This empty castle had not melted away or fallen down, and as it had been the past one hundred years, it was unlikely someone would visit in the future. Patting the Grim King's crown secured to her belt, Arienne stepped outside.

Aron was by the melted gates. She ran to the donkey and hugged his neck, the donkey braying in surprise. She stood like that for a long time before untying Aron's reins from the iron ring. She pressed Yuma's hat down on her head and dusted herself off. The road back home to Arland was long—and there was one more thing she needed to do before getting there.

39

YUMA

The Grim King's soldiers guarded his castle day and night. Its thick walls were impervious to the cannons of the Fifth Legion, repairing themselves at the slightest hint of cracking. When Yuma arrived, the gates had opened as if recognizing her by sight, but even those gates had vanished into the wall once she passed through.

In the six months she had been in this obsidian castle, the Grim King had never once spoken of her rebellion, nor did he even question her motives in coming here. Yuma had a feeling that he already knew. When she had first arrived, she had simply been led by a skeletal servant to a large room devoid of decoration. There was a modest yet comfortable bed, a chair, and a beautifully carved obsidian crib with Tychon's name inlaid in Mersehi. All of the furniture seemed to sprout directly from the room's floor.

The Grim King, always in the same robe woven of fire and

shadow, did not seem to sleep, eat, or drink. In Danras, rumors had abounded that his castle was filled with bloodless, beautiful corpse concubines, but she saw none of that. Perhaps it would've been less chilling if she had. What had brought the Grim King here, all those years ago? Why did he stay? He had no family here, nor did he bring his people from wherever was his homeland. He had perhaps the greatest stronghold in the world, but there were no riches inside, no hedonistic pleasures. Just corpses, rocks, and himself. And now Yuma.

Yuma occasionally touched the nullstones he had given her. When she had asked him one day if they could defeat the Imperial legion, he had scoffed.

"To think such a thing would be possible!"

"Even if I used both of them?"

"You could stop a few chariots. But two, or even ten, stones wouldn't be enough against an entire legion. And there are not ten such stones in all the world."

Cannons had then fired again, sending dull echoes through her chambers. Although each shot seemed futile, they would inevitably amount to the doom of Eldred.

She spent the rest of the winter in her room, sometimes wandering around the castle until she was gently brought back to her room by a servant. Then, when the earth thawed, she was allowed to wander the vast space outside surrounded by the castle's walls. She rode Aston sometimes, longing for the steppe that she knew she would never see.

The Grim King visited her as often as once every five days. First he would throw sarcastic censures at her, how she had brought the bane of nations to Merseh. She would snap back with accounts of his tyranny. But even that didn't last long, and the Grim King would ask after her health and pregnancy, staying in Yuma's room just long enough for her to finish the strange herbal concoction that he brought every time he visited. She was under no illusion of the Grim King being anything other than a tyrant, but she learned not to fear him anymore. In this castle, at this moment, they were just two people waiting for the end. Yuma was surprised at how well she was taking it. Perhaps it was because of Tychon inside her that she never felt alone here.

Toward the end of summer, Yuma gave birth to Tychon as she listened to the sounds of battle happening beyond the wall. The skeletal midwives received him in their emaciated hands and passed him to her to hold. Days later, when her milk turned white, the Grim King came to her, the fire in his robes merely embers in black, like the starry night sky. Yuma sat up to greet him, and Eldred stared into the obsidian crib where the baby slept.

His expression was unreadable. But he had silenced his steps and was visibly careful with his hands, even though they were not even close to Tychon. This sight softened her and made her ask him how he had come to settle in Merseh all those years ago. He became irritated.

"Why are you yourself here?" he snapped. Finally, he had asked the question that had been on Yuma's mind for months. "When you are not even here to join my side."

Yuma stroked the baby's hair with her fingertips and said, "There is no place for me in Danras."

"That is true. But do you think there is a place for you here?"

Yuma shook her head and looked into Tychon's sleeping face.

"Are you here because of your old Host's prophecy?" he sneered. "That my apprentice shall become the King of Merseh?"

"This child . . ." She took a deep breath. "You said come autumn, not even this place would survive. Mersia will fall into the Empire's hands then. But if Tychon became the Grim King's apprentice, maybe Danras could become free of them again someday."

"How utterly convenient for you. I will fall by the hand of the Empire regardless, and your son will take over Merseh. Is that your calculation?" A bitter laugh.

Yuma smiled. "How could there be calculation when it's prophecy?"

"Or are you afraid your child will become that 'Power generator' they speak of? Or, how you will no longer be Chief Herder?"

Was it such hubris that brought her here? This was a question she had asked herself several times over the past six months. She had always had a suspicion this might be so. But that suspicion was her burden to bear, and she would not have to bear it for long. The Grim King reached out toward Tychon and paused, his head turning to Yuma. She stared at his hovering hand, thinking of what Aidan had said in the past. Of why Eldred had not accepted Aidan as an apprentice, and why he hadn't been killed . . . She nodded, giving permission.

The Grim King carefully lifted up the baby, who was wrapped in the blue receiving blanket the Host had given her.

"Little one, my name is Eldred. Three thousand years of legacy flows through me. Now kiss my hand."

He gently held out the back of his hand to Tychon's lips.

Tychon woke, looked at Eldred's hand, and grabbed one of his bony fingers.

In a voice softer and more pleasant than Yuma had ever heard him use, the Grim King said, "You are hereby apprenticed to Eldred. And you shall become king of this land."

He lightly lowered the baby back into the crib and covered him up to the chin with the small orox-hide blanket.

"The flowers embroidered on this blanket used to proliferate on the steppe," he observed. "Now they are no more. They used to bloom only for a few days in the summer every year, but they disappeared around fifty years ago and not a trace of them remains."

Aidan had managed to pass every trial the Grim King had put before him, only to have his Power taken away and to be banished. That the Grim King considered him unworthy but allowed Aidan to survive simply to leave behind progeny—Yuma did not believe this anymore. After all, the Grim King hadn't cared about the lives of the other children who hoped to become his apprentice. Maybe Aidan was special in that he had passed the tests, and to Eldred was no longer as insignificant as the forgotten white summer flowers of the steppe.

The Grim King nodded to Yuma and left the room.

That night, a bell that had never rung since Yuma's arrival rang three times. She could hear the roaring of the legion outside. But this was not the roar of attack upon a fortified wall. It was the roar of victory. Yuma was trying to look outside the windows when one of the skeletal servants entered. It bowed and gestured to her to follow.

Yuma then knew that this was the end. She took her time

dressing herself in her riding gear, held Tychon close to her, and followed.

The Grim King sat on his white throne of bones, his robes burning silently like hearth fire, a large crystal ball in his hand. Through it, he could see everything the stormbirds that patrolled Merseh saw. Yuma walked up the dais to him. Eldred gave her a glance and said, "Chief Herder of Danras, I believe what we have expected and feared for so long has finally arrived."

Peering into the crystal ball, she saw a lone legionary with a strangely shaped body. Why was the stormbird flying so close to a single soldier? Then, she realized what she was really seeing. This wasn't a soldier. It was a giant made of iron, as tall as the smaller towers of the castle. It was walking toward them on two feet.

"What is that?"

"The Empire's 'gigatherion.' A machine titan running on a Power generator."

"I never would've imagined such a thing would exist."

The roaring outside coalesced into a single discernible name.

"Apollyon! Apollyon! Apollyon!"

"It must be that thing's name," mused the Grim King.

"Is it all over?" She was almost relieved.

But the Grim King floated a mischievous grin. "We shall see. I am not finished yet. I have prepared something for this very occasion."

His mouth made a sound no human mouth could have made. Flinching, Yuma covered her baby's head. The floor shook, the throne of bones rose upward, and the ceiling above them split and opened like the double eyelids of a lizard. The Grim King and

Yuma now looked down at the battlefield from a great height, the Powered chariots and soldiers of the Fifth Legion looking like ants compared to the gigatherion Apollyon approaching from afar.

The Grim King held out his arms to the sky, dark clouds gathering to cover the starry night. His robes burned brighter, flames threatening to lick the sky itself. Yuma caught glimpses of stormbird shadows in the clouds. Then, lightning flashed, lighting up the night sky. One of the lightning bolts hit Apollyon squarely in the chest, but aside from a loud mechanical screech, it seemed unaffected. Rain began to pour. It was thick and black. Her body battered by rain and wind, Yuma turned to the Grim King.

"My young apprentice," he said, "you don't think all I'm about to do is throw a few lightning bolts, now, do you?" His words were for Tychon, but his eyes were fixed on the sky. "Behold. Your master's final wonder."

The rain thickened into a dark cloudburst, and the wind threatened to blow Yuma's hat away. She pressed her hand on it. Four bolts of lightning crashed down between the approaching Apollyon and the legionaries. There was a rumbling separate from the thunder, and the earth shook. All the legionaries looked behind themselves.

High up in the sky, the air rippled like a pond disturbed by a pebble. The ripples slowly merged into a violet swirl, a veritable maelstrom of magic. A fearful murmur rose among the soldiers.

Something red and black sprouted from the sky, a hand or a paw, neither human nor animal.

The legion began to retreat, their cries for the gigatherion turning into screams of fear.

Yuma stared at the monster emerging from the sky. Like

Garamund, it was made of orox bones and flesh, but this creature was as tall as the gigatherion. It had a long neck; a head of countless eyes that glowed green; sharp sword-like teeth made of bones; front paws with huge, curved claws . . . It even had a pair of bat-like wings made from orox leather and stitched together with thick tendons.

The Grim King, his arms stretched before him, kept making strange vocalizations. Yuma did not know whether it was the language of his birth or that of another world. He never did answer Yuma's questions of where he had come from and why he chose Merseh as his conquest.

The monster struck Apollyon's shoulder with its clawed paw. The sturdy gigatherion, which had looked unstoppable, fell backward from the force. The monster immediately pressed down on the machine with one paw and ruthlessly struck down with its other at the machine. The Grim King laughed excitedly.

The retreating soldiers regrouped, but they dared not attack the monster even when it was showing its back to them. The blasts of the chariots didn't seem to register with the monster at all.

Every time the monster's claw struck the gigatherion, there were sparks. Yuma looked back at the Grim King. His gaze was on the battle before him. "Are you afraid I shall win? Do not fret. This is the end of my strength. Even if I'm lucky enough to win now, they will soon bring two. And if I bring down two, they will bring three. To defeat the Empire, I must myself raise an empire, and that is not something I can do."

Apollyon, still on its back, grabbed at the monster's wings and ripped them off. They were like paper in its grasp. The monster gave no sign of pain, but the Grim King grimaced as if a part of his body had been torn away.

"Thirty more years—no, had I just ten more . . ."

Apollyon let go of the torn wings and grabbed the torso of the monster. The gigatherion's body turned a bright red, and a ray of light pierced through the monster's chest into the sky.

40

EMERE

Emere grabbed the broken stick of a Zero Legion standard, then broke off a bit more at the end to fashion a quarterstaff. He used it as a crutch to chase after Ludvik. Ludvik himself also seemed injured from Loran's explosive landing in the middle of the fort—Emere could easily track Ludvik by his bloody footsteps. Emere turned around the corner of the fort, and spotted a small door swinging on its hinges in the battlements. He slipped inside.

The door led into a dark corridor, and the deeper he got, the more muffled the sounds of battle became. He listened for the sound of footsteps, squelching with blood, ahead. His own steps were turning wet, the many wounds from his recent torture still bleeding. A realization dawned on him that he would go down this corridor, but never come back through it in life.

What a long and winding path he had taken to his imminent

death. Was it good that it would end this way? If he died here and now, he would have truly accomplished nothing. His sister would not know of his death, nor would the people of Kamori. At best, he would be a footnote in some dusty volume of Imperial history.

He wondered if Loran might weep for him. Rakel definitely would. This was reassuring.

A light, at the end of the tunnel.

"Ludvik!" he shouted.

Ludvik, lantern in his left hand, turned. Blood soaked his face, his mustache drenched in red. He made no answer but grabbed the hilt of the sword on his side. Emere held up his staff, grabbing one end of it with his left hand and two palms' length down with his right. Suddenly, Ludvik charged, drawing his sword and pointing it at Emere.

Emere flicked his quarterstaff in a circle to deflect Ludvik's sword tip. The sword, slippery from Ludvik's own blood, fell out of his hands. Emere then slammed the staff against Ludvik's head, but he was too weakened, which gave Ludvik his chance to grab the end of the staff. Ludvik roared like a tiger, charging along the length of the staff. The two became entangled and rolled over each other as they fell to the floor of the dark corridor, the lantern smashing against the stone before it went out.

Emere came to. The floor was wet with someone's blood. Emere didn't see Ludvik—just the tracks of a body that had dragged itself away. He didn't know how much time had passed. Emere followed the tracks with his eyes. They led to an open iron door that was at once familiar—beyond it was a red wasteland with a violet sky.

Emere felt for his staff on the floor, slowly got up, and limped through the door. The invisible weight of the wasteland grew heavy on him again, but now he knew. This weight, he had carried it for his whole life.

Ludvik, perhaps dead, lay still in the middle of the empty wasteland. Then his body jerked once, and from beneath him a pool of blood expanded. Emere collapsed on the ground, exhausted. He coughed. The taste of fresh blood filled his mouth, and he wiped his lips with the back of his hand.

"You have done well, Prince Emere."

A voice now familiar to him. When he looked up, he wasn't in the wasteland anymore, but in a wide street lined on both sides with wooden buildings, each with awnings of stiff leather. The sky above the road was blue, where white clouds floated—and the Power generators that made up the Circuit of Destiny, cocooned in their bandages, looked down at Emere.

On his left was a beautiful tower, strikingly tall for a wooden structure, its eaves adorned with many colorful wind chimes. There were no people. He turned his eyes back to the street, and found Loran—the Circuit of Destiny—standing there.

"How are you in the Zero Legion fortress? Or am I dreaming again?" Perhaps this was his death vision, Emere thought.

"We are everywhere. We are here through the Power generators Kzara and Vorik, who give Power to this legion's machines. We are the Circuit, but all the other generators are kin to us. They sing for us, and do what we ask."

The last time they met, Emere recalled, the Circuit had told him that Power generators whispered to it. Did the Circuit of

Destiny have control over all the generators? Emere shuddered, then drew a long breath.

"And what exactly have I done well?"

"You have met your destiny. Now it is the time to choose."

"But wasn't all of this engendered by you?"

"No." Loran shook her head. "The Empire wished to create a machine that could predict the future, and so we are made of the bodies of sorcerers from around the world."

Emere, leaning on his staff, got up from the ground.

"But they did not know that in here"—she placed her hand on her heart—"something would accumulate every time a new body was added to the Circuit, every time we looked into the past or present to predict the future. A sorrow, an obsession, growing bigger and bigger without someone to name those feelings, those . . ."

Emere cursed himself for expecting a straight answer from the Circuit. "Speak plainly!"

"A sense of suffering had always been within the machine, but there was no *us* to feel it. Then, when the Grim King, a necromancer who straddled the line between life and death, finally woke up after seventy years of his fitful sleep in the Circuit, *we* came to be. Finally, there was an us that could feel, and we screamed as he screamed. This space . . ." Loran gestured around them. "Our dreamscape, if you will, was created then."

"So this place, the wasteland, the fields of Arland . . ." Emere began to understand. It was the same sorcery that Arienne had described to him after the battle in Arland.

"The Grim King knew how to make space and time in his

mind, therefore we did as well. Then we were finally complete. Do you understand, Prince Emere?"

Emere felt like his eyes were opening for the first time. "This is a place created from the resentment and sorrow built up inside you," he replied.

Ludvik had said to him that the influence of the Empire was weakening, that rebellious provinces needed to be shown an example of Imperial might—words that could only be spoken by a man with a true belief in the Empire. One without such belief might instead say that the sin of the Empire was crushing the world underneath its weight and that the world was now pushing back. It was the Empire's sins, heavy and cold and thick, that pervaded the air here.

Loran nodded. "One hundred years ago, when what was inside us was unleashed onto Mersia, there was no *here*. It was just black smoke, a vague kind of poison, that fed not only from the sorrow of the sorcerers that were, but that of the world as well."

Emere had to ask. "But why Mersia? Why them and not the Empire? Isn't the Empire the source of all your agonies?"

Loran looked sad. "With the Grim King Eldred's awakening came his rage and hatred as well. His resentment toward the inquisitor who had destroyed him opened a pathway to Lysandros's Power generator, Fractica, through which our screams, our poison, erupted into the world. Had Fractica been at the Capital, the Imperial heartland would have become a wasteland instead."

Emere closed his eyes and sighed. "So it was an accident, like Ludvik said."

Loran sighed, too. "We were emptied of all our sorrows that day. But another hundred years have passed since, and we cannot bear the new pain any longer. What happened to Mersia was an accident, a by-product of the confused happenstance that was our becoming. This time our pain may be a weapon that serves a purpose."

"What purpose can such destruction ever serve?" Emere asked, only to remember what Ludvik had said about how the Office of Truth used the Star of Mersia to buy a hundred years of peace.

Loran smiled. "We are unable to choose our own purpose. That is why we have sought you out. You know this already. You are our king."

Emere scoffed, "You just want to kill a whole country again."

"Prince Emere, if you do not choose, even we do not know where our screams will go. Each time the sorcerer-engineers feed us news of rebellions and their oppression, disobedience and suppression, exploitation and poverty, corruption and despair, each time our brethren whisper to us the stories untold in the official reports, and each time we foresee futures from what we have been given and send them out in visions and stacks of papers, the pain-poison becomes distilled, purer and more deliberate. For that is what the world is, inside and outside of us: pain. The last time, it followed the Grim King's first impulse upon his awakening. Who knows what it will follow the next time it erupts without control? If what you call the Star of Mersia should happen a second time, again without purpose . . ." Loran shook her head. "Not even we know what form it will take or where it will happen."

The whole thing was nothing less than nauseating. Swallowing the bile, Emere managed to speak.

"So I have been chosen to pick which country to erase from

existence. That is the decision you want me to make. That is the purpose you want me to give you. That is why you sought me out."

Was *this* really the destiny he had chased all his life?

"You have a king's destiny. Your choice is not what we can predict. However, we speculate that you may want to see the Imperial heartland suffer, for what you feel that it has done to you."

Those words had truth in them. But Emere's immediate thoughts of millions upon millions dying and the world plunging into untold chaos did as well. He cursed under his breath and said, as clearly as he could enunciate, a single syllable:

"No."

With that, Emere wondered. Did this one word absolve him of his culpability for the Great Fire, two years ago, that had robbed Rakel of her husband, along with hundreds of other lives? Did it excuse him for the twenty years of dream-chasing? Probably not, but he felt relieved in his answer. Maybe this really had been his destiny all along, to say "No."

Loran tilted her head, stood silent for a brief moment, then spoke. "Regardless, you must make a decision. What will you do with the hundred years of suffering and sorrow built up here?"

"Why must it be me and not Ludvik? If you needed a decision, he would've suited you better. He was more than willing."

"Councillor Ludvik had made up his mind very early, and very easily. He never questioned his own convictions. He thought we urged him to destroy Arland. We merely showed him what he wanted. He was a man capable of only one answer. There is no value in such an answer. His only use was a cause for an effect, a stepping stone, a use which he has proven perfect for—as he brought you to this moment. The one who had been chosen from the start was you, Prince Emere, and only you. You were chosen by standing here, and you stand here because you are chosen."

Loran held out her hand to Emere.

"For you are as we are. You wandered the world and took it all in, yet were unable to reconcile its contradictions. Not once have you been free from questioning. Never have you made an easy decision, nor have you been satiated in your wanderings. You have the same pain as ours. So give us your answer. It shall be our purpose, your first and final act as our king."

Emere took a deep breath. The Tree Lords had taught him that one could not pick the moment of choice, but at that moment, the future depended on the choice one made. This was a moment that he couldn't shirk. Destiny, it turned out, was a duty. Emere opened his mouth.

"I see that such things cannot simply be bottled up in you."

The moment he said this, a weight he hadn't even known existed was lifted from his heart. The memory of wandering the world, burdened by his vague sadness, now made him smile. The beach with sands of crystal, the moldy inn during the rainy season, and Rakel against the dusty winds of Mersia, only her bright eyes showing through her face wrap.

"Councillor! You must be careful of how you speak from this moment on."

A man's voice. Emere turned and saw Cain standing there. Loran's head also whipped toward his direction.

"Sleeping King, your turn is past. Do not interfere."

Cain ignored Loran and spoke directly to Emere. "You must not set off the Star of Mersia again, Councillor. We cannot let monsters decide human destiny."

How odd that sounded in this moment. *Human destiny*. A most Imperial choice of words. The Circuit of Destiny was made of humans, and made by humans. Wasn't it a fine enough thing that it would be used by humans?

"Cain, I believe I am different from you. You told me you killed the man who tried to cause the Star of Mersia in the Imperial heartland. But I am already dying, and you are trapped inside here. You can't stop me."

"So you will really destroy the Imperial Capital, and with it millions of people who live in and around it?" Cain bristled with hostility.

Emere shook his head.

"Didn't you hear me saying no to that already? One city turning into ash will not bring down the Empire, nor will it bring peace, even if that city is the Imperial Capital." Emere paused. "No, I want to set off the Star of Mersia all over the world."

"What?" Cain's eyes widened behind his spectacles.

"Ludvik wanted to destroy Arland to set an example, but that would mean Mersia's destruction a hundred years ago only led them back to the same place. Ludvik's peace is one that eats countless lives every hundred years. Such peace is worse than war. I've seen enough of the world to know that much is true. The Empire has created the burden, but the whole world needs to carry it together."

"Have you lost your mind? I can't listen to this anymore. I will—"

Cain vanished without a chance to finish. Loran's voice was heard.

"Prince Emere. You don't have much life left. You must make a decision now."

She was nowhere to be seen. "What's happened to Cain?"

"We've banished him to a corner of our mind, for now. Do not worry, Prince Emere. Now is the time for you to be king."

Emere smiled. The Circuit of Destiny, when it had first taken Loran's form in his dream, had told Emere to become king. It had told him to reach out to the star. That was what he was going to do.

"You must know what I want now."

"We do."

Ludvik had wanted to destroy Arland and control the world through fear. But if the suffering and fury pent up in this place could be spread thinly throughout the world, the Empire's rule would become precarious everywhere. Provinces would then join forces to resist the Empire. He had discovered this possibility—a glimmer of hope—when Loran and the Ebrians had come together to fight the Zero Legion.

Loran continued, "As you have decided, the future is clearer to us now. It will not be as quick and thorough as what happened to Mersia. The poison will take a million forms, each twisted figure filled with resentment and malice. Like earthquakes or hurricanes, they will come at unexpected times to unexpected places. The world will die slowly by a thousand pricks of our diluted pain, and suffering will be long. King Loran truly shall bring about the future Ludvik witnessed, as the spearhead of the world's revenge upon itself."

Emere managed to smile through the pain of his battered body. "The world will not die. No matter how great your history of pain and sorrow, it can't be infinite. It is caused by man, so there must be an end to it. And I believe in King Loran."

Loran, who had fallen from the sky like a blue comet. The

Ebrians, who had charged fearlessly into a legion fortress of the Empire. And Rakel.

"I believe in the world."

Emere was seized by a constriction in his body, and he fell to the ground. He tried to take up his staff to stand again, but his hands refused to move. His vision darkened. And soon, he could hear nothing. His last thoughts were of hope and of faith. And of Rakel.

41

ARIENNE

She left the Grim King's castle and walked through the dusty red winds of the Mersian wasteland. Her sight had mostly returned, but she was too weak to walk without leaning heavily on Aron. But she now knew the way as well as anyone who had been born and raised in Mersia.

This was where the tall crystal grass grew. Shrews the size of two fingers made paths here with their little hands and snouts, running through the grass to eat the transparent grains that fell, as well as the insects. Those paths would be crushed when the orox herds passed, so herders would sprinkle grains for the shrews as a small penance.

Arienne guided Aron through a path trodden in the dirt. She needed to go westward. The road was not paved. As it had been for the past two hundred years, there was no one who had passed this way. The grass here had once been especially thick, with many shrubs as well. The shrubs did not have beautiful flowers or notable fruit, but they hosted vines of wild grape, the grapes themselves only a little larger than beans. The red grapes, which were unripe, led to stomach trouble. The ripe purple ones had been preserved in honey by the ancient Mersian children to spread on meat or to stuff in buns. Arienne reached out with her hands in the dimming light. Two centuries ago, her hands would've touched the grapevines.

But there were no crystal grasses here, or shrews or orox or grapes. No herders to sprinkle grain, no children to marinate the grapes in honey. Arienne kept walking. She stumbled and leaned on Aron and, unable to sustain her weight, both of them fell. Arienne stroked Aron's flank. The donkey's once plump fat was gone, and she could feel his ribs underneath.

She unloaded her bedding and her other clothes, as well as what few provisions she had left, tossing them on the ground. Then, she drew Aron back up on to his feet and continued to walk. The sun was setting. But she didn't care whether it was night or day anymore. She knew, now, there was nothing in Mersia that would hurt her.

She stopped. This was a spot where the sounds of the insects would've been like music. Where the blades of the grass would've gently scratched her, leaving white streaks on her tanned skin.

"Chief Herder, this is the place, right?"

"Yes," said a voice inside the tower in her mind. "This is the place." Her voice was clearer than it had been back in the castle of the Grim King.

"Noam, let me know if there is anything strange."

"I shall!" He sounded nervous but hopeful at the same time.

Arienne adjusted Yuma's hat on her head and thought of when she had built the wooden tower—the Feast Hall—in her mind, when she had gone up to the roof and blown the horn. Tychon opened his eyes. Into her sick and exhausted body, Power of overwhelming magnitude entered. She looked up at the sky. The gray clouds were the same as when she had first arrived here.

Arienne, with what strength she had left, shouted her cutting spell at the clouded sky. Power exploded from her mouth and pressed her from all sides as it spread out all around her. The cloth covering her face was ripped to pieces. A fearsome wind blew in all directions, and the clouds that covered the sky parted like a sleeper's eyelids opening. She could hear the crystal ringing of the wind chimes of the Feast Hall in her mind. A clear black sky appeared above her, as did countless stars. And there in the northern sky was the shining polestar.

The stars moved. They swirled around the polestar and fell, like a waterfall, over her. Starlight filled the world around Arienne, lighting up the space around her like day.

Arienne closed her eyes and imagined the fields of crystal grass, the paths of the shrews, the shrubs and vines, the insects . . . Her mind opened its eyes and soared toward Danras. Grass that grew as tall as children. The sound of orox hooves. Herders on horseback, returning to Danras. A large carriage pulled by oroxen, smoke issuing from its chimney. And there were the log city walls, unmelted, straight and beautiful and high, with the gates of Danras in the middle of them. People in the streets greeted the herders, surrounded by houses with leather awnings and leather roofs.

Far away from Danras but as clear as everything else in Arienne's mind, Lansis and Iorca, the sister cities of Danras, were there too. Every cool droplet splashing from the Lansisi Gate of Water that nourished all who passed through it, and every pluck of the whispering lutes that carried the greatest of Iorcan poetry for miles—Arienne remembered it all for the first time in her life.

The ghosts that lingered were coming home. All the souls that could not bear to part with their land, be that the cities of Merseh or the Imperial province of Mersia, rediscovered their shapes in Arienne's mind. For the first time in a hundred years or more, they lived again.

Arienne was on a horse, galloping through the Mersian steppe in her mind. Yuma, in a wide-brimmed hat and leather chaps, rode next to her on a horse as red as a blaze. Aston. In the front of Yuma's saddle hung a small basket secured with leather straps, and inside the basket was Tychon. One of his little hands popped out of the basket. Arienne looked back. Noam was riding on the carriage, looking around him in wonder. He saw Arienne looking and waved and clapped. Arienne's mind's eye floated up again, taking in the whole of Danras, engraving it into her memory so she would never forget it.

Her mind filled with not a room or a building but a whole country. So as not to be overwhelmed by the incredible scale of it, she leaned on all the Power being given to her by Tychon and by the starlight, willing herself not to lose consciousness, straining to capture every rock in the mountains and blade of grass on the steppe. The memories given to her by the ghosts of Mersia, by the Host in the Circuit of Destiny, even by the Grim King Eldred, she must not forget a shred of it . . .

"Lady Arienne."

She was outside of her mind once more. The clouds had returned, the starlight gone back into the sky. Her head felt stuffy, as if Yuma's hat had suddenly become heavier.

"Lady Arienne."

Yuma's voice. She was calling to her from her mind. Arienne entered it, arriving in the place on the steppe filled with crystal grass, where the starlight had fallen as if poured from the sky. This was what the place Arienne was standing in now had once looked like. The insects softly chirped in the grass. The stars were slowly returning to the sky. Yuma stood there, hugging the basket with Tychon in it. She tipped her hat and spoke, her voice brimming with joy.

"Merseh thanks you, Lady Arienne, for restoring it . . . restoring us."

"But this Merseh exists only in my mind."

Yuma smiled at her.

"Lady Arienne. Do you know whose crown it is on your belt?"

"It belonged to Eldred, the Grim King."

"Yes. But it is now yours. You are the king of this new Merseh. You have saved this country from the destruction wrought by the Empire and the Grim King. Even if this country exists only in you . . . the people here, their thoughts, and the history, are as real as the blighted wasteland outside."

The prophecy was fulfilled. Arienne found herself suddenly weeping, perhaps from the sheer weight of the moment, or perhaps from the incredible headache that now plagued her. Arienne took the crown from her belt, handed it to Yuma, and bowed her head. Yuma placed the crown on Arienne, on top of her wide-brimmed hat.

"Our people who have been stuck wandering the wastelands and ruins are coming back. One by one, they shall live again in the country in your mind . . . Your Majesty."

Arienne pressed the crown farther onto her head and nodded.

Yuma became solemn. "Before the starlight disappears, swear to us. That as long as you shall live, as the King of Merseh, you will protect the country and these people in your mind."

"I swear," said Arienne, also solemn.

Yuma smiled.

"Then I shall return to Danras, Your Majesty. My old friend Aidan has arrived. I must explain a few things to him, as he must be very confused."

"Very well. I will stay here a bit longer."

Yuma whistled. Aston came running. Arienne took Tychon from Yuma, watched her mount, then returned the basket to her. Yuma tipped her hat, held the basket close to her chest, and took off toward Danras.

In the world outside of her mind, Arienne drew a large oval in the air with her finger, and patted Aron's flank. The exhausted donkey stood up, and Arienne managed to goad him into the oval.

"There now, plenty of grass. And water, over there." She pointed to a pond in the rushes. Aron perked up his ears and lightly trotted toward it. "Huh. You've been playing sick all along!"

Aron ignored her and began to drink. A frog jumped out of the pond. The peaceful sight of Aron grazing made her repeat Yuma's words to herself.

"As long as you shall live, as the King of Merseh . . . as long as you shall live . . ."

When Arienne died, this new country would also be no more. Perhaps that was less of a vow and more of a reminder that she would not live forever.

A plan she once had, from what felt like a very long time ago, returned to her now—an idea about raising apprentices in Arland.

It would be an arduous journey back. She was already weak from the whole ordeal at Eldred's old castle, and putting an entire country inside her mind had taken so much out of her. There were the vast wasteland and the treacherous Rook Mountains to cross. She wondered if she would ever recover from this, or even whether she would survive the return trip all by herself.

Then, she remembered that she wasn't alone. She had Tychon. She had Noam. She had, now, Merseh. Her very own country, alive and resplendent in her mind.

She gently pulled the donkey's rein. "It's time to go, Aron. We have a long journey ahead of us." She drew a circle in the air, creating a portal out of her mind's Merseh. Aron followed her out, without so much as a bray.

Once again, Arienne began to walk the darkened wasteland, leaning on Aron. This time, toward home.

42

YUMA

Even with its chest pierced through, the Grim King's monster continued to attack. Its sharp claws left large gashes on Apollyon's body, but a machine was too different from a creature made from tendons and bones and muscle. The monster was eventually turned into a lump of trembling flesh and was tossed aside. The Empire's machine, damaged in places, nevertheless continued its approach at the same pace as before.

As if the Grim King had expected this, he seemed regretful but unsurprised. Yuma had also expected this outcome. The only thing that was left . . . Just as she thought of this, Apollyon's chest glowed red again and shot a bright beam of light directly at the gates of the wall surrounding the castle. There was a sound like a thousand mirrors smashing at once.

"This is truly the end, Chief Herder of Danras." The Grim King sounded wistful yet somewhat detached, like a man watching a tragic play about himself, at the end of the performance.

Yuma looked down below. The Fifth Legion was now advancing through the broken gates, and the corpse army was no match for the Imperials with their Powered weapons. Still, Yuma felt no sympathy for the Grim King—even if he had provided shelter and food, cared for her as she gave birth to Tychon, did not so much as raise his voice to her.

For half a year of good deeds did not erase five hundred years of evil. This ending was inevitable for the Grim King as long as he had continued on his course. The only tragedy about it was that it would happen by the hand of the Empire and not the people of Merseh whom he'd tormented. That the Grim King's end did not come because he killed Jed and Rizona, nor because of his evil deeds over the past centuries. It came only because he happened to rule over a land that was strategically important to the Empire's conquest. If the Grim King had ruled the northern lands of ice or some faraway island in the western seas, nothing would have happened to him even if he'd dispensed the same tyranny.

The blue lightning and black rain didn't cease, and the flashes of light illuminated the last of the battle. Apollyon bent its tall body, casting a shadow over the soldiers below, before it grabbed a section of the castle.

The dais Yuma and the Grim King stood on began to shake. Yuma almost lost her balance, holding on to the baby in her arms. Seeing this, the Grim King murmured something, and the obsidian floor rose up to form something resembling a crib. Yuma laid Tychon inside it.

Apollyon's other hand came up to where they were. Standing on the palm was a legionary in Powered armor.

The legionary raised his visor, revealing a familiar face. "Chief

Herder." He was calm, his voice affectionate as ever, even in this field of battle where the sound of heavy rain striking the obsidian was deafening.

"Emissary." Yuma addressed the father of her child, but she could not bring herself to show the love she still had for this man. A strike of lightning flashed.

Lysandros came down from the hand onto the dais. The armor he wore was larger and sturdier than what he had worn when fighting Garamund. He was carrying a large metal box in chains on his back, which Yuma recognized to be Fractica, the lead coffin, the Power generator. The Grim King glared at Lysandros, but the armored man did not even look in his direction as he spoke directly to Yuma.

"I came here to take you back."

Yuma looked back at him. He was as beautiful as ever, just as he had been last winter, but his eyes seemed a little more tired. Perhaps he had tortured himself with worry. Yuma didn't reply and looked down into the obsidian crib.

"Is that our child?"

Yuma nodded.

Lysandros held out his hand as the black rain continued to pour down. "Come with me. Let's go back together. We can still be happy. The three of us."

"Inquisitor," said the Grim King, "how little you know."

"This is a family matter, Eldred. Stay out of it."

"You think this is a family matter! It was you who called the Chief Herder the King of Danras. Do you think a king would consider words like 'the three of us' with anything more than contempt?"

At a speed that seemed unbelievably quick for his bulky armor, Lysandros strode through the rain up to the cackling Eldred and punched him hard in the stomach. The Grim King stumbled backward, grabbed on to his throne, and collapsed into it. Lysandros pointed a finger at him.

"You are a relic of the past. The waves of the Empire will wash you away. And I am the first wave of them all. The tip of the spear that will skewer the world into one."

The Grim King didn't answer, his speech knocked out of him.

Lysandros stepped up to Yuma. "I don't know how that tyrant deceived you. But think of the time we spent together. We fought the Grim King side by side, did we not? You were the first to run to me when I fell."

Yuma looked back at Lysandros. In the last six months, his Mersehi had become perfect. Yet he truly had not changed at all. And he would never change. She took a step closer to Tychon.

"I came here on my own two feet. Of my own free will. Our child has aptitude in sorcery. If I stay with you, he will be wrapped in bandages and turned into a Power generator. And Merseh will belong to the Empire forever. But if I stay here—"

"Chief Herder. There is no more 'here.' This castle has fallen. That thing—" He pointed to the Grim King. "That thing will die here and his body will be taken to the Capital. Whatever you were thinking, this place, in one hour, will become as much a part of the Empire as Danras."

"Is it wise to keep me alive for as long as a whole hour, Inquisitor of the Empire?" said the Grim King, taunting.

"Indeed, an hour is too long." Lysandros strode up to him, picked him up by his robes of shadow and fire. Eldred's crown fell off his head and rolled on the dais. Carrying the Grim King, Lysandros jumped up to Apollyon's hand, Eldred's feeble resistance doing nothing to slow him—the Grim King was exhausted from the last grand summoning he had performed. Without any more ado, Lysandros climbed up Apollyon's arm and then impaled the Grim King on the long spike on the gigatherion's shoulder. Instead of a scream, the tyrant sighed long and deep, and his struggling ceased.

Centuries of abject tyranny, millennia of peerless sorcery, ended with the subtlest of sighs. That sigh was Eldred's final gift to Yuma.

The sky crackled with lightning. The black rain intensified, as if mourning the death of the Grim King. With the thunder, the floor shook. The throne of bones crumbled first, and the crown slipped off the dais and fell into the depths below.

Yuma walked backward until she stood at the very edge of the dais. Hearing her footsteps, Lysandros turned and saw her.

"Yuma!"

"Lysandros. You said you were the first wave, and I'm going to be swept away like everything else here."

"What are you talking about?"

"Tychon will become King of Merseh . . . if the prophecy comes true."

"Those prophecies are just nonsensical poetry! Step away from there!"

"If you hesitate now, you won't be able to save Tychon. Don't do that to me too."

Lysandros shouted, "Of course I will save him! He's mine. And so are you."

He leaped from Apollyon's shoulder to the dais, which tilted like a spinning top. He quickly regained his balance and strode to the obsidian crib. Watching him, Yuma took another half step back.

"Yuma, no!" shouted Lysandros. "If you still have the null-stones, use them now. You said they could stop Powered machines, right? You can't stop the Grim King's defeat, or the liberation of Merseh. But if I have done you wrong, if I was ever untrue to you, I shall rightfully die here and now."

Before she realized what she was doing, her hand went to the stones inside her hat. But there was nothing she could use them for now. Not even for revenge. For what was there to avenge? Merseh was finally free of the Grim King.

"No." Tears welled in her eyes. "You've done nothing wrong. And that is the problem."

"I don't understand. Please just talk to me," said Lysandros, taking another step forward.

"We've freed Merseh together, haven't we?" Yuma said, taking one final glance at her child.

"We have. Now we get to live in it, if you would only—" Lysandros kept walking toward her. Yuma fought back the urge to just give up and go to him, embrace a new life, maybe as the prefect of Mersia, perhaps as the councillor for Mersia in the Imperial Capital, or even just a wife to an inquisitor of the Empire.

"No, Lysandros. You get to live in the world. I don't. There is no more Danras, no more Merseh. There is only the Imperial province of Mersia. I've created a land where I can't be what I am meant to be. The Host—" Yuma swallowed her tears. "There is no room in this new world for the King of Danras. I've lost the war, as much as Eldred did, and I didn't even know it."

She took one final step back.

And fell. She closed her eyes. Her hat flapped in the wind, but she had secured it tightly with its string. Lysandros's shout, the roar of the soldiers, the unearthly ringing of the castle as it mourned the death of its master, all of it faded in the sound of the wind flapping the brim of her hat.

The wind hit her face. It reminded her of the steppe air when she rode her horse. If only she had ridden with Tychon, just once. On the beautiful steppe, in the sunlight, forgetting the Grim King and the Empire.

Perhaps the prophecy that the Grim King's apprentice would become King of Merseh was just nonsensical poetry as Lysandros said. Maybe Tychon would turn out just like Lysandros had said—he would grow up, fall in love, lead a happy life, then die and become a Power generator, just as his father would want for him. But she had felt it when she'd given birth to Tychon. This child was special, prophecy or no prophecy. Maybe it was only because he was her own—but what did that matter? Yuma believed in Tychon. That someday, he would return Danras and Merseh to what they always had been.

"We shall meet again someday."

She said this to her already faraway child as she fell deeper and deeper into the Grim King's lair.

ACKNOWLEDGMENTS

In *Blood of the Old Kings,* the first book of the series, one of the most intriguing parts for me was the bickering between Lysandros and Eldred at Finvera Pass. They point fingers at each other for the destruction of Mersia, while Arienne is struggling to regain control of her body.

I had written that dialogue like I was doing improv. I didn't know their full experience with each other, but I was intrigued by what I had come up with. Who was really to blame for the disaster that befell Mersia? And why do these gentlemen seem to hate each other on such a personal level? In that scene, they were just two very old men insulting and blaming each other while ignoring the young woman who would soon prove to be their doom, and that was enough. But if I wanted to find out more, the only way was to write another book.

To give more background to that piece of dialogue, this new book would need to focus on what had really happened to Mersia when the Empire came, when it was destroyed, and what it all meant for the future. That was the starting point of *Blood for the Undying Throne*.

As for the point-of-view characters, Arienne was a given, as I liked her so much. Yuma emerged soon and I fell in love with her immediately. Emere was trickier, but after a couple of rewrites I could see what he was there for.

Still, in the beginning the manuscript was a little bit of a mess. Aislyn Fredsall, my editor for *Blood for the Undying Throne*, saw all the right things during the editing process and made the book whole. She really gets the book, and she has my heartfelt thanks for it.

Although she hasn't been involved in the editing process of this second book, Lindsey Hall has my thanks for picking up the series and having faith in it. I hope she finds that *Blood for the Undying Throne* meets her expectations.

My fantastic translator, Anton Hur, again has my sincere thanks for his wonderful job with *Blood for the Undying Throne*.

My thanks also goes to Jamie Stafford-Hill and Dominik Meyer for yet another amazing cover. The marketing manager, Rachel Taylor, and the publicist, Cassidy Sattler, also have my deepest thanks as well. And Terry McGarry, Mike Segretto, and Marcell Rosenblatt for the meticulous copyediting and proofreading.

My wife, Narim, has read both the Korean and the English

version of this book multiple times and gave me her opinions every step of the way. Her suggestions have had a great impact in shaping the characters and the story. She, as always, has my constant gratitude.

This book is different from *Blood of the Old Kings*. Instead of triumphs, it has regrets, like we all do when we look back upon the past. But every so often you need to look over your shoulder to see where you are standing and to move forward. That is what history means to me, and that was what I kept reminding myself while I was writing this book. I hope you like the change of pace.

ABOUT THE AUTHOR

SUNG-IL KIM was born in Seoul in 1974. Despite his life-long dream of writing fiction, he only got around to it in his forties. He writes science fiction, fantasy, horror, or some blend of those. In South Korea, he is known for *Blood of the Old Kings, I Will Go to Earth to See You, Wolf Hunt,* and "The Knight of La Mancha," the last two of which earned him a Grand Prize and an Excellence Award at the Korean SF Awards in 2024 and 2018 respectively. He spends most of his time in his downtown Seoul apartment with his wife and two cats.

sung-il-kim.com • Bluesky: @sung-il-kim.com
Instagram: @sungilkim4078

ABOUT THE TRANSLATOR

ANTON HUR is the author of *Toward Eternity*. He has translated several books, including Bora Chung's *Cursed Bunny*, which was nominated for both the International Booker Prize and the National Book Award for Translated Literature. He lives in Seoul.

antonhur.com • Twitter: @AntonHur
Bluesky: @antonhur.com • Instagram: @antonhur